THE DROWNED QUEEN

ELSPETH GREGORSDÓTTIR

First published by Astral Queen Press 2026

This novel is entirely a work of fiction. The names, characters, and incidents portrayed in it are the work of the author's imagination. Any resemblance to actual persons, living or dead, events, or localities is entirely coincidental.

Elspeth Gregorsdóttir has no responsibility for the persistence or accuracy of URLs for external or third-party Internet Websites referred to in this publication and does not guarantee that any content on such websites is, or will remain, accurate or appropriate.

First edition
ISBN: HB: 979-8-9941885-1-4; PB: 979-8-9941885-0-7; eBook: 979-8-9941885-2-1

Cover art, map, and internal illustrations by Elspeth Gregorsdóttir
Typesetting by Astral Queen Press

Author portrait by Caitlin Ross Photography

For those who have stood at the water's edge.

AVYNNE
Frost
Blinding
Mist Marshes
Silvermist
Bridge
Cisqa River
Silverwood Forest
Keepers' Farmhouse
Mistwater
Starfall Trench
Twilight Isles
Shadow Market
To Duskhold

Court
Peaks
Loch
Rime
Amber
Iron Mountains
Vale
Amber Palace
Verdant
Depths
Montumbra
Obsidian
Isles

THE DROWNED QUEEN

he Whispering Sea stretched endlessly before me, an infinite expanse of inky darkness, where the sky and water blurred together without horizon or seam. No stars reflected on its surface. No waves disturbed its stillness. Only the occasional ripple suggested that it was even water at all, like a shuddering breath drawn by some vast, sleeping entity just beneath.

I stood barefoot at its edge, my toes sinking into the gray sand. The journey here had taken... what? Days? Weeks? Time meant nothing in the Duskhold.

During my century of servitude in these shadowlands, I had painstakingly collected whispers and rumors of this sea. And when my master finally cast me from his household as nothing more than a broken tool too gnarled to serve, I followed those fragments *here*.

I lifted my trembling hand into the sullen light, inspecting what I'd become as if it might have suddenly changed. Parchment-thin skin stretched over swollen knuckles. Bare, scarred nail beds. Hair—whatever color it once had—hung in brittle waves around a face that I no longer recognized.

Pain, my steadfast companion as the decades ticked by, riddled every joint, every hinge, every screaming vertebra. The human body was never meant to age to one hundred and twenty.

But mine had.

And that was the particular cruelty of this realm: to age without death; to suffer for eternity without release.

My mind betrayed me just as thoroughly as my body. Some days, I'd wake with perfect clarity—taunting memories of sunshine and laughter so vivid I could almost taste freedom. Other days, I couldn't even recognize my own breath fogging a window.

That torturous mental tide proved far worse than the physical deterioration.

Hope rekindled.

Then extinguished.

Again and again. On and on. Across a timeless, empty space.

A century at least, I was told when I first arrived. A century of service to pay for my *transgression*. Whatever that had been, I could no longer say. Something about boundaries crossed. Love where it was forbidden. The memory faded like footprints washed away by endless, identical days. Only the punishment remained.

I was sold at the Shadow Market beneath a sky where the stars never moved. I knelt on an auction block of cold, unground stone.

Spindly-limbed creatures with rotted breath circled me like livestock, gauging the worth of a human kissed by 'forbidden magic.' My new master had been rather pleased. A mortal with lingering traces of Fae enchantment was rare—even here.

He yanked me by the chain shackled around my neck, hauling me behind him like a leashed mongrel too broken to fight back. When I collapsed—starved, dehydrated, barely able to stand—he slung the chain over his shoulder and dragged me across the crumbling asphalt. Grit embedded itself into my skin as it split open, but the pain kept my thoughts from drifting to the bleak eternity ahead—even as he hauled me through puddles of piss and manure as we passed some stables, my torn flesh burning and shrieking in protest.

"Don't worry, love," he said gently as he shoved me into a tiny wooden crate, folding my emaciated body into unnatural angles. "The infection won't kill you. Nothing will."

With a crooked, yellow smile, he slid the lid closed, and rusty nails secured my fate.

I performed whatever tasks he demanded without question. I cleaned caustic residues that blistered my skin. I entertained his depraved guests—painted and half-naked—retelling stories of a mortal world I could barely remember. I endured his experiments as he tried to extract the Fae essence he believed lingered in my blood.

Eventually, when my body aged beyond beauty and usefulness, my duties dwindled. When my hands grew too arthritic to clean even a spoon, his more able-bodied servants deposited me in the Gray Wastes—the dumping ground for possessions no longer worth the trouble to keep.

It was there, among the others abandoned to slow dissolution, that those whispers of the sea were confirmed. The only way out of the Duskhold.

"There is no boundary there," an ancient creature rasped. Its form had deteriorated beyond recognition. "No distinction between here and beyond. Those who enter the sea never return to these shadowlands."

"Then why don't more seek it?" I asked.

"Oh, many try. But the path shifts. Misleads. Those few who reach the shore—" It shuddered. "They hear dissonant voices. See calamitous visions. Most turn back, believing even this half-life preferable to what waits in the water."

"Voices?"

"The sea whispers what you fear most. Or what you desire most." Its milky eyes fixed on me. "Sometimes they are the same."

"I have nothing left to fear," I said. "And my only desire is death."

The creature's laugh rattled through its hollow ribs. "Death is the Mother's blessing, child."

I stepped forward.

The frigid water lapped at my ankles, making my toes curl instinctively. The cold was jarring against the tepid decay of this prison—a place where nothing ever burned or froze. Only curdled. Only staled.

I closed my stiff fingers around the shard of blue sea glass in my palm. My only possession. My only connection to a life I didn't remember. Once upon a time, it had shown me slivers of memory that never quite felt like mine—a face I once loved, a voice that spoke the name I once carried. Now it held only the faintest echo that something, *someone*, might exist beyond this veil.

Countless times I had pressed it to my forehead or clutched it to my chest, desperate for a glimpse of that face. Once, early in my servitude, a fellow servant noticed me gazing into its depths.

"What are you looking for in that bit of rubbish?" she asked. Her voice was cracked with age, but her eyes remained eerily young.

"Home," I answered, though I was hopeless to describe what

home actually meant.

She nodded, averting her eyes from mine. "That's how they trap us. Leave just enough hope to keep us from seeking the sea."

Then she shuffled back to her Sisyphean duties, and I collected my first whisper.

But she was wrong.

The sea glass hadn't trapped me. It had sustained me—through beatings and degradations, the betrayals of my failing form, the erosion of my very self. While the rest of me died an agonizing death, it had endured.

And thank the gods it did.

Even if my prayers went unanswered. The nobler gods held no jurisdiction here.

The Four Pillars governed all existence. The Father blessed the Fae with immortality, unfurling their lifespans like spools of ribbon, weaving their days into millennia. They were beautiful, ageless creatures who spoke of bygone centuries the way mortals spoke of seasons.

The Mother blessed humans with death, the sweet escape from mortal suffering. As I aged beyond my body's mortal design, I begged Her for that birthright. *Please*, I prayed. *Please make it stop.* Yet each morning, without fail, my chest rose with breath and my weary eyes opened.

The Son, Gwenael, blessed the Fae with magic, threading his own divinity through the elements and anchoring them to their will. I knew nothing of its splendor. Only its cruelty. I saw air ripped from servants' lungs for speaking out of turn, shards of ice impaling hearts that dared to want.

And the Daughter, Alezae, who twisted her blessing into a curse. Once the guardian of transition, the shepherd between life and death, she reshaped her realm into a prison between worlds, trapping souls like flies in endless twilight.

I saw her at the Shadow Market. Not directly, but in the putrid smile of the merchant who shackled me, then in the jaundiced twinkle in my master's eye when my price was named.

Alezae was not wicked. She *was* the wound from which wickedness festered and seeped into the aether. She birthed the first shadow, and she would cradle the last.

Another step.

Water soaked into the tattered hem of my gray nightgown as it rippled against my thighs. The fabric billowed around my legs, then clung to my skin as I slowly inched deeper. The needle-sharp cold bit into my flesh, and my knees nearly buckled with relief. The sea was already taking years of pain from me, and I would gladly give it the rest.

I tried to keep track of those years at first, scratching tallies by my pallet. Until the day my master caught me. He wrenched me upright and pried my fingernails from their beds one by one so I could never mark time again... except for the last one.

He forced me to scrawl it in the blood that poured from my fingertips.

Time belongs to my master and so do I.

I only had enough left to sign the letter *M*.

Another step.

The freezing water reached my waist, stealing my breath. I inhaled sharply, and the briny darkness carried its first whiff of something *real*, reminding me that sensation indeed existed beyond this place. The Duskhold air held nothing. No earthy scent of grass and dirt after a hard rain. No blooming sweetness of fresh honeysuckle. Not even the acrid stench of rot, even though decay lay around every corner.

If I thought my body could have allowed it, I might have swum across the Whispering Sea just to see what lay beyond. Another hell. Or something else.

For some reason, I looked back.

The shore was empty; the landscape unchanged. My life still a hundred years in the wrong direction. I expected nothing, yet the instinct remained—final habit of being human. The urge to wonder what we might be leaving behind.

But I left behind nothing. I didn't even have a name for anyone to call me back to myself, or to sign at the bottom of a goodbye. Even my blood, once written on the wall, had long since flaked and faded.

The only way forward was to surrender whatever life I had left to something less stagnant.

Even if that something was nothing at all.

The water rose to my chest. Then my shoulders.

The sea glass was pinned against my heart, an indelible habit I couldn't remember forming. I lifted it to my lips in a gesture somewhere between a prayer, a farewell, and an apology. When I had nothing, this blue fragment had been my conscience. Soon it would sink to the bottom as the last tangible relic of my wasted life.

Thank the gods it would not remember this.

My last pathetic moments.

I was chin-deep now. I thought of the Pillars one last time— the Father, the Mother, the Son. And Alezae, the cruel Daughter of the dusk. Maybe she would be disappointed that I found my way out.

I hoped so.

I had already said my prayers, and I offered none up to them.

One more step, and the water closed over my head.

The drowning wasn't peaceful.

My lungs burned, and my body lashed against the sea, instinct betraying my resolve. My grip on the sea glass tightened until its edges bit into my palm. Panic surged like lightning.

I gasped with an overwhelming need for air, and the first gulp of water felt like lava shooting down my throat, up my nose, burning through my sinuses. My arms thrashed, windmilling as I spasmed against the fiery band tightening around my chest and throat, trembling on the edge of collapse beneath a thousand molten knives.

I expected surrender.

I expected release.

I never expected my body to fight so viciously against its own extinction.

My heart misfired in my chest, skipping and stuttering as it hurled the last scraps of oxygen through me.

Then my body made its last hopeless bid for survival before the world dissolved into a blur.

Spots of color exploded behind my eyes, the first spectrum I'd seen since the entire world dulled to that hideous gray. Crimson flared like dying stars. Violet coiled through failing synapses. Azure rippled across a crystal pool. The hues fractured into impossible shapes, memories splintering into an impossible looking glass.

In a blink, I saw everything.

Even *him*.

Then the looking glass shattered again, and I remembered nothing.

I sank deeper. The crushing weight of the water warped my skull, the pressure mounting inside my ears and pressing against my temples. Cold pierced beyond sensation, creeping through me until my nerves disconnected, one by one, and my body no longer registered itself as whole.

A curious calm washed over me as my awareness disintegrated. The last fragments of self bubbled upward and vanished. Dying thought flared blindly as consciousness slipped away, leaving a single pinpoint of clarity before darkness claimed me.

It wasn't a revelation of the meaning of life, or a lyrical eulogy for my wasted existence.

It was a simple yet profound sense of complete and utter failure.

Then it evaporated. Along with everything else.

But death was the Mother's blessing, and Her reach did not extend to the Whispering Sea.

arkness.

It wasn't familiar like the blacks and grays of the shadowlands, nor was it the terrifying nothingness I'd imagined *oblivion* to be. It was something in-between, as if it had slipped through a rip in the seam of time and swelled into something alive. It saturated me, permeating every atom, squeezing and scrutinizing all at once.

I should have been dead. Why was my existence so tenacious when I'd long since given up on it? My lungs stretched with water, my heart sputtered and failed, my life force all but slipped away. Yet my awareness—disembodied and hazy—persisted through the dark, like stars scattered across the sky.

The serenity of surrender didn't last long.

The pain returned more intensely than the drowning itself as every fiber of my being was tediously torn apart. My skin sloughed from bone like soggy parchment; tendons and ligaments unraveled in sinuous ribbons. I tried to scream, but my vocal cords were wrenched from my mouth, and my lips peeled back while my teeth melted from my jaw.

I was being unmade, splayed wide on a cosmic workbench.

Please, no. I wanted death, I thought desperately. *Not this.*

But the Whispering Sea gave no more consideration to my desires than the Duskhold ever had. It unwound me for its own inscrutable purpose—indifferent to my suffering, unmoved by my confusion. The Mother had abandoned me once more, and I somehow had managed to fall into something bleaker.

When the ripping and tearing of my physical body subsided, my consciousness expanded beyond the shreds of my dissolving form. My perception wove through the hollow spaces between stars, each one thrumming with potential, waiting to ignite. Some hollows held shapes of things I couldn't name, vague sounds without language, motion without direction. Others opened like windows.

One of those windows revealed the shadowlands as they had once been: the Twilight Shores, a wayward realm of peaceful transition where souls rested before continuing their journey to whatever lay beyond. The shores darkened, its waters stilled, Alezae's bitterness twisting it into a fly trap.

And then...

A small blue light floated nearby, a tiny beacon pulsing like a lighthouse in a fog.

My sea glass!

It must have drifted from my grasp during my unraveling.

In my disembodied state, I reached frantically for it, desperate to hold on to my one solid anchor as I continued to dissolve into complete nothingness. With no fingers to grasp it, no fist to hold it, I enclosed myself around the glass instead—absorbing it within the safety of the infinite chrysalis that contained me.

I did not pass by the next hollow.

I rested.

Bands of ancient power poured from its mouth, a deluge of starlight flooding the shape of what I had once been. A pulse quaked through the darkness, beat by beat, while celestial lifeblood trickled into a steady flow. My unbecoming turned, at last, into remaking.

Time slackened and spread outward.

Gradually—painfully—a new form coalesced around the scattered fragments of my consciousness. Shimmering bone crystallized from starlight. Muscle and sinew wove themselves together from umbral threads. Skin and veins forged themselves from the fringes between darkness and light.

My senses returned one by one, each intact, yet weirdly unfamiliar.

Hearing came first. The whispers of the sea swelled into a near-deafening dissonance. Hisses and shrieks spoke in languages I shouldn't have understood, but somehow did. Haunting melodies drifted through the currents like mournful lullabies sung to empty cribs. They sang of something always meant to be stolen—and always meant to return.

Touch followed. The water was comfortably tepid now, swirling with a gentle, sentient pressure against skin no longer withered, but taut and youthful. The sea glass pressed into my remade palm, and I curled my fingers tighter around it, gripping the stability of its unchanging contours.

Vision came last, tangling with the others. Spots of light

clouded my sight, bubbling from beneath my eyelids and bursting against my cheeks. Layers of colorful shock waves rippled through me—echoes of what had been, and peals of what could be.

As my consciousness compressed back into my skull, I finally understood.

The Whispering Sea was the opposite of emptiness. It was not oblivion, nor a place of nonexistence. It was *everything.* Every choice made and unmade, every idea and notion, every infinitesimal piece of existence across infinite dimensions swam beside me. I felt them brush past, the lives that had almost been mine.

The beginning, middle, and end of every story were—and would always be—written right here.

Including mine.

Once my awareness had sharpened enough to pierce the primordial fog and my body remembered itself, the sea heaved me from its depths. The surface rushed toward me, then shattered into spray as I broke through. Air, heavy with salt and river grass, whipped my hair across my face, wet strands slipping into my mouth and clinging to my eyes as I arced above the water.

I landed hard on the dark soil and smooth stones of a riverbank. I lay gasping, choking, my lungs demanding air once more. Inky water erupted from my mouth in violent retches, pooling around me on the shore. Instead of seeping into the earth, it slithered back toward the river with intention, as though answering some distant summons home.

When I spat out the last of it, I collapsed onto my back and stared up at the sky.

I hadn't seen a sky like this in over a hundred years.

Feathery clouds drifted lazily across the indigo expanse. A sliver of the moon, curved like a toothy grin, cast its light in ripples across the river. And, gods, the stars...

They winked and flared in rhythm with my steadying pulse. I felt a pull of kinship toward them, each one bearing a different name and temperament from the millions beside it. Without thought or intention, I raised my hand toward those knowing heavens and plucked a star from the fabric itself.

I held it between my fingers like a grain of rice. It was surprisingly cool, purring and tingling against my fingertips. With a gentle pinch, I snuffed it out like the head of a match, and it reappeared above me, glittering and waving.

I had no idea how long I lay there, eerily unburdened, breathing in the unoppressive air. Eventually, I pushed myself up to survey my surroundings. The sharp curve of the bank, the alabaster stones clustered at the water's edge, the enormous oak towering above it all—something long-lost stirred in my gut.

Whether in this life or another, I knew this place.

I knew it intimately.

The Cisqa.

The name surfaced from a place beyond my immediate recollection as I listened to the gentle slosh of the current and caught the perfume of the blooms that crept along the river bend.

My legs shook from the alien grace of this new body as I stood. My tattered nightgown was gone, replaced by a shadowy, ethereal robe. The fabric was suspended somewhere between substance and mist, its edges dissolving into wisps of smoke.

Cautious but curious, I padded to the water's edge and looked at my reflection.

The pale moonlight illuminated an unrecognizable face. High cheekbones, full where they were once hollow. Supple lips, plump where they had thinned and cracked. Eyes flecked with shifting light, irises swirling with watercolor nebulae orbiting my pupils.

My hair fell around my shoulders in damp curls of midnight black—save a single ringlet of silver framing my face—so dark it devoured every speck of light. As it dried, iridescent hues wavered within it like an oil slick.

I couldn't remember what I looked like before entering the

Duskhold, but I knew this wasn't it.

The woman staring back in the river wasn't a woman at all. That word suggested someone human. Something mortal. None of the uncanny flawlessness of my reflection belonged to me. Not the symmetry of every pore, not the balance of each precisely placed freckle. I recognized only something wholly *other*.

The sea glass was still clenched protectively in my fist, unchanged despite whatever transformative chaos I had just survived. I pressed it to my heart, savoring its constancy, even if its blue depths still buried its secrets from me.

It had never given me strength to endure, nor bravery to resist. It was never a relic worthy of bard song or legend. It was only ever a reminder that I was not born of suffering. That I had been loved once.

That truth was the last thing that kept me from rotting all the way through, even as I welcomed death. And now, somehow, it had guided me here.

Perhaps it had even guided me *home*.

Hope sparked as I turned away from the river—not the desperate, manufactured kind the Duskhold peddled so freely, but something genuine. Quiet. Alive.

Maybe whoever loved me then might love me still.

If I survived that unforgiving century... perhaps they had too.

Chapter Three

The first rays of sun struck the distant peaks and set the Cisqa River valley aflame. I trudged from the bank, warmth brushing my face and forcing me to squint—sensations so ordinary they should have been forgettable. Instead, they felt foreign, like memories borrowed from someone else's life.

I hadn't seen a sunrise since I was shoved into the Duskhold. There was no sun there. No lavender bleed of dawn, no vermilion hush at evening. Only a sullen ceiling of shadow, cast by nothing at all. I had to remind myself not to stare straight into the light as it spread across the world, no matter how fiercely I might've missed it.

So I headed westward, away from that blazing star—and away from whatever else called to me from the east.

As the sun climbed higher, the world revealed itself in full, aching color. Dew clung to grass and caught the light like scattered emeralds; birds with cyan wings and rust-red breasts flitted between trees whose leaves yellowed with summer's slow surrender. The beauty was almost too much to behold.

And then there was my skin.

My flesh that glowed in the moonlight now shimmered in the sunlight with an inner luminescence, glittering motes swimming just beneath the fuzz and freckles. I swiped at my arms as if I could simply brush it away, undo the past century plus a day through sheer exfoliation.

A pair of fluffy clouds drifted in front of the sun, and the motes dimmed, settling back into me like dust waiting to be kicked up again. Only then did it sink in.

This wasn't the residue of resurrection.

This was something otherworldly.

Something the universe would surely notice.

I was breaching the edge of the forest, thin strands of light slipping through the canopy, when something brushed my face.

Then stuck there.

I staggered backward, gagging as panic surged hot and fast. A thick spiderweb draped itself across my cheeks, my neck, and my shoulders. My arms flailed upward, clawing at my skin, scraping at invisible strands caught in my mouth and my eyelashes. The sensation clung with desperate insistence, sinking into me like a second skin of lace armor.

I squeezed my eyes shut, forced a breath, then another. When I looked again, there was nothing. No web. No enormous spider.

No surviving silk.

Only a pool of darkness at my feet, ink-black and spreading, swallowing me to the ankles. My heart still raced from whatever the hell that was as I stepped back, trying to move away from the shadow.

But the shadow stepped with me—unhurried, unbothered—slinking underfoot like a black cat deciding it belonged to me. I stopped; it stopped. Slowly, carefully, I bent toward it, barely daring to breathe, and reached out.

A tendril unfurled from the mass and lunged.

I hit the ground hard, scrambling backward as terror ripped through me. But before I could scream, the darkness stroked my face. Cool, curious. Like the searching lick of a dog.

"What in the Mother's name—" I mumbled.

The tendril hovered, upright and still, its impenetrable stare piercing through me, though it had no eyes. We regarded one another, matching breath for breath. It didn't move until I did.

I shifted my weight, bracing to stand. The shadow curled around my wrist, slid up my forearm, and hoisted me to my feet with an unsettling, disembodied strength. Once my feet steadied, the friendly tendril melted back into the black puddle, continuing its vigil at my feet.

"Is this me?" I whispered to nothing in particular. "Or is this a trick of the forest?"

The darkness answered by snaking up my leg, looping around my waist, and draping itself across my shoulders like a shawl of cool night air. Its weight was barely there—just a prickle, a ghost of a sensation.

It was me. The shadow was somehow *mine.*

Not a blessing of the Son, for I was no Fae. Perhaps a parting gift from the Whispering Sea. A prize for my survival. And I intended to honor it, befriend it. Maybe even wield it.

I continued on my way, following the peeking speckles of light as the sun stretched higher across the open sky. The shadows cast by towering trees seemed to notice me, bending and reaching unnaturally as I passed. They skittered over the carpet of leaves like a cluster of dark ducklings imprinting on the wrong mother. After a while, I stopped pretending not to notice the constant barrage of shadow-babies nipping at my heels.

Fine. If they wanted my attention, they could have it.

I halted mid-step, curls bouncing forward, and raised my hand in command. The rustling around me ceased as the shadelings gathered and waited, obedient and expectant. I held up two fingers, then flicked them in a slow circle.

Leaves lifted around me in a soft gust, spiraling into a tiny black vortex as the shadows caught and tossed them around. I held up my hand again. The vortex reversed, then stilled, the leaves drifting lazily to the ground as the shadows sat at attention once more.

"Let's see how strong you really are," I whispered, a smirk tugging my lips at the eager shadows buzzing with anticipation.

I raised both arms high, fingers splayed wide. The shadows shot upward, slicing through the canopy and blotting out the sun. Then, I flung my arms down in a sharp sweep, palms catching the air.

The shadows crashed through the treetops, snapping branches that tumbled down. Birds burst from their nests and wailed in the sky. Burrowing bugs exploded from the soil as the leaf bed blasted outward in a violent ring. Leaves and debris rained down—the darkness twisted around me, sealing me into a cocoon that held fast against the ruin we'd conjured.

The forest was stunned into silence. My chest heaved as the booming echo faded. The shadows quivered, ready for more, but my hands trembled at my sides.

I hadn't known I could be that powerful. Or how good it would feel.

The sun sank lower, its edge kissing the river as the cerulean sky bled pink and purple. I didn't feel as tired as I expected following hours of trudging through the woods—but once twilight surrendered to true night, the forest would belong to unseen things. I had no desire to meet them alone.

I found shelter among the massive roots of a sequoia, curling into the hollow they formed. I pulled my knees into my chest and listened to the sounds of the woods. Tiny heartbeats nestling into their burrows and dens, wingbeats of nocturnal birds taking flight for a hunt.

When nothing else stirred, I wove a dark curtain that solidified between me and the rest of the world, and settled in. Sleep crept close, my eyelids turning heavy by the lulling frog song and babbling river.

Voices drifted through the forest. And they were coming closer. I sat up, my instinct to flee flaring, but something in their conversation made me pause.

"The disturbance was definitely here, Tomas. The currents don't lie," a woman said with an accent I couldn't place.

"I don't dispute that, Elidra. But whatever came through here may be long gone," the other voice, a man, said with practicality.

"No, it's close. I can feel it." The woman sounded certain, and the man sighed. "Something crossed from the Duskhold."

Fear scraped through me, and the darkness twitched protectively around me. These were no ordinary travelers out for an evening stroll in the Silverwood Forest. They knew my hellscape prison, and they were actively seeking whatever being that had crossed over. Me.

They were on top of my hiding spot, and a beam of torchlight sliced through my shadow barrier like a cleaver. It dissolved into mist, leaving me bare and vulnerable.

And cornered.

I shielded my eyes from the blinding intrusion. Standing before my hollow was a copper-skinned young woman with intricately braided gray hair, with colorful threads and beads woven within the plaits. Positioned defensively behind her was a much older, weathered-looking man, eyes calm and deep, much like the sky before opening up for a storm.

"There you are," the woman said casually, not a hint of surprise. "I told you, Tomas." She poked the man playfully with her elbow.

I braced myself against the roots—prepared to defend myself, but unsure of my capabilities to do so. "Who are you? What do you want?"

The man—Tomas—raised his hands in a gesture of peace. "We are Keepers of the Cisqa. We mean you no harm."

"Keepers?" The word meant nothing to me.

"Guardians of the boundary," the woman—Elidra—explained, her coffee eyes glinting with something like mischief. "We monitor crossings between realms. Ours, yours... and theirs." She inclined her head toward the east.

"You've caused quite a stir," Tomas added. "The river hasn't behaved this way in generations."

I remained wary. Not sure what to say, but refusing to abandon my guarding posture.

Elidra's mouth gently formed a disarming smile, warming her youthful face. "Standing here in the dark seems like a poor place for conversation," she tittered. "Our home is nearby, with food and a fire... and privacy from prying eyes."

I said nothing.

"You distrust us," Tomas observed perceptively. "Not surprising, considering what you've endured."

"And how would you know what I've endured?" I asked sharply.

"I have seen the Shadow Market. Walked its aisles, in fact," Elidra said softly, knowingly. "I've seen the Masters' Auction, the way slaves are prodded and carted off, and I've seen those *things* driving the caravans."

I narrowed my eyes in her direction. How could a human possibly see the Shadow Market without also being shoved inside the same shit-stained kennel they shipped me in?

"I'm more familiar with the Duskhold than I would like to be, and I will leave it at that."

"We've met no one who actually escaped that realm," Tomas added, his voice filled with wonder as he glanced toward Elidra. "In all our generations of keeping the boundaries, there are only legends of souls lost to the Duskhold, never to return."

"No one escapes?" A stupid question to ask. Escape from the shadowlands wasn't improbable. It was impossible, a fool's notion that served only to prolong one's suffering.

"Never," Elidra confirmed. "Something *extraordinary* must have happened for you to break free of Alezae's grasp." Her interest in me seemed to intensify as her deep brown eyes swept over me, *through me.*

"I sought death."

"And you found us instead," Tomas observed, his gaze lingering on the subtle glow beneath my skin as his knuckles gently brushed against Elidra's.

This all seemed far too convenient to be coincidental. A silence gathered between us as we sized each other up, the trees towering menacingly while the indigo sky finally turned black. A mournful howl sounded nearby, too close for comfort, and I flinched.

"What is your name, child?" Elidra asked gently, making the smallest movement toward me.

"I..." I searched blindly through the fog of my being. The Whispering Sea hadn't given me a name, and whatever sound belonged to me before the shadowlands took it remained lost. "*Myr'Caenith*," I answered, the only name I could remember answering to for the past hundred years. It served as the only identity I had while in my master's household.

The two Keepers mirrored an expression that I couldn't quite interpret, something between concern and dismay. Elidra pressed her lips together into a flat line, dropping her shoulders and extending her hand toward me. The gesture set off feral alarm bells in my head, and the howling grew louder.

After a century of captivity, of being used as a tool and an object, trust didn't come easily. Kindness often concealed ulterior motives, and a hand up usually ended with a slap across the cheek. These people seemed genuine, but I had been deceived by that before.

"We won't force you," she said with a sigh, seemingly reading my thoughts. "Our door is open if you wish, closed if you don't."

"Why would you help me?" I finally asked.

"The Cisqa Valley allowed your passage," Tomas said simply. "That means your crossing serves the balance between realms. Those with ill-intent don't make it past the forest's edge."

"And frankly, we're curious," Elidra added with a laugh.

The howling grew near deafening as I studied them for a long moment, weighing my options. I could push past them and flee, but to where? I had no destination, no plan beyond putting as much distance between myself and the Duskhold as possible. And these Keepers might have had information I needed. Not to mention, a home-cooked meal and a crackling fire sounded heavenly.

So, I emerged from my hiding place, gingerly accepting their offer, choosing for the first time in a century to grab a hand offered to me.

And then the howling stopped.

The Keepers' home was a sturdy stone farmhouse. I glanced around, studying the variety of their collection while Elidra served me a hearty stew, flitting about with ageless grace. Protective herbs hung from the ceiling beams, and intricate patterns and symbols were carved into the wooden supports.

"Before we really get to know each other," Elidra said as she sat down at the table, "let's give you a proper name."

"I have a name," I said, mildly annoyed. "My name is *Myr'Caenith*, and I rather like it."

That was a lie. But it was mine—the only sound I was allowed to answer to for a hundred years. I held it like a shard of glass and dared anyone to pry it from my bloody grip.

"That's not a name," Tomas said, delicately blowing the steaming broth in his bowl. "It means—" Elidra hurled her spoon across the table at his face. Tomas swiftly dodged it with unexpected ease, and it clattered against the wall.

"What?" I asked, suddenly self-conscious. "What does it mean?"

"It doesn't matter what it means," she said, still shooting daggers at Tomas as she stood up to retrieve a clean spoon. She slammed the utensil drawer, and Tomas lowered his eyes in submission. "What matters is that names have power. Power over us and those who use them. *Myr'Caenith*—" She said it like it tasted foul in her mouth. "That word is not a name suited for someone like you."

"Someone like me?" As if they knew anything about me to make assumptions about my character, about who I could have been, this half-naked stranger eating at their table.

Elidra nodded as she glanced over my luminescent skin, then to the shadows beneath my chair that crept up to curl in my lap.

"A fairytale comes to mind," she said. Tomas raised his head, eager to hear what she had come up with. "Lyra. That's what we will call you."

"Lyra," I repeated, testing the name, the sound it made, the way my mouth moved. I sat with it for a moment, allowing the identity to settle over me, to permeate me. It didn't feel borrowed. It felt right. I allowed *Myr'Caenith,* the enslaved husk, to fall away, and invited Lyra to stay. "That will do fine."

Elidra's smile crinkled her eyes, and I wondered if I saw a tear well.

"So... you're *Keepers,*" I said, feeling lighter having shed the false part of myself. "What does that entail?"

"The margins between worlds require tending," Tomas explained as he and his stew settled by the fire with a piece of wood he was whittling—a rough form of a duck. "Not all have Fae guardians. Some places where the worlds grow thin require a more... human touch." He sent a wink over his shoulder to his wife, who turned away with a hidden smirk.

"The Cisqa has been kept for countless generations, but the role was made formal after the Severance," Elidra added, her fingers tapping a rhythm on the table that seemed to match the crackling of the fire. "A border both sacred and dangerous." She leaned forward, expression momentarily serious, but then interrupted by a snort. "Much like my mulled wine, but that never stops Tomas from ruining it every winter."

Tomas didn't look up, but the corner of his mouth twitched upward.

"I improve it," he countered under his breath.

"The point is," she continued, "boundaries matter, as they give definition to the worlds. But they're not meant to be impermeable. There's always been movement between realms, just... regulated movement."

"Last night, the Cisqa turned black as pitch for about half an hour. Tossed like a maelstrom, but the sky was perfectly clear," Tomas recounted as he maintained his whittling. "And then it calmed. Just like that. That's only occurred thrice before in the history of the Keepers."

I set down my spoon carefully. "And what happened those

times?"

"The balance between realms shifted," Elidra said. "Twice for the better, once… not so much."

"What does that mean, exactly?"

They exchanged another of those meaningful glances. The fire gave a hard crack, as if it disapproved of where the conversation was headed.

"The first time, the old stories say that the Four Pillars withdrew from the world," Tomas said carefully. "The second, the Duskhold was born. And the third time—" He trailed off, his expression darkening.

"The third time," Elidra said, grasping for words to describe a clearly traumatic history, "the world damn near ended, and we will keep it at that."

I looked around at the carved symbols in the beams and along the doorframes; the patterns seemed less like art and more like warnings. "What caused it?"

"The Keepers before us didn't know. Or if they did, they didn't record it," Tomas replied with a shrug. "They knew only the signs that preceded it. The river turning black was the first."

The implications settled heavily over the wooden kitchen table. Whatever transpired in the Whispering Sea might have been far more significant than just my personal transformation. How large was the domino that inevitably fell when I emerged from the water?

"Is that why you brought me here?" I asked. "You think I'm connected to this… shift in the balance?"

"Your crossing from the Duskhold may be a sign of changes to come. Whether those changes bring flames or fortune remains to be seen." Elidra paused again, weighing the conversation before she asked the burning question between us all. "How are you *here*?"

I hesitated. How, indeed? The first in a long line of questions

I was hopeless to answer.

"I don't know," I said plainly. "I tried drowning myself in the Whispering Sea. Instead of dying, I'm...this."

"The ancient texts speak of that sea as a boundary no one crosses twice. Yet here you stand." Tomas nodded as if confirming a brewing theory. "The Whispering Sea remade you."

"Your form bears the signature of the astral plane," Elidra said thoughtfully. "A realm beyond both Fae and mortal domains. It's the in-between, the void that cradles creation itself."

My lips parted as my mouth became suddenly dry.

"Is that why I can do this?" I bid a tiny star from the fold to form in my palm, its silver-blue light casting strange shadows and eliciting a tingling heat.

Elidra drew a sharp breath. "Astral manifestation. Never in my life did I..." Her words trailed off as she beheld my pet star.

"And this?" I closed my hand around the star, extinguishing it, then reached toward Tomas's shadow that stretched across the floor. It responded to my call, a ribbon of darkness curling around my hand and sliding between my fingers.

"Shadowmancy," Tomas whispered, watching with fascination rather than fear. "The counterbalance to your starlight. Together, they form the complete expression of astral power. The yin and yang of the very cosmos."

Heat rose up my neck and reddened my cheeks as this potential was finally named.

"Well," Elidra said, shaking off her bewilderment as she shooed the shadow in my hand back to its residency with Tomas, "I think that's enough *illumination* for the evening." A small snort escaped her at her own quip. "Come, Lyra, let's get you comfortable, hm?"

I placed my bowl—scraped clean despite my not being hungry—in the washbasin and followed her to a small room at the back of the house. It was scarcely furnished, with nothing more than a bed, a side table, and a lantern. She left me with some sleeping garments and a bowl and cloth to wash my face.

I sat on the edge of the bed, admiring the sea glass as it captured and refracted the glow from my skin, casting faint blue patterns across the walls. I pressed it between my palms, seeking any memory it might still contain.

It managed a single internal flicker, which was more than I'd gotten from it since I lost count of the days. I pressed the shard to my lips, an evening ritual.

I will find you.

I lay in the darkness, listening to the soft tones of conversation in another room, the words indistinct. Beyond the house, a breeze picked up over the river, carrying its crisp scent through my open window.

And at the very edge of my awareness, almost imperceptible, a presence watched. Not human, not animal. Not Fae, not beast. But something ancient, omniscient. Even as sleep claimed me, the weight of its gaze lingered—patient in the dark, waiting to see what I would become.

Chapter Four

S o," Tomas said as his hands worked a different piece of wood, a songbird this time. "You wish to seek out the Fae."

Not a question.

I looked up from the egg and mutton scramble Elidra had prepared. It was the kind of breakfast that clung to your ribs, reminding you throughout the morning that someone wanted you fed.

"How did you know?"

"Your sea glass." Elidra gestured to the blue shard that now hung around my neck. "It holds remnants of Faen enchantment. And you keep looking eastward, where the Amber Vale lies."

I touched the glass instinctively. I had no idea what lay to the east, just that I felt divinely drawn in that direction. "What do you know of that place?"

"The Amber Vale is the nearest Fae realm." Tomas did not look up from his carving, whittled shavings now scattered over his lap.

"Ruled by the Amber King in his court of eternal sunset, made up of smaller territories that he has *collected* during his reign," Elidra said.

"And a dangerous destination for someone like you," Tomas warned.

She sighed in agreement, scooping her braids from her neck and gathering them on top of her head. As she tied them together, I noticed very delicate points at the tips of her ears.

I held back the urge to ask why. For one, I had no desire to pile more uncertainty on top of my existing identity crisis, and two, it wouldn't have mattered anyway. My resolve outweighed my caution when it came to this second chance.

"I can't allow my suffering to be in vain. I want to go there," I insisted with unwavering certainty. *I need to go there.* The shard vibrated beneath my touch.

Elidra sighed, long and dramatic, the battle already lost. "Wait here," she breathed, and disappeared into another room.

When she returned, she bumped into a doorframe, then the kitchen counter, awkwardly carrying a large traveler's chest.

"You'll need more than just courage and a trinket!" she said as she heaved it onto the table, clattering my half-eaten breakfast. "You'll need a good story to tell."

The smell of cedar and mothballs carried the weight of years and far-off places as she threw open the chest, revealing magnificent and expensive-looking jewel-toned garments.

"Tomas and I traveled to the ends of the earth before we settled in this farmhouse."

"And spent a lot of money," Tomas muttered over his shoulder. His tone suggested the rhythm of an age-old argument, one they likely had in bazaars on every edge of Avynne. Perhaps even farther than that.

Elidra scowled at him before she started picking through the clothes. "He helped me spend it," she whispered to me, though I was sure he heard, because he smirked in his spot by the hearth before changing the subject.

"Lyra was a celestial maiden who tended to the stars, polishing them every night so they would twinkle." Tomas's voice slipped into the cadence of a practiced storyteller. Part of me was convinced he might believe his tale. "From her heavenly perch, she heard a Fae shepherd who would play his flute for his flock every night. Enchanted by his haunting music, she descended to Earth, disguised as a falling star."

Elidra nodded, half-listening as she rifled through the chest, tossing its contents around like old rags.

"The shepherd found her in a smoldering crater, wounded from the fall and covered in stardust, and he offered her shelter."

"Much like our meeting," Elidra said to me with a wink, though I wasn't sure if she meant meeting me, or meeting him.

"He cared for her while she recovered, and they fell in love despite their different natures. The gods eventually discovered Lyra's absence from the heavens when the stars began to dull, and they sent their hunters to retrieve her. But when they arrived, the shepherd played a melody so beautiful that it captivated the hunters as well. So the gods offered a compromise: Lyra would spend half the year on Earth with her shepherd, and the other half tending to her stars."

"But the shepherd grew old," Elidra continued. "As his death grew nearer, Lyra gave him a star crystal containing her eternal light. Upon his death, his soul joined with her gift, transforming him into a constellation that now bears his name—Melatheon."

She smiled as she pulled out a stunning piece, holding it up to me with pride. The dress had a bodice made from indigo-dyed suede and a skirt of the finest midnight blue silk. Thousands of intricately placed crystals were arranged on the entire dress like filigree, glittering with a full spectrum of color.

She paired the dress with a black velvet cloak, opals and sapphires meticulously stitched around the entire hood.

I circled one of the beads with my thumb, admiring the silver thread that trailed it like the tail of a falling star. "These are much too fine," I protested. "I can't possibly accept—"

"They've sat unused for decades," Elidra interrupted. "Better they serve a purpose more than just gathering dust."

I reluctantly agreed and changed behind a screen while Elidra outlined her plan. "The Amber Vale has invited performers from across the realms to entertain at court as they celebrate their prince's return."

"I'm no performer," I objected, emerging in the midnight-blue dress that fit like it had been tailored specifically for me.

"But you have talents no one has seen before," Tomas said, finally looking up from his carving. "Even on a small scale, your magic would make for extraordinary spectacle."

Elidra nodded, circling me with an appraising eye. "Not to mention, a performer would have access to the palace without the scrutiny faced by diplomats or merchants."

I furrowed my brow as I flexed my fingers, shadows barely buzzing at my fingertips. The thought of using this new magic for spectacle felt both obscene and thrilling in equal measure.

"You'll need a place of origin," Tomas said. "Somewhere that might explain your unusual magic."

"The Twilight Isles," Elidra suggested matter-of-factly.

Tomas looked to her adoringly. "That would explain everything."

Elidra nodded. "Because it explains *nothing*."

"I'm not following," I said as the two communicated silently about this vaguely brilliant idea.

"The Twilight Isles are mysterious for good reason, and most Faen don't care to find out what those reasons might be. They have ways of channeling magic beyond the Son's blessing."

My mind circled the plan, looking for holes I might fall through. "If I'm questioned about my... *art*... what would I possibly say?"

"You could say nothing," Tomas offered.

"Nothing?" I repeated incredulously.

"Anybody would be too nervous to ask something twice of an Islander, especially a Twilight Islander."

"Perfect," Elidra agreed. "The mystery of the Isles works in your favor. Your reluctance to explain your techniques would be respected."

"Out of fear?"

"Fear equals respect in the Amber Vale. Wield it wisely."

I let the idea settle, then nodded. Fear was a language I could learn to speak.

Elidra beamed as the pieces of my new identity fell into place. "Lyra, starlight illusionist from the Twilight Isles." She tasted every syllable like the title of a prized memoir.

My hand quickly shot up to touch the curve of my ear. Distinctly not Fae. "Will my human appearance raise questions?"

She shrugged in dismissal of my worry. "The Faen realms have become more... accepting of outsiders in recent decades," she explained, sorting through the other garments in her chest and pausing to reminisce as she held each one up to the light. "You'll find humans in the Vale. Not many, but enough that your presence won't raise suspicions."

"Since when are the Fae welcoming toward humans?"

Tomas inclined his head thoughtfully. "The Fae in the north softened their boundaries first, about fifty years ago. Humans with particular talents or trades can now petition for temporary residence in most Fae territories."

"The Amber King resisted longer than most," Elidra continued, "but even he couldn't ignore the benefits of human innovation. Your ears won't be what draws attention." She looked at Tomas, and he rose from his chair and headed toward a cabinet in the corner of the room.

"What changed?"

"The world kept turning," Tomas said plainly. "Even immortals must eventually adapt or be left behind."

He returned with a delicate chain draped over his knuckles. The pendant, an unembellished oval, bore an etched design that seemed to hold no proper shape.

"A dampening charm," he explained. "It won't hide your power completely, but it will mute its signature enough that you might pass as an unusual Semi-Fae rather than something entirely *unnameable*."

I accepted the pendant cautiously. "Why would you have such a thing?"

"With our travels have come many interesting baubles," Tomas said, his voice solemn. "And as Keepers, you never know when the opportunity for unique intervention may present itself."

As I clasped the chain at the nape of my neck, a subtle shift settled against my chest. The ever-present power that rippled beneath my skin receded to a comfortably faint hum.

Over the next hour, they instructed me on Fae customs and court etiquette, or as much as they could glean from a life spent skirting the borders.

Elidra demonstrated the proper way to bow—head inclined just so, eyes lowered but not fully downcast—while Tomas explained the intricate web of favors and debts that governed Fae dealings.

He corrected my posture with a quiet click of his tongue. "Too low," he said, lifting my chin a fraction, "and you offer submission. Too high, and you invite a challenge. Either can bind you to a bargain you never meant to make."

It wasn't long before Lyra the illusionist looked back at me from the polished metal mirror Elidra held. Exotic, mysterious, with just enough otherworldliness to intrigue rather than alarm.

"You'll pass," Tomas said with approval. "At least long enough to find what you seek."

"And if what I seek isn't there?" I asked, voicing the fear that had lurked beneath my determination.

"Then you will at least be richer for the experience," Elidra said gently. "How you get there is just as important as where you're going."

Without another word, Elidra reached for her traveling cloak. Tomas followed suit, tugging his own from a peg by the door, his other hand curling around a rolled map.

I blinked. "You're coming with me?"

Elidra flashed a smile. "Only as far as the bridge."

Tomas grunted. "Just making sure you don't get eaten on the road." Elidra elbowed him in the ribs before we all piled out the door.

The cart rattled over the dirt path; the map was spread across my knees as I traced the thin black line from the Silvermist Bridge to the tiny painted spire marking the palace. "If I'm walking from the bridge... how far will it be?"

Elidra shrugged. "Depends on how the realm feels that day. Could be half a day. Could be three."

Tomas pulled the horse to a slow halt, hopped down, and began tucking wrapped parcels of bread and dried fruit into a small satchel.

"That doesn't make any sense," I said, frowning down at the

map.

"The sun never moves in the Vale," Tomas replied. "So it's fair to say time doesn't exactly follow the same rules you're used to."

Elidra's tone softened. "It's better to think of the distance as... negotiable. The Vale keeps its own rhythm."

Tomas handed me the sack he had prepared as he climbed back up and urged the horse forward again. "Eat when you can. And don't lose that map," he said, eyes forward. "I would like it back." His tone made it sound less like advice and more like a devotion he had prayed over many travelers before me.

The bridge's sweeping arch of pale stone floated above the widest part of the Cisqa River, ethereal mist clinging to it, marking the end of mortal Avynne and the start of Fae Avynne.

"It's guarded," Elidra noted as she craned her head, somehow able to scan the distance. "They'll want to know your business in the Vale."

"What do I tell them?"

"The guards are trained to identify deception, but they struggle at discerning half-truths." Tomas advised. "So you tell them the truth. Part of it, anyway."

"You're a performer who wants to share your illusions with the court," Elidra declared. "No more, no less."

She then turned to face me fully, eyes shining the way a mother's might on the edge of goodbye.

"How can I ever repay this kindness?" I asked.

"Remember us," she said. "And when the time comes to choose your path, choose what serves the balance, not your own desires."

Her fingers squeezed mine once before she let go. Tomas gave me a single, gruff nod. These were the last bits of warmth before my world turned to strangeness yet again.

I hopped down from the cart, and we went our separate ways, though I knew they were still close. I could hear their horse's impatient whinnies just around the bend.

Two guards were stationed at the mortal end, wearing armor the color of burnished copper, their postures alert. I approached them with confident steps, my performer's clothing and the dampening charm bolstering me.

"Halt," the taller guard commanded as I reached the bridge's threshold. "State your name and purpose in the Amber Vale."

I bowed just as Elidra had taught me.

"I am Lyra, illusionist of the Twilight Isles. I seek to offer my talents at the court celebrations."

"Another performer?" The shorter one sighed. "The Vale teems with entertainment already."

"None like mine," I replied, letting a hint of pride lace my words. "May I demonstrate?"

They exchanged bored glances before the taller one gave a curt nod.

I extended my palms and summoned the stars to hover in my hands. With intention, just as I had practiced, I willed them into the shape of a tree, branches flowing in a phantom breeze. Leaves of shadow fell from the branches, each dissolving into a puff of mist before touching the ground.

Their skepticism softened to mild interest. "Peculiar magic." The taller guard tilted his head, his eyebrow lifting as though he were tempted to pry at my cover story.

"My talents lie in the manipulation of light," I explained smoothly. "Mere illusions to tell stories."

The shorter one's expression eased. "The court has been keen on such novel entertainments since the prince's return. You may pass."

I bowed again. "I appreciate your consideration."

The shroud of mist deepened as I made my way across the bridge. It licked at my feet and curled along every inch of exposed skin, like fingers eager to drag me across.

Halfway over, the air changed. Scents of wildflowers and spice drifted in the sticky breeze, and each breath felt clearer somehow. One taken on this side of the river had more life than a lifetime on the other side.

When my boots landed on the far side of the bridge, the landscape looked like an illustration torn from a storybook. Trees spiraled in impossible patterns. Flowers bloomed in colors that should not exist in nature. The dirt path from the bridge became a road of shimmering stone, each gap filled with mortar that glinted like weathered gold.

This was the Amber Vale.

The sun stayed nestled behind me, where it would sit forever. Since it hadn't moved once I crossed the bridge, I couldn't tell how long I had been walking. Certainly more than a few hours. Probably less than a full day.

I stopped for bread and water when the Amber Palace appeared on the horizon. It was a behemoth of crystal and stone that trapped the sunset and scattered it back a thousandfold across the hills. Sharp spires rose like flames; open courtyards and terraced gardens cascaded down the hillside in varying shades of warmth.

By the time I reached the gates, my legs trembled from the trek, lungs burning raw and sweet. Merchants, messengers, and fellow performers crowded together in a messy queue, seeking entry to the palace.

A steward wearing pearl-trimmed robes stood at the front, consulting a ledger in his hand as if it had offended him.

"Another performer?" His quill hovered menacingly, like it might want to stab me instead of taking down my information. "Specialty?"

"Illusions of light and shadow," I replied, and gave a smaller, neater version of my bridge demonstration.

His gaze tracked every flicker with an apathy that only comes from hundreds of years of seeing too much and caring too little.

"Not Faen magic, is it?"

I kept my tone easy. "My techniques are unique to my lineage."

He gave a noncommittal grunt, then scrubbed something down so violently I was sure he'd rip the page. "Wisteria Wing, with the other performers. The next round of auditions is at midday tomorrow in the Golden Hall." He looked at me, realizing I was too green to know how to tell time here. "Listen for the chime. Don't be late. Don't wander without your token. And by all means, do not defecate in the communal baths, and any glitter you leave behind, you must clean up yourself."

I almost laughed at the absurdity of it. A realm that could bend time still fretted over sequins clogging the drains. I bowed as he shoved a silver token into my hand.

"I am honored by the hosp—"

He shooed me off with a hiss, followed by a sharp snap of his fingers to summon the next in line.

The Wisteria Wing was removed from the palace proper, separated by a manicured promenade. It resembled a gilded greenhouse, drowning in fragrant purple blooms and flooded with light as the panes of glass burned like solar flares.

My assigned room was modest, furnished for function, not luxury, but it was far from unkind. A narrow bed pressed against the wall, dressed in quilts that smelled faintly of lavender and wood smoke. A small writing desk sat in the corner, its surface scarred with ink blots and knife marks, supporting the scrawling laments of countless travelers before me. A single lantern swayed gently from a hook in the ceiling, casting honeyed light through the room that blended with the sunset bleeding through the lace curtains of the window—a window overlooking a strange garden that was somehow untouched by the sunset, blanketed entirely in the shade of night.

A chime sounded as I settled in, echoing through the palace

like an omnipresent bell choir—*bing bong bing bong!*—the signal that it was now considered nighttime, though the sky glowed its endless orange. I sat at the window, looking out at the palace proper, hoping the smudged face from my distant memories was somewhere within those walls. Perhaps he was the prince who had recently returned from some unknown travels.

I wondered what kind of woman I must have been, if that was true, to have fallen so recklessly in love with a Fae.

An incredibly stupid woman, no doubt.

And yet, here I was, sneaking into a den of predators, hoping to rekindle a flame I couldn't even remember first setting ablaze.

Chapter Five

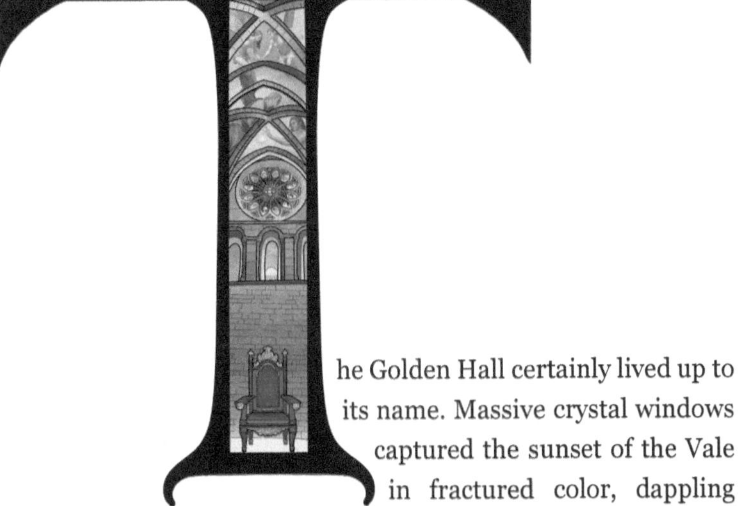

The Golden Hall certainly lived up to its name. Massive crystal windows captured the sunset of the Vale in fractured color, dappling the polished marble floors and gilded columns in shifting, distorted illustrations. The domed ceiling soared impossibly high, painted to depict scenes from Fae history that moved when viewed from different angles. Their shifting made me dizzy, like the room itself wanted to remind me that its fortunes were not my own.

The light spilled across the marble until it caught on me, painting half of my face while leaving the other in shadow. Two people stitched together, neither of them whole, neither of them having any idea what we were doing here. Perfume wafted through the air, the clicks of heels and snaps of fingers bouncing off the ceiling.

I willed my thoughts down to a whisper, worried that if I was too loud in my head, it might echo through the entire palace.

I stood among two dozen other performers in the antechamber, each of us waiting for our turn to audition. We were a diverse collection of artists: musicians with instruments I'd never seen before, dancers whose feet never touched the ground, and other illusionists who manipulated the elements—though none played with celestial darkness like I did.

I scanned the gathered crowd and noted with relief that I wasn't the only non-Fae present. Among the performers waiting in the wings and courtiers scattered through the hall, there were smaller faeries with wings and horns and gangly bipedal creatures whose skin shimmered in shades of powder blue and lilac. Several humans stood among them as well, their skills—whatever they were—having earned them a coveted place in this realm of immortal beauty.

They were far fewer in number than the Fae, but their presence meant I might not be seen as the imposter I felt to be. Still, I counted each breath, attempting to hide the fact that I was shaking in my skin.

"First time at court?" asked a voice beside me, pulling me out of my daze.

I turned to see a lovely Fae with autumn-red hair woven into a crown with rose gold silk. Her feline yellow eyes rested upon me with a quaint ferocity, and it was unclear if I'd been chosen for conversation or cataloging, though her smile was friendly enough.

"Is it that obvious?" I asked, smoothing over the bodice of my dress unconsciously. I winced as a contortionist twisted herself into a lacquered dress box, bones cracking with deliberate rhythm.

"Only to someone who watches people for a living." She extended a slender hand adorned with rings engraved with strange symbols. "Lysara, Court Historian and Keeper of Records."

"Lyra," I replied, using my adopted name with growing ease. "Starlight Illusionist."

"From which realm do you hail?" Her eyes sparkled with peculiar interest. "I can't quite place your accent."

"I'm well-traveled." A half-truth.

"Aren't we all?" Lysara laughed melodically.

"I claim the Twilight Isles." I purposefully did not meet her eyes.

"Before my role here in the Amber Vale, I did some tutoring in the archives of the Twilight Isles. Fascinating magical traditions there. Though they never grant outsiders the truth of the sources from which they conjure." Her head tilted as her expression tinged with hope.

I tensed at her mention of the Twilight Isles. If she had spent time there, she could easily poke holes in my paper-thin alibi.

"I'm not quite sure what you mean," I deflected, hoping my evasion read as sacred as opposed to specious.

Her disarming smile didn't seem suspicious, even as it fell slightly in disappointment. I prayed she meant nothing more than pleasant conversation, and perhaps a nugget of forbidden knowledge that I did not possess. A pause stretched between us as I continued wiping my palms along my dress.

"You seem a bit nervous," she said, her tone softening. "I remember my first court performance. Before I could officially establish my role as the Historian's apprentice, I had to recite the entire catalog of magical artifacts in the royal treasury. Over three hundred items, and I was certain I'd forget half of them."

"And did you?" I asked, grateful for her timely change of subject.

"Worse." She grimaced. "I misnamed one artifact named in the old tongue. Instead of naming the Scepter of Truth, I basically called it the 'Dick of Justice.'"

My hand flew over my mouth, but not before a cackle tore past the antechamber, rattling the poor fire-eater currently mid-audition. He nearly swallowed his torch as his fiery gaze shot to me, and I was certain I'd made my first foe at court.

Lysara chuckled under her breath. "It was pretty minor in the grand scheme of things, but in the world of ruthless court politics..." She dragged a finger across her throat dramatically.

"And yet here you stand," I noted, warming easily to her self-deprecating humor.

"Surprisingly, the King found it amusing, rather than having my head for the vulgarity. He even joked that he might rename that particular article in honor of my blunder."

Her candor helped untie the knot that had formed in my stomach ever since taking my first step onto the bridge. I had convinced myself that she was simply being kind to a newcomer and reminiscing about her own first days in court.

But that notion didn't last long.

"I am rather intrigued by your timing." Her forehead wrinkled as she raised an eyebrow.

I knew it. A truth for a truth. Here was the first of those pesky favors the Fae dealt like a hand of cards.

"You, with your curved ears and pretty dress, arriving just as whispers about our returned prince fill every corner of the continent," she said, eyes narrowing with curiosity. She tracked the subtle shift of my feet as the unease seeped back into me. "As court historian," she continued, "I document patterns and coincidences. They're often more telling than any officially made statements."

"My schedule is dictated by whatever opportunities present

themselves," I said plainly. "The prince's homecoming sounded lucrative, and my purse needs lining."

"Very practical," she nodded, making a mental note of my evasively damp reply to her burning question. "Most visitors claim to be drawn to the Vale's beauty or its renowned hospitality. Few will admit to a payday."

A steward appeared then, granting me a reprieve from her questioning as he called the next performer. A musician with a crystalline harp stepped forward, the last act before it was my turn.

The harpist was joined in the middle of the hall by a spectral beauty, white hair that defied gravity hidden beneath a shawl. The first string of the harp was plucked, and the mournful sound that came from the hooded creature was chilling as it was shrill.

Her keening hit a pitch that rattled the crystal chandeliers and stained glass panes of the Golden Hall. Courtiers pressed hands to their ears, silk sleeves muffling gasps and cries as her ghostly form billowed like a sail in a storm.

"Get that banshee out of here!" The King commanded as he stood. Guards descended upon the performers from all sides.

Their hands gripped their scabbards, preparing to draw, as if their tempered steel could cut down grief incarnate. Without another shriek, both she and the harpist evaporated in a burst of ash-scented smoke, leaving only scorched marble and the taste of iron in the air.

No one applauded this time. A few courtiers scurried to the wings, faces pale and hands over their mouths.

"Is the prince's return unusual?" I asked, keeping my tone casual as the court wrestled with its discomfort. My cup had run over when it came to ill omens, and my nerves refused to make room for more.

Let the banshees wail, as far as I was concerned.

Lysara remained unfazed as well, her casual interest flipping to calculated pursuit. "A century-long political errand, even for lesser diplomats, is atypical at best."

"How do you mean?"

Her gaze swept the antechamber before she leaned in. "Court historians are meant to record facts, not gossip. But since you're new—"

Before she could continue with whatever juicy detail she almost divulged—a personal hypothesis, a well-rounded rumor, or perhaps another hopeful favor—the steward returned. Nobody was ahead of me this time.

"Lyra of the Twilight Isles."

Every eye in the antechamber burned into my back, willing me to either shine or choke. I wiped the sweat from my palms as I prayed for the former, my skirt surely threadbare by now with my constant soothing.

I followed him through the ornate doors into the Golden Hall proper. At the far end, on a dais of gold-veined marble, stood three throne-like chairs fit for the royals.

The Amber King was unmistakable, power and authority radiating from him like the scorching heat of a white-hot flame. His features were classically Fae—ageless and uninterestingly perfect, not a single flaw or asymmetry to snag the eye.

Beside him sat a female whom I was sure was the Queen, her ethereal beauty seemingly distant, as if part of her existed in an entire realm apart. Her gloved hands were folded neatly in her lap, hair draping over her bony shoulders in a perfectly straight sheet of silver, her gaze fixed somewhere far beyond this chamber.

The third chair, set on the Queen's far side, remained hopelessly empty.

"Your Majesties," the steward announced, "Lyra of the Twilight Isles, illusionist."

I bowed. *Head inclined, eyes lowered, waist parallel to the floor. Breathe in. One, two, three, four... breathe out. Rise.*

"I am honored by your consideration," I said, the formal phrase feeling strange to my otherwise informal tongue.

"Proceed with your demonstration," the King commanded, his voice carrying an intimidating coolness.

The dampening charm hummed from the space between my skin and bodice as I centered myself. I reached ever so carefully into the well of my power, not daring to exhale as I drew the finest thread.

I raised my hands, and darkness bloomed around them in a mist that solidified into a tiny, velvety night sky. Pinpricks of light peeked through to create constellations that moved slowly while I turned the world beneath it, telling the ancient Fae story of the first stars.

From the darkness, shadowy figures emerged—dancers, lovers, warriors, and killers—acting out the tale within the moving heavens. They felt a bit too real, too reactive, as if I had invoked long-dead spirits for this dance instead of my own imagination. A murmur rippled through the watching courtiers as they realized this was unlike any Fae illusion they'd seen before.

Playing on their growing captivation, I deepened the illusion, sending tendrils of shadow eagerly zipping around the hall. Those intrigued murmurs quickly turned to fascinated sighs as they corkscrewed through the crowd like ribbons of ink in water. The sweet validation washed over me like a warm bath—along with the temptation to keep feeding them until I burned myself hollow.

The darkness expanded above, blotting out the ceiling as the stars pulsed brighter, burned hotter. The room's temperature climbed as I teetered on the edge of losing myself in the layers of magic orbiting around me.

Then, the air was sucked completely out of the room.

The doors behind the royal dais opened with an unapologetic force, and a figure entered. A male, tall and graceful, who moved with the fluid economy of a natural-born predator. He slid into the empty third chair, his features lost to the backlighting of the doorway and the blur of my overexcited shadows. Something sleeping within me opened an eye and lurched toward him.

Darkness shook. Light flickered. The illusion wavered as I clawed for focus, my heart battering against my sternum.

Could it be him? The stranger whose ghost lived in my sea glass?

As if echoing the question, the sea glass warmed where it sat against my chest.

The prince, for he could be nobody else, leaned forward slightly, and the light finally revealed his face.

Among the countless immortal beauties of the court, he was more striking still. Dark blond hair flowed in perfect waves, catching the light like fresh honey dripping slowly from a comb. High cheekbones gave way to a chiseled jaw shaded by morning stubble. Even in his formal wear, his powerful physique was truly a display to behold—broad shoulders tapered to a narrow waist, the posture of someone trained in both court and combat.

But it was his eyes that truly seized my attention. Irises of gold ringed with bronze, shrouded in a way that had nothing to do with my illusion. They rivaled the very sunset we basked in, near holy. I hated how easily it made me want to kneel beneath his gaze. His expression remained unreadable, almost vacant, yet those eyes studied my performance with such intensity that it seemed like he pierced through the magic and saw right to the core of me.

As the prince watched me with detachment, the heat of his stare boiled me alive from the inside. Whether it was my body remembering a long-lost love, or simply the infamous, predatory charm of the Fae twisting my emotions into a wiry bramble, I could not deny that something primal churned within me at his presence alone.

My shadows responded in kind, growing more nebulous and unstable as my emotions bled into them, making them far too bold. My illusion shifted from a sweet, traditional folktale to a feral dance of separation, longing, and stumbling home in the dark with the taste of love stuck to your tongue.

My awareness of him became suffocating, and a rogue shadeling wriggled free from my control and snaked up to the dais. Straight for him, forward in a way I could never be. It slithered between the thrones and curled around the prince's ankles, pouring smoke over his toes. A flash of amusement lit up his face for only a blink before I yanked the shadow to heel.

The scene poured out of me then, mortification and turmoil making it impossible to rein in. It was like trying to lasso a winged horse with nothing but a shoelace. Ridiculous, impossible. The whimsy of the shadows warped into violent clouds, writhing with unintended ferocity; stars threatened implosion as they slipped beyond my control.

For a single, terrifying moment, I imagined what this power could *truly* do—to me, to the realm, to the universe—and I wondered if I might have already gone too far by reducing it to nothing more than a parlor trick.

Blood pooled in my fists, pattering onto the pristine floor as my fingernails bit deep into my palms. Pain became a vessel to knit together my fractured attention, knot by knot. Sweat beaded at my temples, my cheeks blistering hot, as I willed the chaos to obey.

My relief was palpable when the shadows and starlight finally calmed, then blew away like ash on a gentle breeze, as if nothing had just roiled like a tempest and nearly destroyed the entire court.

When the last spark blinked out of existence, and the illusion was finally over, the hall was silent for three excruciating heartbeats. I stood there, frozen solid, heart pounding violently, acutely aware of every breath taken and held in the vast chamber. Courtiers exchanged uncertain glances, their expressions suspended between awe and unease at the strange magic they'd just witnessed.

Then, as if the gathered audience took their cue from the King's subtle nod of approval, applause erupted, startling in its enthusiasm. The courtiers were impressed. Perhaps more by novelty than skill, but impressed nonetheless.

The King raised a hand, and silence fell like a shroud. "Odd magic," he said flatly. "Unlike traditional Faen illusions."

I idly brushed my fingertips up to my ear, relieved to note my hair had stayed in place enough to hide its curve. *Good.* Though I was sure he could scent the imposter before him.

"No, Your Majesty," I agreed, bowing again.

"I've witnessed many forms of magic across the realms," he remarked, eyeing me with cold calculation. "Yet nothing quite like that. Which *traditions* inform your craft?"

"My techniques blend various traditions," I said, begging my voice to remain steady and my breath to catch up with the rest of me. "Traditions from my *homeland*."

The King's brow furrowed as he leaned forward, gripping the clawed arms of his throne. His lips parted, his tongue prepared to launch a spear right for my head, but the prince spoke instead, slicing through the tension like a cleaver.

"Father," he said. His voice was deeper than I expected, the edges of his register rough, as if rarely used. "We invited performers from across the realms specifically to bring new arts to court. Revealing her secrets under your order would ruin the wonder."

Oh, if he only knew.

Wisps of smoke rose from the King's knuckles as the velvet of the throne singed under his palms. He slid his gaze slowly to his son, and some unspoken, venomous communication passed between them.

After a moment, he nodded.

"Indeed. Novelty, of course, has its place in celebration." He turned his attention back to me. "You will perform at the Haust-blót Feast three nights hence."

"You honor me," I replied with yet another bow.

The steward escorted me back to the antechamber, where Lysara waited, her eyes now bright with exhilaration.

"That was magnificent!" she exclaimed, clasping my hands in hers as if those few minutes in the antechamber were actually years of close friendship. "I've seen nothing like it. Truly, it was like watching the night itself dance!"

"Thank you," I mumbled, still reeling from almost leveling the hall. Or was it that *voice*? The one that cut through the thicket and pulled me to the other side of the thorns to safety?

"You've earned yourself a place at the Feast," Lysara continued. "That's quite an achievement for a newcomer. Most performers wait months for such an honor."

"The prince intervened."

What did he see? What did he recognize? A magician? A damsel? A victim? Was there something that stirred as deeply in him as it did in me?

Lysara's expression grew thoughtful.

"Yes, that was rather unusual. Prince Torian has rarely involved himself in court matters since his return. He attends functions when required, but seldom speaks." She studied me with renewed interest, her eyebrows raising just a hair. "Yet he spoke for you."

"Perhaps he simply appreciated the novelty, as the King suggested."

"Perhaps." She didn't sound convinced. "In any case, you've made quite an entrance. The court will talk about your performance for days."

"Is that good or bad?"

"Both, usually." Lysara smiled wryly. "Renown at court is a double-edged sword. Opening doors while also inviting scrutiny."

I could already feel the blade tip against my throat, sharp and humming.

"Just what I've been craving," I said under my breath.

"If you'd like to learn more about court dynamics before the feast, I could show you the archives. It might help you navigate the political currents."

I hesitated only briefly. She was right. I needed help. I also needed a friend. At this point, I did not care if I owed her a favor. If maintaining my cover and keeping my head from rolling off my shoulders was the outcome, she could have whatever she wanted.

"I would appreciate that greatly," I said.

"West Library, mid-day chime." And without another word, she threw a quick wink over her shoulder, then departed from the antechamber without watching another audition.

I guess mine was all that mattered.

CHAPTER SIX

Lysara was waiting for me when I arrived, dwarfed by the twenty-foot double doors of the library.

"Lyra," she greeted me enthusiastically, her eyes twinkling and glowing gold. "I'm delighted you came. Few visitors appreciate the *real* treasures of the Amber Vale."

Her fiery hair, braided loosely into an intricate fishtail, flopped over her shoulder, contrasting vividly against her deep blue velvet robes, embroidered with silver and black threads. At least ten earrings lined her elongated ears, and single freshwater pearl studs sat right at their pointed tips.

"I appreciate the invitation," I replied as she pulled open the double doors almost effortlessly. I tried not to gape as I glanced around the impressive space. "I've always found history fascinating." A half-truth.

The West Library, which took up an entire wing of the palace, was the most impressive sight I had seen so far. Its curved walls were lined with shelves that soared three stories high, with narrow staircases spiraling between levels and rolling ladders providing access to the uppermost reaches.

Between each bookcase hung larger-than-life paintings— some horrifyingly grotesque, others indescribably beautiful. Where one would make me cringe, another would make me sigh. My least favorite was a depiction of an emerald and onyx wyvern, flames spiraling from its mouth as it set a naked woman ablaze, her face melting off her skull.

"Then you've come to the right place... and to the right person." Her smile turned almost conspiratorial. "The library is open to all court guests, but it is specifically designed to be enigmatic without the guidance of an historian."

My fingertips trailed over the gilded lettering on the spines of decaying books while we strolled through the maze of towering shelves. Lysara's eyes flicked to me, to the shelves, to the increasingly winding path ahead of us, back to me. I realized a bit too late that I had no idea where in the labyrinth she had led me, and I would be hopeless to find my way out alone.

"I've cataloged hundreds of magical demonstrations in my decades here," she finally said, sounding almost out of breath. "But never anything quite like your stars and shadows."

"You've been the Court Historian for decades?" I asked, surprised by her apparent youth, even for a Fae.

She laughed. "One benefit of our longevity. I've held this position for nearly seventy years, though that makes me relatively new compared to my predecessors."

"And you've never seen magic like mine before?"

"Never." Her eyes darkened as she stopped near an alcove, ears perking slightly as the pearls twitched from side to side. She was listening for something. "Well, at least not of the caliber of yours. Which is precisely why I was so eager to speak with you further." Her ears stopped twitching, and she continued into the labyrinth.

"I'm uncertain if I can satisfy the questions you seek answers to." The weight of my own ignorance—along with the magic that tore through me at the audition, wild and half-divine—pressed down on me as I followed her deeper into the maze.

She continued as if I had said nothing at all.

"Court historians are charged with documenting each instance of magic that appears in the Vale. Every detail from every performance is tediously chronicled."

She reached up her sleeve and held out a small journal to me. I leafed through it, skimming over her surprisingly messy handwriting.

There were a couple of sentences about the wards around the kennels, a mention about sightings of ice wielders, and the most recent entries about the fire-eater and the banshee from the audition yesterday.

"It's incredibly tiresome. But yours," she hesitated, sliding a fingernail down an empty spot on the page, presumably where my magic was supposed to be written. "I need more information."

Her explanation made her interest in me much clearer, and a chill shot through me. So it was never just a friendly overture. And this wasn't the historian's duty to document blindly, or else she would have. She needed to understand, and she had a plan to do so.

We reached a section where the spiraling path of the labyrinth tightened into a cozy nook. Lush armchairs circled a hearth that was carved into a circular bookcase against the wall, and massive tomes lay open on reading stands and tables. Dust motes and wisps of long-abandoned cobwebs swayed and danced in our wake.

"These are the doldrums," she sighed. "These archives contain court proceedings, diplomatic histories, magical taxonomies. Carefully curated, but dreadfully stale."

I flipped through one of the open books, an abandoned edition of a stuffy etiquette manual that detailed an eighteen-course place setting, complete with illustrated bits of silverware whose purposes I could not even imagine. For some reason, '*scooping eyeballs from a skull*' rang a bell for one of them. No doubt something I witnessed—and quickly repressed—during my enslavement.

"So, what exactly are you hoping to learn about the court?" She asked, glancing over my shoulder at the book.

I needed to be careful in how I proceeded. Aside from a nice foot rub, I was impoverished of favors worth the information I truly sought. Either Lysara would offer it willingly, or I would have to stumble upon it myself. And I wasn't entirely sure what *it* was that I needed. But even a breadcrumb might cost me dearly.

"Aside from how to avoid committing any *faux pas* or walking through the wrong set of doors, I find myself curious about the prince and his return."

Lysara hummed in acknowledgment, flattening her lips into a line, as if I said exactly what she had expected.

"As you said yourself," I continued, "a 'century-long political errand' seems important, albeit unusual. If I am to perform for His Highness in celebration of his homecoming, I would like to fully understand the weight of the occasion."

Her eyes narrowed on me for a second longer than was comfortable before she slid a book from one of the nearby shelves. The threads of binding looked new, and the pages creaked with freshness as she opened it.

"These are the official accounts of Prince Torian's diplomatic mission. It details his conversations with the High Lords from both the Frost Court and the Obsidian Isles. Such careful negotiations of peace and trade with our bristliest neighbors. Here is an interesting one:

> *Following the flooding of the Rime Enclave and the egregious genocide of its people, I, Prince Torian of the Amber Vale, have come to an agreement with Lord Iäen Thrymskaldr of the Frost Court, in the presence of Lord Daeran Noctis of the Obsidian Isles, that in penance for his callous actions, he shall pay reparations to any surviving family members of those so carelessly slain who have permanent residence in the Vale. He has also agreed to temper hostility at our borders in order for trade routes to remain safe for merchants, and to ensure safe passage of refugees fleeing his tyranny.*
>
> *Let this record also show that Lord Daeran Noctis and his entire council are to be held to full accountability by association for the crimes committed against Faenkind by their closest ally, and his allegiances will not be quickly forgotten.*
>
> *It is also my pleasure, as is my duty, to recover the bodies of those killed at the border who merely sought a simpler life in the sunset eternal. It was their gods-given right to a peaceful life away from villainy and starvation, and we will claim them as our own posthumously.*
>
> *With this agreement, both High Lords have agreed that any show of force against the Amber*

Vale or its people, as well as any further spread of authoritarian rule past the currently established borders, will be met with necessary martial intervention until the threat has been purged.

My attention snagged on that single word—*genocide*—and refused to move. Lysara's finger pressed harder into the page, as if she, too, felt its weight.

A flush had risen in her cheeks by the time she handed me the book, and I was met with curling letters and symbols that I did not recognize. Lysara huffed as I turned the book around at different angles, attempting to orient myself to the direction of the language.

"Eldertongue—the language of the gods," she explained. "Few can translate it; fewer still can speak it fluently. Its primary use these days is to keep secrets in plain sight." She clocked the confusion on my face right away as she took it back from me. "But what secrets could possibly lie between these pages?" She said it as though she already suspected the answer.

"What else does it—"

"The secret," she cut in softly, "is that these accounts are not written in Prince Torian's own hand."

The admission took me by surprise.

"Perhaps a steward went along with him? Chronicled their steps?"

Lysara shook her head almost angrily, and I could see the gears turning behind her eyes.

"They do not send lowly, illiterate stewards along to document politics of such weight," she bit out. "They send historians, or at the very least, an apprentice. But I was conveniently shipped away to the Twilight Isles, and my predecessor..." Her words trailed off as her throat tightened with rising emotion. "She did not go with him."

"Surely there is an explanation—"

"The only explanation is that it did not happen. That *this*," she said, waving the book in the air, "is just beautifully written fiction."

I suddenly felt bare, like I was not supposed to be hearing the words coming from this female's mouth. A disembodied fire popped in the grate, spitting embers and making me jump.

"These notions seem very dangerous even to consider, let alone speak aloud," I whispered.

Lysara's dwindling air of mischief sank from her cheeks.

"They don't scare me." Her eyes budded with a craze I had no interest in seeing bloom larger.

"Who?" The constant bobbing of her thought process was dizzying. She did not answer, but simply shook her head, her braid sweeping across her back and her earrings tinkling against each other.

"Why did you bring me here?" I asked directly.

"You have something I need," she said sharply.

"And what is it you think I have?"

A sudden coldness radiated from her, making the hair on my arms stand on end. No matter how disarming she seemed, she was still Fae, after all. She was a predator, just like the rest of them.

She brought her face within inches of mine. Her eyes darted between mine, then at my quivering lip, at my trembling nostrils, searching my face for anything she could use.

"Everyone brings something with them to the archives. A piece of the puzzle, a fiber of truth."

"I don't—"

"I know you don't. At least, not yet. But you will." She watched my pulse hammer in the soft spot beneath my jaw as her presence pinned me to the spot. "I'm not playing with stupid favors, Lyra. I am concerned only with truth. I want it to *make sense*." She tapped her finger at her temple, then finally pulled away from me. Her voice was strained, as if she were trying to hold a thousand thoughts at once, each one unraveling at its edges.

"W-why not just ask the prince himself to recount it?" I stammered. I knew immediately that it was a useless recommendation. Lysara rolled her eyes as she gently placed the book back on the shelf.

"Believe me, I have tried. He refuses to say anything that isn't a parroted response from his advisors. I stopped prodding after he threw an unopened bottle of wine at my head."

I winced.

"There are rumors," she continued, "regarding his sudden detachment. Some think he fell victim to the mirages of the sirens in the Isles. Others say gathering the charred bodies at the border likely fractured him."

I imagined him trudging through thick snow, chunky flakes of white sticking to his hair, to his eyelashes, as he hoisted blackened corpses over his shoulder, whispering a vigil for each one. Then I thought of him during the audition, of those shadows that clung to the whites of his eyes, the sorrow that weighed on him so heavily. But it did not feel *correct*.

"And what do you think?"

She studied my face briefly before her expression completely fell, and her eyes shifted to the hearth, the flames within crackling much more violently now. She did not open her mouth to answer.

"If there was no political mission, why welcome him home with such jubilation?" She continued to stare into the fire. "Why fabricate negotiations that could so easily be disproven otherwise?" Still not a word. Her sudden silence was near maddening now. "Why am I here, Lysara? *Really*?" I asked again. But this time, I did not know if I meant here, now, in the library with her, or in the Amber Vale in the first place.

She finally looked back at me, her jaw slackened as if the dance of the fire had put her into a trance she struggled to escape.

"I don't know," she sighed. She blinked away whatever scene

was playing behind her eyes, and I could tell that those words did not pass her lips often, and certainly did not do so easily.

My frustration with Lysara and her weaving, conspiratorial conversation threatened to boil over when someone behind us cleared their throat in announcement. Both of our heads whipped around at the intrusion, our clandestine meeting now exposed. My heart stopped.

Prince Torian stood in the doorway, tall and regal, wearing a tunic of deep bronze that accentuated the gold in his eyes. For a moment, he seemed surprised to find this secluded area of the archives occupied, his gaze sweeping over us with a tinge of annoyance.

Lysara straightened immediately and curtsied. "My Prince, we did not expect you. The archives are yours, of course. We will take our leave posthaste if you wish it."

I followed her lead and dipped as well, keeping my eyes lowered, though I longed to study his face for any sign of familiarity.

"No need, Lysara," he sighed roughly. "I merely sought a quiet place to think."

"Of course, Your Highness," Lysara replied. "We'll be silent as the shadows."

Her formal words, though flustered, belied a comfortable friendliness in the slight tilt of her head, the ease of her gaze meeting his. There was clearly a history between them that transcended their official roles—and the wine bottle incident.

He moved swiftly past us, entering an even more removed reading nook nestled on the other side of the hearth. As he went by, his eyes lingered on me with an unsettling intensity, though his face revealed nothing of his thoughts. The sharp scent of alcohol and smoke clung to him, dragging the remnants of whatever storm he had just weathered through the archives.

Lysara and I took seats in opposite chairs in front of the fire, the heat between us now cooled. I wanted to bolt from the library and hide in my room until the world ended, to escape *both* of them. But I couldn't. So I simmered and sat, pretending to study the place-setting again, not a word spoken between us. Meanwhile, Prince Torian remained absorbed in whatever book he'd plucked from a nearby shelf.

After perhaps half an hour of this painfully uncomfortable silence, Lysara leaned forward. Her eyes twinkled again, as though nothing out of the ordinary had transpired.

"Would you mind showing me your magic?" she whispered. "I've been dying with intrigue ever since witnessing your audition yesterday."

I hesitated, glancing toward the prince.

"Here?"

"The tiniest demonstration," she urged, poking her bottom lip out in an exaggerated pout. "Please?"

I nodded reluctantly with a sigh, and against my better judgment, cupped my hands together between us. I summoned a single constellation, cradling it gently as it turned slowly on a tiny celestial axis in my palms.

Lysara's eyes dilated with delight as she leaned closer to see the intricate details of each star. "Extraordinary," she breathed. "They move with such purpose, as if—"

Her thought was interrupted by a sharp gasp from across the room. We looked up to see Prince Torian standing rigid beside his reading table, his book forgotten on the floor where it had fallen from his hands. The pages of the book glowed with heat, curling in as they burned.

"Your Highness!" Lysara sprang from her seat, concern evident in her voice as she rushed over to trample the growing flame. "Are you unwell?"

He didn't respond, transfixed by the stars cradled in my palms. His stare was so disconnected from the expression of raw shock on his face. I closed my hands quickly, extinguishing the illusion.

For a long moment, he remained frozen, his knuckles white where he gripped the edge of the reading table. Then, with visible effort, he composed himself, bending to retrieve the smoldering book with movements that seemed unnaturally stiff.

"My apologies," he stammered, his voice strained. "A momentary... distraction."

He turned abruptly and replaced the half-burned book on its shelf with meticulous care. As he did so, he murmured something under his breath, words in the ancient Fae tongue I could not understand, clearly not meant for us to overhear.

Recognition dawned on Lysara's face at his words, though she gave no other indication of having heard, aside from a slight frown of pity. With no further inclination in our direction, Prince Torian strode from the archives, his departure just as jarring as his arrival.

"What was *that* about?" I asked Lysara. "What did I do?"

She shook her head, her expression troubled. "It wasn't you. Not directly. Something about your illusion must have triggered something long forgotten within him, I think."

My stomach swooped at the idea that my magic had that stark an effect on him.

"What was it he said? Was that Eldertongue?"

"Yes," she hesitated. "He said, 'Emergence from eternal grief is an illusion.' A strange turn of phrase."

"What is that supposed to mean?"

"I believe..." she paused, sifting through her words carefully, "he was chastising himself for whatever reaction your magic elicited in him. As if he doesn't believe he deserves to feel anything aside from his unending grief."

My heart ached at the thought.

"I wonder why he tortures himself so," I mused, trying to keep my voice steady.

Lysara shrugged. "There are no records of any recent personal tragedy. Whatever haunts him must have occurred during his absence." She studied me with renewed interest. "I've never seen the prince react so viscerally to anything since his return."

I shrugged, feigning disinterest in order to deflect. This trip to the library had become nothing short of exhausting, and I did not feel any wiser for the experience. If anything, I had even more questions that I dared never ask out loud.

"We should conclude our research for today," Lysara said. A shred of guilt tinged her voice, though I knew it was not her intention to make things as uncomfortable as possible. "The Haustblót Feast is in two nights," she continued as we traced our steps back to the entrance of the library. "If you wish to learn more about Prince Torian, simple observation might prove more revealing than anything historical records might provide."

"I'm honored by your insight," I said, "and genuinely grateful for your help."

"My pleasure." Her eyes twinkled. "It's rare that I find someone as interested in uncovering truths as I am."

I nodded with a small smile before starting off down the hall toward my rooms.

"One last thing!" Lysara called out to me. "It's meant for oysters!" Not eyeballs, thank the gods. "Until the feast, Lyra."

Until the feast, indeed.

Chapter Seven

I stand at a river's edge, the clear water flowing swiftly over moss-covered stones. Bankside trees drop their jewel-toned leaves in vibrant spirals. The light of late afternoon warms my skin, pink and tender from a full day of harvesting herbs to restock our dwindling supply.

I'm gathering pale blossoms, their petals glowing from within, not yet unfurled in the deepening twilight. Moonflowers. My fingers know their stems, how to cut them at just the right angle for longevity, and their leaves—how to crush them clock-

wise, then steep them in boiling water.

"Those flowers are more potent if picked under the full moon, you know." A voice tolls like a cathedral bell from behind me, warm and rich, but dripping with something I only imagined in storybooks as a girl.

My breath is snatched from my throat as I keep my back to him, afraid of making any sudden movement likely to end in my demise. Every story I'd ever heard whispered by firelight rises to the front of my mind, crowding out reason, paralyzing me.

"The full moon isn't for another week," I reply calmly. "We need them for a sleeping draft today." I say 'we' as if I'm not out here all alone, as if an extra pair of mortal hands could fight off just a single one of his kind.

Fae.

He steps closer, moving with the hunter's finesse our elders warn us about—the very reason I didn't hear him sneak up on me. I plead for my breath to remain steady as I slowly turn toward him, and it is stolen from me a second time.

Such treacherous, immaculate beauty. Which is exactly how they get so close—how they get you to desperately invite their mouth to your throat, right before ripping it out with their perfect teeth.

"Most humans run when they see one of my kind," he says, head tilted slightly in animalistic curiosity.

"Shall I start running then?" My pulse hammers in my neck as he steps even closer. Then he hands me a flower from behind his back, petals spread wide. I take it.

The scene shifts, fragmenting to the same familiar riverbank, the ground now carpeted with yellowed leaves, and the air crisp with the approaching winter. The Fae and I sit on a fallen log along the shore, shoulders barely touching with a forbidden, yet inevitable, intimacy.

He reaches down and scoops a handful of sand from the

ground at our feet. The grains slide between his fingers as he closes his fist, but not before the tiniest flicker materializes in his palm.

The air between us hums with a new warmth that brushes against my cheek. The skin at the edge of his hand glows from the heat blooming within his grasp. His face strains as his grip tightens, knuckles blanching against the effort. The sand pops and crackles as it burns, and then cools. The light dims, and the heat recedes, leaving me chilled once more. But I do not notice.

His fingers open toward me, revealing a piece of blue sea glass that catches the fading sunlight with an unnatural inner fire.

"It will capture moments so they can never be lost," he explains, dropping it in my palm in sacred bestowal.

The shard warms instantly at my touch, and from within its depths I glimpse a moving image: this very moment, the two of us, his gift, my awe.

"It's... beautiful," I whisper, my voice catching as his fingers linger against mine.

Beautiful. Far too small a word for what it truly is.

"As are you," he says, his eyes of molten gold piercing through me with such intensity that my heartbeat stills, and I am suspended in time.

His lips find mine at long last, the universe narrowing itself down to exist within this single point of contact. It is nothing more than a nervous whisper against my mouth at first, like the first careful step taken while crossing a stream. He slides his hand into my hair, still warm from his magic, and cradles my head as if I might shatter at his touch.

He tastes like summer melting into autumn. He tastes like too-ripe fruit on the vine. He tastes like everything I have ever loved, yet like nothing I have ever had before.

I press into him, my human inhibitions surrendering com-

pletely to my need to be closer. Closer. Closer, despite the stories told to children to keep them from wandering, despite the poultices and remedies I ought to be mixing, despite our natures as prey and predator.

The sea glass grows warm in my fist again as it captures this exquisite transgression in perfect detail.

Before I'm ready—I will never be ready—he pulls away from me, leaving me feeling bare and trembling. The look in his eyes borders on promise and warning. It's as if he would risk everything he has for a single morsel of what has now blossomed between us.

Whatever 'everything' might be.

"I—" he stutters, "Forgive me." He turns his face from me, but not before I catch the reddening of his cheeks. "I should not have done that."

"Why not?" I can still feel the prickle of his lips on mine.

"There are laws against—" He gestured between us. "—this. My father holds fast that there are certain boundaries which should never be crossed. In this world, or any other."

He releases a defeated sigh as I study him—the wrinkle at the corner of his eye as he winces, the end-of-the-day stubble that shades his clenched jaw. I run my hand along his forearm and tug him to look at me.

"Perhaps we could be the exception."

Without permission, without thought, I bring my lips to his again, refusing any answer other than this.

The dream dissolves at its edges; the riverbank fades; his face blurs even further. I reach for him, desperate to hold on to the memory, but he's already gone, leaving only the faintest whisper of a vow that didn't quite fit the scene: "I will find you."

I tore awake with a gasp, my lungs tight and heart aflutter. That dream—though it was more than just a dream—clung to my mind, sticky and unshakable. The riverbank curve. Blooms in hand. The taste of him. Those weren't fading shreds of imagination. It was all too specific, too *real*, to be anything but genuine memories, though his face remained frustratingly blurred.

Light filtered delicately into the room, which felt much too small to contain the echo of him that pressed its weight against the walls. The shadows in my chambers stirred alongside me, responding to my distress. They gathered at the edges of my vision, their sentient wisps reaching toward me to offer their comfort. I drew a deep breath and willed them to recede. They obeyed, albeit reluctantly.

I withdrew the sea glass from beneath my nightdress and pressed it to my aching heart, trying to make sense of the scattered fragments that had played so vividly behind my eyes. This morning it was surprisingly cool, as if to remind me that memory cuts both ways. I drifted to the window, tossed the curtains open, and conviction hit me along with the soft orange light of the sunset.

No more wishing. No more waiting. No more squeezing this bit of glass to feel something when *he* might be within my reach.

Tonight at the feast, I would seize my chance. Perhaps through my illusions, I could reach past whatever walls surrounded him, his memories. Our history might only be buried, not entirely lost. But only a faultless illusion would wake Prince Torian's recognition while shielding my true nature from the rest of the court.

The day slipped by in a storm of restraint. Every twitch of magic was measured, every detail excruciatingly honed as I rebuilt the splintered dream, piece by piece. Each drop of water that splashed against the stones was meticulously placed; each filament of the petals was lit one by one.

Finally, the constellation. The one that had affected Prince Torian in the library, those twelve little lights that sent him reeling.

That moment was when I *knew*. He was once mine.

I fastened the last button at my back and smoothed my palms down the midnight-blue gown, taking a deep, steadying breath. Almost ready. Almost *Lyra*. A knock startled me, soft yet insistent.

When I opened the door, nobody stood waiting. Only a garment box lay at the threshold. It was tied shut with a blood-red ribbon, and a handwritten note rested neatly on top.

By order of His Majesty King Oranth, for the Twilight Isles performer.

My stomach turned as I flipped the box open and held up to the light what I was expected to wear for the feast. It was a topaz silk gown with fabric so sheer that the faintest glow of light passed clean through it. Gold stitching curled along the curves and seams—beauty without mercy, design without decency.

I tossed the dress onto the bed and swallowed down the nausea that crept into my mouth. Even from across the room, it reeked of mockery, delicately tailored with the King's derision.

This was a test. Perhaps of my willingness to comply, of my desperation to remain at court. Perhaps it was a test of his own prowess in humiliation. No matter which, the King was asserting his power in the most demeaning way possible. I hesitated. Refusing a royal 'gift' would draw attention I couldn't afford, yet accepting meant parading before the court like an exotic pet rather than an artist.

In the end, survival won.

Two thin strips bound at the back of my neck and plunged past my navel, turning the gown into a spectacle, drawing the eye down, down, down. The yellow silk was clearly made to gild Fae complexion. Against my skin, it leached the life from me, leaving me pallid, almost sickly.

I hated it.

But if the King meant to humble me, he would be disappointed.

I draped my pendants around my neck, the glimmer of my skin settling under the dampening charm, and I caught sight of my reflection. Despite the King's intentions, the woman staring back at me was neither victim nor object. She was neither the aged prisoner who had walked into the Whispering Sea, nor the naïve girl who had once gathered moonflowers by a riverbank.

She was the woman who still sought connection, pursued truth, and believed in the possibility of reclaiming what had been lost despite outlasting a century of chains and enchantments.

The prince might not recognize her, but I did. And even if he didn't, he might at least take notice of the curves of my body in a barely-there dress.

The Haustblót Feast was held in the High Ballroom, which dwarfed the Golden Hall where I had endured my audition. Crystal chandeliers hovered overhead, cradling captive flames that cast the chamber in a warm, burnished glow. Satin-laden tables trimmed the walls, bright with calendula and butterfly weed, each displaying curried meats, candied fruits, and exotically spiced dishes from every corner of the realms. The center of the ballroom remained open, reserved for dancing and entertainment.

The court nobility had already assembled, a dazzling display of Fae beauty and finery, waiting for the royals to descend so the night's revelry could begin.

I stood in the wings, teeth pressed into a nervous row, my powers caged beneath the dampening charm. Around me, other performers carried on with their final preparations—fiddlers tuning their strings, dancers pushing up on their toes, pyromancers warming their hands. Across the crowd, Lysara's gaze found mine, sharpening as her eyes traced the indecency of my gown.

A hush fell over the assembly as the doors swung open. The Amber King and Queen entered first in glimmering orange and gold, every inch the distant pair as her gloved hand hovered over his. They acknowledged the court's bows with the slightest of nods as they floated past.

Behind them came Prince Torian.

An invisible hand closed around my throat, robbing me of breath and sensation. Even from across the room, his presence hit me like a gale on the sea. His polished mask of princely decorum barely hid the restlessness roaring beneath as he dragged those citrine eyes coolly across the crowd.

He took his seat beside his father, moving with such graceful indifference that it shrugged off the formality of the entire evening. Several nearby courtiers followed his every movement with appreciative glances. I understood their reactions all too well. Even without rank or regalia, he would be impossible to ignore.

The evening ticked by with droning formal speeches from sycophantic dignitaries and plate after plate of food. I wondered how the Fae stayed so trim, or how they danced so spiritedly with such full bellies. I was scheduled to perform between the sorbet and the syllabub, apparently a position of honor. Or simply the King's idea of a little tart before the rich dessert.

Once the entremets had been cleared away, a herald's voice split the hall with a flourish: "Lyra of the Twilight Isles, starlight illusionist."

I wiped my palms along my dress, but the sheer fabric did nothing for the clamminess of my nerves. I forced myself not to imagine how the chandeliers surely laid me bare. Every curve and line, every dimple and freckle, even the private shades of my breasts and the cleft of my bottom, illuminated for the entire court.

Before I had even crossed halfway to the dais, the reactions throughout the room confirmed my dread about my appearance. Courtiers' eyes lingered, whispers fluttered behind jeweled hands, and the King wore a satisfied smirk that made my skin crawl. But it was Prince Torian who unsettled me most.

The entire room seemed to fade around him, chased away by the storm beneath his stillness. His gaze held no lust or wonder, but barely restrained anger. His hands clenched the arms of his chair, knuckles white, as he shot his father a look of such raw accusation that several nearby courtiers physically recoiled. The King paid him no heed, and the prince's mask carefully slipped back into place, though white-hot anger radiated from him like a firestorm.

I bowed, drew a steady breath, raised my hands, and began.

Darkness unfurled at my fingertips, spilling a blanket of black velvet into the air. Stars glinted to life against the void, constellations gathering as I told the age-old tale of Lyra, the Star Maiden.

As the illusion expanded, filling the space above the court, I threaded my dreams into the tapestry I wove. The stars rearranged themselves to mirror the night sky, just as it had appeared over the river in my dream. From the dark, two silhouettes stepped forward: a woman plucking flowers, and a tall figure watching from beneath a gnarled oak.

Prince Torian tensed, his attention sharpening as his guarded stare now locked on the blackness above us. My heart thundered as I clenched down on my control, begging myself not to look away.

Tiny leaves of shadow fell, curling delicately around the figures as they inched closer among the bowl-shaped blossoms. The male shadow extended his hand, offering a glowing shard of blue.

Appreciative murmurs rippled through the court, but I barely heard them.

The prince's mask slipped again, his expression shifting from controlled tension to confusion, then pain, and beneath it all, a desperate dawning of recognition.

The final scene showed the shadow figures by the river in winter, its current slowed to slush, while snow flurried around them in star-flecked swirls. The male figure cupped the woman's face with such tenderness that several courtiers audibly sighed at the romance of it all.

All the while, throughout each season, every dance, every flicker and swell, I kept that single constellation constant. Melatheon, the shepherd.

When the last shadow had dissolved and motes of starlight rained down on the court, I finally met Prince Torian's stare directly. His eyes were wide, pupils blown with an emotion I couldn't name. His hand had risen to his heart, pressing against it in the exact gesture I was shown to use the sea glass.

For a single breathless second, the glamour waned between us, and the masks of time and punishment fell away. We knew.

Then the court erupted in applause, shattering the moment that electrified the air in my lungs. With a quiet word in the Queen's ear, and a single brush of his knuckle beneath his eye, the prince rose from his seat and strode from the ballroom.

I ended my performance with a formal bow, accepting the court's enthusiastic approval with appropriate gratitude. But all the while, my mind sprinted around the chaotic question: Did I reach him?

As I stepped away from the center of the hall, a handful of eager courtiers descended upon me like bedazzled birds of prey.

"Even the prince was moved by your craft!" one of them said. "I wish I had a love like in the stories you tell," sighed another one.

They grabbed at my hands, stroked my curls, cooing and fussing to get close to me, as if I were some legendary creature in a circus menagerie. Compliments and propositions were spat into my ears. Then, amid their perfume and wine-soaked breaths, I heard the distinct jingle of coin in my ear.

Its effect was immediate.

Bodies surged inward in a tidal crash of jewels and silk. An elbow landed in my ribs; a hand slid boldly down my spine. They sniffed at me hungrily, inhaling me with their hot, greedy breaths.

Drunken hands trailed over every inch of my exposed skin. And out of nowhere, a comically large chocolate-covered strawberry was shoved between my lips as I tried to protest their adoring assault.

I was dizzy, near sickened, from the attention when slender fingers curled around my wrist and yanked me out of the tangle of admirers. Lysara pulled me into her and practically hissed at the overzealous courtiers, her lips curling in a snarl like they were vermin.

"Fix your dress," she murmured, still shielding me. The flimsy, gauze-thin fabric had slipped, baring the entire left side of my chest. I ought to have been mortified, but the dress did nothing to hide my anatomy anyway.

"Thank you," I mumbled as I adjusted myself against her.

"So, that was rather… pointed," she said, barely loud enough for me to hear, eyes blazing with impatience. "Those weren't random images, were they?"

I shrugged and stepped back from her guard.

"Every story has its inspiration."

Lysara chuckled, low and dangerous.

"And the prince's reaction suggests he acknowledges that inspiration." Her voice dropped even further. "Be careful, Lyra. You're playing with fire."

"Ice tends to thaw over a lit match," I replied softly, resolve taking root in my gut.

"I wouldn't call that a match. I'd call that a pyre." I did not budge as she studied me. She finally nodded with a huff, eyes flicking to my revealing gown. "He left through the eastern door, toward the Night Garden."

She unfastened the clasp at her neck and pulled her shawl from her shoulders, then slung it carefully around me. "And take this. Just looking at you is making me want to freeze."

I understood her underlying meaning immediately. "Thank

you."

"Don't thank me yet," she cautioned. "Whatever game you're playing, it has higher stakes than you may realize." With a half-smile and a shake of her head, she melted back into the handsy crowd, and I slipped unnoticed toward the Night Garden. Toward my prince.

Chapter Eight

Stars winked brightly overhead against the onyx sky of the Night Garden. I slipped free of the Vale's enchantment as I crossed the threshold between the golden afternoon and this private, hushed midnight. Disembodied flames hung like votives between the branches of cherry blossom trees, illuminating the stone pathways and hidden alcoves. Water trickled from a nearby fountain; mourning doves cooed sadly from above.

The Night Garden breathed like a living creature. Dainty

petals opened and closed with the rhythm of a sound sleeper, exhaling the faintest breath of sweet perfume. An aquamarine silk moth the size of my palm stirred from a blossom's trumpet, trailing pollen like faerie dust as it fluttered into the shadows.

And everywhere I looked, moonflowers bloomed. Their luminescence pulsed like synchronized heartbeats, the blooms turning their faces to follow me as I passed. They were watching me, waiting for whatever sin I meant to commit among them.

I padded further in, the thunder of the Haustblót merriment softening to a dull murmur behind me. It was beautifully dizzying; the paths twisted too tightly, the garden too dense. How would I possibly find the prince without getting lost myself?

The head gardener and his apprentice hovered at the main arbor, pruning the climbing vines and carefully clipping blooms. I nodded casually as I passed, but they paid me no heed.

"This particular bloom," the head gardener said as he delicately inspected a clipping, "is ideal for propagation. Five equal points in the center, six-inch diameter, at least one foot-candle of luminescence. A perfect replica of the original bloom that Prince Torian gave me over a century ago."

The apprentice studied it closely, noting each trait with earnest focus.

"The prince? With the way Queen Krivnya tends to them, I assumed this garden was all hers." The gardener shook his head and smiled as he twirled the stem gently between his fingertips.

"Oh, no, my boy. A mother's devotion, perhaps. Before Prince Torian crossed the realms, he made this freckle of darkness his own private sanctuary. That being said—" The gardener paused to look at me as I pretended to admire the night sky. "You saw him walk by just now?" The apprentice nodded. "He comes here to think—to be *alone*. Do not approach the willow while he is present, or he might have your head for it."

And there was my answer.

I pulled Lysara's shawl tighter around my shoulders and made my way through the labyrinth of winding footpaths. Each turn led me deeper into the garden, and the moonflowers grew more abundant, spilling out of their beds in luminous folds. They climbed tree trunks and trellises, blotting out the night, until all I could see ahead was a giant weeping willow, towering at the garden's center.

There he stood beneath the sparse starlight, half-concealed within the drooping branches, his back toward me as he slumped against the tree. His shoulders were tense, his posture rigid as his hand rubbed the back of his neck.

I lingered at the edge of the clearing, suddenly uncertain despite the proof that had led me here. Every choice, every thought, every breath carried me to this moment, yet a lifetime of doubt rooted me in place. The shawl slipped as a gentle breeze nearly knocked me off balance.

"Your performance was... unexpected." His voice cut the air, slicing clean through my paralyzing indecision. He did not turn to face me, but he knew exactly whose presence called to him through the night.

I brushed aside a sweep of branches, stepping in as the ground softened beneath my feet by fallen catkins. The curtain swung shut behind me, and all the sound was swallowed up. No trickling fountain, no melancholy coos. Just the blood hammering in my ears and Torian's sharp respirations.

"I am pleased to know it moved you," I offered, voice steady despite my quivering pulse.

He turned slowly, and his weary, bloodshot eyes found mine before his gaze drifted to the flowers surrounding us.

"Cisqa moonflowers," he murmured. "Not the common garden morning glories. These are descendants of a single clipping from the river's bend in mortal Avynne. A personal favorite."

His fingers brushed a bloom and lingered a beat too long. For a male who could burn the court with a look, he handled the petals like they might bruise at a whisper.

"Yes. They're quite beautiful indeed."

"They're also remarkably specific." His eyes locked onto mine, searching, waiting for me to give something away. "As were the other details in your performance this evening. The river, the oak tree." He paused. "Why those images, Lyra of the Twilight Isles?"

His emphasis on my false name suggested he already doubted it. I took a step closer.

"They came to me in dreams," I said carefully.

"Dreams," he scoffed. "Of places you've never been?"

"Who says I've never been?"

His eyes narrowed in suspicion. "You claim to be from the Twilight Isles."

"I claim many things," I said, holding his gaze. "As do you, Prince Torian."

His careful composure briefly cracked. "What is that supposed to mean?"

"You claim to have spent the last century on diplomatic missions," I whispered, wary of the invisible ears that might be listening through the breeze in the trees. "The records of which appear to be forged."

He stiffened, face paling as his expression hardened into a wall of ice.

"I understand now," he said as he pushed away from the tree and stalked toward me, golden eyes now simmering with malice. "My father sent you, didn't he? He found some pretty little tart with rounded ears to parade around the palace wearing—" He gestured vaguely to my immodest gown, making me want to shrink inside myself. "—wearing *that*, having her recreate my cursed memories. To what end? To keep me in line?"

I clenched the shawl even tighter around me, the fabric slicing into my skin, though not even a fleece cloak could spare me from feeling so naked under his scrutiny.

"I've paid his price for my so-called crime," he continued, "and you can tell your King that if he doesn't stop twisting his knife in me, then his cruelty may very well cost him his heir."

His voice quaked under the weight of his declaration, the air between us embrittling at the threat he just made against himself—a desperate male's only leverage.

"Torian," I said gently.

"Your familiarity is grossly misplaced, given your station." The crack of a whip.

"*Prince* Torian, I—"

"This is a private garden." He turned his back to me. "Be on your way before I summon the guards."

"Prince Torian, please. The King didn't send me. He has no idea who I am."

"Then who are you?" He spun toward me again, eyes of golden flame charring the night. "How could you possibly—" He raked his fingers through his hair, then dragged his hands roughly over his face as the frenzy grew inside him.

He was coming apart right in front of me. The proud prince of the Amber Vale, unraveling thread by thread. I had come here to find him, to bring him back to me. Gods, how truly lost was he?

"Because I lived those moments!" My desperation spilled out of me, the searing truth between us burning a hole in me. "With you! The river, the flowers, the constellations we would trace on each other's palms. You'd trace the lonely hunter, and I'd trace—"

"The shepherd," he whispered. "I ask again, who are you?"

"I think you already suspect," I said, moving closer. "I think something in you recognized me the moment you saw my stars in the library. Just as something in me recognized you, despite everything that's changed."

He shook his head. "This is madness."

The pulse in his forehead thumped faster with each word I

dared to speak. "Isn't it? I know things about you no stranger should know."

"Stop this."

"The first time you kissed me," I continued, pushing past his royal command, "you apologized afterward. You said you shouldn't have done it. And when I asked why—"

"I said *stop*."

"*And when I asked why*," I repeated, bulldozing the consequences of the liberties I refused to stop taking, "you said there were boundaries that shouldn't be crossed."

"Enough!" The word tore from him, raw and forceful. He staggered backward, pressing both hands to his temples. "You have overstepped your bounds. Those are private moments. Sacred. How dare you—"

I should have stopped, but the words kept spilling out, each one flung toward a minefield, and I could only pray they wouldn't detonate this fragile thing I was trying to rebuild.

"And I said, 'Perhaps we could be—'"

"*The exception*." Not an answer—an echo. But his eyes still smoldered stubbornly with ruthless denial.

I reached for him instinctively, but he recoiled.

"She's dead."

I froze. "What?"

"The human woman. The one who..." His voice caught in his throat at his jagged confession. "She was executed for our dalliance. I watched her die."

No wonder he didn't recognize me. I had died long ago, and even the magic of the Fae cannot undo death.

But if not mine, then whose death did he witness? My chest heaved.

Gods, an innocent.

"Then they must have killed someone else in my stead," I said quickly, desperately, now troubled by the death of someone whose only crime was wearing a similar face. "Because I am *alive.*"

A silence gathered between us, ragged breaths and pounding hearts. The words had come out of me sharper than I meant them to, as if I were trying to convince both of us. Trying to convince myself that my accidental existence was worth condemning the guiltless.

"What were her last words?" I asked meekly. Not to pry, not to prove. Perhaps to honor the woman in my place, the one who received her blessing from the Mother far too early, while mine was held behind lock and key.

He frowned as he watched my expression fall from determination to guilt. I couldn't meet his eyes after that. My fingers wrung the edge of the shawl until the threads frayed.

"I..." he began, searching his mind for the details of the execution that he had so deliberately filed away. "She had no last words."

Tears welled in my eyes, but for some reason, I *laughed.*

"It definitely wasn't me, then."

His golden eyes flashed with sudden anger. "Do not dare to mock my grief."

"I'm not mocking anything."

"Do you think me so vapid that I would not know her if she were standing right in front of me?"

I took another careful step toward him, finally within arm's reach. Though my body would have never known how to move any closer than this.

"What's more likely?" I asked softly. "That the King would grant a human a swift death for consorting with you, or kill someone else in front of you, then send your lover somewhere she could suffer for eons?"

"The Duskhold," he whispered, the color draining from his face.

"Yes," I confirmed. "A century of servitude in the shadowlands, though the intention was an eternity, I'm sure."

He stared at me, conflict raging behind his eyes. "You don't smell like her—" His grief was fighting to maintain control of him as his nostrils flared with the breeze that carried my scent, but I could tell its grip was slipping.

"The Whispering Sea changes those who survive it," I said simply, as if more than just me had endured those waters.

His gaze raked over me, taking in my otherworldly features— the subtle glow of my skin, the galaxies in my eyes. I could see him struggling to reconcile what he saw in front of him with what he vividly remembered.

"You gave me this," I continued, pulling the sea glass from beneath my bodice. The blue shard caught the moonlight as it hung limply from its chain. "You said it would keep our memories safe so they could never be lost." I held it out, shoving it closer to him, like this little gem could bridge the gap a lifetime had carved between us. "You showed me to press it against my heart whenever I needed to see you. For a hundred years, I kept you with me. This was all I had."

He was near-hypnotized as he watched the sea glass dangle in front of him like a pendulum. I saw the war being waged behind his eyes as he analyzed my trinket, analyzed *me*, the memory of my execution battling against the truth I was forcing upon him. This final, undeniable truth. For a long moment, we stood in silence while the night air became electrified with new possibility.

He made a movement toward me, attempting to close the remaining space between us at last, when heavy footsteps approaching on the stone path made us both freeze.

"Your Highness," a guard's voice called from just beyond the clearing. Unhurried boots ground against gravel, as if he knew exactly when to interrupt. Halting at the willow's veil, he pushed the branches aside and flicked his eyes to me briefly before dropping them respectfully.

Torian's expression hardened instantly, the vulnerability I'd briefly glimpsed vanishing behind that frustrating mask of princely composure. He stepped away from me, putting the proper distance between us.

"Excuse the intrusion, sir, but your betrothed has officially arrived and is awaiting your formal introduction," the guard said.

He cleared his throat, shaking off any last remnants of our heated encounter. "I'll return immediately," he replied, his voice once again the controlled tone of a prince rather than the raw whisper of a male confronting impossible truths.

The guard bowed and retreated, but the moment was shattered. The fragment of intimacy we'd built, the tentative bridge across a lifetime of separation, had dissolved in an instant.

Torian hesitated just long enough for the mask to barely slip again. A tiny tremor shook his hand as he adjusted his collar. His jaw tightened, teeth clenched. He turned only halfway, not enough to fully face me.

"I must go."

"Prince Torian—" I began, but he was already moving away, his stride purposeful.

He gave me no other inclination as he turned a corner at the other end of the clearing and disappeared down the garden path toward the palace proper. The sudden shift from the heat of the conversation to the emptiness of the brisk night air left me feeling exceptionally bare. And nauseously shaken.

I wanted to scream, to claw at the air and demand that the night give back the moment it had just stolen from me. So close. We had been so close to a breakthrough, to recognition. I had seen it in his eyes—the moment when the denial began to crumble beneath the weight of the heaviest truth. But now, doubt would have time to reassert itself, to regain its hold and continue to smother him in his eternal guilt.

And now mine. The blood on my hands for the sake of a reckless love story.

Not to mention this betrothed I hadn't expected. Yet another complication in an already impossible situation. It was too much to bear all at once.

I wished I had never come to the Amber Vale.

Never found him.

Never knew about the innocent I killed.

Never emerged from the water.

I didn't remember walking back to my room, peeling the silk gown from my chilled flesh, vomiting in the bathroom sink, slipping into bed, wishing for sleep that didn't end in another morning.

But sleep claimed me anyway.

Moonlight silvers the frosty Cisqa River as I wait beneath the ancient oak, my heart racing with the familiar anticipation of seeing Torian. He appears between the trees, and I run to him without hesitation, our embrace desperate after days apart.

"I've missed you," he whispers against my hair. "Court functions have kept me prisoner all week."

"You're here now," I say, reaching up to trace the shaded line of his jaw. His eyes are heavy and troubled as he leans into my touch. "What's wrong?"

"I can't live like this anymore."

My heart stops. Is this the end of us? Did my prince finally come to his senses and realize that love from some twenty-year-old mortal woman could never satisfy him?

"What do you mean?" I make to pull my hand from his face, but he places his hand over it.

"Stealing moments with you, lying to my court, feigning interest in political matches I refuse to accept."

"What other choice do we have?" I ask, fear solidifying into doubt.

"I could renounce my title. Give up my immortality." His

voice is barely a whisper, full of resolution. Shock renders me speechless for a moment.

"I can't allow you to make that sacrifice," I protest.

"A mortal lifetime with you is worth countless centuries of power and privilege. It wouldn't be a sacrifice." He laces his fingers through my hair and pulls my head into his chest. "In three days, there will be a new moon on the winter solstice, perfect conditions for the Nyaeleth vyr Aeoneth. I will bind myself to you completely, age as you age. Say yes, Aevra Nightwind, and we will live and die as one."

"Yes," I breathe. "A thousand times, yes."

Aevra. My name is Aevra.

I woke with a gasp, my true name echoing in my mind like a bell being struck. Aevra Nightwind. The name felt right, settling into place like a key turning in a long-rusted lock.

"Aevra," I whispered into the darkness, reclaiming those fundamental syllables that had been stolen from me, even though they tasted like ash in my mouth.

"My name is Aevra.".

CHAPTER NINE

TORIAN

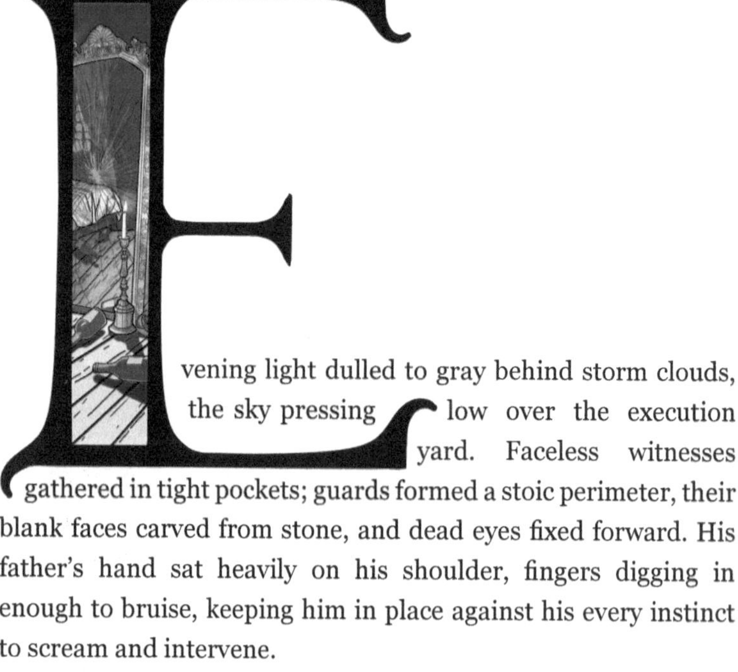

Evening light dulled to gray behind storm clouds, the sky pressing low over the execution yard. Faceless witnesses gathered in tight pockets; guards formed a stoic perimeter, their blank faces carved from stone, and dead eyes fixed forward. His father's hand sat heavily on his shoulder, fingers digging in enough to bruise, keeping him in place against his every instinct to scream and intervene.

And then there was her. Gods, *her*.

She knelt on skinned knees, hunched on the stone scaffold as each lump of her spine jutted from her back like spikes. A tattered dress hung loosely over her emaciated frame, stained red from the flogging she'd received moments earlier. Her dark curls, matted with blood and dirt, flopped forward to hide her swollen face. The silver streak—that godsdamned silver streak from the fever—peeked through the grime, flapping weakly like a tatter of surrender.

They took their sweet time bringing his love to her final end. She was shoved into a dungeon cell barely fit for animals. They gave her enough food to stave off starvation; an old pipe dripped sewer runoff into her cell, which she licked from the floor to wet her cracked tongue.

There were no corners to hide in, no separation between sleep and piss, blood and breath. Just a single slab of raw stone where she'd softened and spoiled in her own humiliation.

He swallowed hard. This was his fault.

But in just a few agonizing moments, she would receive her blessing from the Mother and finally escape the suffering his arrogance had caused.

"Watch," his father commanded in his ear, his tone like splinters of ice slicing across Torian's cheek.

A guard wrapped his fist in her hair and yanked her head up, forcing her to look out at the crowd. Though the rest of her was feeble and mottled, her eyes retained their luster. Those eyes, swirling with blues and golds like the sea glass he had once given her, found his instantly. They did not well with tears. They sought no bargaining or retribution. No love, or hatred, or forgiveness. Just intense emptiness, which felt infinitely worse.

"I'm so sorry," he mouthed, chin trembling.

He wanted to look away, but unseen magic kept his head forward in a locked vice, his eyelids pried open by invisible fishhooks. A ghost of a quiver touched her split lip as the executioner stepped forward, ceremonial axe gleaming in the dull light.

"Witness the consequences of your actions, boy," his father hissed. "Watch your mortal cur die for your adolescent delusion."

The blade rose and fell in an excruciatingly slow arc. The sound it made when it hit its target—that wet, terrible sound—would nauseate him for millennia. Her body slumped forward as her head... *her head*—

It tumbled from the scaffold, bouncing down the stone steps with a sickening thud. It came to rest at Torian's feet, those blue eyes still wide open, still staring straight through him. Blood seeped from the slice at her neck, pooling around his boots and soaking into the leather.

His father released his shoulder as a satisfied smile crept across his lips. "Remove the prince to his chambers," he called. A guard stepped forward, placing a steadying hand on Torian's chest as he faltered. "He has much to contemplate before his diplomatic journey begins."

He couldn't move. He couldn't look away from those eyes that had once sparkled with laughter by the riverbank, now fixed and clouded, staring past him at nothing.

Somehow, the world did not end with her. His lungs still drew their ragged breaths, heart still stubbornly thumped. That was the cruelest part of all.

He thrashed against the guards as they dragged him backward, boots scraping uselessly against gravel. Somewhere behind him, the yard began its grim reset. Soapy water sloshed and turned pink as horsehair brushes scoured her blood from every surface.

A servant bent to collect her head with a stained rag. Then clumsily fumbled it. A sharp, startled curse followed as the weight proved uneven and that disgusting noise sounded again.

Only then did he tear his gaze from her, bile surging up his throat. He couldn't watch her being handled like a bruised melon, already forgotten and tossed out. His legs barely worked as he allowed himself to be led away.

Once the doors to his chambers slammed behind him, the scream finally came. It tore out of his chest, shredding his throat until blood filled his mouth. But the sound of his anguish was swallowed by the void opening in his ribcage. Grief collapsed in on itself, dense and absolute, devouring anything that dared shed light.

He was a black hole. Nothing escaped except the fractured apathy that had taken root and overgrown into what he was now.

The wine bottle slipped from Torian's fingers. It hit the floor with a hollow thud, rolling until it bumped softly against his boot. Wine spilled from its mouth, bleeding across the polished marble. For a disorienting moment, past and present fused—blood and wine, memory and reality indistinguishable.

With a strangled grunt, he kicked the bottle away. It spun across the room, shattering outward as the last dregs of crimson spattered the wall like blood spray.

He barely noticed, didn't care.

It had been three months since his return to the Amber Vale, and still, every morning began the same. With panic, with the impossible task of reconciling the drafty mountain cave with his opulent chambers. The comfort of the bedsheets felt like a straitjacket. The freedom of the palace felt like an elaborate, gilded prison.

For a century, he had starved. Hunted. Climbed. He *suffered* under the searing light and blistering cold, with nothing for company but the memory of her. One hundred years of exile in the Blinding Peaks—sunburnt, frostbitten, half-mad—reduced to nothing but a few scraps of paper, and a lie signed in his hand and stamped with his seal. A tall tale of heroic diplomacy.

And he was *congratulated* for it, exalted by his people as an altruist, a peacekeeper, with no mention of what he truly was.

A murderer.

The first week following his return had been a spectacle—carefully staged, meticulously rehearsed, and utterly revolting. His father had greeted him in the Coronal Vestibule, arms outstretched in a public display of paternal pride that made Torian's skin crawl.

"My son returns from his diplomatic mission," the King announced to the assembled court, voice carrying through the vaulted space, "having secured alliances that will strengthen the Amber Vale for centuries to come."

Applause followed right on cue.

The King's hand came down on the prince's shoulder in the exact spot where he had gripped him that fateful day. Torian fought the instinct to flinch beneath it.

He stood there, mouth dry, the familiar courtly phrases and gratitude refusing to surface. Words that once came effortlessly now tangled on his tongue. Years piled on years of speaking only to himself and shouting into the wind left the polite lies and elegant deflections a foreign language he no longer trusted himself to speak fluently.

"I am... grateful to return," he managed.

The pause was noted. He felt it ripple through the court like a dropped stitch.

His mother approached next, breaching the awkwardness. Her beauty remained unchanged, though something in her eyes had dulled since he last saw her. When she embraced him, her touch was light, almost reluctant. Not a single word passed her lips, not then or in the months since. Her silence pressed on him heavier than his father's hand ever could.

So the court welcomed their darling back as a hero. He acknowledged their scrapes and bows; he allowed them to kiss his knuckles. He could almost see her among the crowd, barefoot and laughing at the absurdity of it all. But it was his father's satisfied smirk that made his blood run like slush in his veins.

◐ ◑ ◕ ● ◕ ◑ ○

The announcement came on his third night home, delivered with the same casual indifference as discussing the weather.

"Lady Valeraine of the Obsidian Isles will arrive soon enough," the King said, spearing a slice of meat. "The arrangement was finalized during your... absence."

Torian's fork froze midway to his mouth.

"A union between the Vale and the Isles will secure our southern borders," his father continued, as though outlining a trade agreement rather than the rest of Torian's life.

"You arranged a marriage without my knowledge or consent?"

"You forfeited your right to make those decisions for yourself. Don't you remember?" A sneer curled across his face. The matter was not open to negotiation. "Lady Valeraine is of palatable lineage and considerable political value. You will find her suitable."

Suitable. The word lodged in his chest like a shard of ice. He stared down at his plate, appetite evaporating and replaced by anger and shame.

That night marked the first of many dinners he did not bother to finish.

◐ ◑ ◕ ● ◕ ◑ ○

He approached the shattered mirror, snatching up another half-empty bottle that sat on his desk amid scattered papers and overturned books. He tipped it back, letting the wine burn a familiar, stinging path down his throat.

The sophistication of the Faen wine never brought the same oblivion the nightshade rotgut punished him for brewing in the mountains. He traded the feral hallucinations and endless bouts of vomiting for this civilized haze that just barely kept him staggering through his duties as the perfect crowned prince.

Every day blurred into the next. Every decision, every step, was another fantastical parade in his honor that made him want to hurl himself out the nearest window. Today's event would be no different.

The audition promised to be a tedious affair, but he would attend if only to dodge his father's scrutiny. He had no interest in feigning amusement for the elemental wielders conjuring the same tired dragons of fire and ice, harpists recycling concertos, or humorists whose jokes never landed.

With polished efficiency, he assembled the princely mask in the mirror, cracking his face into a dozen jagged edges. He straightened his morning coat and strolled out of his chambers without a glance at the mess. It was his silent rebellion; the only thing he could control was the trail of destruction he left in his wake for his father's menials to clean. What the hell else were they being paid for, anyway?

He arrived at the Golden Hall fashionably late, just as intended, slipping through the rear entrance behind the dais. He ignored his father's cutting side-eye as he sank into his chair.

Overhead, darkness played across the vaulted ceiling. Torian barely registered it. His thoughts floated sluggishly along, struggling to stay afloat in the sea of wine he'd drowned them in.

He leaned forward, elbows on his knees, squinting through the intoxicated glaze blurring his vision. The performer before him was little more than a shifting silhouette. His eyes fixed on it stubbornly, as if sheer will might coax a single sober thought to his face.

He hadn't meant to arrive this impaired, and scandalizing the court with his vice wasn't on today's agenda. So he stayed still, blank-faced, and let the wine sink beneath the surface like a hidden undertow.

And then—

A tendril of shadow slipped from the performer's grasp and

slithered toward him, curling up the dais like a curious serpent. He watched it slide along the floor, its reach stretching for him *specifically*, a whimsy that nobody dared offer him anymore. For the briefest moment, genuine amusement flickered within him, a notion he had thought long since dead, buried somewhere between the mountain snow and bloodstained stone.

With a quick yank from the performer, the shadow serpent withdrew reluctantly, unraveling from between his feet and slipping back into formation.

The space it left behind felt soberingly hollow. That little sentient shadow had noticed him. Had liked him. Perhaps he was once likable before everything happened.

Perhaps he could be again.

When she finally pulled the darkness from the air, the incessant questioning of her craft began, and Torian stifled an annoyed groan. The magic they had all just beheld was like none other, and whether it was a true rarity or a simple parlor trick was no one's entitlement to know. Not even the King's.

"So, he *does* know how to speak before his court," his father said spitefully once the performer had exited to the wings.

Torian did not turn. His face remained composed, though heat rose up his neck like flames.

"I'm *elated* to see you put down the bottle long enough to participate," the King continued pleasantly, "but never undermine me in front of my subjects again, or you might find yourself exploring other diplomatic opportunities."

His meaning was unmistakable. And as swiftly as it had come, the little spark of optimism he felt from that little shadow guttered and died.

Nothing had changed in the hundred years he was away, and nothing would change in the countless centuries to come.

He awoke the next morning with a roaring headache as light splintered behind his eyes. Images strobed beneath his eyelids, fragmented and relentless. Flowing water. White petals. A shimmer of blue. None of it made sense.

Groaning softly, he reached blindly for another bottle and took a long swallow, hoping to soak up the visions before they had time to fully surface. The wine was sharp and sour on his tongue, immediately making everything worse.

So much for that.

He pressed his palm firmly to his temple and let his magic unfurl, smoothing carefully over the ridges of his brain. The pain dulled to a manageable throb, and the images blurred and sank into a muffled murmur.

He needed air, a change of scenery. A tunic was yanked over his head; the wardrobe door slammed shut behind him. He left the stale smell of his chambers in his wake, giving the servants a chance to change the sweat-soaked bedsheets and clean up this morning's fresh pile of vomit.

The archives had always been a refuge.

Even as a child, Torian had retreated here when the palace grew too loud, or his father's temper grew too hot. Stone walls swallowed sound; dust softened the air. Time slowed to something almost merciful between these shelves. Here, at least, the King rarely lingered, and the court's insufferable sympathy only reared its head in front of an audience.

Ancient texts rose in their orderly rows, spines worn smooth by centuries of hands searching for answers long since lost. He breathed more easily the further he wandered along the bending paths, the pressure behind his eyes ebbing just slightly. Memories weighed less here. Or perhaps they simply had more company to occupy themselves instead of incessantly plaguing him.

He rounded a corner and stopped short. Lysara stood wild-eyed in the heart of the archives. Beside her was the shadow wielder from the audition, though his recollection of the prior evening was foggy at best. The sight of her hit him with a peculiar sense of dislocation, as if he were staring at a ghost. His gaze swept over the translucence of her skin in the lantern light, and he wondered if she truly might be one.

Their hushed conversation died the moment he stepped into their view, guilt flickering across their faces like shadows. He felt nothing. Let them talk about him. Let them whisper their little rumors. Nothing they could say would ever come close to the truth. Compared to that, gossip was a kindness.

He read the same sentence at least ten times. The words blurred, refusing to settle as his focus frayed with every soft murmur behind him. He was dimly aware of Lysara shifting her weight, of the performer's voice lowering further. None of it mattered more than a minor annoyance.

Until he saw it. A faint string of twinkling lights bloomed between the woman's palms. They winked at him as they formed an instantly—and violently—familiar constellation.

The book slipped from his hands as pain lanced through his skull like a white-hot needle, driving the breath straight out of his lungs. He clawed at it with his magic, desperate to scrape it away, but the assault only intensified as more of those unwelcome images detonated behind his eyes.

Water rushing over stone. Petals of white drifting endlessly. The same impossible shimmer of blue cupped in his fiery grasp.

He gripped the edge of the table for dear life, paralyzed, eyes glued to the stars trembling in her hands even as his vision swam. And she noticed.

Whether in offense, alarm, or instinct, she snuffed the constellation abruptly, crumpling it like wasted paper. The stars vanished, and the migraine loosened its searing grip, leaving him shaking in the silence that followed. He sagged in relief, breath uneven as he stooped to retrieve the fallen book, forcing his hands steady and his face into neutrality.

Nothing to see here. Nothing to question. He prayed Lysara would look away from her faltering prince instead of checking the welfare of her oldest friend. But of course, she didn't.

He needed to get out of here, to rebuild the dam around his mind to keep any more agonizing memories from flooding back. He replaced the book on its shelf and muttered that single line on the page that he had read so many times over, only now it made sense to him.

Adaelith vyr drôrith aeonïs esth mærlûsith.

Emergence from eternal grief was indeed a grand illusion. Perhaps even grander than that blinding constellation that had just ripped his mind in two.

◖ ◑ ◕ ● ◑ ◐ ○

The Haustblót Feast was yet another exercise in endurance, another celebration designed to distract. The Amber Vale hadn't celebrated this northern tradition in its two thousand year history, but the King claimed he wished to honor his queen. Torian didn't believe that explanation for a heartbeat. When had he ever honored anything but his own self-absorption?

The hall groaned under the excess. Tables bowed under roasted meats and sugared fruits. Wine flowed with nowhere near enough restraint. Courtiers guffawed too loudly, ate far too much, and reveled in the palace's permission to forget themselves for another pointless evening.

The prince understood the strategy perfectly: keep the court gorging themselves and cavorting mindlessly, then perhaps the whispers about the true nature of his absence would dissolve with their hangovers.

Ironically, it was the first event he'd managed to attend neither drunk nor late.

"Lyra of the Twilight Isles," the herald announced. "Starlight illusionist."

The ghost from the library. So he hadn't frightened her away after all. His attention sharpened as she made her way to the center of the ballroom. The crowd quieted as their hunger shifted focus onto the fragile little human. She was utterly breathtaking, but anger rippled through him at the sight of her careful, self-conscious movements.

His gaze flicked up the dais to his father. Of course, he had dressed her.

The diaphanous amber monstrosity clung to her like deliberate provocation, sheer enough to invite scrutiny while masquerading as generosity. Humiliation that demanded gratitude. A reminder to her and every onlooker of exactly where they all stood in this court: beneath the crown's thumb.

His hands clenched the arms of his chair, knuckles blanching as he leveled his father with a sharp look of accusation. The King met it with a satisfied smirk. Something primal surged awake within him—hot, unrestrained, and deeply inconvenient. He wanted to rip something to shreds with his teeth, protect her from something he couldn't even stand against himself.

But the moment she began to weave her magic overhead, even that notion fell away as the rest of the world dissolved around him.

Without the glaze of alcohol numbing his senses, Torian could truly behold her art for the first time. As her darkness unfolded at her fingertips, an unexpected sense of relief washed over him.

Relief that the King's accusatory questioning hadn't driven her away. Relief that his own jarring episode in the archives hadn't chased her into retreat. Relief that the damn bit of gauze she'd been forced to wear had not broken whatever resolve carried her into the ballroom.

He was completely enamored.

Her night sky took shape above them, stars igniting one by one in their deliberate patterns. She told the story of her namesake—or seemed to—but it wasn't a version he had ever heard. The Star Maiden met her shepherd in a mountain meadow, not on a riverbank. He ensnared her with his flute, not moonflowers. And the eternal gift was a star crystal, not...

Blue sea glass.

How could he have known that from an infinitesimal glow? How could he be sure it wasn't just chance? But he *did* know, with bone-deep, logic-dodging certainty. This tale poured from his soul's own inkwell, an inkwell shared with only *her*. And her death replayed for him every morning he woke, every night before he fell asleep, without mercy.

Then, as if she had climbed inside his spiraling skull, she placed a single, unmoving constellation right above his head. Melatheon. The shepherd.

Recognition slammed into him with the force of a tidal wave. His hand rose unconsciously to his chest, his body reacting to something the rest of him had neatly tucked away and forgotten.

The illusion fell away like ash on a breeze, her eyes met his, and the world tilted beneath him.

He knew her. She obviously knew him. In another life, in another world, in another timeline, with a version of himself he no longer recognized.

Applause thundered through the hall, shattering her final, silent illusion. The ovation rose overwhelmingly fast, and Torian rose with it, carried on the noise.

"That magic was rather dizzying," he murmured to his mother, the cracks in his voice masked by the crowd's awe. "I require a moment to compose myself."

She gave no reply, not even a nod, and he slipped from the ballroom without looking back. If that spectacle had truly been meant for him, she would follow.

◐ ◑ ● ● ◑ ◑ ○

He drifted through the corridors in a daze. Habit guided his footfalls; muscle memory carried his body forward while his mind remained elsewhere. In the Night Garden. With *her*.

The guard's interruption had come at the knife's edge between them—just as he had moved toward her, not knowing whether his intention was to embrace her or silence her, to kiss her or kill her. Perhaps it was a mercy that they did not learn which.

He reached the door to the Council Chambers far too quickly. He adjusted his coat and smoothed his expression into something close to princely control. His hand froze around the doorknob, knuckles locked, forearm shaking. This was all wrong. The timing, the intrusion, the maddening *insistence* of it all. He wished for nothing but a bottle in his grip instead.

When he finally opened the door, his father stood beside a slender Faen female with sea-blown black hair and eyes like frosted sapphires. She bore an uncanny resemblance to the woman whose head rolled against his foot every night. No coincidence, just another punishment. The King was adept at finding doppelgängers to dangle before him: to taunt, to marry off, or perhaps even to kill.

"Prince Torian," the King said, his voice smooth and edged with warning. Torian felt it settle into place like a familiar collar. "May I present Lady Valeraine of the Obsidian Isles, your betrothed?"

She curtsied gracefully, completely unaware of the sadistic game in which she had been made an unwitting piece.

"Lady Valeraine," Torian said, bowing automatically. He took her offered hand, brushing his lips across her knuckles in the bitter gesture protocol demanded. "How predictable of my father to secure a political alliance while I conveniently could not object."

She smiled ever so carefully. "The honor is mine, Your Highness. I have long awaited our eventual meeting."

"Have you?" Torian laughed cruelly. "How long, exactly?

Were you even of age when the King began shopping for my bride? Or were you still at your mother's breast when he promised you to a prince who didn't even know you existed?"

"Torian—" his father warned.

"It's quite alright, Your Majesty," Lady Valeraine interjected smoothly. "If I may—might His Highness and I have a moment alone?"

The King's eyes narrowed on her, her eyelashes fluttering downward as she properly averted her gaze.

"Very well," he said at last. "I shall leave you to become acquainted." His gaze lingered on her a moment longer than necessary, tracing the shape of her bodice, the rise of her skirt in the back. His empty smile turned toward Torian, thin and promising. "The official betrothal ceremony will take place shortly after Mabon. I expect you both to have warmed to each other by then, hm?"

The door closed behind him, and Valeraine's pointed ears pricked at the sound of the latch clicking into place. The sound had barely settled when she whipped toward the prince, her diplomatic smile vanishing entirely.

"Prince Torian," she began coolly, "I believe the tone of this exchange ought to be corrected."

"Is that so?" His words were unimpressed, almost mocking. "I believe the tone is appropriate, if not lacking deference, for a female of your station making the acquaintance of her royally intended."

"Then allow me to clarify," she continued, refusing him another of her polite smiles. "I was well over two centuries old when the formal negotiations for this betrothal began—two hundred and forty years your senior, in fact. I find your concern for my agency grossly misplaced, if not outright condescending."

Torian opened his mouth, perhaps to speak, perhaps to scream in protest. But she did not afford him such a courtesy.

"Let me be perfectly clear, Your Highness. If you require someone to belittle in order to feel powerful, I suggest you look elsewhere. I was learning to rule realms while you were still attending charm school—lessons which you seem to have forgotten during your absence."

He stood there, slack-jawed at the sheer audacity. No one spoke to him that way. No one *dared.*

"I represent the Obsidian Isles in this alliance," she went on, barely pausing to breathe. "My people's interests are my priority, not your self-importance."

Torian blinked in the silence that fell like a shroud as the temperature dropped ten degrees.

"Now," she said calmly, "shall we begin again with the courtesy befitting our *stations*? Or would you prefer to continue this fragile display and confirm what your court already whispers? That your time away has left you—" She raked her eyes down and back up. "—*diminished?*"

The word was a spear launched straight from her mouth.

"You mistake me, my Lady," he said finally, his tone far more civil after the devastation of his ego. "I merely wish to understand the arrangement made in my stead."

"Then ask directly," she replied. "I value clarity over civility when forced to choose between the two."

It took him a moment to recalibrate, eyes fixed on her while the gears in his head sputtered and lurched.

He had assumed she'd be young. Inexperienced. *Grateful.* His mother wasn't even a century old when she wed the King.

He expected—absurdly so, apparently—that Lady Valeraine might offer admiration, or interest at the very least. That he would easily establish dominance, intimidation, so she'd never question him when he disappeared in the middle of the night. But she dismantled every one of those assumptions in a single breath.

He cleared his throat.

"You must be tired from your journey," he said, retreating to safer ground, unable to muster the strength to meet the challenge she presented. "I'll have a servant show you to your quarters."

"Of course, Your Highness," she replied, composure restored. "We shall have ample time to get to know one another in the coming days."

His hands trembled even worse now as he turned the knob. He watched his betrothed depart, her posture flawless, steps unhurried as the hem of her gown floated a hair above the floor—as if she hadn't just eviscerated him without spilling a drop of blood on the marble.

◗ ◖ ● ● ◕ ◑ ◯

The windows were flung open, and the breeze blew freely into his chambers when he returned. The chilled evening air swept through the room like an invisible maid, carrying away the worst of the stench and leaving behind a trail of lemon and fresh linen. It helped, but just barely. Torian's nerves still thrummed too close to the surface, skin itching with everything he should have said. Should have done.

Back and forth. Back and forth. He paced like a caged animal, kicking the armoire as he passed. The wood cracked inward, splintering as a shard flew loose and skittered across the floor. He reached for the nearest bottle, hands shaking so badly he missed the wine glass on the first pour. On the second pour. He cursed softly before abandoning propriety and bringing the bottle straight to his lips.

Two truths stared him down from opposite corners of the room. The head and the illusionist. They could not coexist. Yet they did.

His throat stopped stinging, so he took another sip before setting the bottle down with a sharp click. He crossed to the hearth, and his fingers traced the ornate carvings along the mantel, finding each notch from a thrown knife, every dent from a piece of hurled furniture. It was habit, muscle memory.

Until his fingers found the stone, wiggling like a loose tooth. His heart thudded against his ribs as he pried it free, holding his breath in case the walls might be listening. He reached into the narrow cavity hidden behind it, and his hand closed around something solid and worn. Something that must have been hiding there for a century or more. A leather journal.

His journal.

Its cover was cracked with age, darkened and peeling from time and handling. He opened it carefully, the leather creaking in protest and the pages stiff and fused together. Old tear stains marred the parchment—ghosts of a night when grief had been a freshly torn wound rather than an old scar.

The handwriting within was unmistakably his, though softer than his current script. More hopeful. Each curve of ink seemed to reach forward, pleading with this future version of himself.

Most of the entries were smudged beyond clarity, but fragments remained:

"Looking for Hermia... a woman by the river today... gathering flowers—"

His held breath refused to release.

"... gave Aevra the sea glass... wanted to preserve... never forget—"

The walls seemed to slide inward, pressing in on him from all sides.

"The way Aevra laughs... like music... never heard in the Vale—"

Aevra.

The name jolted through his nervous system, sharp and electric. Pain flared behind his eyes again, but he didn't push it away. He hadn't realized he had forgotten her name. Forgotten damn near everything except her death.

Aevra.

Not Lyra.

The trembling in his hands had miraculously subsided—from the wine, from renewed purpose—though the pressure in his skull mounted with each line he read, memories surging up at last and crashing against the dam he had built to contain them.

The last entry was dated the day before his so-called diplomatic mission began.

"Father's punishment... Aevra to be sold... not killed. Worse... Duskhold... I will never see her again—"

The blade, the blood, her final breath...

A lie.

"What did you do, father?" he whispered to the empty room, fury icing over every fiber of his soul. "Who have I been mourning?"

The silence gave no answer.

He closed the journal and tucked it into his tunic, right over his heart, as if it might steady its calamitous hammering. Tears burned his eyes, and he scrubbed them away with the heel of his hand.

He needed to find her.

Aevra.

Not Lyra.

For the first time in a century, the grief that had hollowed him out cracked and bled just enough to let something else root within him. Not hope. Hope was far too dangerous a word to name outright. But curiosity. Determination. Even anger. Those he could acknowledge.

Those he could wield.

Chapter Ten

barely slept after that memory resurfaced. I drifted in and out, like sleep was a tide and I was caught in the roil. My wild thoughts melted into half-dreams, which twisted into waking hallucinations I couldn't blink away.

I saw Torian in the corner of my room, wavering in my vision with his hand outstretched toward me. Every hour, I'd wake and look for him in the corner, reaching for me from the shadows, and wishing he'd take a step closer. Wishing he'd say something, like the sound of my true name pouring across his lips.

Aevra.

The possibility that maybe I had left an irreparable crack in his stone wall of doubt, just wide enough for him to glimpse the truth on the other side, gave me something sturdy to stand on. But even then, my legs wobbled beneath the weight of the other life that ended so mine could continue.

I tried not to picture her face, but my shame sketched one for me anyway. She shook her head as she watched me walk into the water, squandering her sacrifice. I shook my head in return.

It wasn't my fault.

I tossed the bedsheets aside, letting the chill of the air on my bare skin help shake off the last dregs of sleep, and padded to the wardrobe. I didn't own a single stitch hanging there, but it was stocked all the same. Another quiet courtesy of my strange captivity.

I threw on a simple tunic and pants, my groggy fingers fumbling at every button. Maybe I'd head to the kitchens for something to eat. Or maybe the baths to wash away some of the fog, and perhaps some of the guilt along with it. I wasn't quite sure where I was headed, or what I needed. I just knew that I wouldn't find it alone in this room whose walls were pressing in tighter by the heartbeat.

It wasn't my fault.

I repeated the mantra like a ward while my feet took me wherever they pleased. My attention drifted somewhere behind my eyes, to a disconnected corner of my brain where intrusive thoughts might not find me.

As I rounded the corner on my trip to nowhere, I slammed into an unyielding chest. The impact knocked the air from my lungs and jostled my feeble awareness around in my skull. The world swayed, but a pair of strong hands caught me at my shoulders, steadying me before I could stumble backward.

I blinked, still half-stuck in my sleepy daze, and looked up with an apology already forming behind my teeth. Burnt-honey irises seared through my morning haze, and the sluggish flow in my veins stilled at once.

Prince Torian.

For a moment, neither of us spoke. The air of the surrounding corridor froze with us, the distant sounds of the palace fading to nothing but the wild drumming of my heart. I managed a weak curtsy, my eyes fluttering down like nervous butterflies. 'My Prince,' I think I murmured.

"I would like to speak with you," he said. "Privately."

I nodded, my throat too tight to allow any sound. He looked around, quickly scanning the corridor for any prying eyes, then lifted the edge of a tapestry—an old rendering of the founding, or the fall, of some ancient kingdom stitched in dusty gold thread. He inclined his head toward the shadowed alcove, and I wordlessly stepped through.

I pressed myself tightly against the wall as he followed behind me, letting the tapestry flap back into place. His body filled the remaining space, despite my efforts to appear small. There was barely enough room to breathe... so we shared the same breath.

His scent coiled around me, sage and something volatile, like the warning that curls in the air before the sky breaks open. Even in the faint light that filtered through the fabric, I could see the tiny copper rings around his irises, the fan of his lashes, the grain of his freshly shaven jaw.

"Tell me your name." The demand of a prince, not the plea of a lover.

I hesitated as my voice disconnected from the rest of me, and I forgot how to form a single word.

"Your *real* name."

Whatever dangers lurked beyond the tapestry faded beneath his scalding urgency, crackling the air as if my silence might burn straight through me.

"Aevra," I finally said, the name scraping across the lump in my throat.

He closed his eyes and took a long, shaking breath. His chest expanded fully, closing the dwindling space between our bodies, as the fabric of his tunic skimmed delicately against mine. He held it there, suspending us both in a tiny, excruciating limbo.

When he finally released it, his breath washed over me, stirring the loose ringlets around my face. His shoulders dropped, his jaw relaxed, and when he opened his eyes to look at me—to *really* look at me—I knew he saw Aevra, not Lyra.

His gaze fell to the sea glass nestled against my skin, the shimmer of blue peeking out from the slit of my open collar. Slowly, tenderly, he reached toward it, toward *me*.

He grazed my skin with his fingertips as he traced the chain down the delicate hollow of my neck to where the pendant rested. I suppressed the jolt that shot through me and into the ground. His touch was lightning, fanning out to the ends of the earth, so strong that I was sure the entire palace felt it.

"You kept it," he whispered, his voice vibrating through me like plucked harp strings. "After everything, you kept it."

My throat scorched even as my mouth watered from his lingering touch. "Of course I did."

He slid his hand up from my neck to cradle my cheek, electricity trailing his touch. I leaned into him, letting him hold the weight I had carried for a century in the tilt of my face. I exhaled into his palm, a breath that had been trapped in my chest for lifetimes. He brought his other hand up to wipe a tear I hadn't realized had fallen.

"Aevra," he said, his thumb brushing across my temple. "My Aevra."

I don't know which of us moved first; both of us pulled violently together, like twin planets snatched into the other's gravity. Our lips collided with the momentum of a godsforsaken century.

One hand settled at the back of my neck, the other slipping into the tangle of my hair. I pressed my palm over his, while the other rested firmly against his chest. There was no hesitancy to overcome, no permission to ask. Everything had already been given.

It felt like only moments had passed between us instead of decades. Continuation, not reunion.

His tongue glided over the seam of my lips before slipping past in a gentle, greedy sweep. That first soft scoop against mine sent a rippling shudder down every nerve. It was a pleasure so acute it bordered on pain after eons of numbness. He must have felt the way my skin prickled at his touch, because his mouth curved into a smile as his thumb brushed the corner of my mouth.

His hand traveled from my neck down to my waist, pulling me tighter against him as he pressed deeper into my mouth. His name bloomed in my throat before I could stop it. *Torian.* He caught the sound before it passed my lips, swallowing it like every other thought he'd devoured from me.

I could still feel him when his lips left mine, my ribs aching for the air he'd taken with him. But he didn't pull away. Instead, he dipped his head to the slope of my shoulder. His nose brushed across my skin, breath catching as it passed over the mess of curls gathered there, as if he were drinking me in, sick of being sober. He lingered there for a moment, not kissing, not claiming. Simply existing, carving out a safe space within it all, while my pulse hammered against his cheek like a war drum.

"You were dead," he whispered into my hair, voice scraped raw. His arms locked tighter around me, as if he could shield me from any damnation already endured. "What my father did—" He choked on the thought.

"We're here now," I said, anchoring us in this one stolen moment instead of the thousand others stolen from us. Stolen from her.

He lifted his head from my shoulder as the actual weight of our situation settled between us, shattering the fragile sanctity.

"He will try again."

"I know."

"We must be careful."

"*I know*," I repeated with a sigh. "But I don't want to pretend anymore."

His thumb traced my lower lip, still glossed from our kiss. "Then let this be the last lie we tell, *F'Elvænith*." He named me in the tongue of the gods, which felt like a sacred offering laid at the altar of something older than reason.

I knew we should have stepped away then, smothered the lit match before it had the chance to burn down everything in front of us. But his grip on me was a warm homecoming after a desolate exile. I couldn't move. *Wouldn't*. Not yet. Not while his thumb still rested against the corner of my mouth.

"Kiss me again." My caution surrendered to aching, impossible need. "Before I become a stranger once more."

He answered my plea with a longing that mirrored my own. His lips met mine, softer this time, like his mouth already mourned our inevitable separation. We lingered there, unmoving aside from the tremble of my lower lip as he pulled it gently between his teeth. As if our stillness could slow down the bitter reality that loomed ever closer.

The sea glass flared between us, its light casting ribbons of blue and silver across the stone of the alcove. My own magic stirred alongside it, strands of glittering shadow swirling around in a melancholic dance.

Torian pressed his forehead to mine as the last grain of sand fell through the hourglass. "Tonight," he whispered. "Under the willow." The willow where he reprimanded—then cracked. "Not another night without you."

I nodded, unable to deny him anything of myself. And then he was gone.

The absence that his body left in its wake made room for the heaviness to finally release its held breath. My back met the wall, and the threads of my tunic scratched down the stone as I slid to the floor.

I did it.

I found him.

I brought him back to me.

And now that my stupid, pig-headed hope, kept so tightly wound, could unravel at last, I wept.

It wasn't my fault.

I changed my clothes three times. Then, somehow, I ended up right back in the same tunic I had worn this morning.

Unacceptable.

I sniffed the tunic, then yanked it back over my head and threw it against the wall. I refused to let him think I didn't try. But then again... what if trying made me seem desperate?

The fourth was another tunic, but black.

I finally resigned to just leaving it alone and left my room before I could second-guess it too much. But that didn't stop the thoughts spinning in my head. What if I was too dark to see, and he missed me entirely?

Or worse—what if the tunic blended in with the darkness and I appeared as just a floating head bobbing around the garden?

My body carried me through the winding paths of the garden while my mind lingered in front of the mirror, cursing myself for not trying harder to look less ridiculous.

But my dissociation didn't survive the sight of him. He stood broad-shouldered and still under the willow, its trailing branches casting long ribbons of shadow across his back.

He turned at the sound of my footsteps, hands limp at his

sides like they hadn't received their instructions yet. For a moment, he just... stared. His mouth opened, then closed. One hand twitched up halfway, like he meant to give me a handshake, or maybe touch my shoulder, or maybe knight me—gods only knew. Then it just aborted its mission entirely, falling uselessly into his pocket.

The prince was flustered, it seemed. But then, so was I.

"Prince Torian," I said, dipping midway into a curtsy before I caught myself and paused. Torian smiled through a wince.

"Should you still do that around me?" he laughed under his breath.

"I don't know," I said, still hovering in a semi-crouch. "Should I?"

He raised his eyebrows, peeking at the hem of my collar where it dipped just enough to allow a whisper of cleavage to show. I shot up out of the pathetic curtsy and smoothed my hands over my torso, cheeks flooding pink.

So the tunic *was* a bad idea after all.

"On second thought," he said, a smirk tugging at the corner of his mouth as his confidence slid back into place, "do that every time you grace me."

I willed the blush to recede from my face. "Ah, there's that charm I hear so much about."

He gave a low chuckle and took a step closer. "Good to know my reputation precedes me. Though I can't say I mind earning it properly."

He gestured to a stone bench beside him, and we sat, leaving a careful space between us as a comfortable silence swirled. How strange, I thought, that the reckless hunger from this morning had somehow surrendered to this—a sudden shyness at our proximity, his knee bouncing, my hands wringing, our shoulders hovering but never quite touching.

Now that the danger of the alcove had receded, neither of us dared reach again for what had already been taken.

Maybe it was easier to be brave in the face of the consequences of hesitation. Adrenaline and carelessness overthrew sensibility. But here, now, where the stillness was security and the moonflowers pulsed with their lazy glow, we were left with nothing but our unadorned selves. No tortured souls. No desperate bargains. Just the fruit of everything we'd survived... and neither of us had any idea how to take the first bite.

He reached into the inside pocket of his jacket and pulled out a neatly wrapped, slightly crushed parcel of silk.

"I brought these straight from the kitchens," he said as he unfolded it, revealing two honey cakes glistening with freshly poured syrup. "I received a few strange looks. I suppose it's not every day their beloved prince goes rummaging for a midnight sweet." He shrugged as he handed me one of the cakes, tucked in its own bit of silk.

And it *was* strange.

The kitchens had mostly emptied for the night, save a few stragglers wiping down surfaces or storing pans. A wary hush had swept the room when he entered. Not necessarily out of respect, but out of caution, surprise. A flicker of fear. All but one of the staff had lowered their eyes as he passed.

"Prince Torian," the head cook, Uksana, said with a slight nod and a soft smile.

Torian bowed properly to her, a gesture he did not offer lightly to the help. But Uksana's hands had fed him since he was in the womb, and that alone deserved more respect than a crown.

"If you want something to eat, I can have something brought up to your rooms," she offered, wiping her hands on her apron.

"No need," he said with a wave. "I just wanted something sweet on my way to the garden. Some night air."

Uksana nodded again and plucked a single honey cake off a passing tray. He cleared his throat. "Two, actually. If it's no trouble."

She raised an eyebrow as she grabbed a second one. "Two?" She smirked. "I won't pry. But are you sure you don't want something finer? A petit four, or perhaps a mille-feuille?"

"This is perfect," he said gently. She wrapped the cakes with such care—in silk, no less—as if she knew they were an offering.

"What's a mille-feuille?" I asked.

Torian smiled, eyes flicking to mine. "It's a bit messy for a garden-bench tryst."

Right on cue, a slow drop of syrup slid over my lip and down my chin. I reached up to wipe it away, but his thumb was already there. He caught the drip and then brought it to his mouth, licking it from his thumb without a thought. I felt like I should have been embarrassed again. But I wasn't.

"Well," I said with a chuckle, "I suppose this isn't any less of a mess."

"I suppose not."

We nibbled in companionable silence for a few moments, stealing glances and smirking when we caught each other. It all seemed very tame on the surface, but beneath it all, *gods*, my tastebuds were bursting and the flesh of my cheeks burned with flavor I had forgotten to crave. Honey, spice, warmth, and a certain sweetness that had nothing to do with the bake of the ingredients. It was like a part of him remembered what I might need, far removed from physical intimacy, but still incredibly real.

I leaned in closer to him, my pinky deliberately brushing his as I noticed a scar on the back of his hand. I hesitated before clearing my throat.

"Where did he send you?" I asked. Torian released a long sigh as he slowly wiped a crumb from his lip.

"The Blinding Peaks," he answered. "After the execution, they held me down and drugged me. I woke up half-covered in snow, and my skin had already started to burn from the unfiltered sun. I was left with nothing but the shirt on my back. No knife, no food."

"You survived," I murmured, picturing the perfect prince beside me as a wild beast, alone in the mountains. At least my misery had company.

"So did you," he said with a gentle smile.

"Just barely."

I tilted my gaze to the night sky, desperate for a change of subject before I might have to revisit the details of my own whereabouts.

"Are the stars real?" I asked.

"Of course they're real," Torian said, hooking his pinky around mine. "The garden's enchantment doesn't manufacture the sky. It just draws a veil so the stars can shine through it."

I answered with a barely audible hum.

"This was the first place I came when I returned from the Peaks," he continued. "Not for the quiet—I had plenty of that in a hundred years. For the stars." I turned toward him, but his face was stilled toward the sky. "There are no stars in those mountains. Just the blinding sunlight."

"Hence the name," I said, attempting to brush aside the intruding tension.

"Hence the name, indeed," he agreed. "And you command them."

I scoffed half-heartedly as I slid my hand into his. "I wouldn't dare say I command them. They're not my minions. They're more like friends, I think."

He shifted his body to face me as he took my hand fully.

"Friends who are doing me a favor each time I beckon them."

"Loyal friends, it seems."

I gave an uneasy shrug. "I'm rather certain they will eventually call in those favors." He laughed quietly as his hand tightened around mine.

"I'm remembering your gift of making the impossible sound

inevitable," he said, bringing our joined hands into his lap. "I used to imagine what I would say to you if I ever got another chance."

"And now?"

"And now," he continued, rubbing his thumb over mine and studying the way our fingers entwined, "I find all of those imagined words wholly inadequate."

I understood perfectly. There were no words that could bridge the span of a century; no turns of phrase could erase the ache of all we had endured. And yet, that ache was lessening.

"I think you've done well thus far," I said, bringing the last morsel of honey cake to my mouth. "Plus, who needs driveling, apologetic conversation when there is cake involved?"

Torian's eyes met mine, surprise warming to resignation. He huffed through a soft smile as he brought our clasped hands to his mouth, grazing his lips across my knuckles.

"Then I shall promise to keep my drivel to myself."

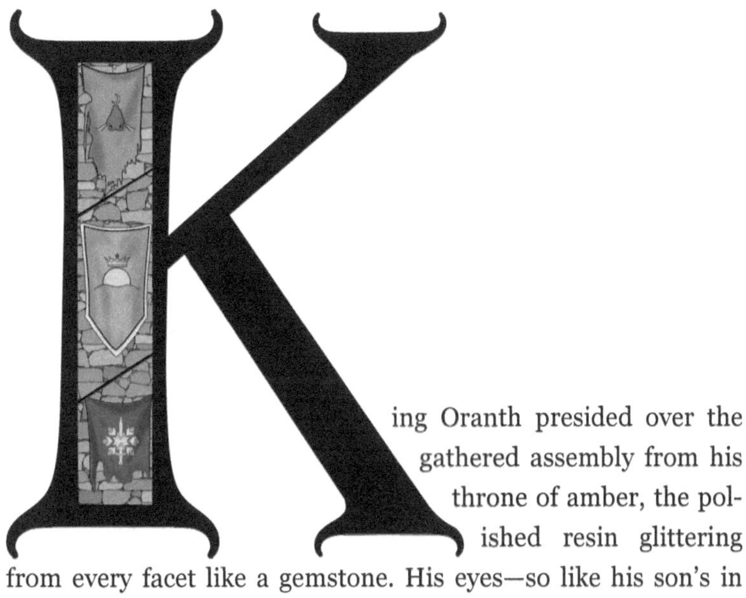

ing Oranth presided over the gathered assembly from his throne of amber, the polished resin glittering from every facet like a gemstone. His eyes—so like his son's in color, yet freezing where Torian's burned—narrowed with an unsettling calculation.

Lysara and I stood at the fringe of the audience. We hugged the wall, quietly observing as nobles from across the Amber Vale arranged themselves by a hierarchy I was only beginning to grasp.

Those closest to the throne basked in his shadow, while others lingered at strategic angles, near enough to catch the King's eye. Or far enough to avoid it entirely.

Among the crowd, a handful of humans: a band of musicians, a master craftsman, and a scholar with ink-stained fingers. Their spines held stiff, shoulders rounded inward, as if appearing as small as possible might keep their fragile welcome from crumbling. They had all been granted coveted residence in the Vale, but they were *guests* all the same.

To the King's left, Queen Krivnya sat in her vigil of unending silence. To his right sat Torian, posture uncomfortably perfect, expression painted into majestic boredom. His eyes flicked to mine for a fraction of a second, and my stomach jumped so violently that I nearly lost my breakfast.

"Boundary patrols report increased activity along the western territories," a copper-armored commander announced. "Three incidents of unauthorized crossings from the mortal realm this month alone."

King Oranth leaned forward. "What manner of crossings?" he asked with a sneer. "Pilferers of our enchantments, or criminals seeking refuge among the faeries?"

"Unclear, Your Majesty. Traders. Herb gatherers who claim they 'lost their way.'" The commander's tone dripped with skepticism. "Their identities have been logged, and they were escorted across the bridge with the standard warnings, per protocol."

"Ah, yes. *Per protocol*," the King echoed. "Do you find the standard warnings sufficiently memorable, Commander?" A sadistic smirk ghosted along the King's mouth as he raked his eyes over his gathered audience.

A ripple of unease masked by pockets of strained laughter moved through the court. The commander inclined his head in acknowledgment, his stone-straight face unmoved. "The mortals will not forget easily, Your Majesty."

The King gritted his teeth as the earlier buzz of excitement dulled to a thin hum.

A courtier in elaborate leather robes stepped forward to stand beside the commander, dwarfed by his silhouette. "If I may, Your Majesty. The increased human activity presents a unique opportunity. Their craftsmanship continues to prove... useful."

The King's posture shifted. "Explain, Weapons Master."

"Human smiths have achieved advancements that our own artisans cannot replicate. Perhaps controlled trade at designated points would benefit the Amber Vale more than separatism."

The court erupted in murmurs at the suggestion—some eager, some disgusted, some intrigued. King Oranth let the chaos swell before gesturing to a different courtier, an enormous, severe-looking male who towered over the rest of the court. "Lord Caenan, as Captain of the Amber Guard and heir of the Keepers of the southern boundaries, what say you?"

Lord Caenan stepped forward with such seismic footfalls that I swore the chandeliers swayed with each step he took. Unaware courtiers stumbled aside as he muscled his way to stand on the other side of the weapons master.

"Boundaries exist to be maintained, not erased," Lord Caenan began, his voice thunderous. "The mortal realm has its place, as does ours. Too much interaction breeds familiarity. Familiarity breeds contempt."

"Interesting," the weapons master interjected, now squeezed between the two mountainous figures, yet holding firm against their intimidation. "Prior to being absorbed by the Vale, the south held more progressive ideals regarding human interaction."

"A regrettable laxity of standards," Lord Caenan countered coolly. "The Vale's maintenance of stricter separations has preserved the purity of Faen bloodlines in the south."

"Purity?" The weapons master laughed. "Or stagnation? The few survivors of mixed blood resulting from the Cataclysm are some of the strongest wielders we've seen—"

"The Cataclysm must not be diminished to the fire beneath a melting pot, as its name commands. These boundary disturbances ought to be contained, not embraced."

"And yet, complete isolation limits our growth."

"Growth for growth's sake is not a plausible reason to endanger our people," Lord Caenan said through gritted teeth, barely having caught his voice from rising to a shout. "What this weapons master has failed to mention is the nature of this weaponry the humans possess. Projectiles smaller than gumdrops, faster than arrows—capable of piercing stone and exploding on impact."

Faces that were once stern with conviction suddenly fell into uncertainty, some even worry. A child clutched his mother's skirt while she petted his head, as if she were assuaging his fear of the bogeyman.

Lord Caenan's voice hardened, his tone dropping even lower. "The humans destroy anything they cannot understand. And now they have the means to do it from fields away."

"I believe you underestimate—"

"How could a creature who lives in the blink of an eye possibly understand our way of life without setting fire to it simply for making them feel inadequate?"

The air was snatched from my lungs. Snatched from the entire room. My pulse hammered in my ears, deafening me.

The human scholar turned pale, quill trembling in his hand as a muscle jumped in his jaw. The craftsman edged nearer to the exit as his stare fixed on the floor. The musicians huddled closely together, ready to vanish into the wall.

Lysara nudged me, flicking her eyes toward my exposed ears. I teased a few curls loose from my neatly tucked bun, letting them fall just enough to hide their curves.

"Don't react," she cautioned under her breath, placing a calming hand on my arm. "Court has eyes everywhere, on all of us."

I leaned in, unable to stop myself as heat flushed my cheeks. "Why open the Vale to humans at all, if we are so clearly despised?" I whispered.

"The cruelest voices are often the loudest," she offered. "Most here do not believe in isolationism. But it's—"

"Easier to remain silent than risk the consequences of dissent?" I finished for her. Her mouth pinched, but she did not reply.

The debate continued, heated exchanges erupting in pockets throughout the audience as a new wariness flared. Throughout it all, Torian remained silent. I wondered what he might say if asked directly, the perfect Fae who had once loved a human enough to risk everything. If I hadn't been trying so hard to blend in, I might have piped up to ask him myself.

"I'm curious where Prince Torian stands in all of this?" I muttered. Lysara wrinkled her nose as she shot her eyes up the dais where he sat, unbothered by any of the surrounding noise.

"I don't have the privilege of knowing what goes on behind that mask he wears." Her tone was sharp, almost spiteful. "I can't imagine he would agree with all this posturing, but he has surprised me countless times of late. So I would wager nothing regarding the prince."

The clamor reached a high, and King Oranth raised his jeweled hand, effortlessly silencing the entire room. He had heard enough.

"Double the patrols," he barked to the commander. "And double the punishments. The humans require a much firmer hand."

The commander nodded, bowed, and fell back to his post in the corner of the room. The King peered over the assembly like a viper, daring anyone to challenge his decision.

No one did. Of course they didn't.

Before the next matter of discussion could be presented, the doors at the far end of the room swung open. The herald's staff struck the marble floor three times.

"Lady Valeraine of the Obsidian Isles!"

All heads turned as she entered, her midnight blue gown shimmering with shards of volcanic glass. Her hair spilled over her bronze shoulders in dark ripples, adorned with silver hairpins shaped like crested waves.

The name was already burned into my skull. A sharp pang of jealousy pierced me right through the gut as I watched her approach the thrones with assured steps. Not a strand of hair out of place, not a freckle speckling her complexion, not even a single crease in her gown as she seemed to float across the floor—untouchable.

The King stood, offering his hand to her as she stepped onto the dais. I expected her to accept it with a curtsy. Instead, she knelt and kissed his rings. His face warmed as she pulled her lips from his knuckles, the closest thing to genuine pleasure I had seen from him since I arrived. It was repulsive.

"Lady Valeraine," the King greeted her. "Your presence honors us." His hand lingered low on her back as he guided her to her place beside Torian.

"Your Majesties, I am humbled by the Vale's welcome. Your Highness." She curtsied as she turned her attention to her betrothed. "A pleasure as always." Torian simply inclined his head, averting his eyes from her piercing sapphire gaze as she sat.

"Onto the next matter of business—"

"The Frost Court requests leniency at their borders," a lilting voice blurted from the middle ranks. A young guard, cheeks blotched red, hunched his shoulders as every glare snapped to him.

"Leniency?" the King drawled.

"Y-yes, Your Majesty. Formal channels have been blocked."

King Oranth rose from his throne with a terrifying slowness, his eyes locking onto the inexperienced guard across the sea of anxious faces. "The Frost Court would do well to mind their own side of the mountains. Patrols will remain firm as long as their dead refugees continue to be jettisoned onto our side of the Peaks."

He summoned him forward with a crook of his finger. The guard stumbled forward until he stood exposed at the foot of the dais.

"What's your name, boy?"

"I—" the guard stammered. "Corporal Isca, Your Majesty."

The King nodded with a frown, his eyes finding the guard's shoulder patch.

"*Lance* Corporal," he corrected. "Do not steal valor in my court where your insignia clearly states otherwise."

"My apologies, sir." The King raised a malicious eyebrow as a glimmer of sweat beaded on Isca's temple. "S-sorry, Your Highness. Your *Majesty*. Sorry."

I winced at the palpable embarrassment.

"From where do you hail?"

"E-east, Your Majesty. The Iron V-Valley."

"Ah, I might have guessed," King Oranth mocked. "Your family still lives there?"

"Y-yes, Your Majesty."

The King pursed his lips as he began pacing the dais.

"Imagine for me, Lance Corporal Isca, that you go home to visit your family. You expect a hot meal, maybe your favorite dessert." The King paused, tilting his head slightly.

The lump in Isca's throat bobbed with uncertainty. "R-rhubarb pie, Your Majesty."

The King hummed. "Rustic. You imagine playing with your nieces and nephews in the field outside." He held out his palm and summoned a flickering flame into his hand. The guard's eyes fixed upon it as it danced delicately in the King's grasp. "Maybe a cozy fire in the hearth. But when you arrive—"

He closed his fist, extinguishing the flame with a hiss, and a pile of ash spilled onto the floor.

"—you find nothing but a slab of ice where your house once stood. You look down. Beneath your feet, you see your mother's face, frozen in a scream. Your sister clutching her baby to her chest. And your father is scattered around them, his body cleaved into pieces. Everything you loved—buried, massacred."

The young guard swallowed hard as the King circled above him like a vulture. The stale air of the chamber turned heavy as the temperature seemed to drop ten degrees.

"Would you loosen safeguards against such beasts because they expressed *discomfort*?"

Isca wobbled on the spot, knees buckling at the thought. "N-no, Your Majesty."

"I thought not." He was dismissed with a wave. Relief and shame clung to him as he retreated, swallowed into the crowd.

"Let's test the sharpness of our newest knife on the rack. Lady Valeraine," he said, eyes burning as he turned his sadism to her. "What say you about the Ice Giant's request for clemency?"

The entire court leaned in for her answer as she stood.

"Though Lord Iäen has weakened in his old age, his barbarous ideals have spoiled the north," she said evenly, her gaze lifting to meet the King's without wavering. "While he himself might not pose an immediate threat to the Amber Vale, his court of monsters certainly does."

She looked to the crowd, pausing just long enough for the weight of monsters to settle over them.

"Following the events preceding Loch Rime," she continued, "the Vale's vigilance and severity with the Frost Court must be maintained."

Valeraine neither smiled nor bowed as she concluded her stance. A slight inclination of her head was all she offered as a growing murmur swept through the room.

"Hear, hear!"

"Well said!"

The court's approval of their new soon-to-be princess echoed through the audience chamber, making me shrink into myself as envy ate me alive. I couldn't look at Torian. I couldn't stomach seeing admiration on his face.

"Well spoken, my Lady," the King said, approval sharp as glass. "I am pleased to see such political instincts despite your barbaric upbringing on that rock."

Lady Valeraine smiled congenially, curtsied flawlessly, and eased back into her seat without so much as a single feather ruffled.

"The celebration of your betrothal approaches," the King changed the subject, his smile not quite reaching his eyes. "This union will strengthen the Vale eternally."

I bit my cheek, heart twisting and churning at the casual bartering of my future. Lysara noticed my fidgeting and elbowed me.

"You'll bite a hole through your face," she whispered.

The King gestured, and half the crowd jumped in surprise, then sighed in annoyance, as an exceedingly petite figure flickered out of thin air. Her skin glittered as if it were dusted with crushed opals, and butterflies floated around her rose-gold hair. The whimsy of her arrival seemed absurd amid the tension that still clung to the chamber like smog.

"Of course, the preparations proceed as planned, Your Majesty," the faerie said as she adjusted the tiniest pair of glasses on the tip of her upturned nose.

"That's Miravelle," Lysara whispered as she leaned in. "She's half woodland faerie, so she flits from place to place around the palace. She can be rather *startling*."

"Although our immediate efforts are focused on the quickly approaching Mabon festivities," Miravelle announced with shrill enthusiasm as she waved a clipboard in the air. "Both events will showcase our finest talents, naturally. Bless the harvest and bless Prince Torian!"

"It shall be so," King Oranth stated plainly, concluding the audience without entertaining any further questions.

Lysara and I slipped into the hallway as the rest of the crowd filed past, reliving some of the heated topics of the session.

"Instructive, wasn't it?" she muttered.

"Very," I agreed. "A tad alarming."

Lysara gave me a sympathetic half-smile and hooked her arm in mine as we strolled along the corridor.

"It's mostly posturing and pageantry." Her expression grew serious as she glanced over her shoulder. "But be careful, Lyra. The King's interest in the boundaries isn't merely political. He will hunt for a scapegoat."

"For the disturbances?"

"Yes, because it's more than just humans wandering where they shouldn't," she replied, her voice dropping. "He will wield the fear of his people to tighten his grip and capitalize on the weakening boundaries. He will blame the Frost Court. He will blame the mortals. He'll point to everyone until the mob believes that expansionism is the answer to security."

"Surely, they will see through that," I offered hopefully, naïvely. "How could anybody be responsible for cosmic alignment?"

I thought of my own crossing from the Duskhold, how much easier it had seemed than the rumored impossibility. A chill ran through me. Was my own crossing of a boundary the result of its weakening, or was I the root cause of everything? I shook my head clear of the thought.

Lysara shrugged.

"Fear of the unknown is blinding to the masses. And they will follow the one who says he can see, trusting he won't lead them off a cliff."

And that might have been the most terrifying truth of all.

Chapter Twelve

I am burning alive from the inside out. My skin feels like parchment stretched over smoldering coals, so hot that the cool cloths my father places on my forehead sizzle and steam. Through the haze of delirium, I see him hovering above me, his face gray with exhaustion, deep hollows beneath his eyes from days without sleep.

"Please, Aevra," he begs, his voice cracking with desperation. "You must fight. You must stay with me. I cannot lose you too."

I try to respond, to reassure him that I don't want to go, but *my throat is so parched that breathing feels like inhaling shards of glass. Each labored breath I take rattles in my chest. The taste of copper fills my mouth, blood from where I've bitten through my tongue during seizures I don't remember having.*

I drift in and out of consciousness. In lucid moments, I hear scraping and sloshing as my father mixes a poultice at his work-table, muttering incantations to blend the salve with desperate prayers. His remedies, which had saved others up until now, have failed to break my fever.

"This one will work," he whispers, more to himself than to me. "This one has to work."

When the stone bowl touches my lips, I convulse, my body re-jecting even this last hope. The bowl crashes to the floor. My fa-ther makes a sound I've never heard before, a sob torn from the depths of his soul.

"I've tried everything," he pants, collapsing to his knees be-side my bed. "Everything I know. Everything I've learned in thirty years of healing."

Through half-closed eyes, I watch as my father—the man who has stood strong through every crisis, who has faced death with quiet dignity as he fought to save others—buries his face in his hands, his shoulders shaking with silent tears.

"Not her too," he pleads to gods who remain indifferent to his sorrow. "Please. Not my baby."

Darkness blankets me without warning, taking hours with it. Maybe days. When my awareness returns, night has already fallen. My father is slumped over in his chair, exhaustion finally claiming him. Through the window, I see towering flames burn-ing on the distant shore, more victims of the fever that has been ravaging the village for weeks now.

Half the village has fallen ill, many never rising again. I've seen the processions, the small shrouded forms of children car-ried to their final rest, parents hollow-eyed with grief following behind. Now my father faces the same fate, watching helplessly as the Mother claims his only child for herself.

In my delirium, a name drifts across my cracked lips. A name I shouldn't speak, a secret I have promised to keep. But death hovers so close now, its shadow falling across my bed, and I long to see those golden eyes one more time before that visiting darkness embraces me forever.

Torian.

The dream shifts, fractals of memory swirling like leaves in a windstorm. My father ages before my eyes—lines on his face deepening, hair turning from brown to gray to white, shoulders bowing under the weight of years and solitude. I reach for him, but he drifts further away with each passing second.

His last words echo as I struggle to reach him through the dense fog: "Be happy, my child. That is all I ever wanted for you."

The dark envelopes me, taking me from him again.

I woke with tears streaming down my face, the memory of my old home, the ache of my father's love excruciating in my chest. How could I have spent a century in the Duskhold without holding tight to the memory of the man who had raised me, cherished me, sacrificed for me?

The guilt was overwhelming. While I had clung to fragments of memory about Torian, I had let my father fade from my mind. The sea glass had preserved one love while the other slipped away almost entirely. I had forgotten him. And it felt like losing him twice.

I rose and dressed mechanically, my mind still trapped in the memory of my father's desperate vigil. The image of his face, lined with fear and exhaustion, refused to fade. The sound of his voice breaking as he begged me not to leave him echoed in my ears. And despite his fervent requests, I did just that.

A soft knock at my door startled me from my reverie. Torian stood there, dressed in a simple olive tunic to avoid attention. The servants would be changing shifts now, leaving a brief window where his presence might slip by unnoticed. But if anyone saw...

The wildness that danced in his golden eyes darkened with concern as he stepped gracefully into my room.

"You've been crying," he said, closing the door quietly behind him.

"Just a dream," I said lightly, as if it weren't already shelved high among the guilt I was steadily collecting. "Or a memory. Of my father during the fever that swept through Mistwater."

Mistwater. Its name surfaced like a gasp for air. My home.

I floated to the window and pulled the curtains shut, shrouding the room in shadow. The darkness pressed against me, holding me firmly in place. I swiped my hands across my arms, pretending to rub away a chill.

Torian's face softened as recognition flickered across his gaze. "The fever that nearly took you from me."

"You were there?" I asked, watching his expression shift as the buried memory emerged.

"It was how your father discovered us," he said quietly. He leaned against the edge of the small desk in the corner of the room. "You were delirious when you called out to me. Nothing more than a whisper. The wind carried your plea, clear as if you had breathed it directly into my ear. I came to you immediately, certain that you were soon to be lost to me."

I padded over to him, bare feet silent on the polished stone floor. He pulled me gently against him, his fingertips resting on my waist. He was warm, solid.

"Tell me," I urged, needing to fill the gaps in my fractured recollection. "I remember being ill, and my father's fear, but little else."

Torian brushed aside the silver ringlet from my forehead and tucked it behind my ear. His gaze grew distant as he looked back across the century that separated us.

"Dozens from your village had already perished from the fever. I watched from the forest's edge as the funeral pyres burned night after night. Then word reached me through the breezes in the trees that the healer's daughter had also fallen ill."

He took a shuddering breath, hands tightening at my waist, as if revisiting it in his mind might result in a different outcome. "I went to the river bend every night, hoping for news, hoping for you to be recovered, waiting for me. When you didn't appear for five moons, I feared the worst. On the sixth night, I felt it. A pull, like a thread tugging at my heart. Then I heard you."

"I was dying," I breathed into his chest, his heartbeat patting my cheek.

"You were dying." He cleared his throat as his voice failed to form even a whisper. "I slipped into the village just after midnight, following that pull straight to your cottage. Your father had forgotten to lock the door."

I could picture it clear as day—the heavy wooden door with the burnished handle that was always stuck, the herbs hanging from the rafters, the worktable cluttered with failed remedies. Imagining Torian's imposing figure emerging through that rickety, mortal doorway seemed almost comical.

"When I found you," Torian continued, "your breathing was barely a rattle. Your skin burned like fire; your lips had turned gray. The scent of death clung to you, that sweetness that comes from your body breaking itself down."

He rose from the desk, gently moving me to the side as he paced my small bedroom. "I sat beside you, took your hand in mine. You were so fragile, so close to slipping away. I couldn't watch you—couldn't stand the thought of—" Words became more difficult as he raked his hands over his face, and I realized what he had done.

"You saved me," I said, touching the silver streak in my hair, still tucked neatly behind my ear. The mark of magic.

"I poured everything I had into you," he nodded. "My light, my strength, my very essence. I felt the fever like a living thing. It fought against me, trying to tear you in half and drag you into darkness. For hours, we battled over your body—the illness and I."

A ghost of a smile touched his lips. "Then, just before dawn, you took a deep, easy breath. Your skin cooled beneath my hands. The gray faded from your lips."

"And my father found you," I prompted.

"He was asleep in his chair beside you. And he woke along with you." Torian's smile faded. "I've never seen such fury in a mortal's eyes. He grabbed a cleaver off the hook and lunged at me."

I gasped. My father was not a violent man. He would patiently usher spiders and hornets outside when killing them was far easier. "He attacked you?"

"He saw a crazed predator looming over his unconscious daughter," Torian said, understanding in his voice. "But then he noticed the change in you, that your breath was steady and your skin was pink. He felt your forehead, and the knife clattered to the floor."

"And then what?"

Torian's voice grew quiet as he crossed back over to me. "He wept, Aevra. The stern, stoic healer crumpled to his knees and cried over you with relief. And I just stood there, frozen, uncertain whether to flee or stay."

I imagined my father, my unwavering protector, his defenses crumbling after days of his desperate struggle to save me—and the stranger who had accomplished what all his knowledge and skill could not.

"When he finally spoke," Torian continued, "he asked who I was and why I had come. So I told him the truth. I had been meeting his daughter by the river for months, and I felt her calling to me."

"What did he say?" I asked, trying to imagine my cautious father's reaction to discovering his daughter's secret Fae lover.

"He asked if I loved you," Torian said simply, stroking his thumb along my cheekbone. "I told him I did, beyond reason or sense. He studied me for a long time, then said something I never expected from a human who had just discovered a Faen in his home."

"What?"

"He said, 'Then you understand the danger you've placed her in.'" Torian's voice took on a deeper cadence as he impersonated my father's speech. "'If harm comes to her because of what you are, I will find a way to make even an immortal suffer.'"

I laughed despite myself, tears springing to my eyes. That sounded exactly like my father—impractically protective, and utterly fearless even when facing a predator who could destroy him with a thought.

"I swore to him I would protect you," Torian said, his tone solemn once more. "He didn't trust me, of course. But we reached an uneasy understanding."

"He never told me he knew," I said, wondering what other secrets my father had kept to protect me.

"He loved you enough to accept what most humans would have fought against until their dying breath."

The weight of it settled over me. My father had known about Torian, had allowed our relationship to continue despite the dangers. He had placed my happiness above his well-placed fear of the Fae, above the village's suspicion of what lay beyond the bridge, above his own paternal instincts.

And I had abandoned him and his memory in return.

"I need to know what happened to him," I said suddenly, the words spilling out before I'd even fully formed the thought. "I need to go to Mistwater, to find out if he's still alive, or how he died, or—"

"Aevra," Torian interrupted gently, "it's been a hundred years. Even if he was a young man when we were separated—"

"I know," I said, the reality of human lifespans a cold certainty. "But I *need* to know. Did he spend years searching for me? Did he believe I was dead? Did he die alone, grieving for his lost daughter?" My voice broke on the last word. My father held me with relief when I escaped death, only for me to die shortly after, without even a body for him to bury beside my mother's grave.

Torian took my hands in his, then brought them tenderly to his lips. "We will find a way," he promised. "It won't be easy since the bridge is guarded twofold. But if this is what you need, we will find a way."

"Thank you," I whispered, leaning into him with my full weight which now seemed impossible to carry.

As his arms encircled me, I thought of my father's warning to him all those years ago. *If harm comes to her because of what you are, I will find a way to make even an immortal suffer.* He never could have imagined the harm that would come. I wondered what he would think of me now. Would he recognize his daughter in these star-filled eyes? Would he still love the being I had become?

"I should go," Torian sighed as he placed a kiss against my hair, glancing toward the window as palace life emerged. "The servants will be making their rounds soon."

I nodded and stepped back from his embrace, though every instinct in me rebelled. The loss of his warmth sent a chill straight through me.

"Tonight?" I asked, hopeful despite myself.

"Not tonight," he said through an apologetic smile. "I have some tedious court details to comb through. But..." He caught the disappointment I failed to hide and tilted my chin with his knuckle. "I will see you at dinner tomorrow."

A gentle peck brushed my mouth, and then he was already turning away, slipping out the door before I could gather my thoughts.

"Dinner?" I called after him.

He answered only with a wink over his shoulder before vanishing into the morning bustle now blooming through the palace corridors.

Dinner.

The word echoed as I paced my room, worry gnawing at the edges of anticipation. Did he mean another stolen picnic with treats and sweet nothings? Or something riskier? Something public? Or worse... had he simply forgotten that I was not the one he was seen beside, that I would never be the one he paraded openly through these gilded halls?

I was mid-spiral when I was interrupted by a curt knock at my door. Torian must have returned. To clarify. To apologize. To admit he'd misspoke and I was still doomed to eat alone in my rooms.

I swung open the door, my mouth half hanging, ready to tell him off for confusing me with such a tantalizing image of enjoying a meal with him. But my eyes landed on Miravelle, the glittering half-faerie I had glimpsed during yesterday's audience.

"Miss Lyra," she said with high-pitched formality, extending a sealed parchment bearing the royal crest. "I have the honor of delivering your formal invitation to tomorrow evening's Patronage Dinner."

Her lavender eyes narrowed slightly behind the tiny glasses perched at the tip of her nose as she beheld my hesitancy. Somehow, this felt like a trick.

"Prince Torian has expressed particular admiration for your illusory work," Miravelle explained, her tone suggesting this was an exceptional honor. "He has offered his royal sponsorship for your continued residence within the Vale. The King has approved the arrangement, of course."

As I accepted the parchment, Miravelle's usual brisk efficiency softened slightly. She glanced at the royal seal, a flicker of nostalgia crossing her features.

"I received one of these myself, ages ago," she said, her voice taking on a rare personal tone. "Shortly after Queen Krivnya's marriage to the King. I was arranging flowers in the east corridor, just a minor assistant to the decorator at the time. The Queen stopped to watch me work."

One of her butterflies fluttered from her hair, landing briefly on the invitation in my hand before returning to its perch.

"I thought I'd made a world-ending mistake when she approached me. But it turned out she wanted to sponsor me herself." Miravelle adjusted her tiny spectacles, a small smile playing at her lips. "Official court records state it was for my 'exceptional attention to aesthetic harmony,' but between us, I think she mainly just wanted a friend. Especially after I once paired crocus and marigold in a bouquet. Gods preserve me, it was hideous."

She shuddered at the thought, then sighed as she pulled out her enchanted ledger, which flipped open to a precisely marked page. "Your seating assignment is here," she said, showing me a miniature diagram of the dining hall where a tiny glowing dot marked my place. "Three feet seven inches from the eastern candelabra, four feet two inches from the salt cellar, and precisely eighteen inches from Prince Torian's chair." She slammed the ledger with satisfaction.

"I... I'm honored," I managed, genuinely surprised by both the invitation and her extraordinary precision. "Please convey my gratitude to His Highness."

With a curt nod, she flitted away, disappearing to adjust whichever earth-shatteringly important detail in the palace needed her attention.

Alone once more, I broke the wax seal with enthusiasm and unfolded the crisp parchment, which bore the official crest of the Amber Vale in gold leaf:

By Command of His Royal Highness
Prince Torian of the Amber Vale

IT IS HEREBY DECLARED THAT LYRA OF THE TWILIGHT ISLES, HAVING DEMONSTRATED EXCEPTIONAL MASTERY IN THE ART OF ILLUSION, BRINGING FORTH TRUTH FROM THE DARKNESS AND ILLUMINATING WHAT WAS THOUGHT LOST, IS GRANTED ROYAL PATRONAGE UNDER THE DIRECT PROTECTION AND SPONSORSHIP OF HIS ROYAL HIGHNESS PRINCE TORIAN.

UPON ACCEPTANCE, SAID ARTIST IS COMMANDED TO PRESENT HERSELF AT THE ROYAL PATRONAGE DINNER TO BE HELD IN THE BANQUET HALL OF THE AMBER PALACE ON THE SIXTEENTH DAY OF HARVEST, WHERE FORMAL RECOGNITION SHALL BE MADE BEFORE THE ASSEMBLED COURT.

IN RETURN FOR THIS PATRONAGE, THE ARTIST PLEDGES HER LOYALTY TO THE CROWN AND AGREES TO REPRESENT THE ARTISTIC TRADITIONS OF THE AMBER VALE WITH DIGNITY AND EXCELLENCE.

GIVEN UNDER OUR HAND AND SEAL ON THIS FIFTEENTH DAY OF HARVEST IN THE THREE HUNDRED FIFTIETH YEAR OF THE REIGN OF HIS MAJESTY KING ORANTH.

King Oranth

Prince Torian

I traced a finger over the embellished *T* of the prince's signature. The swoop of his script beneath my fingertip felt intimate, like it shouldn't be in my hands, shouldn't be addressed to me at all.

But it was, and I could finally sit beside him as more than just a stranger.

he Banquet Hall blazed with light that refracted from countless crystal surfaces. It was almost as if the palace was determined to burn away every familiar shadow I might have hidden in. Even the brocade fabric of my dress glimmered blindingly as I stepped timidly through the gilded archway, the knots in my core tightening as the impostorism crept in.

I stood paralyzed at the entrance of the dining room, scanning the merriment for some kind of instruction. Was I to hunt down my seat like a lost servant? Approach the prince unannounced? Gods, no doubt that would be considered graceless, if not actionable.

Before my sheer awkwardness drew any notice, I spotted Miravelle tearing into a copper-haired courtier. He looked terrorized while she gesticulated furiously at him—a comical sight, her tiny frame dismantling the Fae twice her size.

"Lord Caenan cannot sit beside the Iron ambassador without violating three separate protocols," she insisted, her voice rising with frustration. "The precedent from the Winter Solstice celebration of 1742 was quite clear on the matter!"

I approached her carefully, clearing my throat.

Miravelle whipped around at the interruption, her lavender eyes still blazing with the impudence of the seating arrangement.

"Lyra of the Twilight Isles!" She beamed, the fire within her now doused. She looped her arm in mine, leaving the male open-mouthed and dazed. "Allow me to show you to your seat." One of her butterflies kissed my cheek as we headed to the heel of the horseshoe-shaped table.

"Your Highness," Miravelle addressed Torian, who was clad in a tan evening coat made of worsted wool, "Lyra, the illusionist, has graciously accepted your patronage."

I caught the briefest flicker of mischief in his golden eyes as they met mine. "Thank you for extending my invitation, Miravelle," he said as she nodded in gratitude. "I am truly humbled by her acceptance."

She flitted away, and Torian rose from his seat, pulling my chair away from the table.

"It's wonderful to see you this evening, Your Highness," I said, lowering my eyes as I sweetly dipped into a curtsy, then allowed him to push my chair in beneath me. "Though I must confess some surprise at being granted such an honor after so short a time at court."

"Exceptional talent deserves equal recognition, Miss Lyra," he said as he took his seat beside me.

A steady trickle of nobles and dignitaries briefly greeted the prince before taking their own spots around the dining table. I glanced around at the other patrons and their charges, taking mental notes and trying to remember names that Lysara had rattled off to me earlier this evening. I knew I would be tested on my attentiveness later.

On Torian's other side sat Lady Valeraine, deep in conversation with her sponsee, a flaxen-haired female with pointed features and crystalline blue eyes. Beside her sat multiple scholars sponsored by the merchant prince Thio, who had recently returned from the distant continents with more than just a few trinkets. From what I could glean from my view across the table, his party included an historian, a linguist, and a seer.

Further down, Lord Caenan's exceedingly large frame was squeezed between the King and his own sponsored charge. I blinked away my surprise at the weather-beaten man. His face was sun-carved, wind-torn, with stubborn scruff scattered along his jaw. He wrung his calloused hands, deep-set eyes shifting around the room, assessing for a threat. His tattered, mud-caked jacket looked so out of place among the finery of the court that I wondered if he had been plucked straight from the wilderness and plopped in his chair.

I nudged Torian as the lingering courtiers found their seats, and he followed my gaze down the table.

"That seems rather unusual," I muttered, barely moving my lips.

"Miss Lyra," he said with a mock scold, "we mustn't look down our noses at the less fortunate."

I scoffed. "I shall keep my nose properly aligned, then."

Torian took a measured sip of his wine, attempting to hide the smirk at his lips behind his goblet. Only a prince could turn the mundane act of drinking into a poised maneuver.

"The court delights in its oddities," he murmured. "They polish them until they glitter, and discard what no longer shines."

The musicians in the corner began a light trill as the first course was served—a fragrant squash soup served in dainty platinum bowls, placed before us with ceremonial precision.

"Is that my fate as well?" I asked under my breath, stomach dropping as I dipped my spoon and stirred the heavy cream.

His eyes slid to mine, softening as the corner of his mouth curved. He did not hide behind his wine this time.

"They will never cast aside what is *mine*." His pupils dilated, swallowing gold into black, and I looked away before the blush could creep into my cheeks.

His knuckles brushed against mine beneath the table, so slight it might have been an accident. But then his pinky finger deliberately hooked around mine, sending warmth spiraling up my arm and making my scalp prickle.

I glanced to the other side of him, where his betrothed sat. Still engaged in conversation, still oblivious that beneath the tablecloth her prince had chosen another. My pulse thundered at the surge of power that shot across my skin, a thrill I could easily grow addicted to.

"Your performance at Haustblót was extraordinary," he remarked, his tone now pitched perfectly to sound like casual interest rather than intimate knowledge. "The way you wove the stars and shadows together surpassed every court expectation."

"Thank you, Your Highness," I replied, my voice remarkably steady despite the lightning crackling through my veins. It was absurd how a single hooked finger made me feel more claimed than any contract or crown ever could. "The manipulation of light and shadow is a specialized art in the Twilight Isles."

His fingers now fully entwined with mine, squeezing tenderly. "And do all illusionists from the Isles conjure such *stirring* displays, or is it a craft only you possess?"

I was acutely aware of his thumb tracing circles on my palm.

"Only the most practiced of hands can rouse the most pleasing of magic," I said as I lifted my spoon, blowing soft ripples across the soup. I let the flavor linger, savoring the mouthful longer than necessary. His body temperature spiked as I slid the spoon slowly from my mouth.

His hand released mine and began lazily exploring my thigh, bunching the fabric of my dress little by little.

"Practiced hands are disciplined hands," he hummed in agreement. "Where idle hands tend to be reckless. Wouldn't you agree, Miss Lyra?"

I brought my water goblet to my mouth as he brushed his fingertips over my exposed knee. My breath stalled in my throat, the rim of the glass clicking against my teeth and betraying the shiver that quaked through my body.

"There is charm in recklessness," I breathed, "if one knows exactly where to find it."

His free hand flexed once against his thigh before smoothing the napkin in his lap, masking the subtle shift of his hips in his chair. He tipped back his head, draining the last of his wine, the faintest purr escaping him through his burning swallow.

Before the sound of his suppressed growl even faded, Miravelle materialized with a startling shimmer at Torian's elbow.

"Your Highness," she chirped as she adjusted his goblet a precise half-inch closer to his plate before signaling a servant to refill it.

Her keen eyes flicked between his hand beneath the table and my reddening face. My pulse battered in my neck as her gaze narrowed on me. I held my breath as she opened her mouth to speak.

"What's—" She was interrupted by a calamity of clattering dishes and indignant shouts at the far end of the table.

A server had spilled an entire tray of pheasant and potatoes right on top of Lord Caenan. Miravelle gasped sharply and reappeared over him, fussing over the food in his hair, in his lap, as he attempted to bat her away. I let out a shaky breath as the main course was placed in front of us. Torian did so as well, chuckling, while his hand continued creeping insistently upwards.

"Is there not danger in summoning the very heat of the stars themselves?" he asked, voice low, as the hem of my gown pooled in my lap. The cool air whispered against my bare skin, sending a quiver up my spine. "The depths of such magic must be volatile without proper restraint." His fingertips toyed with the edge of my undergarments.

"The particulars are rather—" I smothered a heaving gasp as his touch slid past the thin slip of fabric and glided over the tender swell between my legs. "—*sensitive*."

His fingers lingered there, teasing me with maddening, barely-there strokes. Every time I shifted my hips beneath his hand, angling for more, he would retreat, setting my nerves on fire with his exquisite denial.

"Though it does require the proper direction—" Frustrated, I clenched my thighs around his hand, trapping him there.

A silent demand.

He gently tried to ease himself free, and I hooked my ankles together, tightening my grip. Helpless, his eyes burned into me as I spoke so evenly. He knew if he ripped his hand from my lap, he'd risk notice.

Knuckles splayed, he pried my knees apart, skin sheering against silk as he did. His strength was undeniable against the stubborn clamp of my thighs, as he reclaimed the spot he so torturously relished.

"—as well as surrender to achieve the desired effect," I finished.

His feather-light touches finally deepened into deliberate swirls, and I nearly shattered at the sweet relief of it.

The roasted pheasant cooled in front of me, its savory aroma mixing with the scent of the spiced wine. I forced my hands steady as the juices dribbled from the meat with each slice of my knife. I lifted a forkful to my mouth, pressing the morsel past my lips and chewing with exaggerated calm. I tasted nothing as savory as the distraction unfurling beneath the tablecloth.

I met his hungry eyes as I licked the lingering spice from my lower lip. He mirrored the gesture, his tongue sweeping lazily along his mouth. I could tell it cost him every fiber of restraint to contain the fire within him, as the circles he delicately traced pressed harder, faster.

"So mastery is achieved only when control is saturated by surrender," he said, curving a finger downward and finding the slick heat of me gathering between my legs. His jaw tightened as he sank deeper, my composure splintering as the swell of each knuckle slowly pressed further into me. "*Breathtaking.*"

A blush of pink rose up my neck as I raised another bite to my mouth. I shyly removed my gaze from his, attempting to maintain whatever shred of poise I might have had left.

"Indulge me, Miss Lyra," Torian went on, intently watching me fray with each wet plunge of his hand.

I suppressed a gasp as he slid a second finger inside me. His thumb continued circling the swollen bundle of nerves with agonizing patience, the tempo building steadily with the hammering of my pulse.

"Do you find satisfaction in the penetration of your senses, or does it only leave you wanting *more*?"

He might as well have groaned it against the shell of my ear.

I nearly choked at his forwardness, the bite snagging in my throat as I coughed quietly into my cup. My eyes watered as I sipped, heat racing up my cheeks. Meanwhile, his touch was merciless—unyielding even as I almost gave away the scandal of the millennium. Every exquisite stroke of his thumb sent waves crest-ing and breaking in my core. In and out, up and down. Over and over, faster and heavier.

I was so enraptured, and so focused on not showing it, that I almost did not hear my name coming from Torian's other side.

"Miss Lyra," Lady Valeraine said, eyes boring into me with either concern or suspicion, "are you quite well?"

I realized I was still holding my water goblet, gripping it so tightly that my knuckles were white. I set it down carefully, terrified my trembling hands might betray me. Torian remained unbothered. Still circling, never slowing.

"Yes, my Lady," I said, clearing my throat. A tremor shot through my belly, through my thighs. He felt it. A razor-thin smirk spread across his mouth as he brought a forkful to his lips to hide it. "The seasoning is just a bit strong for my sensitive palate."

A scrape of his knuckles brushed the perfect spot, and my hips bucked involuntarily against his hand. He withdrew slightly, hovering at my entrance in agony. Lady Valeraine chuckled lightly as she pushed food around on her plate.

"I must agree with you," she said. "The Vale's kitchens tend to bury flavor in spice."

I reached for another sip of water, drowning a squeak as Torian dragged his fingertips across me before sliding back in. Deeper this time. My legs quivered, fluttering the tablecloth at my lap.

"To my taste," Torian interjected, "the spice is exactly what makes the dish memorable."

"Ever the contrarian, my Prince," Lady Valeraine said. She dabbed her lips delicately as they started to purse, the jest in her words barely giving way to the barb just beneath.

Right as I approached the precipice beneath his smoldering touch, a broad-shouldered male stumbled forward, bowing low. He was red in the face, eyes wide. His worn trousers were caked with mud and slobber, and he wore the musky scent of nature.

"Your Highness," he murmured, "the kennels require your immediate attention... and, ah—" His eyes flicked to the King at the other end of the table. "—your discretion."

I blinked at the state of him. To come barreling into a royal banquet looking like that, it had to be serious.

Torian's eyes narrowed on the male, his circles slowing from the distraction.

"It's Hermia, then?" His tone suggested it was less of a question and more like a statement of fact.

With maddening calm, Torian withdrew his hand from inside me, leaving me bare and trembling on the edge of bliss. "Of course, Kennel Master," he replied, his voice betraying nothing of what had just transpired. "Please inform her I will be at her side shortly." *Unruly hound*, I heard him mutter under his breath.

As he pushed away from the table, he brought his fingers to his nose, inhaling with quiet satisfaction. Then, without haste, he drew them into his mouth, savoring my arousal. A glint of possession flashed across his golden eyes, leaving me breathless, my body still pulsing with unfulfilled need.

"Lady Valeraine, Miss Lyra," Torian said, inclining his head to each of us. His eyes met mine briefly, molten gold burning with promise. "I would love to continue our conversation when the *night* permits."

No elaboration was needed.

Tonight. Under the willow.

With that, he departed, leaving me to regain my composure while seated beside his betrothed. I prayed she couldn't scent her intended on me... within me.

Lady Valeraine turned toward me, smile poised, a diamond bracelet catching the lamplight. She was so enigmatic; I had no idea if she knew, or what she knew.

"Miss Lyra," she said evenly, "allow me to introduce Miss Brella, my sponsee." The flaxen-haired female inclined her head shyly in my direction. "She plays the mandolin for The Chordilleras. Their music has become quite indispensable in the Vale of late."

"That's a clever name," I said, my voice more timid than I intended it to be. As the exhilaration ebbed, a prick of shame rushed in to fill its absence. Here I sat, exchanging pleasantries and introductions while the embers of Torian's possession cooled to ash. "Are you from the mountains, then?"

"Not originally," Brella said meekly. "I hail from the Rime Enclave."

Her answer landed like ice down my back. The Rime Enclave, the northern ghost, drowned and frozen over. She noticed my throat bob as I swallowed.

"I—I'm sorry," I murmured, selecting each word with care. "I imagine it is difficult to revisit every time you're asked about your roots." Brella shrugged as she sipped her wine, avoiding my eyes.

"My family fell to tragedy before the rest of the Enclave did. But, yes. The sting never leaves."

Lady Valeraine's eyebrows twitched inward as she laid a hand delicately on Brella's wrist.

"She has a gift for weaving harmony out of grief."

"Music endures," Brella said, her blue eyes frosting over. "Even when stones and blood do not."

A brittle silence stretched between the three of us. Discomfort slotted itself beside the guilt that had taken up residence within me. I glanced around the Banquet Hall, looking for something, *anything*, worthy of a subject change. Aside from mentioning the perfect placement of the sconces on the wall, I came up with nothing.

Thankfully, Lady Valeraine cleared her throat.

"Miss Lyra," she said smoothly, "how do you find the Vale? I must admit, it is nice to have another islander among the court's company."

"It's... dazzling," I said, "though I do occasionally find myself missing the sunrise."

"I haven't traveled to those isles since I was a girl," she said, her crystal goblet humming low as she idly circled the rim with her fingertip. "Though I remember the sunrise being... unlike any other." Her smile lingered, though something about it stripped me completely bare.

"Perhaps a visit is warranted in the future," I added calmly. "Much has changed within the last few centuries." I could have missed the tiny shift in her countenance. The luster in her eyes dulled slightly, her knitted brow casting a shadow across her fluttering lashes.

"Perhaps."

A single word, sharp as ice. She turned her attention back to Brella with such unhurried grace that I hardly noticed I had just been politely dismissed.

I did not engage much in the conversation that followed. I sat motionless, hands awkwardly placed in my lap, as they discussed The Chordilleras playing at the Mabon Festival, and the unwanted advances from the troupe's hurdy-gurdy player. I desperately wanted to know what a hurdy-gurdy was, but I could not stop chewing the inside of my cheek long enough to ask.

The remaining courses passed in a blur of wine and politicking, nobles trading barbed compliments as servants cleared plate after plate. When the last of the trifle bowls had been licked clean, the majority of patrons and their sponsees stumbled out of the dining hall, their bellies full and their minds swimming in wine.

"A word to the wise," Lady Valeraine said, voice low, manicured fingernails clicking rhythmically against her glass. "Dangerous secrets are best kept behind lock and key."

I blinked, smile faltering. She stared at the remaining dregs of wine as she swirled her goblet.

"I'm not sure I quite catch your meaning, my Lady."

She rose suddenly from her chair with liquid elegance. I lurched halfway to my feet, fumbling for the proper etiquette befitting my station. Her hand met my shoulder, fingers curling as she pressed me back into my seat as if I were a child. Her lips drew a genteel smile as she leaned down, close enough for her breath to stir the wisps of curls at my temple.

"You are not nearly as discreet as you think you are, Lyra of the Twilight Isles."

I parted my lips to answer, but the sound of my voice was lost to the pulse hammering in my ears. She linked arms with Brella, and they both strolled from the Banquet Hall.

She knew something.

She knew.

And it was only a matter of time before that knowledge became a blade she would drive right through me.

My head spun as my legs carried me back to my room. I didn't remember the clack of my heels bouncing off the walls as I rushed through the hallways. Or the rips in my dress as those heels bit through the hem that got caught in my haste. I didn't remember fumbling for the doorknob, slamming the door behind me, tearing off my shoes and hurling them against the wall.

But I did remember approaching the window, watching the male in the worsted wool evening coat amble into the Night Garden. I rested my forehead against the cool windowpane. The glass fogged under my shallow breath, blurring Torian as he strolled further along the dimly lit path. Every instinct urged me toward him. My unfulfilled need was so sharp that I might've just tied the bedsheets together and rappelled down to the garden just to save a measly minute with him.

I pictured him leaning against the willow, hidden behind its branches, his hand still faintly smelling of me. I imagined those exquisite fingers unfastening the brass buttons of his evening coat, one by one, exposing his rugged chest beneath. The effortless pull of his shirt over his head. The sight of him, bare in front of me. Finally.

I pushed away from the window before I completely undressed him in my mind. I did not climb out the window, nor did I take the stairs.

Instead, I crawled naked into the bed. The idea of a nightgown touching my charged skin nearly suffocated me. I groaned dramatically as I rolled over, tossing the sheets, begging sleep to take me so I didn't have to feel anything else tonight. The images of him persisted, flashing through the dark. The frustrating ache between my thighs intensified, smothering the gripping paranoia.

My hand traveled slowly down my body in the same way I imagined his would. A finger tracing the side of my neck, a palm kneading gently the peak of my breast. The lightest touch sliding across my stomach, along the ridge of my hip, up the skin of my inner thigh. I was just as slick from the sheer image of him as I was an hour ago at his mercy.

My fingers echoed the memory of his touch, moving in such knowing and precise circles, pretending it was him. The heavy duvet was his weight on top of me. The crumpled linens against my cheek were his lips nuzzling against me. The draft from beneath the door was his breath on my skin.

The release came quickly, violently. Stars burst behind my eyelids as I bit into my pillow, muffling the moan that forced its way out of me. The waves of pleasure crashed over me, then ebbed to jerky, rhythmic tremors as my hand slowed, my body going limp.

It was a poor substitution, as the fleeting satisfaction left behind yet another strand of guilt. He was probably still down there waiting for me, while I lay here, shuddering from the release he should have given me. Too scared to meet him because of a threatening riddle, courtesy of his betrothed.

I didn't watch as he exited the garden, hands in his pockets, head hung low. I couldn't bear to witness the disappointment I had caused.

Chapter Fourteen

Petals of marigold and chrysanthemum clung to my fingertips, staining them yellow as I wove their stems through the lattice of the gilded trellis. Like every other performer Miravelle had guilted into service, I'd been commandeered to help dress the Vale for Mabon. My hands had almost gone numb. The flowers slipped clumsily in my grasp, my fingers cramping from the repetition. I had just tucked in the final blossom when Miravelle's voice cracked like a whip across the courtyard.

"The lanterns are to be placed on the main processional path, twelve inches apart. Do not scatter them about like dead lightning bugs!"

I stepped back, wiping my palms on my trousers as I inspected the last three hours' labor. My shoulders ached from the strain; my knees popped in protest as I shifted my weight. Miravelle had demanded perfection, and as I admired the cascades of color, I believed I had delivered nothing less.

Paisley ribbons of warm blooms swirled through every curve of the golden arch. Chrysanthemums blazed gold, marigolds glowed orange, and dahlias bled red. Violet lilies brooded to near-black. Every petal carried its own omen, the flowers weaving a tale of glory, endurance, blood, and shadow. The story of a hard-won kingdom.

I flexed my stiff fingers, admiring the mesmerizing design, when I was jolted out of my stupor. Miravelle popped into existence beside me, unmoved by my undignified shriek of surprise. She stood there longer than was comfortable, arms crossed, gaze sweeping over every inch of the arch.

I braced myself for the eventual nitpicking. Surely, there were petals out of order, stems tucked too loosely, or some symbolic faux pas I had made without realizing.

But the criticism never came.

Instead, she tilted her head, gave the flowers a single calculated sniff, and—to my absolute shock—nodded. It was unnerving to see her wearing satisfaction behind the tiny pair of glasses that sat at the tip of her nose. She felt so as well, it seemed.

"Yes," she said flatly. "That will do just fine, I believe." Her tone carried the same weight as a gavel strike.

An audible sigh of relief escaped me as she pivoted, skirt flaring and butterflies whirring around her head.

"Come, come!" She beckoned sharply as she scurried toward the center of the courtyard. "Much still left to do!"

I trailed behind her as she bobbed through servants and other performers, barking orders as she passed. The string lights were hanging too low. The flames in the lanterns were burning white instead of gold. The leaves on the ground were strewn too haphazardly.

"I can't control the trajectory of falling foliage, miss!" The words snapped from the dancer before she could catch them, sweat shining on her temples.

I winced on her behalf at the verbal lashing she was about to receive for her perceived arrogance. Miravelle stilled, then vanished in a shimmer. She reappeared within an inch of the dancer, so close that their noses nearly brushed.

She inhaled once, slowly and steadily, then delicately cleared her throat. The dancer's lip trembled ever-so slightly.

"Then I suggest you find a broom," Miravelle said, her dulcet tone far more bone-chilling than a shout. "Lest I notify Her Majesty of your insolence?"

The dancer blanched, dropping into a sloppy bow.

"Brooms are in the gardener's shed yonder. Make haste." She did not spare the female another glance, already sweeping onward. I kept pace behind her until she stopped at the very heart of the preparations.

A weathered old Fae knelt at the edge of a mosaic, examining the colored glass, knuckles tucked under his chin. The mosaic spread wide across the courtyard floor. Its pattern was half-laid, half-empty, catching the lamplight in fractured glimmers of topaz, sapphire, emerald, and ruby.

A handful of others were gathered around it, some on the edge, some toward the center, each carefully placing bits of tile and gems within the circle. Brella sat at the crown of the mosaic, bringing each shard to her forehead, then her lips, then her heart, before laying it reverently on the ground.

"Master Finvarra," Miravelle said. He grunted in acknowledgment, but did not take his shrewd gaze from the mosaic. "Miss

Lyra will assist you with the Pattern of Balance."

Master Finvarra stood, hands on knees as he straightened his back, vertebra by vertebra.

"Well met, Miss Lyra," he said, placing a friendly pat on my shoulder.

"And the glow—" Miravelle paused, then with exaggerated precision corrected, "—the *auroragourds*. See that they are accurately placed by the evening chime."

Her face blazed a light shade of pink before she flitted out of sight, though her enthusiastic demands still carried through the breeze. Master Finvarra shook his head and smiled.

"She could wring thunder from a clear sky, that one," he muttered under his breath.

I continued watching silently as Brella maintained her ritual. She would place a square of tile and then set a single gem atop it. Over and over. Forehead, kiss, heart.

"Every stone and square tells a story within the Pattern of Balance," he said, noticing the hypnotic vigil I was trapped in. "Topaz for the golden age of the Vale, rubies for the blood of the south, sapphires for the western river, emeralds for the eastern hills." He then gestured toward Brella and her vigil. "And diamonds for the souls of Loch Rime. All of them must meet in the center, else the Pattern has no voice."

A jar filled to the brim with gemstones sat on the ground beside the Pattern. I dipped my hand in and plucked out three sapphires. One for the woman who went to the Duskhold, one for the woman who emerged at the river, and one for the woman who took her place with her death.

"And around the outside?" I asked, noting the burning shades of orange that surrounded the entire Pattern as I knelt to place the stones neatly within a spiral of blue.

"Sunstone, for the eternal glory of the Vale and all of its inhabitants. What's gained, what's lost, and what yet endures. The Pattern steadies our realm against the fabric, for equinoxes and solstices thin the veil 'til it's threadbare. Come," he said, clapping me on the back as I stood. "We mustn't keep the *glowbellies* waiting."

I could not suppress my light chuckle as I followed him toward a shaded corner where gourds of orange and white were being gutted and shaved. "Glowbellies?"

"The gourds swell so fat in the mountain soil they look fit to burst. We carve them up, set candles inside, and those giant bellies grow warm enough to keep the shadows at bay," he said.

He looked across the yard at Miravelle, now flitting haphazardly between tree branches. She yanked a paper lantern from a musician's inept hands, muttering something about symmetry as if her life depended on it.

"The prim and proper around here call them auroragourds. But that little faerie, she's a bumpkin just like the rest of us. Only she's not as proud of it."

We approached the largest of the carved gourds. They sat four in a neat row, each one hollowed out, skin shaved in intricate designs that curled around precisely cut lines and shapes. I stepped closer to a cream-colored pumpkin whose stem sat at the same height as the knot of curls on the top of my head. The carving spiraled in tight swirls, the lines opening like fingers into a scene in the middle. Four figures, one kneeling with its face buried in its hands, while the others loomed above, judging, merciless.

"Ah, the Ascension," Master Finvarra said as he turned another of the massive gourds on its side and rolled it back toward the center of the yard. I did the same, astounded at how incredibly light it was despite its mammoth size. "Just before my time, so I can't guarantee that it is an accurate depiction. Make way!" He laughed as he rolled the giant pumpkin onto a distracted decorator. "But we all know the stories of the Pattern."

"I don't," I admitted softly. "Not like this, anyway."

"Ha! Then you are in luck, my dear," he said as his grin

widened, deepening the lines on his face. "Allow Master Raconteur Finvarra to regale you with the oldest story the universe has to offer."

He ushered me and my pumpkin to the bottom of the circle, helping me align it just right so the curve of its 'belly' kissed the curve of the mosaic. Others around the courtyard paused their decorating when they heard his echoing theatrics. Some stayed put, leaning in while idly continuing their assignments, while others abandoned their work completely to sit around the Pattern and listen.

"The Ascension sits at the northern pole, because every story begins at the top of the page," he explained. "The gods once lived among us. Not high on thrones, but shoulder to shoulder. For centuries, millennia even, they bent their backs in our fields, broke bread at our hearths. They were as common as rain, and just as taken for granted.

"Eventually, their presence among their creations bred dependency instead of innovation. Our hands grew idle even as our demands became excessive. Houses stood unfinished. Fishermen refused to cast a net. The bathhouses overflowed while the fields lay fallow. The balance teetered for the first time.

"The Son, Gwenael, who was the favorite among the Faen, sought to redeem us. He begged the others to reconsider, stating that we simply needed guidance, not desertion.

"'We cannot simply abandon them to starve and collapse,' he pleaded. The other three disagreed with his sentiment.

"'It is their own hubris that will lead to their ruin,' the Father said.

"'Who will worship you once they have all perished from your negligence?' Gwenael said.

"But the others remained unconvinced, and they dragged him five hundred leagues across the seabed as punishment for his indignance. Barnacles tore through his skin, salt burning the wounds deeper. His cries were the last echo we heard of the gods.

"And when they withdrew from this plane, oh, how we wailed at the injustice! But they did not shed a tear for us, and the sky dried up for fifty years. Our crops withered, the wells soured, and famine stole through the streets. Mothers held their babies to their breasts, but they produced no milk. Lifespans shortened to those of mortals. Faenkind had been robbed of its livelihood, though it was we who robbed ourselves of it for the sake of our own entitlement.

"Such is the tale of the first imbalance."

Master Finvarra wiped his palms on his trousers and shuffled to the bright orange gourd he had placed on the eastern edge of the circle.

Its carving twisted into two halves, a beach cleaved down the middle. Three figures stood together on one side of the fracture, while the fourth stood alone, head thrown back. He patted it with a heavy hand, as if it were the rump of a horse he meant to ride.

"The Severance sits on the right side of the Pattern, symbolizing the correction of order. See how she walks into the circle, toward her fate on the other side," he said as he drew a line in the air with his finger, trailing to the gourd that was now being placed on the western edge.

"The Daughter, Alezae, was once a benevolent shepherd, a courier of wayward souls across the sands of death. But she was not satisfied with this eternal kismet. She watched as the other gods were worshipped for their generosity, temples erected in their names, sacrifices made at their altars. Her jealousy curdled into resentment. Her resentment spoiled into wickedness.

"Fewer and fewer souls crossed into the Mother's reach, as if death itself had stalled. Troubled, the Mother traveled to the Twilight Shores. She found the glittering sand dulled to gray; black billows of storm clouds blotted out the once violet sky. The Whispering Sea was still and silent. She found Alezae seated atop a spectral throne of shattered souls with her feet propped up casually on the back of some unrecognizable, emaciated creature.

"The Mother wept for the souls that Alezae had sworn to guide, their mortal coils reduced and molded into the shape of a chair. The Mother demanded their release, but Alezae refused.

"'You have no power here,' she said. 'For I am the Adumbral Queen, and all that I reap, I will only ever keep.'

"She could not be struck down, for if one Pillar falls, the cosmos itself collapses with it. And thus the covenant of the gods was sundered as the other three bound her to her own hideous creation. Her throne unraveled, its innocent captives wrenched free from beneath her, and the bitch goddess fell to the floor, cursing her kin for their persecution.

"Alezae would keep her prison, but she would forever remain a prisoner within it.

"And such is the tale of the second imbalance."

Master Finvarra's voice faded, and the silence that followed clung like smoke, the tale itself unsettling the surrounding air. The only sounds were the faint crackles of the lantern flames and the scraping of tiles being placed on the cobbled ground. Workers who had only meant to pause for a moment now stood around the Pattern, enchanted by the spell of his cadence. Even Miravelle, who had been buzzing in near hysteria all afternoon, had stilled in her frenzy, hovering at the edge of the circle despite herself.

The crowd flowed with him as he moved toward the next gourd, a speckled green and yellow pumpkin that was laid on the left curve of the circle. The entire courtyard breathed in unison, waiting for him to begin again.

He took a long, steady inhale as he traced a finger down a sunken groove in its skin. Only one figure was etched into the rind this time. Its arms spread wide overhead, hair sprawled and spiraling in wild tendrils, while curling flames engulfed the entire circumference of the pumpkin.

"The Cataclysm," he continued, his voice betraying a tiny shudder as he exhaled.

We watched him in silence as he worked to stifle the trembling of his chin, still idly running his hand over the enormous auroragourd. He blinked quickly and began again.

"The Cataclysm is set on the left side of the Pattern, symbolizing the ruinous evil that ravaged the realms three hundred fifty years ago. Many of us remember—" He paused, clearing his throat once more. A few sniffs echoed around the circle. "—the ones we lost. Let us take a moment now to honor their memory."

An impenetrable hush lay across the courtyard like a shroud. He bowed his head in reverence, his palms sitting firmly on the gourd, as if it might try to escape the discomfort it caused. Hands clasped hands all the way around the Pattern of Balance, thumbs tracing circles of remembrance. Even Miravelle uncrossed her arms to join in the moment's solidarity.

I took Master Finvarra's free hand in mine as names of the dead were raised in prayer around the courtyard:

> *Elya Airsong*
> *Lorenzyn Rife*
> *Maggie Pellelec, Maddie Pellelec, Cece Pellelec—*
> *my little girls*
> *Synnøve, Bjørn, Kaspyr*
> *Copper and Sylvia del Ayne*
> *Flaryn Marconju*
> *Missy Mae—the best girl*
> *King Anthurium, Queen Marceline, Princess*
> *Seraphi*
> *Milicynth Finvarra*

He shifted on his feet as the tribute waned, looking up to see his listeners watching him with admiration. A ghost of a smile touched his lips as he squeezed my hand before releasing it.

"Thank you," he muttered to the group. "Let's continue." His voice now carried the same theatrical rhythm it had before the tragic memories flooded his talent.

"Four centuries, Alezae stewed in her resentment, her prison twisting darker, its unwilling denizens meeting crueler and crueler fates. She fashioned a new throne, and with each unfortunate soul she absorbed, her power grew stronger. But it was never enough for her to break the manacles forced upon her. Her chains cracked, but never yielded.

"Her rage peaked, bursting the seams between the realms, and she shattered the barriers that separated us from the gods. On the first day, flames poured from a blood-red sky. Some were mere flickers of a match, while others were balls of fire the size of palaces, sparing no roof, no field, no beast. The world blazed until we could barely breathe for the stink of charred flesh and timber.

"On the third day, the rivers boiled over, scalding fish into pale husks, running black with ash and scorched bone. Some were desperate enough to drink from the river, hoping to quench their arid throats. Their blood thinned, spilling from their noses, eyes, and every single pore until they were completely drained of life.

"On the fifth day, the sweltering air betrayed us. Without homes for shelter, or canopies for cover, blisters blossomed on every face and hand, swelling until they burst and ran with poison. The sickened wept pus and fire, their cries echoing like hymns of agony. Those who survived were left mangled, their bones corroded within their flesh.

"On the seventh night, the fire stopped falling. Rain broke through the burgundy sky, the tears of the gods as they wept for what their fallen kin had carelessly obliterated. The embers hissed as they stitched the fabric of reality back together. We collected our dead in the downpour, laying blackened corpses shoulder to shoulder. We tended to our wounded, cataloging missing limbs, granting mercy to the moribund. The rain washed away the blood and ash, carrying it all to the rivers that ran clear once more, and out to the sea.

"Such is the tale of the third imbalance."

The circle of listeners loosened, as if the grip of the story released their rigid postures all at once. But Master Finvarra did not step back from the Pattern, did not take a bow. Instead, he turned to the final gourd that sat at the southern pole of the circle.

It was the largest of the four, but it had no intricate, swirling carvings, no godly figures hovering over a scene. Its skin was shaved and peeled off, and the rind was painted solid black. Tiny holes the size of the tip of a quill were bored through it. I imagined the candlelight shining through it would make it look like constellations against the black sky.

A shadow flashed in the corner of my eye as it scurried from between my feet, slinking through a hole in the gourd like a frantic lizard. I couldn't suppress the shiver that crept up my back and into my scalp.

"Four?" Miravelle's voice rang out, her question biting through the scarred silence that had gathered. "There have always been only three!"

The communal solemnity dissipated. Feet shuffled against the cobbles as Miravelle's sharp tone knocked everyone back into themselves. Some scurried back to their tasks, grateful for the excuse to retreat to busyness, while others lingered, unwilling to abandon this potential encore of Master Finvarra's performance.

"Only because the balance has never demanded a fourth," he answered. "The signs are clear. Something is coming, and it demands to be honored."

Miravelle rolled her eyes, arms crossed tightly across her chest. "I think you are asking for trouble with that."

"Or perhaps we have invited trouble all along by neglecting the fourth."

The tension between the two was cleaved in half by the metallic groan of the front gates. Two guards in copper armor stepped through, dragging a disheveled, nerve-wracked man between them. Round ears. Small. Mortal.

Their grips clamped down like irons on his elbows. His bare feet smeared skid marks of mud as they hauled him forward. Whatever work had continued following Master Finvarra's tale stopped as we watched the man struggle against their unwavering grips.

"Please, sirs! Please, I just want to go home! Back to—"

"Mistwater. We know." The guard's voice was flat, almost bored, but the name rang like a struck bell in my chest.

"My wife will worry if I'm not home by supper, m'lords, please—"

"That's the least of your worries at the moment, human." The other guard gave a brutal yank on his arm as he tried to dig his heels into the stone. "Once you tell us why you're here—"

"I told you already, I don't know why I'm here!" The man's voice cracked with desperation. "I'm just a fisherman! I cast my net into the river, and the mist swallowed me up. The sun wouldn't move, I couldn't find west—please!"

He sagged in defeat, but the guards pressed on, unrelenting despite his pleas.

"Save your breath," one muttered. "You'll need it for the Captain."

"Hopefully, your superior will see more reason than you brutes!"

"Don't count on it."

The guard's hand dropped to his hilt. Metal rasped against leather as he drew his short sword, the sound slicing the air like a warning song.

My stomach lurched. *Gods, not here. Not now.*

The man froze, eyes wide, chest heaving. "No—please, I'm sorry—"

The guard raised his blade, its edge glinting in the lantern light. Gasps rippled through the courtyard, sharp and panicked. But none of us looked away. None of us moved. No one did anything.

I stood paralyzed in my horror, waiting for the sword to drive through his skull. But the steel flipped. The guard caught the blade in both hands and smashed the pommel across the fisherman's nose. Bone crunched. Blood sprayed.

The man shrieked, staggering back, only to take another crushing blow to the temple. He crumpled limply onto the cobbled ground.

Without pause, the guards hooked him beneath the arms in one smooth, synchronized motion and continued dragging his unconscious body forward. A steady trail of bright red followed them through the courtyard and into the palace. The double doors slammed behind them, and the yard was quiet as death once more.

"See?" Miravelle whispered through the stunned silence. "Trouble."

Chapter Fifteen

I stood on black sand and stared into an empty sky. The Whispering Sea was gone, its tide sucked backward into a horizon too far, too *wrong*. A breeze lifted my curls gently from my shoulders. I shivered, though not from the chill, but from the impossibility of it. There was no wind in the Duskhold. If one stirred now, either a draft had entered through the perilously thinning veil, or something colossal was breathing down my neck.

I turned. A shadow loomed in the distance. Too tall, too thin, stretching upwards until it vanished into the void. I reached toward it on instinct, but it was not mine to claim. It bent slightly in my direction, tilting its head as if amused by my audacity to communicate. I staggered back, breath catching in my throat as it grew darker, drew nearer.

I ran toward the sea, my bare feet pounding over brittle shells. It had saved me once. If I could just reach it again, find where it had hidden itself away and throw myself into its arms once more...

But the further I pushed, the worse the ground betrayed me. With each step, I sank deeper into the wet sand, dragged down ankle-deep, knee-deep, until my strides became a desperate trudge. The tide was nowhere, only endless black. Panicked whimpers escaped me as I tried to wrench my legs from the sludge of the seabed.

The shadow heard my pitiful mewls. Laughter—low, resonant, unmistakable—rippled through the emptiness, quaking the earth and knocking me off-balance. I fell forward, my hands sinking into the sand and sticking there just as hopelessly as my legs. I was snared. Hogtied by the very place I had defied with my survival. The laughter turned maniacal. The shadow reached for me.

I gasped.

I cried.

I awoke to starlight.

Not dawn, not the familiar amber haze that never shifted, but dozens of silver-blue sparks hovering just beneath my ceiling. They drifted in lazy constellations, painting my walls in an eerie, alien light.

For a moment, I couldn't catch the breath that I had lost in the Duskhold. I was certain the shadow had followed me here, lodged in my chest. Then my panic receded, and I recognized the stars as my own.

Stars that I had created in my sleep.

The frenzy slammed right back down my throat. I scrambled up, clutching the blankets with trembling fists as that phantom laugh still vibrated in my skull. A floorboard creaked outside my door. The servants were beginning their morning rounds, and if one of them peeked in…

I waved my hands above me, sweeping in an arc and swatting them away like pesky flies. The stubborn stars only flickered.

"Shit," my voice cracked. "Please."

Sweat ran hot down my temples as I poured every ounce of will into banishing them. Slowly, reluctantly, they guttered, one by one, like candles in a sudden wind. The last few clung viciously to the stale air of my room, pulsing at me, mocking me. I snatched them down in a furious sweep and crushed them tightly in my fist.

I sagged against the headboard, pulse rattling against my ragged breaths. My palm throbbed from where my fingernails had dug deep. When I opened my hand, the fine stardust spilled across the sheets like pulverized bone.

I went to the window, pressing my forehead to the cool glass. Before the fog of my breath coated the pane, I caught a flash of my reflection. The nebulous clouds in my eyes had turned stormy; the motes beneath my skin swam like trapped glow-worms.

I reached up to my neck. Surely the dampening charm had fallen off in my fit of sleep. But there it was, warm and humming, nestled against the sea glass. I yanked the curtains closed and did not want to look in the mirror for the rest of the morning.

I stood there for a long moment, waiting to see if the stars would spark back to life without my blessing. They didn't, and the stillness of it left me half-relieved, half-troubled.

I opened my hand again, skin still stinging. Red crescents bit into my flesh, encircling tiny scorches, perfect black pinpricks edged in feverish pink. The stars had left their mark before dying, branding me with their last betrayed sigh.

Never before had they turned on me, and I wondered if this was a cruel trick of Mabon, or if I was losing my grip on my magic.

I pulled myself out of inaction and began to dress. My body

protested in exhaustion with every garment as I fumbled with the clasps and laces. But there was no room to sleep the day away. Not with rehearsal looming. Not with Mabon less than two days away.

As I fastened my sequined skirt at my hips with careful fingers, palm still biting, something rustled in the bathing chamber.

I froze.

"Hello?" I called out stupidly, my voice too thin in the stillness.

No answer. But then the scrape of movement across the floor, too deliberate to be a draft. A shadow slipped along the threshold, slick and slow, ignoring me as it slid into the bathroom. My skin prickled.

I crossed the room with careful, silent steps. The chamber was dim, the curtains drawn tight. I peeked in and saw the floor mirror, which was always left facing the room, turned backward against the wall. My mouth went dry as I reached out and rotated it back around.

My reflection stared back at me. The same glowing, ethereal woman. Then something darted past in the glass, moving fast, just outside the doorway behind me.

I whirled around. Nothing. I peered around the doorjamb. Nothing. Bedsheets still in the same tangle, wardrobe door still open, clothes still strewn. I grabbed my shoes and exited into the hall barefoot, slamming the door behind me.

Just another day in the Amber Vale. Another trick of the thinning veil.

The corridors were worse. The warm light of the palace wavered like a heat mirage. A tapestry I had passed a hundred times—the coronation of Beloved King Anthurium, stitched with solid gold thread and encrusted with sunstone—shifted as I walked by; the King's hands, once steady with scepter and orb, were now closed tightly around a dagger dripping with glittering rubies.

I turned away from his hollow eyes that seemed to follow me, judging my bare feet. I couldn't make myself look back to see if the stitching had righted itself.

I quickened my pace, but not for long. A bloodcurdling wail ripped down the hall, freezing me where I stood. My veins hardened to ice. The banshee. The same shriek that rattled glass and crystal in the Golden Hall, but it was worse, somehow. Drawn out. Distorted. It ricocheted off the walls like a blade dragged over stone.

I clutched the sea glass at my throat, whispering to myself: *Not for me. Not for me. I am nobody, a shadow in someone else's house.* Nobodies never warranted a lament. But her keening was thick as smoke, gagging me to prove me wrong.

The servants around me carried on, their chattering undisturbed, errands unflinching, their hands full of garlands and candles. To them, the corridor was silent as death, and I was the only one caught in the dirge.

I bolted. My feet slapped against stone, raw and bare, shoes still clutched uselessly in one hand. The sequins stitched into my skirt tinkled and clicked like broken glass as I ran, wild percussion accompanying the banshee's song. Servants flattened themselves against the walls as I tore past. Their wide-eyed stares followed me, some muttering under their breaths, others snickering nervously as if I wasn't the first one to get spooked in the halls around Mabon.

I didn't stop until the banshee's echo thinned to silence, leaving only the clatter of my sequins and the pounding of my heart to fill my ears.

Not for me.

The rehearsal for the equinox ceremony took place that afternoon in the Golden Hall, which had transformed into an unmatched autumnal bounty under Miravelle's exacting supervision.

"Three degrees clockwise, if you will," she instructed a servant who staggered beneath a wreath weighed down with gourds and fall fruits. Then she vanished in a shimmer, reappearing across the hall in the blink of an eye. "The candles must be equidistant, exactly eighteen and three-quarter inches apart," she snapped at another before she flitted again, this time to my side, startling me.

"Your performance space will be prepared according to your specifications," she declared. I didn't recall making any specifications, but she barreled on, pointing to the northwest corner of the room. "The shadows will be deepest there, as requested."

The servant under the wreath buckled, sending oranges and small pumpkins bouncing across the freshly polished floor. Miravelle darted after them, muttering something about how difficult it was to make bruises look symmetrical.

Performers from across the court gave clipped demonstrations of their crafts, while Miravelle's orders cracked like whips. I'd grown so used to her tirades by now that I barely heard them over my own wandering thoughts. My performance was scheduled near the culmination, when the sunset's light would strike the Pattern of Balance at precisely the right angle.

So the sun here moved after all.

I waited at the edge of the hall, listening as a trio of musicians played a haunting melody on crystal bells. The sound lingered unnaturally long in the vast chamber, reverberating as though the painted figures on the ceiling were humming along. When the last note faded into silence, Miravelle gestured to me.

"The starlight illusion next. Center position, please."

I stepped forward, lightheaded. The air shimmered with potential, thin as a spider's lace stretched to breaking. I raised my hands, summoning the simple illusion I had prepared—a celestial map of the equinox stars.

They appeared as expected above my palms. But then, without warning, the stars expanded outward in a violent burst.

Within seconds, the ceiling of the Golden Hall completely dissolved and was replaced by a boundless night sky. It devoured the lamplight, snuffed the chandeliers. Uncharted constellations careened overhead. Nebulae flared like wounds torn through the dark.

My skin thrummed with unchecked power. Silver starlight streaked through my veins, each heartbeat sending it rushing through my body, through the floor, quaking the palace. Threads of light zapped from my fingertips, streamers of green and violet and pink, forming a waving curtain across the sky—an aurora, radiant and impossible. Its beauty was unbearable, sharp as broken glass, and the longer it shimmered, the more it felt like it might split the world open.

This was not an illusion. This was not mine. This was a communion, where my body was a dissolving vessel for a thousand distant suns. For a single, breathless moment, I was back in the Whispering Sea, seeing all cosmic paths in the expanse beyond.

Gasps echoed. Someone whispered, "Magnificent." A crystal bell clanged and shattered as it fell from mesmerized hands.

Then...

One star collapsed. It swallowed its own light, then the entire sky around it. The silence that sucked the room into a vacuum was absolute, suffocating. Then it burst, the shock wave knocking everyone to the ground with heat and shrapnel.

Fragments of starlight rained down in jagged streaks, sizzling through fabric, hissing against stone. The hall erupted in shrieks as the others scattered, taking cover beneath tables and behind singed curtains. I staggered, heat lancing my arms and chest as sparks went straight through my clothes. A sharp metallic taste flooded my mouth. Blood dripped from my nose, bright red against the silver glow still twisting beneath my skin.

"Enough!" Miravelle's voice sliced through the chaos. Stardust scattered as she flitted between falling sparks. "End it now before it takes us all with it!"

Her words jarred me back. Hands shaking, I yanked at the aurora streamers, pulling the curtain from the sky grommet by grommet. I severed each thread that still clung to the swallowed stars, painfully choking my power from them. The sky collapsed inward until only my intended illusions remained beneath. The harmless little map of stars sputtered out in a pitiful flicker.

I bent forward, bracing myself on my thighs. Sweat dripped freely down my spine, between my breasts, while blood from my nose dotted the floor. My breath sawed ragged in my chest; my skin screamed beneath charred velvet.

Miravelle's heels clicked sharply until she loomed over me. I decided then that I preferred her popping in and out of existence. Her expression was polished to ice.

"Unexpected," she said flatly, lavender eyes sitting a bit too long on the blood that trailed from my face. "Balance will not tolerate improvisation. And neither will I."

"Of course," I rasped. I steadied myself as I stood, wiping a sleeve across my nose. "It won't happen again."

She leaned in close, her voice a silken hiss for my ears alone.

"Your patron sees everything." I followed her line of sight, which narrowed across the hall. Torian stood in the shadows, still as a carved idol, golden eyes fixed on me. "If you mean to keep his sponsorship, you will *mind yourself*. Clean yourself up."

She flitted away and screeched for the next performance, as if she hadn't just threatened to strip me bare in front of the court.

I retreated to the edge of the hall, wiping my face again, smearing crimson and silver on the back of my hand. My stomach churned, my skin still stinging.

"Impressive display."

Torian's voice cut through the ringing in my ears. His face was forced into neutrality, but the fire behind it was unmistakable. Hot as those falling stars. His gaze darted to my nose, to the smear on my hand.

"Gods, are you bleeding starlight?"

"A simple illusion," I said, straightening myself and swallowing back the nausea.

"Was it?" His voice dropped lower, softer, dangerous. "Because it seemed remarkably... *authentic*." He caught my wrist before I could swipe my face again, his grip firm but careful. His thumb brushed against the scorch marks on my skin. "Or are these burns also part of your *simple illusion?*"

His touch might have seared more than the burns. Everyone could see. I ripped my arm free as heat rushed to my cheeks, embarrassment nearly crowding out the pain.

"Don't," I hissed.

"Let me see," Torian said through clenched teeth, a prince's command.

"Not here."

Too many eyes. Too much heat already searing straight through me.

His eyes narrowed, but he did not argue. He only guided me with a light touch at my elbow. We slipped through a narrow arch and up a spiraling stair, Miravelle's barking orders fading with each curving step.

The gallery was empty, washed in dust and amber light. Below us, the Golden Hall still reeled in the wreckage of my failure. Musicians knelt to gather splintered crystal bells. Pages swept up charred fragments where stars had fallen, scrubbed the marble where it had scorched. My catastrophic performance lingered everywhere, and even from up here, I could not escape it.

My stomach twisted as I watched them down there, cleaning up my mess while I hid above them. I clenched the railing, tears blurring the world I had nearly reduced to ash. Torian's hand closed over mine, steady and sure, loosening my grip before he turned me gently to face him.

I couldn't bear to meet his eyes as they swept over me. His gaze lingered on my bloody face, then lower, catching on the wisps of smoke still curling where the starlight had sparked through the fabric. My velvet blouse clung in melted tatters at my ribs, exposing angry pinpricks beneath. What a sight I must have been, caked in blood, burnt to a crisp. At least I was wearing shoes.

"Take this off," he breathed. Not a suggestion.

I stared at him. Surely he didn't mean—

I searched for hunger in his eyes, for some flicker of amusement at my vulnerable state. But there was none. No smirk, no mischievous glint, no wolfish edge.

I reluctantly obeyed, though the motion pulled at the scorches along my ribs, and I hissed at the pain.

"Let me." His voice was a patient rumble. His fingers grazed the bare skin of my stomach as he took hold of the hem of the ruined blouse. Carefully, prayerfully, he eased it upward, tugging the fabric over my head without jostling the burns.

I stood bare before him, exposed and trembling, wearing ugly blotches of the starlight's cruelty. My stomach clenched at the sight of my ruined blouse as it slipped from my shoulders.

My body folded in on itself before I could think. My arms crossed hard over my chest, shoulders curled forward, legs pressed tightly together. Every instinct begged me to stay hidden. But Torian's hand found my wrist, and he drew my arms gently aside as I unfolded inch by reluctant inch. My arms slackened at my sides as he stepped closer, claiming the space I wanted to collapse into.

"Don't hide from me, Aevra."

I flinched as he lifted his knuckles beneath my chin, tilting my face up as though he might claim my mouth. Instead, he pulled a handkerchief from his pocket and dabbed at the blood on my upper lip. His movements were careful, each touch so deliberate it hushed the ache. Then, before I could even breathe, he leaned down and pressed his lips to the bridge of my nose.

The kiss startled me in its almost playfulness. But when he pulled back, the throb that had been hammering behind my eyes was gone. The blood no longer trickled.

He traced lower, and my breath hitched in my throat as his gaze swept over the burns that marred my flesh. His mouth met the first mark, a singe along my collarbone. The kiss was unhurried, unadorned. His lips parted just long enough to cool the sting.

Another followed across my ribs, then beneath my breast. His mouth brushed against the angry marks, one by one. The pain dissolved beneath him until the memory was harder to bear than the burns themselves. When he pulled away from the last one at my hip, I thought he was finished. But then he grabbed my hand.

For some reason, I tried to close it, to hide the damage that my stars had done this morning. As if it made any difference what time of day the white-hot betrayal occurred. He caught my fingers before they curled and pressed the final healing kiss against my palm. In that tiny, tender moment, all I knew was the heat of his lips sealing over my wounded skin, the pain and comfort exquisitely intertwining.

A boldness sparked in me when he lifted his head and looked at me. He flattened his palm against mine, locking our fingers together.

"My mouth hurts, too," I murmured, eyes half-closed in the relief he had just given me. He rested his forehead against mine, lips hovering half a breath away, close enough to taste the words on his tongue.

"Answer me this first," he whispered. "Have you been avoiding me?"

Not intentionally, I thought. But the spiny truth prickled all the same. I hadn't sought him out since that night, hadn't lingered anywhere he might find me. Valeraine's 'advice' carved deeper than I cared to admit, bleeding into every step I took in the Vale. I forced a crooked smile.

"I nearly turned the palace into a supernova, and that's what you ask me?"

"Yes. Because this—" He picked up my scorched blouse and tossed it behind his shoulder. "—and this—" He brushed the tip of his nose against my bloodied face. "—and that—" He gestured to the chaos that was finally dying down below us. "—are all far less important than whether you still want to look at me."

His words landed hard, forcing my gaze downward. "Dinner didn't sit well with me."

"The food," he asked lightly, tilting his head just enough to needle the source of my shame, "or the company?"

"All of it," I sighed.

"I waited for you."

"I know. I'm sorry."

A muscle ticked in his jaw. "I even brought more honey cakes. They went stale while I sat there like a fool."

His admission landed like a blade to the gut. I looked at the floor, pulling my lips between my teeth while I bit down the sharp heat rising again in my eyes. He had waited. And I had left him there. And he wanted me to feel it. I had nothing deserving to say in my defense while the pause between us grew damn near menacing.

When he slipped his morning jacket from his back, I wondered if his disappointment in me had warmed to anger. But he slung it around me, draping it over my bare shoulders. My body curved inwards as he pulled my head to his chest.

"As luck would have it," he added at last, a silken-wrapped parcel materializing in his hand from somewhere I couldn't see, "there were fresh ones this morning."

he Mabon Festival transformed the Grand Courtyard into something near holy. The Pattern of Balance was spread wide in its completion, gems glinting in the sunset. Lanterns hung from branches, swaying in the air that shimmered with spice and smoke. From the balconies above, streamers of burnt orange and gold silk drifted in the breeze like flickering flames. From below, music from the territories meshed together into a single chorus—coral flutes, tree-bark drums, guttural voices that sang impossible notes.

But I barely heard any of it, barely smelled the roasted apples, the honeyed wine, as I watched the creatures that teemed in the Vale to celebrate the turn of the season.

A bark-skinned dryad strummed a harp made of creeping vines, the leaves singing with each pluck. A pair of nymphs flitted and zipped between nobles like mischievous moths to lamplight. One perched herself on a guard's shoulder to braid his hair, while the other whispered something in his ear that made him blush. Tiny sprites rooted around in lily trumpets, scattering pollen and glimmering dust over the crowd as they sampled each flower.

Lysara's arm brushed mine as we walked the length of the courtyard, our steps falling into the same leisurely rhythm. We'd barely made it past the pastry stalls when the crowd ahead slowed to a hush. The music faltered, and even the warm scent of iced sticky buns seemed to stall in the air.

Then I saw it.

An enormous shape loomed among the lanterns, creaking with every slow movement it made. It walked on four legs made of tree trunks, roots shooting out of its soles like overgrown toes. Antlers of living branches crowned its head, heavy with dried flowers and decayed ribbons from festivals long past. It looked as if the Silverwood Forest had simply picked itself up from its leaf bed to attend the festival.

"Father and Son," Lysara breathed as her hand floated to her chest. "That's a Harthorn."

The creature shook its head once, sending a storm of birds erupting from its antlers, screaming into the sky. I gripped Lysara's arm in a vise, as if she could protect me from the thing that towered in the middle of the courtyard.

"W-what exactly is it?" I whispered.

"A forest spirit. A protector of the realms," she whispered back. "One hasn't been spotted in the Amber Vale in decades."

I swallowed as it bent forward, kneeling on its forelegs until the ground shuddered beneath its weight. Children crept toward it slowly, strips of silk clutched tightly in their little hands. One by one, they looped their offerings through the lower branches that adorned its monstrous head, until its antlers looked like a spun crown.

"Did you make a wish?" a mother said as her son skipped back to her side.

"Yes, Momma. I made a good one!" She rubbed the child's back as they stepped away, though she never took her eyes fully off the Harthorn.

"Why has it shown up now?" I asked.

Lysara shook off my grip and laced her fingers through mine. "It's rumored they only wake when they sense a threat to the balance. Although—"

A little girl ran a trembling hand over the Harthorn's moss-covered muzzle, while another gently stroked its broad taro-leaf ear. The creature gave a deep, resonant snort, like wind through hollow bark, and the girls squealed in delight. It then wiggled its lips before ripping one of the girls' caramel apples clean off its stick.

"—I suspect it just wanted dessert."

The laughter that rippled through the awestruck crowd shattered the silencing spell, and the music began again. I was still watching the Harthorn as the children clambered up its legs, swinging from its kudzu vines like ribbons, when a lilting voice chirped through the merriment.

"First Mabon in the Vale?"

A woodland faerie hovered at my right with a tray of glasses strapped around her neck. Her butterfly wings, which were tapered like a swallowtail's and sparkling clover green, beat lazily at her back. She poured a decanter of gold liquid into two crystal goblets.

I blinked at her as the breeze from her wings brushed across my face. "Is it that obvious?"

She grinned, the natural glimmer of her skin glinting in the dimples beside her mouth. "You have the look of someone seeing the eternal with fresh eyes. And what a fine Mabon for your first," she added, gesturing toward the Harthorn, which now trotted in slow circles with a dozen children clinging to its back.

She offered the brimming glasses to Lysara and me.

"Thank you," I murmured, hesitating.

"Aureate spirits," the woodland faerie said. "Harvested under last year's harvest moon. But drink carefully. It lets you taste time itself."

I had already downed nearly half the glass before her warning landed. The taste was warm, almost electric, as the spice buzzed over my tongue. A drop slipped over my lip and down my chin just as she flitted away, wings scattering dust as she went to befuddle more festival-goers.

The wine burned sweetly all the way down. It warmed my chest until the crisp air felt alive on my skin, and its swimming fingers prickled along my scalp. My heartbeat thrummed with the kick of distant drums. The lamplight seemed to drip like honey over the cobblestones beneath my feet. The blood-red leaves of the maple trees sang my name as they swayed. I was near the bottom of my drink when another hush fell over the courtyard.

The royal procession had arrived.

Lysara guided me toward the edge of the crowd as courtiers and visitors parted to make way. King Oranth strode first, adorned in crimson and gold and wearing a modest crown encrusted with rubies. The Queen followed a step behind him, her hair veiled in a lattice of crystals, turning her head into a living prism.

And then came...

Prince Torian and Lady Valeraine. Arm in arm, regal and radiant. His suit gleamed with threads of the sunset itself, while her gown shimmered with the first breath of night. They were the very picture of balance that the realms craved. Perfect. As if the gods themselves had arranged them just so.

Her manicured hand rested lightly on top of his, while I gnawed on my cuticles. The sight was a fiery blade sliding between my ribs. My chest tightened, refusing air. I downed the rest of my drink in a single searing swallow, the sweetness turning bitter on my tongue.

Lysara tilted her head, studying me with a sidelong stare. "Parched, are we?"

I couldn't tear my eyes off the pair of royals, couldn't hide the raw flicker that crossed my face. I didn't answer her, just shrugged as the glass somehow disappeared from my hand. Whether it was taken by the woodland faerie, or dissolved into thin air to escape my blazing jealousy, I was unsure.

I was grinding my teeth when Lysara pressed her own glass— still mostly full—into my clammy hand. "By all means, drown whatever that is before someone notices."

Her words might have stung if they hadn't been so gently spoken. I took it without polite declination and drew in another sip. I could feel the bars caging my jealousy buckle under the wine as it continued to seep into me.

Lysara didn't say a word as the procession strolled past us. They waved, they nodded, but I might as well have been just another peasant or merchant in the crowd, begging for a chance to kiss their hands. Then, barely a whisper, as if she were speaking to the air in front of her face, she said, "The night of Haustblót... you didn't discuss a sponsorship, did you?"

My throat nearly closed. I opened it with another sip. "Nope."

"I thought not."

The crowd followed the procession toward the pavilion situated at the top of the Pattern of Balance. A low hum thrummed through the festival. Strings struck, low and pulsing, as The

Chordilleras tuned to each other in a single, piercing note. Fiddle, guitar, upright bass, mandolin, and...

"Oh shit," I whispered through the growing haze of the wine.

My eyes fixed on an intricately carved instrument with a hand-crank, nestled against a young male standing a bit too close to Brella. My burning question had finally been answered.

"It's the hurdy-gurdiest!"

I hiccuped as the band bowed to the crowd in a synchronized motion.

The sound that came from the instrument as the rosined wheel rubbed against the strings was haunting. It ushered in the gentle strum of the guitar, then the lilting sigh of the fiddle. I swayed as the music melted whatever thought had plagued me earlier.

"Do you mean the gurdy player?" Lysara chuckled beside me.

"No," I said, too loudly. "I mean hurdy-gurdiest, because—*hic*—nobody has ever hurdy-gurdied so mightily."

"You're incorrigible!" Lysara bumped me with her shoulder, nearly sloshing my drink from my hand. Thankfully, I caught the spill with my mouth, giggling into the glass.

A horsehair bow glided over the fiddle, while the bass was plucked in a quick rhythm. Brella's fingers flew over her jade-inlaid mandolin, eyes closed, lower lip caught between her teeth. Then she lifted her head and began to sing.

> *The fires of vanity burn bright,*
>
> *crumbling all that's sacred to embers.*
>
> *Then trapped in a deluge of white,*
>
> *but the screams baked in stone will remember.*

My head was swimming, thoughts clumsily colliding into each other. My drink was still half-full, and I wondered if I ought to put it down. The clock that was nestled into the arch of the pavilion said I still had four hours until my performance, a distant promise that felt like permission. I took another sip.

Mother, please, keep my mother.

Hold her as she once held me.

Mother, please, raise my brother,

too young, so pure and sweet.

Love and look after my father,

and please, dear Mother, take me.

The crowd clapped to the beat of the chorus. Lysara leaned in and whispered, "They say she can make stones weep."

The air that carried her voice seemed to shimmer as it traveled through the courtyard. My eyes widened when a nearby stone fountain trickled against gravity, flowing upwards over its basin and dripping onto the cobbles like hot tears.

"Sleight of hand," Lysara added. "She has water magic."

My shoulders slumped in disappointment. Even when magic existed in excess, the wonder captivated.

The cinders will weep ever after.

Hear how they wail for closure!

Onlookers watch from the rafters,

their thumb-sucking masked as composure.

Lady Valeraine stepped into the open space between the crowd and the band. She gathered her skirt in her hand and started *dancing*. Not the courtly kind of performative steps, but sinuous, graceful twirls and spins that looked almost ritualistic. She threw her head back, her black waves billowing around her as she spiraled.

The first ripple of clapping spread upward and outward, gathering bodies into motion like the tide pulling in a drift. Laughter loosened, hands found hands, inhibitions fell away.

Mother, please, keep my mother.

Hold her as she once held me.

Mother, please, raise my brother,

too young, so pure and sweet.

Love and look after my father,

and please, dear Mother, take me.

Torian stepped back from the ring of dancing bodies that now engulfed Lady Valeraine, his golden coat catching the ever-setting sun. He said something low to a guard, then turned and slipped away.

My heart twisted before I could straighten my gaze after him. I forced myself to watch the performance instead. Brella's eyes snapped open, and she looked directly at the King.

Crowns are heavy when gilded,

hands are calloused when jeweled,

and empires fall when they're tilted,

and blades are most brittle when cooled.

Whatever mask of reverence and prayerfulness she had worn fell away completely, replaced by something colder. Bone-chilling. Her voice didn't falter as she sang it, but that stare hardened, venomous and unblinking. Unafraid.

The King's jaw clenched, a vein pulsing in his temple.

Even in my foggy state, I felt it—that icy something passing between them. Royal and artist. King and citizen. He who had everything, and she who had lost everything. Whatever wound she was singing about, he had carved it in her.

A reveler, spun by Lady Valeraine's orbit, stumbled and brushed the King's sleeve with a mortified gasp. King Oranth's attention broke, and the nervous laughter forced the tension to shatter.

Mother, please, keep my mother.

Hold her as she once held me.

Mother, please, raise my brother,

too young, so pure and sweet.

Love and look after my father,

and please, dear Mother, take me.

The last note lingered, her voice so low that I felt it rumble into the ground. Brella lowered her mandolin, and the crowd did not wait for the King's blessing. Applause erupted like thunder cracking over an open tomb. And still, her eyes never left the King.

The band slid without fanfare into a reel to bless the awkwardness away, and the dancers continued without mercy. The press of bodies shifted, and a passing courtier jostled me sideways—straight into a warm, familiar chest. Torian's palm steadied at my elbow. My knees buckled at his touch, and I played it off as an ugly curtsy.

"Enjoying the festival, Miss Lyra? Lysara?" he asked coolly.

Lysara dipped down gracefully, her tone smooth as glass. "Immensely, Your Highness. The Vale outdoes itself with every season."

Torian smiled at her, then looked at me as I fumbled to remember how to speak.

"And you, Miss Lyra?" His hand lingered on my arm a moment too long. I had completely forgotten how to move my mouth to form words, how to move my throat so that sound could escape.

"The Chordilleras seemed to have struck a chord," Lysara quipped lightly, saving me from further humiliation. "Though I suspect a few hearts may need mending come morning."

Torian laughed. "Yes, the healing chambers might be full. But

I believe art that doesn't wound seldom endures. Wouldn't you agree, Miss Lyra?"

I swallowed hard, pulse hammering as my glass quivered in my hand. I nodded and threw back the rest of my drink.

"Pardon my boorishness, Your Highness," I said, realizing that being drunk in his presence was surely uncouth. My body felt like it was on fire. "My nerves over my upcoming performance this evening are rather... *persistent.*"

"The saffron fields are fragrant this time of year," Torian said without missing a single beat. "Perhaps some time away from the festivities would do well to calm you."

His gaze held mine, steady, starkly unreadable. Was this a suggestion or a request? He blinked away the spell with the ease of a prince accustomed to hiding behind a mask. Before I could open my mouth, he had already stepped away, offering Lysara a shallow nod before the crowd swallowed him whole.

Lysara gave a low whistle, then looked at me with what I could only describe as exasperated fondness. "You could have set yourself aflame and he would still pretend not to notice."

I laughed weakly. "I might as well have."

"Then, for the love of the gods, cool off before your hair catches light."

"Come with me to get another drink?" I asked sweetly, already knowing the answer. Lysara rolled her eyes and sighed.

"No more drinks. You're hours away from the stage, but you're about a sip away from making headlines." Her hand met the middle of my back with a light push.

"Fine," I said reluctantly, my legs still barely recovered from giving out moments ago. "I'll walk the fields. Clear my head."

"M-hm," Lysara hummed knowingly. "Try not to get lost in it, dove."

But it seemed I already had. My thoughts were doing slow cartwheels in my skull, each one landing crooked. I wasn't drunk, not really. Just pleasantly unmoored.

The reel swelled again as I stepped away from Lysara. Brella's voice echoed through the afternoon, a lingering ghost of unknown defiance. 'A gift for weaving harmony out of grief,' indeed.

I was so enraptured by the wine, so blissfully impaired, that I failed to notice Queen Krivnya standing just a breath away. She watched me as I followed her son out of the festival and toward the Saffron Fields.

Chapter Seventeen

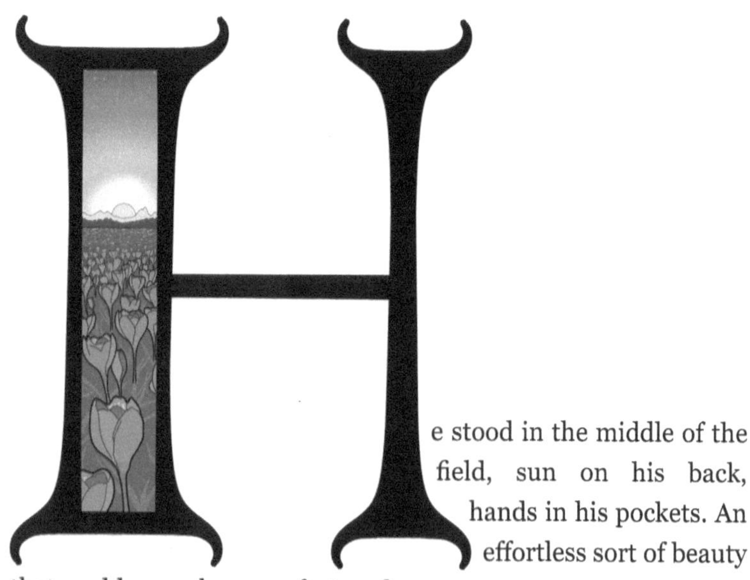

e stood in the middle of the field, sun on his back, hands in his pockets. An effortless sort of beauty that could never be manufactured.

The surrounding crocuses bowed to him in the wind. Their violet petals trembled, scarlet filaments peeking out for a single glimpse of he who stood among them. The breeze was thick with their ambrosial scent, an earthy sweetness that refused to fade as a golden haze blew from their hearts. It clung to him as he turned, his silhouette an eclipse against the ever-dying sun.

I didn't walk. The alcohol coursing through my veins wouldn't let me.

I ran.

Threads of saffron snagged the hem of my skirt; blooms brushed my calves as I leapt off the ground and barreled into his arms. He caught me with a low, surprised laugh. His arms locked around my waist, spinning me in the air as he regained his steadiness.

There were no guards to interrupt us, no duties to intercept or cut our time short. It was finally just him and me. Just us.

The music from the festival drifted faintly through the valley, a whisper from another world. The only sound that reached me was our shared breath, steady and real.

He opened his mouth to say something, but I silenced him with a kiss. A kiss born of too much waiting and far too much wine. My lips moved against his insatiably, pressing into him with every ounce of jealousy that still rattled around in my ribs. She might be perfect, but he was *mine.*

He pulled his head back and eased me back to the ground, but didn't let go. I stood on my tiptoes, chasing him for more.

"Again," I breathed.

He placed a finger to my pouting mouth and clicked his tongue softly.

"Not yet, my star."

He tapped my lower lip once, then slipped a hand into his pocket, bringing forth a little paper-wrapped parcel. The scent of roasted nuts and brown sugar cut through the saffron mist as he opened it. Peanut butter biscuits—another favorite.

"Your laundry must attract ants with as many sweets as you stuff in your trousers."

His mouth curved mischievously. "You'd be surprised how often they come in handy. Open."

He held up a biscuit, but I declined to bite. I swayed closer, my grin lazy and wicked with wine.

"Mmm. There's something sweeter in there I'd much rather have." I pressed my hips into his, placing my hands firmly against his lower back.

The laugh that left him was soft, controlled, but his throat worked as he swallowed. His eyes dipped quickly before returning to my face with the same precision of a blade being sheathed.

"Open your mouth," he said again, cookie still hovering.

"Say that again," I cooed. "Whisper it in my ear."

I closed my eyes as he lowered his head, his lips grazing my earlobe.

"You are very clever, Aevra," he whispered, "but I am growing impatient." His hand tightened at my waist as the buckle of his belt pressed into my navel. "Open. Your. Mouth." The words were gentle, but the command beneath them was not. "*Now*."

Heat flooded my cheeks as I parted my lips against the biscuit, half from the order, half from the way I was dying to obey it. The peanut butter hit my tongue like a salve, sticky and salty-sweet.

He waited until I swallowed, then brushed a crumb from the corner of my mouth with his thumb. I caught it with my lips, drawing him inward for just a heartbeat, just enough to pull a sharp breath from him.

I slipped my hands around his belt, tugging him toward me until the leather creaked against my grip. "Now you must kiss me."

"Not yet," he purred. Ever the prince of restraint and ruin.

I jutted out my lower lip, the lingering taste of peanut butter sliding along with it.

"But I did what you wanted," I hissed, my voice stuck between a plea and a dare. He clicked his tongue again.

"You took a bite. I want you to *finish*."

I rolled my eyes but took another bite, slower this time, deliberately defiant. He watched me as I chewed, his gaze unwavering as it burned into me. He was studying me, studying my descent into obedience while I was at the mercy of a godsdamned cookie.

"Satisfied?" I asked as I swallowed the last bite. Torian scoffed.

"Hardly." His voice was low, almost civil. "You mistake my appeasement for satisfaction."

I ran my hand up his stomach, over his chest, then rested it on the side of his neck. He gently gripped my fingers and removed my hand, then pressed a full waterskin into my palm.

"And you mistake your cruelty for patience."

"Cruelty?"

His voice was so razor-calm that I almost doubted the purpose of our tryst. I felt foolish for wanting. But then his hand found the nape of my neck, tangling in my hair. He tugged my head back, forcing my wavering gaze to meet his molten eyes.

"I'd be cruel to fuck you while you're dulled and sloppy on wine."

His other hand caught my hip, fingers biting in deep as he pressed his hard length against me. He wrenched my head again, baring my throat while he ran his teeth over my hammering pulse. A whimper escaped before I could stop it.

"When I finally take you in this field," he murmured, "I want you to feel every single inch of me. I want you aware of everywhere I touch you." He trailed a finger along the inside of my thigh, heat ghosting through the fabric of my skirt. "I want you to remember how you taste on my mouth." His tongue glided across my lower lip, too quick for me to catch between my teeth. "I want to be the only thing coursing through your veins when you scream my name."

I clutched the waterskin so tightly that it nearly burst at its seams. My chin quivered, shame and want blurring together. He guided it to my mouth.

"Now, *drink*."

I brought the waterskin to my lips so fast that my teeth clinked against the metal spout. The first rush of cold bloomed on my tongue, and I drank like the water was breath itself. Like I'd wandered years across a desert, and he was the first oasis I found.

I barely finished before his mouth crashed into mine.

"Finally," he breathed against my lips. His voice was rough, sparking at its edges like a strike on flint as he traveled to my cheek, down my neck. "I can't wait to finish what I started at dinner."

A wild grin curved through me, sharp as glass. "Don't worry," I sighed, "I finished it for you."

He went still. Just for a second. Then something in him broke loose, like a dam buckling against a storm. His hand tightened in my hair, and his mouth on my skin turned molten, all-consuming. Every breath between us caught fire as whatever control he had been clinging to shattered into pieces.

His other hand slipped beneath my shirt, curling around my waist and toying with the hem as he nudged it upwards. A low purr hummed in my throat when his fingertips slid along the dip of my spine. He smiled against my skin like he'd been waiting for that sound. He pushed the fabric higher, slowly. Far too slowly. The evening air sighed against the strip of exposed flesh between us, cool where his hands were warm as a fever.

I tugged at the edges of his tunic, clumsy with want and the lingering dregs of wine in my blood. "Off," I whispered.

He huffed a little laugh, half-breath, half-growl. "So impatient," he teased. "I want to take my time with you."

"I've waited plenty."

He hesitated then, his mischievous smile faltering just enough to betray something else beneath it. The feral tension simmered as his hands stilled at the hem of his shirt, a flicker of reluctance crossing his face. There was a shadow he did not want the light to find. But he lifted it anyway.

The sunset spilled over his skin, gilding the ridges of his stomach and the faint trail of gold that led upward to the scar bisecting his chest. It was an ugly, beautiful thing—uneven, brutal, and alive. My fingers hovered over it, tracing its course like a river on a map. His muscles jumped beneath my fingertips.

"The mountains were not kind," he said, voice shadowed by the memory of it.

I leaned forward and pressed my lips to the scar's beginning, following its crooked path with slow, deliberate kisses until I reached the edge of his heart.

"I'm sorry," I whispered against his skin. "I can't take away the pain of it."

"You don't have to."

He caught my jaw in his hand, knuckles beneath my chin as he guided my mouth back to his. When his fingers found the edge of my shirt, one smooth pull had it discarded somewhere between us and the pink sky.

I didn't try to hide this time while he looked at me, drank me in. The hunger in his eyes wasn't ferocious. It was measured in its own vicious way. His gaze swept over me as if he were familiarizing himself with something sacred and long-lost.

I forgot about the crocuses, the sweet haze of the saffron, my performance still hours ahead of us. There was only that *look*, and the way he finally rushed to close the space it had created.

One arm looped around my waist, the other beneath me. I barely had time to gasp before he lifted me, smooth as a current taking hold. The flowers bent under us as he laid me down among them. The world tilted with me, golden light pooling in the hollow of his shoulder.

The weight of his body hovered above me while our mouths moved against each other. My fingers fumbled at his waistband, impatient, drunk with want. But before I could pull him closer, his hand caught mine.

"Not yet." He pinned my wrists above my head, his grip firm enough to make me still. "I've been starving for you since I licked you off my fingers."

His palms flattened against mine, then his hands ran down the length of my arms, around my flaring ribs. He paused at my breasts, pressing into them while his lips trailed down my sternum with a growl. He gave my nipples a delicious pinch before moving his hands lower, scouring over my stomach, down my thighs, around my calves.

When his fingers found me, the sound he made wasn't prayerful or yearning. It was possessive. Raw and guttural, like something caged finally tasting the first lick of freedom. His body went rigid against mine, muscles coiled tightly as if he were holding himself back.

"Fuck." Hearing the crowned prince curse at the mere touch of me only made the heat pool deeper. "Tell me you've been this wet for me since dinner."

"Yes," I gasped. No other words existed in my wine-stripped lexicon aside from *yes, yes, yes.*

He pressed his fingers inside me, and we both groaned from hours, days, of empty aching.

"Won't your betrothed miss you at her side?" I managed between gasps, some reckless part of me needing to push.

He scoffed dismissively against the underside of my breast. "Let her miss me," he said, almost indistinguishable. The words were lost in my skin as he moved lower, muffled while his mouth traced its burning path downward. Whatever he continued muttering into my ribs, my hip, the inside of my thigh, it wasn't about her.

He settled between my thighs, shoulders spreading them wide, his breath hot and hovering against the oversensitive skin. It was torture. The sort of torture that was planned over the course of a lonely century. I tried to roll my hips up, desperately seeking his mouth, but his hands pinned me firmly in place.

"So eager," he purred as he lightly glided his lips across me. "And oh so pretty."

Then his mouth was on me.

The first swipe of his tongue was nothing short of aggressive. No gentle explorations or dutiful reacquaintance, just him claiming what he had been so mercilessly denied. A starved moan vibrated against me, and the added sensation had me crying out, gripping the crocuses flat beneath me.

He pulled back just enough to speak. "I locked myself—" His tongue swept through me again, my back arching. "—in the washroom—" Another, deeper this time. "—and came from thinking about you like this."

That confession, delivered in ravenous pieces, was somehow more devastating than if he had managed to say it all at once. Each return of his tongue a punctuation, each breath a revelation.

"Gods, you taste like—"

He didn't finish. Couldn't. His mouth became less precise, more ruinous. Every pull of his lips sent lightning forking through my veins. Then his fingers returned, three this time, stretching me, making my vision go white at the edges.

I was coming apart.

I bowed off the ground, hands fisting in his hair hard enough to hurt. But he didn't stop, didn't slow, just held me there on the knife's edge. The sounds I made were no longer words, just broken things that might have been his name, or might have been begging. Or maybe the noise of a soul trying to leave its body.

Lights flickered above us, stars manifesting unconsciously, silver and trembling alongside me. They cast strange shadows through the field, but I could not find a single shred of myself that cared.

"Please," I begged while his mouth focused on that one spot that had me seeing galaxies behind my eyelids. My thighs shook around his shoulders. "I need—"

The stars above us swirled faster, near violent. The shadows grew darker, denser, gathering at the edge of our clearing. But I was too lost to notice.

And then he stopped, pulling away from me completely.

"No," I whimpered, attempting to tug his head back down into me. "Why would you—"

His lips met mine with bruising force, face slick with the taste of me. Leather scraped against metal as he tore at his belt.

"Because when you come undone," he breathed against my mouth as the button of his trousers popped loose, "when I finally *let* you, I want to feel it all around me. I want to be inside you when you *break*."

"Inside me," I demanded in a pant. I didn't wait for him to decide whether to obey my plea. I reached between us and took what I wanted.

The moment my fingers found him, wrapping around like a hungry vise, we both lost our breath. Prince Torian of the Amber Vale, who was so restrained, so deliberate in his plan for my utter demise beneath him, shuddered in my grasp.

"Aevra—"

"Don't talk," I whispered, drunk on the power of it, on the way his eyes went dark. I stroked him slowly, savoring the second heartbeat pulsing hot in my palm. "All this time, you've been playing with me. Teaching me patience." I pulled on him again as he thrust gently into my hand. "But you're not very patient yourself, are you, Your Highness?"

His helpless, beautiful laugh came out fractured, his forehead dropping to mine. "You're going to ruin me."

"Good," I murmured against the coarse grain of his jaw, shifting my grip as he hummed a groan. "That's only fair."

I guided him where I needed him, but did not grant him entry. I just held him there, letting him feel how ready I was, denying us both for the sake of this power trip I reveled in.

"Is this what you imagine when you lock yourself away?"

The stars above us fed off my brutality, pulsing brighter with each thrust I denied him. They spun in dizzying spirals, multiplying, some popping into darkness, only to come back blazing more dangerously. The darkness at the corners of my vision crept closer, reaching toward me like greedy fingers. But they weren't mine. They felt ancient, patient, with an intense thirst that matched my own in this moment.

And *still*, I did not care.

I shifted my grip on him once more, watching his control unravel as he bucked his hips forward, seeking what I refused to bestow. That's when I felt it—something moving in the air around us. But my awareness flickered too late.

The temperature plummeted. Our ragged breaths clouded silver between us. The stars were no longer stars. They were wounds torn through the threadbare veil.

"Torian," I gasped, releasing him. "Something is wrong—"

The air cracked.

Not like thunder, or the too-heavy bough of a tree, but like existence breaking along an invisible fault. A jagged seam tore open, edges crackling and flaring with a frigid void. It was not darkness. It was nothing. It was the absence of everything.

"Torian," I said again, fear striking through me.

Something reached through the tear. Not hands, not tentacles, but something that had no given name, no form my feeble brain could comprehend. It wrapped around my ankles like frozen chains and *pulled*.

I was ripped violently from beneath him. My body was dragged over crushed saffron, purple petals and blood-red powder scattering as I clawed at the earth, at Torian, at anything solid.

"Aevra!"

He lunged for me, fingers grazing mine for a split second before I was yanked even harder, the force lifting me off the ground entirely. I reached for him as I was dragged upward toward the tear, toward the stars that had once again betrayed me.

The last thing I felt was the phantom pressure of where he had almost been, the ache now replaced with unbridled terror.

I saw him scrambling to his feet, our eyes meeting across the growing distance, his face plastered in horror and rage.

I heard him shouting my name before the void swallowed me whole, and I fell into that nothingness. A silence so complete that I couldn't even hear my own screams.

CHAPTER EIGHTEEN
TORIAN

She was gone.

The world stood frozen in the wake of the violence that had just torn through this sacred space. No insects hummed; no birds dared sing. The crocuses stilled like witnesses to a crime. The air itself was wrong, thin like the mountains but gagging like smog, popping and crackling as the tear sealed itself shut.

Torian crashed onto his hands and knees, gasping for a solid breath. His palms pressed into the crushed flowers that still held her warmth. The imprint of her body lingered in the bent stems, now nothing but an unbearable ghost, mocking him for his inability to save her.

"Aevra!" he shouted into the silent sunset.

No answer.

He lurched to his feet, stumbling through the field, arms outstretched as if he could find a loose thread in reality and rip it open again. His tunic hung partially unfastened, buttons misaligned where he fumbled to dress. Blood streaked his skin from thorn scratches, and fire burned at his fingertips, searing the blooms he pushed aside to ash. His legs carried him toward the music, toward the revelry of the festival that continued on in its ignorance.

"AEVRA!"

The sound of his own panic cracked the universe open for him. She was right there, settled beneath him. She was alive, laughing, gloriously playful. Then she was yanked through that gaping mouth while he'd caught only smoke from the up-kicked dirt.

"Your Highness!" Lysara burst through the rows of saffron, her festival gown catching on the same thorns that bloodied him. "By the gods, you'll bring the entire court running!" She looked at her disheveled prince, standing on the scorched earth, power sparking from him like a live wire, and went still.

"She's gone," he wheezed. "She was here, then she—she—the air, it tore, and something—it took her—"

"You need to breathe." She raised her hands slowly, as if approaching a wild creature. Her scholarly composure hung by a single thread. "People will see—"

"Let them!" He roared. Another flare of magic erupted from his fingers, burning a ring of blossoms to black. "Let them help me find her!"

"And when they see the Prince of the Amber Vale raving in the fields, tunic backwards, while his intended is in the courtyard?" she hissed. "When they ask why your hands are shaking and your charge is missing? Think about what that means. Not for you, but for her."

He was struck still. He turned over his palms, looking at them as if they'd betrayed him, allowing her to slip through them. Lysara held them in hers, cupping them together to muffle their trembling.

"Something took her," he repeated. "The sky opened, and she was gone with it."

"Magic misfires during Mabon," Lysara whispered, gesturing to the field he had reduced to cinders, not entirely convinced.

"This wasn't a misfire," he snapped. "She was snatched away!" The words sounded impossible, but they were all he had.

Lysara's eyes widened, pupils blown with alarm as she chewed the inside of her cheek. She didn't have an answer. "Prince Torian—"

He was already moving, brushing past her, the acrid smell of burnt saffron scattering in his wake. "I have to find someone who can help. Maybe they can open a path—"

"Wait!" she called, catching his sleeve. "You can't rejoin the festival like this!"

He turned on her, wild and unseeing. "I don't care, Lysara!"

"Torian, *please*." She was no longer addressing her prince, but her oldest friend. "You will ruin her if you don't think."

But her plea barely landed on his ears. He shook off her grip and continued storming toward the glow of the festival, toward the sound of laughter that felt obscene against the deafening ringing in his head.

Lysara stood paralyzed as she watched him leave, hands pressed into her cheeks, muttering something that might have been a prayer.

He crossed the threshold into the lantern-light. The music

still played, bright and mocking, but the mood had shifted. Too many eyes turned his way; too many whispers carried across the breeze.

Lady Valeraine stepped into his path, placing a firm hand against his chest, stopping him in his tracks.

"That's far enough." Her tone was low and dangerous, firelight glinting off her diamond jewelry. "The entire courtyard heard your shouting."

"Step aside, my Lady." More heads turned their way, craning for a look at the crazed prince emerging from the wilderness.

"Your Highness," she said sweetly, smiling politely just enough for those watching. "You're flushed. The heat of the festival can certainly be dreadful. Let's find you some shade."

A few nearby eavesdroppers murmured in agreement before drifting back to the pavilion, swiping glasses of wine from passing trays. It seemed they were content that the prince's betrothed had his interest well in hand. Only when they were out of earshot did her face fall ever-so slightly.

"What in the seven hells are you doing?" she hissed through her forced smile.

Her perfectly manicured hands went up, though not tenderly, to straighten his collar, smooth the line of his tunic. From a distance, she was dutifully attending her ruffled fiancé.

"You disappeared from your own festival and came storming back half-dressed and mad as a hatter. Do you have any idea of the position you have put me in?"

"I don't care about optics—"

"Then you are a fool." She pressed the last button of his tunic and patted him with mock affection. "You may not care, but *I* do. And your father certainly does. If you spiral in public, then *I* become the one too stupid to notice the prince unraveling beneath her nose, and your fitness as heir comes into question."

"She's gone," he repeated. "I need to find her."

She gently fingered away the hair plastered to his brow, brushed invisible dust from his lapel, while her tone remained utterly surgical.

"You need to smile and pretend that I found you wandering off to clear your head, not rutting in a field with a magician who left you to face the court yourself."

His eyes snapped to hers, smoldering with barely restrained fury. "She did not leave me. She was taken. She could be dead."

"And she will stay dead regardless of whether you button your godsdamned shirt." Her hand lingered against his chest for another moment, solidifying her endearing illusion.

"But she—"

"You will accomplish nothing by advertising your hysteria to the court. Pull yourself together, or you might lose any chance of seeing her again if she turns back up."

She was right. Gods damn her, she was somehow always right.

"You are a prince, not some heartsick boy in the mud. Act like one."

○ ◑ ◕ ● ◕ ◑ ○

I was scattered throughout the darkness. Not the darkness of closed eyes, but an endless black that penetrated my being, devouring the light from inside me. It pressed against me from all sides, lapping at the edges of my soul like a thirsty animal.

I tried to struggle against it, but my body was disconnected from my will. I couldn't move, couldn't even scream as a voice sliced through the void.

There you are, it sighed. *My little absconder.*

Heavy smoke coalesced into a vague feminine form before me. Her features were cast in shadow, but the devastation radiated from her in frigid wisps.

Alezae.

Her laughter rolled through the darkness, amused and terrible and everywhere. *How witty you must have thought yourself to slip away through my sea?* She mused playfully. *Did you think I wouldn't find you? That you could swim away with what is mine?*

She reached toward me, stroking an icy mist across what might have been my cheek. *I could crush you right here,* she continued with a purr, *but it behooves me to allow your master his entitlement to your fresh mortal flesh.*

Terror surged through whatever remained of me. My horrible master had cast aside my useless, withered husk. He would certainly relish what I had now become.

And oh so pretty.

If I had a throat, I would have vomited.

The surrounding air suddenly shifted, the darkness wavering. Glimpses of light flickered in and out; distorted musical notes and fragments of conversation sounded in scattered pockets in the dark.

Not yet, Alezae hummed in annoyance as she lunged forward, snatching at me. *You will not escape me again.*

But it was too late. Something gave, like a frayed rope snapping under too much tension. The boundary tore open again, and reality seized me with brutal force. The darkness exploded around me like broken glass, and I was falling in all directions.

I hit the ground hard enough to shatter the cobbles. The impact forced the air out of my newly solidified lungs. Crystals and tiles screamed and scattered as the Pattern of Balance fractured beneath me. Pain flared white-hot through my shoulder that hung in the wrong direction. I tasted blood, eyes burning in the lantern light as the world tilted sickeningly. Frightened cries from hundreds of Fae and faeries sang through the courtyard.

"The Pattern rejects her!" Miravelle shrieked, pointing her crooked finger at me. Courtiers pressed against the edges of the crowd, shielding themselves behind each other as they shouted and whispered about the *ill omen. Curse. Abomination.*

I couldn't have blamed them. My festival dress was in grass-stained tatters, blood and saffron dyeing it crimson. I looked like ruin.

King Oranth pushed through the cowering court, amber eyes blazing without mercy. "Seize—"

The courtyard began to tremble.

At first, it was almost gentle—just a shiver from the earth that clinked wine goblets on distant tables and set the lanterns swaying. But then it deepened, finding a terrifying rhythm.

Thoom.

Thoom.

THOOM.

Footsteps. Massive and deliberate ones, each one shaking the palace to its bones.

The ground beneath me bucked as a single enormous shadow fell across the broken Pattern. I was too weak to command it as all the other shadows skittered away. I tried to stand, but my legs betrayed my weight. I couldn't lift my hands, not in surrender, not in defense.

The Harthorn loomed over me.

But it was not the same gentle creature that knelt for children and stole candied apples. The laughter it once inspired was gone. Its moss-covered frame shuddered with barely contained power, antlers scraping the sky, shedding scraps of ribbon that had once fluttered like prayer flags. Golden sap dripped from its maw like rabid slobber. And its eyes—gods, its eyes fixed on me with the weight of mountains, glowing from within like twin furnaces.

The sound it made tore through the air, a wind of warning howling through hollow bark. It clattered my teeth and rattled the palace windows. Birds fled from the trees in a black wave.

Everyone froze. Even the King.

"No," whispered Master Finvarra, his features draining pale

beneath the glow of the auroragourds. "No—this isn't possible—"

The Harthorn lowered its head toward me and stamped once.

Silk ribbons—children's wishes—dangled inches from my face, mocking my whimpers. It exhaled a bellowing snort that reeked of wet soil and death, like the forest floor once a pyre's ashes had gone cold. Its breath hit me like a gale, whipping my tangled hair across my cheeks.

I tried to crawl away, but my palms slipped on the blood-slick shards of tile.

"Father above..." came Lysara's trembling voice from somewhere behind me. "It's judging her."

Its nostrils flared, and every ceremonial rune etched around the courtyard erupted in wild color—gold, silver, purple, blue— each pulsing in time with the creature's booming heart.

Then the first strike fell.

Its hoof slammed down like the fall of a tree where my head had been just a heartbeat earlier. Shards of glass and shattered rock crunched and exploded. The shock wave hurled me aside as pain tore through my dislocated shoulder and my ears rang with white noise.

I dragged myself across the broken Pattern, its sharp edges slicing fabric and skin as I crawled belly over stone. Behind me, another strike obliterated the ground where my legs had been. Its antlers tangled in my ankles, knocking me forward as my face skidded along the rubble.

The Harthorn followed, relentless and patient—herding me inward, toward the heart of the ruin. With every step it took, the runes beneath its feet flickered and died.

The Pattern was failing. The ancient light that had once pulsed in harmony stuttered and dimmed until darkness spread outward like an ink stain.

The creature reared on its hind legs, its silhouette blotting out the sunset. I rolled, trying to escape to the edge of the Pattern, but the ground shuddered again—then split in half. Roots burst through the fractured cobblestone, thick and knotted, snapping the stone apart as if it were brittle shell. They sprouted with purpose, claiming the space around me.

I scrambled backward, but my back met more roots that rose behind me. They writhed too much to climb over and were too smooth to grip. They continued curling upwards and inwards, trapping me in a perfect circle. And the Harthorn stood at its center, watching me with those furnace eyes and sap-frothing mouth.

"Please," I whispered, though I didn't know if I was praying to the creature or to whatever gods might be listening. "I don't understand what I've done."

It tilted its head, then stepped closer. The runes beneath its hoof went black. Another step, more darkness spreading like a plague, creeping toward me in a rising tide. But not like a stain. Like a *void*. A void that would swallow me—extinguish me—so that the blessing could be restored. So that balance could be restored.

"Stop!" Prince Torian's voice split across the courtyard as fire wrapped around his hands. He shoved through the crowd, panic smothering sense, his restraint completely shattered. "Leave her alone!"

The Harthorn's massive head swung toward him, and for a breath, its burning gaze left me. I scrambled for the wall of roots, finding a thin patch and clambering at it uselessly. My hand slipped through a gap in the wood. Before I could pull it away, the roots shifted, filling in the empty spaces and coiling around my wrist.

I yanked. Hard. Again and again, but the roots only tightened their grip. The Harthorn returned its attention to me, snorting in annoyance, and I nearly dislocated my other shoulder trying to rip myself free. The void at its feet continued to tear through the ground, hungry to destroy me.

It stopped right in front of me and lifted its hoof high.

This is how I die, I thought. Crushed beneath a god's foot just moments after escaping another.

"NO!"

Torian screamed, and fire erupted from him—from his hands, from his chest. He was engulfed in his own panicked inferno as he slung fireballs without aim. Without thought. Just pouring everything he was into stopping my annihilation.

Tents and carts exploded into flames; silk banners ignited. Auroragourds whistled and burst, sending scalding chunks whirring through the frenzied crowd. A fiery branch fell between me and the Harthorn, and its flame reached for the hem of my skirt. But I couldn't pull it out of its path. I just watched it, waiting for it to burn me up before I could even be stamped out.

The blaze struck the Harthorn's flank, and it reared and bucked against the flames. They spread over it like hunger, racing along ancient wood, down its legs, up its neck. The creature keened, an earsplitting cry of betrayal and agony so immense that the windows of the palace shattered.

Glass rained down over the courtyard like glittering knives, slicing hands that covered faces, splintering into gems under trampling feet.

Torian didn't stop. He couldn't. His fire poured from him in torrents, crackling along his skin with molten veins as he burned himself hollow.

"Torian, please!" I screamed as the fire licked at my feet.

But he didn't hear me over the sound of the pavilion crashing to the ground, over the festival collapsing into screaming chaos.

The Harthorn turned, a living pillar of flame, and charged him through the wreckage. Each hoofbeat shook the universe, trailing fire like a comet hurtling through existence.

There wasn't time for me to mourn my future as I watched it burn to the ground. No time to wish I had one more second with him in the field. We'd both be dead without a single goodbye spoken between us.

And then a voice rose above it all.

Water erupted, torn from everywhere, from everything all at once—fountains, reflective pools, goblets stolen from trembling hands, moisture wrenched from breath and air. It swept through the courtyard like a coursing river, then struck the Harthorn as a battering ram, knocking the massive creature sideways as steam exploded upward in a boiling cloud.

Through the haze came its confused bellow, the crash of wood hitting stone. Brella swayed where she stood, her skin glowing turquoise. Her hands shook, and her breath came sharp and shallow. She kept her eyes fixed on the ground, refusing to acknowledge the destruction, the attention now snapping toward her small, trembling form.

The steam thinned, and the Harthorn stood amid the ruins, each movement groaning like an old tree splitting as it rose. Every rune lay dark. Water dripped from its charred bark, pooling around its hooves. Burnt ribbons fluttered weakly from its antlers, blackened ghosts of the children's wishes. Flames still clung to its body, stubbornly flickering as smoke billowed from its wounds.

The creature turned its vast head toward me one final time, and in its eyes I saw everything—sorrow for what it had been forced to destroy, recognition of whatever I carried, and the terrible finality of a guardian who failed its sacred charge.

Then it bowed—one immense, grief-heavy gesture—and limped through the shattered gates into the Amber Wilds.

Silence fell like a shroud. It pressed against my eardrums, and I wasn't sure if the world had lost its voice or if I had truly gone deaf from the Harthorn's lament.

Water trickled red with pulverized flowers. Smoke clung to the air like incense from a funeral. The Pattern of Balance lay in complete ruin. And there I stood, slack-jawed and shackled at the center of it all—the obvious cause, the undeniable catastrophe.

King Oranth stepped forward, his face already smoothed over as he surveyed the devastation.

"The Pattern is destroyed," he said coldly, straightening his cufflink at his wrist. "The Balance that has held the realms in peace since the Cataclysm lies in ruin."

His eyes fixed on me like a predator sighting prey, and he gestured to the guards flanking him. "Seize her."

The guards hesitated, glancing between me and the destroyed Pattern as if I might summon another horror to finish what the first had started.

"She is under my protection."

Torian struggled to his feet, his skin still smoking and hands shaking with exhaustion. The King watched as he staggered toward me, pulling the roots apart enough for me to wrench my hand free. He then scanned the crowd, injured and cowering, and opened his arms to address them.

"What is a king without his trust in his successor?" the King asked with a smile. "And what is a prince without good faith in his subjects?"

Low hums and murmurs of agreement whispered through the mewls of pain and fear.

"Your prince has chosen to defend the architect of our undoing," he continued as he strode toward us, his footfalls just as menacing as the Harthorn's before him.

"Let us hope his good faith has not been misplaced."

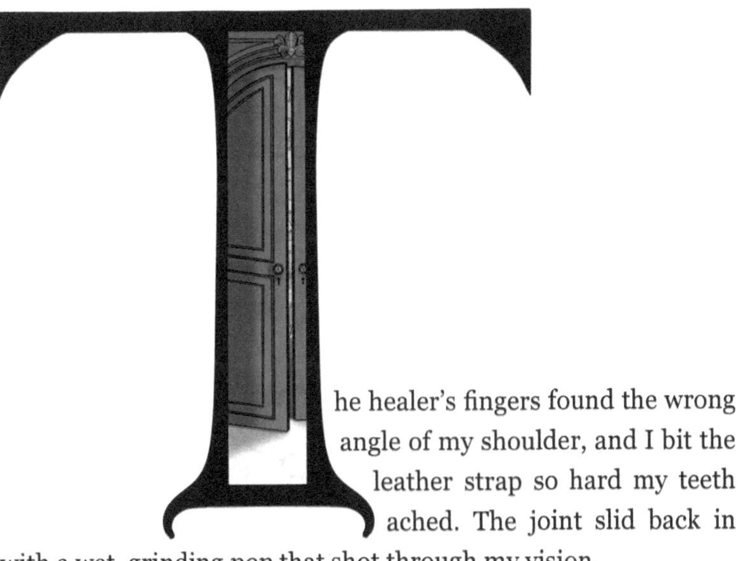

Chapter Nineteen

he healer's fingers found the wrong angle of my shoulder, and I bit the leather strap so hard my teeth ached. The joint slid back in with a wet, grinding *pop* that shot through my vision.

"The prince insisted on being present," the healer murmured, pressing a cool rag to my brow as I caught my breath from the re-alignment. "Claimed he could ease the pain. I barred the door."

So that part of his magic wasn't common knowledge then.

I pictured it with agonizing clarity: Torian pacing the corridors, hands wrapped in fire he couldn't use, desperate to fix what he couldn't prevent. The thought hurt worse than the setting bone.

"You're fortunate," she continued, binding my arm in a sling that reeked of mint and something aseptic. "Most who find themselves beneath a guardian's hoof do not rise again."

Fortunate. I had considered myself many things over the past few weeks in the Amber Vale, and fortunate never came to mind.

I barely had time to sigh before the silk curtain separating me from the rest of the palace was yanked to the side, and two guards stood at the threshold. Their copper-plated armor bore scorch marks, and the smell of smoke still stuck in the seams. Neither of them looked at me directly.

"The King commands your presence." Not an invitation. Never an invitation.

I slid off the bed in a nightdress and bare feet. The cold marble floor bit into my naked soles. Each step jarred my sore shoulder. The guards flanked me as we moved through the halls as if I were a prisoner. No shoes, no dignity. Just the way the King wanted it, I was certain.

Courtiers scattered at our approach, pressing themselves into the frescoed walls as we passed. Someone hissed pattern-breaker; someone else muttered chaos-bringer. Another touched their fingertips to a ward hanging at their neck. Whatever curse I carried was contagious to them.

The council chamber doors loomed ahead. They did not bear the throne room's spectacle, or the banquet hall's sophistication, but something worse in their intimacy. Simply carved mahogany with unembellished gold doorknobs. I swallowed hard as the guards pushed them open without ceremony, revealing the assembly within.

Torian looked like he hadn't slept in weeks. Shadows pooled beneath bloodshot eyes that no Fae glamour could hope to hide. His hands were pressed around the back of a chair, as if he were pinning himself to propriety by force. We met each other's gaze for half a breath. Something flickered there—apology, fury, helplessness—and then he looked away. A muscle jumped in his jaw. Once. Twice.

To his right stood Lady Valeraine, perfect as a painted doll in blue velvet. Not a single hair was out of place despite the earlier chaos. Her composure was its own kind of mockery. *See how untouched I am*, the jealousy of it spat at me. *See how little your disruption bothers.*

Lysara stood on the other side of Lady Valeraine, her autumn hair pulled back so tightly I could feel the ache in my own scalp. Her expression was professionally flat, but her fingers wrung a frayed place at her sleeve. She knew I was hiding something, and she chewed on her cheek over whether that something had almost gotten us all killed.

Near the wall, practically melting herself into the stonework, stood Brella. The mandolin-wielding hero of the chaos, though you might not know it from her hunched shoulders and downcast gaze. Her dress had singe marks at its hem, and she clutched her jade-inlaid mandolin protectively at its neck.

A scribe sat in the corner, quill poised over crisp parchment. He took attendance with a trembling hand, the tension in the room near gagging as the door shut behind me.

King Oranth stood apart at the head of a crescent table, fingers steepled beneath his chin. His golden eyes tracked me with the patient interest of a spider measuring a fly in its web.

"Ah," the King said. "Our distinguished guest."

I curtsied as low as my shoulder would allow, biting back a tiny whimper when I dipped my chin a tad too far. "Your Majesty." I turned toward Torian with another curtsy. "Your Highness." Then I nodded to Lady Valeraine. "My Lady."

"Before we address the previous... disruption," he went on, gesturing for the others in attendance to sit while I was clearly left without a chair, "gratitude is owed." His attention cut to Brella, who seemed to recoil at his consideration. "Brella of The Chordilleras, please step forward."

She moved to the center of the room like water trying not to disturb its own surface. She curtsied flawlessly, though her knuckles were white as she wrung the fabric of her skirt.

"Your quick action saved not only the courtyard, but my son's life." The words should have sounded warm, maybe even proud. But instead, they carried an edge hidden in his tone. "The gods favor those who remember their place. Though I wonder if your musical selection was entirely appropriate for such a sacred day."

A shiver took hold of me when a tiny flinch crossed Brella's face. Her fingers tightened around her mandolin's neck, its steel strings scraping across the wood.

So I hadn't imagined it. Her song was a pointed finger at the King, and this commendation was a leash, not a laurel.

Brella spoke steadily, though barely above a whisper. "The old songs honor the old ways, Your Majesty. I meant no disrespect."

"Of course not." His smile was all teeth, no warmth. "Your service to the Crown will not be forgotten. You are dismissed."

Brella curtsied again with mutters of thanks and stepped toward the door. Lady Valeraine rose smoothly to move along with her, her gracious benefactress.

"Your loyalty honors the Vale," she said as she opened the door for Brella, who curtsied shyly before retreating. "We shall celebrate with tea in the west solar. I will send for you."

"Now," the King said once the latch clicked into place, turning the full weight of his attention back to me, "the matter of the guardian's provocation."

My throat tightened as the flashes flooded my senses. The desecrated Pattern. The burning Harthorn. My nearly lost love.

"If I may, Your Majesty." Lady Valeraine's voice rang through the tension like a wind chime. "I have asked the resident court historian to provide context for this discussion."

Lysara stepped forward. I tried to catch her eye, to reach for the friend who strolled with me through the festival and shared her wine with me, but she did not look at me.

"Historical precedent exists," she said with icy formality. "During both the Severance and the Cataclysm, boundary instability triggered defensive manifestations in the sacred guardians. When the Pattern is disrupted by any solitary will, a guardian may respond... vigorously, perceiving imbalance as intrusion."

The King sat back in his chair and sucked on his teeth. "And what, pray tell, is your explanation for what preceded the Pattern's annihilation? How did this performer come to fall from the sky and into its heart?"

My heart thudded in my ears.

"I have a theory, Your Majesty." Her voice was even, though I saw the quick glance she cut toward me. "Records from the Cataclysm detail many disappearances followed by spontaneous reappearances. Eyewitness accounts describe similar distortions, not unlike what occurred in the courtyard today. It is my belief that Miss Lyra may have been drawn into such a deformity prior to her violent re-entry. The guardian would have perceived this as an act of trespass, not mischance."

She was saving me, saving Torian, and yet cutting me open as she did so. Every word felt like a betrayal, like she was explaining away what we both knew was far from the coincidence she was suggesting.

"Convenient," the King murmured coldly. "Thank you for your insight. You are dismissed."

Lysara dipped slightly, then quietly exited without so much as a click from the latch. He then turned to Torian.

"And you, my son. Why does a sacred guardian lie burned and broken while its adjudged still draws breath?"

Torian stiffened, stifling a barely contained scoff. "Because it would have killed her had I not intervened."

"Precisely," said the King. "That was its purpose. The guardian acts wherever the balance is threatened. One death, contained and meaningful, would have ended the matter. Instead—" He gestured to the shattered window, smoke still rolling beyond the walls. "—we have a destroyed courtyard, a terrorized court, and half the Vale proper wishing to relocate because of ill omens. Tell me, *future king*, which outcome better served the realm?"

Torian's hands curled into tight fists as steam spilled from his back. "You would have had me stand idle while it pulverized her?"

"I would have had you *think*," the King said with a sharp softness I had never heard from him before. "A prince who cannot distinguish impulse from duty endangers far more than the worth of a single girl. You set fire to a god-beast, Torian. Do you understand the weight—"

"I understand the weight of watching someone die while I did nothing to stop it!"

The chamber air froze over. The twin sets of golden eyes locked onto each other in burning fury.

Lady Valeraine rose halfway from her chair. "Your Majesty, the prince's actions were born of instinct. Any delay might have seen the guardian's wrath turned upon the court itself. He acted in defense of the Vale—"

"Don't," Torian snapped, the word cutting through her shield before she could even bring it up. "Do not speak for me."

Her smile did not falter as she sat back down. "Of course. Forgive my presumption."

King Oranth leaned forward on his elbows, eyes half-lidded as if her defense of the prince annoyed him.

"Assumptions," he said after a long silence, "are not facts. We could invent a hundred tales of what the guardian *might* have done. It might have picked up a fiddle and played with the band, for as well as guesses serve us."

A flash of pink climbed up Lady Valeraine's cheeks as she pressed her lips together.

"What is fact, however, is that you self-immolated without proper precaution or authorization, injuring the creature and many festival-goers caught in its frenzy. All to save one human life."

The weight of that single word—*human*—felt like an accusation.

"I acted to protect the court. To protect *you*."

"The court did not require your heroics, nor did I."

The King rose from his chair in one fluid, dreadful motion. His shadow stretched long across the table.

"You mistook mercy for mastery, my son. Until you learn the difference, you will not act without my word. Not in council, not in court, not even in kindness." He walked up to Torian and placed a heavy hand on his shoulder, lowering his voice to a deadly calm.

"You will obey, and you will be silent, until I decide you are worthy to be heard again. You are dismissed."

Torian bowed stiffly, jaw locked, hands shaking. Lady Valeraine rose with him, threading her arm through his.

"Come, my love," she murmured. "A promenade in your garden will soothe your temper."

His garden. *Our* garden. The words hit me like a punch to the gut, and it took every fiber of myself to smother the jealousy furrowing my brow.

Torian's face went white, then flushed. His free hand clenched into a fist at his side, and I thought he might pull away from her. Might actually speak the words burning behind his eyes. But he didn't.

He hesitated for a single, doomed second, his eyes finding mine once more, before she guided him out. The door closed behind them with a soft finality that echoed through my bones.

In that moment, I wondered if I should even care if the King tossed me out of his court. Perhaps it would be for the best.

"Leave us," the King commanded his scribe, who was still scribbling furiously from his vantage point in the corner.

His quill stopped mid-scratch, leaving a wet blob of ink bleeding across the parchment. "Your Majesty?"

"That was an order."

The scribe saw the murderous look on the King's face and scurried out, the tip of his quill tearing through his last sentence as he bolted. The click of the latch left me and King Oranth in a room that suddenly felt much too small, too warm.

He did not return to his seat, and I dared not move a muscle for fear of having my jugular ripped out. He prowled in a slow circle around me, appraising me like a hyena waiting for me to trip. I kept my hands loose at my sides, my eyes fixed on his face.

The shadows resting in the empty hearth stirred at my discomfort, sliding over soot and spilling onto the carpet like oil. *Be still*, I urged them. *Please don't make this worse.* They slowed against the force of my will, but I could tell they were keeping watch. Making up for their betrayal of me to their goddess.

"Curious," the King hissed at length, stopping just behind my wrapped shoulder, his breath stirring the curls at my neck. "Your tenure in my palace has been mere weeks, and yet you materialized right at the heart of my sacred Pattern. Not a step left or right. As if you knew how to land on the fulcrum of a millennia-old design."

His gaze flicked to the pool of shadows across the room. He made no inclination toward them, but the minuscule narrowing of his eyes told me they had his attention. My pulse stumbled as a black finger waved at me from the mass, then playfully slid along the floor.

"I didn't aim," I said. "I was simply... pulled back. I didn't know where I would fall."

"Pulled," he repeated incredulously, flipping the word around in his mouth as if he were tasting it for treachery. "Pulled from where?"

"I don't know." A half-truth. "There was darkness," I said meekly. "No direction, no beginning or end. I heard the music of the festival, and I followed it out. That was when I—"

"Lord Iäen grows bold," the King interrupted, as if my answer bored him. Each step of his clicked like a clock ticking down as he continued his circling. "His borders weaken; the boundary thins near the Frost Court, and he uses it to send his shadows *creeping in.*"

I could not help the confusion that made itself evident on my face. "I'm not sure I follow—"

"Don't play dumb with me, girl. I know there has been movement at the Mist Marshes, and I know there is a Frost Court spy in my halls. Perhaps you thought the festival would cover your return to him. You'd simply slip through my boundary gone soft with Mabon; instead, you tore it wide open and revealed yourself."

"Your Majesty, I have never even met Lord Iäen—"

He moved faster than my eyes could track. A flash of orange flame cracked through the air. A fireball roared past my cheek and struck the hearth, erupting the room in heat and light. The shadows slinking across the floor screamed as the flames burned them away, writhing like snakes. The sound felt human and inhuman all at once, the pain and loyalty tangled together.

I staggered backward. My heel caught on the rug, and I fell straight onto my tailbone, unable to catch myself with my arm in a sling. The air left my lungs as the pain shot up my spine. He bent down, lowering his voice until it rasped the shell of my ear.

"Your shadows and your lord are no match for the Golden King."

The Golden King. Not the Amber King.

I couldn't speak. I could only whimper as he towered over me.

"Get up," he snarled. "Go back to your quarters. No performances. No magic. No tricks. You will not leave these walls until I say otherwise. If you are what you claim—some harmless little conjurer—then you shall find confinement... comfortable."

His face was a hair from mine, eyes darting around my face to find any flicker of dissent. Then he stepped back, as if he were granting me some courtesy I had not earned.

"If I find you sniffing anywhere near the gates, or whispering to shadows that don't belong to you—" A smile sliced his face in half like a knife. "—you will die."

The latch clicked free as the door swung open at the mere flick of his finger. I hesitated, pinned by heat and humiliation.

"Go," he murmured as he stared into the fire, the echoes of my shadows still sizzling in the hearth. "Before I decide to burn something else."

I clambered backward, not even bothering to stand. Pride was a luxury I could not afford in this room. I scooted and crawled across the floor, my good arm dragging along the plush red carpet. If survival meant scuttling like vermin from the *Golden King*, then vermin I would be.

The door yawned wider as I made it to the open doorway. A tall silhouette darkened the frame, disdain carved into every line of his face—Lord Caenan. His gaze slid down to me, a tripod human on the ground, and he curled his lip as though I had crawled from the gutter to stain his boots.

I tried to edge past him, but he stepped forward deliberately, knocking his foot into my knee and forcing me sideways across the carpet like some pathetic slug. I was barely clear of the threshold before he slammed the door behind me, hitting my hunched back and drawing a choked gasp from my throat. The ridges of my spine sang in pain as I hauled the rest of me into the corridor and rested against the cool wall.

The latch didn't sound this time. The door rebounded on its strike, leaving a thin, indifferent seam of light spilling from the council chambers. Through it, I heard Lord Caenan's voice.

"Your Majesty, forgive the intrusion," he said, smooth as an oiled hinge. "Preparations for tomorrow's departure require your approval."

"Show me."

Paper slid against paper as a map was unfurled and flattened on the table.

"The scouts have mapped the western approach. The mortal village of Mistwater is ideal. Farmland, access to the Cisqa and the Western Sea, borders the amenable south."

My blood froze in my veins as the name poured like cold water down my neck.

Mistwater. My home.

I thought of my father's hands, stained with the ink of salves and old recipes. The herb garden I had tended as a child, learning which healed and which harmed. The harbor where I watched the fishermen pull up nets of fish that we would all eat that night.

Then I thought of the children playing in the streets, the old women who told tales of warning around a fire about the cunning fair folk.

They wouldn't stand a chance.

"Excellent," the King replied. I inched closer to the gap and pressed a trembling hand against my mouth to muffle my panicked breaths. The lip of a bottle clinked against a glass. "And our guide?"

"The huntsman has agreed," Lord Caenan said. I could hear his wicked smile in his words. "His price was... quaint."

"Oh?" The King sipped something, sucking his teeth as it burned on the way down.

"His guidance through the forest in exchange for the *Nyaeleth vyr Myr'Faen*," he answered, the Eldertongue phrase rolling rather beautifully off his tongue.

I could hear amusement creep into the King's voice. "He

agreed to what?"

"The *Nyaeleth vyr Myr'Faen*," Lord Caenan repeated matter-of-factly. "The sacred ritual performed during a new moon where a mortal can become Faen."

My heart stopped.

Torian once mentioned its opposite—the *Nyaeleth vyr Aeoneth*. It was spoken as a last resort, severing immortality for a blink of the love we had.

But there was another way.

I wanted to scream, to find Torian and shake him for not allowing me that option. A Fae prince consorting with a Fae commoner might have been met with disapproval, but it certainly would not have resulted in a fate worse than death.

Silence gathered in the council chamber as ice cubes tinkled in the King's swirling glass. I held my breath, my fingernails digging into my palms.

Torian, how could you?

The King's boisterous laughter shattered my spiraling thoughts. Genuine laughter, so unexpected and harsh that I jolted into the wall, my head bouncing off the plaster and echoing through the hallway.

"Idiot's sacrifice?" The King translated, still chuckling. "Direct. Even for you, Caenan."

The angry heat that surged within my chest curdled into shame, leaving me cold and raw. Of course it was a joke, made at the expense of a human foolish for wanting. And I had fallen for it just as easily in the space of a heartbeat.

I backed away from the crack in the door, bracing against the wall as I finally stood. Footsteps approached as the guards rounded the hall to collect me once more. I composed my face before they could read it.

Perhaps I was the spy I had been accused of being after all.

Chapter Twenty

Steam rose around me, feathering the air and doing nothing for the ache set deep in my bones. I submerged myself deeper in the bath, the water lapping at the hollow of my throat.

I dumped too much bergamot oil and lavender salt in the tub, and their scents coiled so thickly that I could barely breathe. I was told they would help with relaxation, but it was taking everything in me not to jump out of my skin. Yet, even as the water grew tepid, I couldn't bring myself to get out.

A sharp knock on the bathroom door shattered my brooding. The door swung open before I could even call out, before I could grab more than just the nearest hand towel to clutch against my bare chest.

Lysara burst in, autumn braid in messy tangles, eyes wild and urgent. She did not seem to care that I was naked, or trying to mope in solitude.

"Forgive the intrusion, but this cannot wait." She snagged a bath towel from a hook on the wall and threw it at me. Water sloshed as I reached for it, catching it just before it landed in the bathwater.

I wrapped the towel around me and stepped too quickly out of the bath, nearly slipping on the marble tiles in my haste. "What's happened? What's wrong?"

My mind sped through every single horrific scenario I could conjure. *Torian is dead. Valeraine killed him. Lysara helped her hide his body in the archives. I'm next.*

"You," she said. Then softer, "and everything you touch."

She crossed to where I stood in the corner of the bathroom. My knees buckled against the edge of the tub as she came within an inch of my face.

"I've been patient," she said. Her yellow eyes, usually soft as candlelight over weathered pages, burned into me with such intensity that it nauseated me. "I've watched you since your arrival, noticed the prince's reaction toward you, observed your unusual magic. After yesterday's incident with the Pattern, I can no longer wait for the truth."

My heartbeat lodged itself in my throat. "I don't know what you mean."

"Don't." The word came out of her like the crack of a whip. I nearly recoiled at the sharpness of it. "You couldn't even recognize Eldertongue on the page. You're clearly not from the Twilight Isles." Her voice dropped to barely above a whisper. "And I'm certain your name isn't Lyra."

The droplets of water felt like frost on my skin. "Lysara—"

"The way Prince Torian behaved yesterday—that wasn't concern for a court performer. He looked like his heart had been ripped clean from his chest."

"I can explain—"

"What I witnessed was distress for someone he loves, and someone he has loved for far longer than the few weeks you've supposedly been here."

The certainty in her voice left no room for denial. I studied her face, searching for any sign of malice, any hint of a trap. I saw only determination, and something hurt. Like a friend who had been lied to.

"If I tell you the truth," I said carefully, "I put you in danger."

Lysara's lips thinned into a straight line. "You already have."

She did not move, did not back away from the human she had pinned in the corner of a steamy bathroom. She would never let this go. I would become a skeleton draped over the side of a tub before she submitted to my carefully constructed lie.

"Let me dress," I sighed. "This isn't a conversation to have while I'm naked."

So she did.

I pulled my sling over my head and wrestled myself into a robe one-handed. The soreness in my shoulder had eased, but I looped my arm through it anyway, hoping to elicit a dash of sympathy from Lysara's disdain.

Once I was all tied in, I sat on the edge of the bed, unsure if my legs could hold the weight of both me and my story.

"My name is Aevra Nightwind."

And then the stones lifted from my chest, one by one. I told her about Mistwater—river-mist and salt-laced mornings with my father—about the Fae prince who tasted like summer and recklessness, about the century of darkness that scraped the edges of me thin, about the Whispering Sea swallowing me, then spitting me out with the stars as a parting gift.

She did not interrupt. Only once did a sound crack through, and a hand flew to her mouth—when I mentioned Alezae and my threatening encounter with her yesterday.

Then I told her about the King's lie, the public execution that took an innocent's breath instead of mine; about the guilt that sat heavier than iron because I didn't even know her name.

"I'm haunted by her," I said weakly, wrapping my arms around myself to hold the pieces together. "An innocent woman took my name to her grave while I rotted in the shadowlands. Her blood is on my hands, and I don't even know—who was she? Did she have a family? Did she know why she was dying? Did she curse me with her last breath?"

Lysara sat in stunned silence, staring at her palms. The afternoon light through the window caught the dust motes floating between us, making them dance like tiny, mocking spirits. When she finally looked up, her face was pale, expression grave as fresh-turned soil.

"If what you're saying is true—if Alezae herself is hunting you, and the boundaries are weakening enough for her to reach through..." She swallowed hard. "The Amber Vale is in danger. Perhaps all the realms are."

"I never meant to bring this danger here," I said. "I only wanted to find Torian."

"Well, you certainly found him." She shook her head incredulously, and a flicker of hurt flashed in her eyes. "I've been helping you research court history, showing you private archives, and you couldn't trust me with that?"

"It wasn't about trust," I tried to explain, but the words felt empty. "Anyone who knows becomes a potential victim of the King's wrath."

"And yet, here we are, with the Pattern in ruins after you dive-bombed it straight from the Duskhold, and the prince all but declaring his love in front of the entire court!"

Her tone carried an edge I'd never heard from her before. Disappointment sharpened by accusation.

"Safety through secrecy has clearly failed you, my friend."

I had no further argument, and my heart clenched at her mention of the word *friend.*

"I'm sorry," I managed.

"What's done is done," she sighed, squeezing my fingers gently in her lap. Her pulse raced through her fingertips despite the calm smile she donned clearly for my benefit. "But the shock of all this... I need a moment. Excuse me."

Lysara disappeared into the bathroom, the latch clicking and locking into place behind her. I fell back onto the bed, my mind reeling from finally sharing my truth. The weight of it had been crushing me slowly, and now I felt like I could almost breathe again.

Almost.

The main door to my chambers burst open without warning—no knock, no announcement. Torian filled the threshold, golden hair uncombed, shirt askew, amber eyes glowing wild with barely contained emotion. His chest heaved as if he had run here.

Before I could even speak—before I could warn him about Lysara—he crossed the room in three desperate strides. His hands cradled my face with trembling fingers.

"Aevra."

My name was a prayer on his lips as his mouth crashed into mine. Not careful, not courtly. Just a drowning lover finding air and taking too much for himself. His tongue parted my lips; one hand tangled in my wet hair while the other slid down the dip of my spine. I tasted honeyed mead on his breath, the smell of smoke on his carelessly unbuttoned jacket.

"I wanted to come sooner," he murmured against my mouth

between deepening kisses. His lips moved across my jaw, down my throat, pressing hot and desperate into my skin. "They wouldn't let me see you—and then seeing you slung and barefoot in front of my father—gods, Aevra! I thought—I was terrified of what he—"

He didn't finish. His mouth found that sweet spot where my neck reached my ear, then down to my collarbone, pushing away the sling to find the skin beneath the fabric. The entire world went fuzzy as I nearly went limp in his arms.

"Torian—" There was something important I needed to tell him. I was sure of it. But whatever it was dissolved when his hands slid across the thin silk of my robe.

"Let me," he rasped, his voice breaking like waves against cliffs. "Let me feel you. So I know you're real. That I didn't watch you die, and this isn't just a—" I wrapped my legs around his waist, my fingers weaving softly through his hair. "—a dream."

His mouth returned to mine, gentler this time, as he nudged me onto the unmade bed. I nearly lost myself in his touch, but the weeds of jealousy had overgrown since yesterday, and I couldn't bite back the venom that was about to pour out of my mouth.

"Was your walk through the garden last night as restorative as intended?" The words felt cheap, but I did not want them back.

He blinked twice, then his hands tightened on my hips as he pulled back just enough for me to see the confusion on his face.

"The gardens? With Valeraine?" The disbelief in his voice was almost comical. "You think—Aevra, no."

"You can't deny she is a smart match," I continued. I hated how petty and small I sounded. Even as he hovered above me, and I could feel how much he wanted *me* in this moment, I couldn't stop it.

He silenced me with another kiss, his teeth catching my lower lip, sharp enough to draw a gasp from my throat. "Stop," he commanded against my mouth. "No more."

I turned my head to the side, pouting, refusing to give him more. He slid his hands up to my face, thumbs brushing my cheeks as he forced me to meet his eyes.

"We talked of weather and wool tariffs while I thought only of you." He traced my lip, still swollen from his warning nip. "Every moment, Aevra. Every godsdamned moment since you stepped to the center of the Golden Hall, I've thought only of you. When I wake, when I dream, when I'm trying to read a book or supposed to be listening in council meetings—it's you. Always only *you*."

The bathroom door clicked open.

"Well," Lysara said dryly, emerging to find us tangled up in sin and each other's panic, "this clarifies several follow-up questions."

Torian lurched backward, stumbling over his own feet and knocking into the wardrobe against the wall. Color flooded his face as his composure shattered like dropped crystal. He fumbled to straighten his jacket and smoothed a hand down the front of his pants.

"Lysara—I didn't—this isn't what it—" He cleared his throat, reaching for his tone of court, but it came out sounding strangled. "I was merely checking on Miss Lyra's wellbeing following yesterday's incident."

"She looks rather disheveled, Your Highness," she said, arching an eyebrow, gaze dropping to my robe that was nearly hanging off of me. "Is she well, or shall I send for a healer to assist—"

"That's hardly necessary—"

"She knows," I said simply, ending his bumbling attempts at recovery.

Torian stilled, a muscle jumping in his jaw. "You told her?"

"I've known for a while," Lysara said, her tone gentle, though the amusement of the situation still danced in her eyes.

"How long?" He asked, curiosity mixing with the ebbing embarrassment.

"Longer than you think," she replied, picking casually at her fingernails. "She's been trying very hard to cover that stubborn love bite for a couple of weeks."

My hand shot up to my neck, heat flooding my cheeks. Not that it hadn't healed this whole time... it just kept getting replaced with a fresh one.

He dropped his shoulders and sank down onto the bed beside me, all pretense abandoned. The mattress dipped under his weight, sending me spilling onto him. "And you said nothing?"

"It was not my place to remark, Your Highness. Even after finding you crying among the crocuses."

"I wasn't crying," Torian protested weakly.

Lysara grinned, dimples peppering the sides of her mouth. "Though I must confess, it is rather romantic. Star-crossed lovers reunited against all odds, and all that."

She moved toward the door, pausing at the threshold to look back at us.

"Which is why I will take my leave. And *Aevra*," she said, forcing the newness of my true name from behind her teeth. "Come to the archives when you're... *finished*. I have something to show you."

With an incline of her head toward me, and a sweet curtsy to her prince, she swept from the room.

The air felt suddenly heavy. The heat of the previous moment had dissipated, and Torian's hand found mine, his thumb tracing circles on my palm.

I needed to get dressed. The silk of my robe felt sticky and too warm on my flushed skin. But when I attempted to stand, he gently tugged me back down.

"What happened to you?" he asked. I swallowed hard, remembering that terrible void and that horrible laugh.

"It was Alezae."

"What?" Torian went rigid, his grip on my hand tightening almost painfully. "The Reaper goddess? She *took* you?"

"She was upset that I escaped. That she lost one of her *possessions*. She's hunting me, Torian. And the boundary is so thin that she can—"

"No." The word was a dagger through the air as he stood abruptly, pacing to the window and back again. "Listen to me," he said, low and certain, firmly bracing his hands on my shoulders. "She will not take you again. If she reaches, I reach back with hellfire. If the shadows open, I will stand in front of you. I will burn every road to the Duskhold before I let it have you again."

He pulled me against him, and his heart thudded into my ear. I wanted to believe him, to believe that it was possible for love to truly conquer all. But the heaviness in my chest sank deeper.

"There's something else," I muttered into his shirt. He hummed in reply, still holding me. "I overheard your father in council. The hunting expedition—he plans to survey Mistwater."

"Mistwater?"

"He's going to take it. Claim it for the Amber Vale." I pushed away from him to meet his eyes, to see if there was worry in them, or confusion. I didn't find either. The closest word I could find for it was *untroubled.*

"Aevra—" I could hear his dismissal coming from a mile away.

"I have to warn them. My people—"

He cupped my face gently in his hands. "One crisis at a time, my love."

"But my father—"

"Your father..." He chewed on his next words carefully as he watched the panic race across my face, my cheeks burning warmer beneath his palms. "It's been a hundred years, Aevra. Your father is not there."

The words stung more than they should have. Of course, he was dead. I knew that the only living pieces of him were in the fractals of my memories.

I turned away from him to swipe a welling tear from my eye.

His posture slumped as his fingers glided from my skin, his hands hanging limply at his sides.

"Aevra," he called sweetly, reaching for me again. I rounded my shoulders, shrinking away from his touch.

"You don't understand," I said weakly, my voice cracking as I held back more tears that I refused to let fall in front of him.

"I understand you've been through some traumatic things." His voice was soothing, reasonable, infuriating. "But rushing into danger will only make things worse. The King's hunting party leaves tonight, and his eyes on us will be gone. Meet me tomorrow, and I will do my best to take your mind off of all of this."

Tonight.

His hand found my wrist, but he did not pull me toward him. He stepped around me, and I pretended to look into his eyes.

"Please?"

I wanted to scream that Mistwater couldn't wait, that my people needed warning far more than I needed to be canoodled in the dark.

"Tomorrow," I sighed in agreement, the lie bitter on my tongue.

He kissed me softly, a promise pressed against my lips that would not be fulfilled. And then he was gone, slipping out the door while leaving me with nothing but the certainty that waiting for a prince's blessing was a luxury my village could not afford.

The West Library felt different at this hour, as if the secrets it held in its endless rows weighed heavier on the air. I found Lysara in a secluded alcove, bent over a leather-bound tome. She looked up at my approach, and something in my weary expression must have betrayed my inner turmoil.

"He dismissed your concerns," she said flatly.

"How did you—"

"You have the look of someone patted on the head and told not to worry." She closed the book with deliberate care, but a cloud of dust still billowed from its weathered pages. "Males often mistake privilege for wisdom, even the best of them."

The understanding in her voice nearly undid me. I pressed my palms into my eyes, trying to push back even more of those stubborn tears. I couldn't tell her what I planned. Torian would be furious with me, and me alone.

Lysara stood, then studied me for a long moment. I wondered if she could see the decision that had already crystallized behind my eyes. If she had, she did not mention it.

"Come. There's something you need to see."

She led me deeper into the archives than we'd ventured before, past shelves undisturbed for decades, dust curling in the candlelight. The shelves no longer held journals and books, but artifacts hidden behind glass cases or crystal caskets. I could feel the eerie weight of ancient magic pressing against me from all sides, like the hot breath of a primordial creature guarding its trove.

"The Forbidden Reliquary," she whispered. "Some of my favorites are tucked away back here."

I craned my neck as I tried to behold the countless items covered in dust and dirt. A simple picture frame was turned backward on its shelf. I didn't dare turn it around. An orb filled with purple smoke sat nestled on top of some threadbare rags. Its contents swirled faster as I examined it, as if it were begging me to pick it up. Again, I did not dare do so.

"I shouldn't be here," I whispered back, though not in my own voice. It was like something was talking *through* me.

"Probably not," she agreed with a grim smile. "But you're already in over your head with things you shouldn't be doing, so what's one more?"

I didn't hear her. Instead, I heard singing, a lullaby that felt like I had heard it in a dream. Lysara followed close behind as I searched urgently for the source of the music.

My mother was singing. My mother was *here*. I needed to find her. I rounded a corner, and the singing stopped. In front of me was a pearl necklace sitting on a music stand.

"A word to the wise," Lysara said from behind me, making me jump. I couldn't remember how I had gotten here. "Never follow the music. And if your parents are dead, they will stay dead. No matter what you see or hear."

I nodded, feeling suddenly bare, as if the lullaby had totally emptied me from the inside.

She inclined her head toward the wall at my shoulder, then pressed her palm against the stone. She muttered a beautiful string of words in Eldertongue that made something stir in my chest.

"*Otvôrynth, caedryn.*"

The wall shimmered and dissolved like morning mist, revealing a circular chamber beyond. The moment I crossed the threshold, I felt it—power so dense it was like trudging through mud, like breathing gas siphoned straight from the sun.

"The Four Pillars," Lysara said reverently.

Four alcoves carved into pale stone, each emitting its own disembodied illumination. Four figures, each only the height of my forearm, yet they bore a presence that could sit atop cathedrals.

The Father stood to the east, hands outstretched with actual light pouring from his open palms. Not carved. Real, warm, almost terrible in its purity. His stone face held such a distant serenity that it made me feel smaller than the specks of dust floating around my head.

The Mother in the west seemed to breathe despite being stone, her robes rippling with invisible wind. Her smile held infinite compassion, along with something wilder. A chaos that could birth worlds, or swallow them whole on a whim.

The Son stood to the north—loving, powerful, and... hauntingly *familiar*. Not in the forlorn expression on his face, or the ring of magic that encircled his prayerful hands, but in his presence. It felt like I had forgotten something, and I could almost remember what it was.

But it was the southern alcove that stole my breath as it frosted in front of me.

"Alezae," I whispered, her name metallic on my tongue.

The effigy was all but ruined. Cracks spread from her heart like veins, only they were full of void instead of blood. Half her face was crumbled to nothing, leaving an absence that seemed to watch me more intently than her remaining eye.

"The Cataclysm," Lysara explained softly. "Her effigy was damaged while the others remained perfect."

My legs carried me closer to her, obeying something deeper than my own intention. The broken stone pulled at me with invisible threads, like calling, like drowning, like coming home to a place that had never existed.

"Don't touch it," Lysara warned.

Too late. My fingertips had already found its fractured surface.

The world shattered and expanded into fragments.

Overwhelming isolation. Loneliness so profound it feels like suffocation. Endless twilight shores. Souls never staying. Never thanking.

Blinding rage. Shadows sprouting teeth sharp enough to tear reality. Waters running black with hate.

And a whisper: mine.

I stumbled backward, ripping my hand from the stone that felt like it had a vise grip around my wrist. My head pounded as the vision released me, still strobing behind my eyes as I caught my breath. The shrine's air felt too thick, too real after the vast emptiness I'd just witnessed. My knees buckled under me, and I fell against the Son, the sharp angle of his praying hands bruising my ribs.

"What happened?" Lysara demanded, her yellow eyes wild with curiosity and fear. "What did you see?"

"*Her*," I managed between gasps, my voice sounding strange to my own ears.

"Aevra, you were standing there for an hour!"

Her hands fluttered near my shoulders, not quite touching, like she wanted to soothe but didn't want to get sucked in as well.

"I tried calling your name, shaking you. You went completely rigid. I thought—"

An *hour*?

The hunting party would be gathering now, servants loading the final supplies. I was running out of time.

I pressed a palm to my forehead, finding it clammy with cold sweat. "I don't feel well."

Not entirely a lie. I felt unmoored, like part of me was still stuck on those shores, still stuck in that vision of borrowed grief.

"You should rest." Lysara slipped her arm around my waist, supporting me as she led us out of the chamber. "I'll help you back to your rooms."

"I can manage," I said quickly, casually shrugging off her grip. "Just get me out of this deathtrap of a reliquary before that necklace starts singing to me again."

Chapter Twenty-One

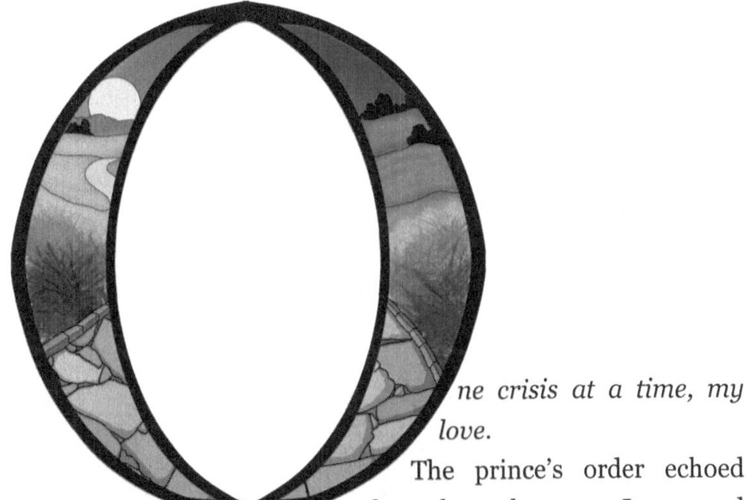

ne crisis at a time, my love.

The prince's order echoed through my bones as I prepared for the most dangerous—and stupidest—risk I'd taken since stepping into the Whispering Sea. My hands trembled as I pulled the servant's garb from the bottom of my wardrobe.

I had found the rough wool tunic wadded behind the armoire like a forgotten rag when I first moved in, checking for any clues or hidden scraps I could use. The fabric smelled of lye soap and something vaguely musty, like it had waited years just for this moment of desperation.

Whether it was a cosmic gift for my predetermined trek to Mistwater, or simply lazy housekeeping, I was thankful either way.

I bound my hair at the nape of my neck, pinning it underneath so tightly my scalp ached. Then I ripped a strip of cloth from my bedsheet and tied it around my head, tucking my distinctive silver curls beneath it. The ochre powder that I lightly dusted to conceal the ever-growing shimmer of my skin was now caked onto my face, neck, and hands. Mascara thickened my eyebrows; rouge ruddied up my cheeks and forehead.

It certainly was not the most comfortable look I had worn, courtesy of the Amber Palace. My trousers were too short, and I tugged at the tunic as it chafed at my neck and wrists. But the discomfort was appropriate. A reminder of the misguided heroics I was about to attempt.

I drew up the hood of my simple traveling cloak and left without another glance in the mirror, worried my reflection might try to dissuade me if I gave it any more consideration. Aevra Nightwind dissolved, and only a forgettable face remained, one that would blur into the background of the King's endless parade of the overlooked.

I'm sorry, Torian, I thought as I slunk through the service corridors, bringing the sea glass to my lips in apology. I was going to let him wait for me again on that empty bench, with honey cakes in his jacket and a string of promises on his tongue. The thought lodged in my chest like a stake. I ached to join him there, to let his hands and mouth erase my worries, to pretend we were stealing nothing but time.

Your father is not there.

No, he wasn't. But others were. There were children who played in the same streets where I'd skinned my knees; fishermen who sang the same shanties I hummed during my house chores. There was probably a new healer in my cottage who gathered herbs by the light of the full moon. All of them were there, blissfully unaware of the party of Fae preparing to ride.

In my skulking, I found a footman completely dozed outside the kitchens, head lolled against the wall and peaceful snores escaping his open mouth. A satchel hung loosely at his hip, its leather worn soft from years of use. I slipped my hand inside, hoping to find something useful.

Crumbs from yesterday's stale bread lunch, a discarded note—~~Dearest Petr, My love,~~ *Petr, I hope you are well.* ~~I miss the way you~~ *I look forward to your attendance at Solstice. It has been too long.* ~~Far too long. Best, Yours,~~ *Warmly, Merek*—a greased metal comb with missing tines. And then exactly what I needed: orders for assignment to the baggage train.

Sorry, Merek. Enjoy your unexpected day off. Perhaps use it to find an alarm clock. Or a better place to nap.

The eastern courtyard already bustled with controlled chaos. Servants loaded wagons with enough supplies to feed a small army; nobles in ridiculous hunting attire discussed the day's prospects as if they were planning a picnic instead of a conquest. The smell of horses and leather and metal polish might have taken me back a hundred years or more, if their purpose wasn't so grotesque.

I joined the queue of other weary-eyed and pallid servants, clutching my stolen papers as if they were burgled jewels. A harried steward, who looked like he hadn't seen a bed in years, was sloppily marking down names and stamping orders.

"Merek of the Iron Valley." He didn't even look at me. "Third wagon. Provisions."

I fell into sync with the others, mimicking their tired shuffle across the cobblestones, their practiced invisibility in their rounded shoulders. We were a river of brown and gray, flowing around the bright obstacles of nobility without ever quite touching them. I learned the rhythm quickly: eyes down, ears up, efficient but never eager.

I busied myself with securing packs to one of the smaller wagons, running my fingers along the ropes, untying and retying knots, careful to look useful while not actually doing anything memorable.

"You there!"

My heart nearly jolted up my throat and out of my mouth entirely. The Captain of the Guard, Lord Caenan himself, stared directly at me with a look of such disdain that I briefly considered caning myself for the crime of existing.

"Sir?" I kept my voice small, choking, so forgettable that it was carried away with the wind.

"Those provisions go on the third wagon. Not the second." His tone dripped with the particular exhaustion of someone who believed themselves surrounded by idiots. He pointed to a faint marking on the canvas tarp slung over the cart. "Can't you read?"

I can read that you're an ass who gets off on yelling at servants; your boots are new enough to rub blisters on your heels, and you're taking it out on anyone smaller than you. I can read that you're so worried about impressing the King that you forgot to snip the tail stitch on your coat and nicked yourself shaving.

"Forgive me, sir. I was never taught."

He grunted and moved on, hunting for his next victim before the expedition even began. I exhaled slowly, tasting copper where I'd bitten my tongue to keep that monologue from pouring out of my mouth.

The provisions made it to the third wagon, each bag placed with the careful precision of an illiterate servant without a single malicious thought.

The courtyard—and perhaps the entire world—hushed as the palace doors swung open. King Oranth emerged in hunting attire of deep crimson and dazzling gold. Subtlety, it seemed, was reserved for peasants who resorted to hunting for food. Certainly not a king with no such intentions while preparing to embark on a 'hunting' expedition.

He mounted his horse in one beautiful swoop of his leg, the leather of the saddle barely creaking beneath him as he sat. His animal—a dappled Shire colossus—stood perfectly still as the King settled atop him, as if he too understood the consequences of fallibility.

"We ride for the mortal territories," he announced. "Let this hunt bring glory to the Amber Vale!"

Glory. Pillaging was now masked by honor. Definitions of words change when someone else is holding the pen.

The party raised their fists in salute as they mounted their own horses, echoing their King's brutal sentiment.

I kept my head down and hopped in the back of the wagon, drowning in the absurdity of it all. A human woman, forbidden to leave these walls by the King's order, now hiding in his hunting party like the world's most dangerous stowaway.

The wagon lurched as we departed, bumping over the cobblestones and tossing me into crates of apples and cheese. I peeked through a slit in the canvas tarp, watching the procession snake across the valley while the landscape gradually shifted around us.

The eternal sunset gave way to actual honest sunlight. I nearly gasped when I watched our shadows stretch and darken as the sun tracked across the sky. This was a sunset as well, but it was a real one. One that would soon lend itself to true night, where the stars would poke through and the rolling meadows would be lit by the moon.

We hadn't been traveling long before we reached land where magic seemed to loosen its grip on nature. Plants followed seasons instead of whims. Birds sang songs that didn't lull with enchantment. Even the air tasted fresh. Like earth and rain instead of perfume and candy floss. And on the horizon, the Silvermist Bridge, the knife's edge between the realms.

My pulse thudded in my ears as the wagon halted, and the canvas flap was tossed open.

"All servants assemble by company," called a stone-faced guard. The few of us who settled among the crates climbed down from the wagon, giving him a wide berth as we exited. "Documents ready for inspection."

I joined my assigned cluster, reminding myself over and over of my name and clenching my papers in my clammy fist.

I'm Merek. I can't read. I love Petr—not sure if he loves me. Third wagon.

They checked each of us with frightening thoroughness. Their eyes lingered on faces, compared documents to mental inventories, occasionally pulled someone aside for blinking too many times. As the line moved forward, each inspection seemed to take longer than the last. The guards grew more suspicious, their patience becoming razor-thin.

When my turn finally came, the soles of my feet screamed from standing too long in one spot. I presented the documents with hands that miraculously didn't shake, though my palms were slick with sweat.

He examined my papers carefully, eyes flicking furiously between the written orders and my face like there was some life-or-death puzzle to solve.

I'm Merek. I'm Merek.

"Merek?" He said it like an accusation.

"Yes, Your Honor. I mean, yes, sir."

His suspicion crawled over my skin like ants. His gaze lingered on my hood, and for a terrifying moment, I thought he might demand that I lower it.

But then, blessed chaos erupted toward the front of the procession. A massive silver hound broke free of its handler, bounding through the crowd and playfully evading capture.

The hound nipped at haunches, sending the horses dancing sideways into their neighbors, who then bit each other for the offense. Nobles shrieked and cursed as they were tossed from their mounts; servants dove out of the way of flying hooves. Handlers scrambled to contain the beautiful disaster, and I was shooed along dismissively with my hood still drawn.

I climbed back into the wagon and watched the havoc continue from the safety of my apple crate.

When we finally made our way across the Silvermist Bridge, it felt like walking through a dream—or perhaps waking up from one. The mist clung to me like greedy fingers, whispering in my ear, showing me things in the fog so I wouldn't want to leave.

It showed me glimpses of what might have been, what *I* might have been—married to Torian, draped in sunshine instead of shadow, children with his golden hair and stubborn chin, a life measured in decades instead of centuries.

This was a mistake.

I needed to go back.

I needed to shout for the procession to stop so I could run across the bridge back to my love. I bolted to my feet, jostled into crates and other servants as I stepped through the wobbling wagon toward the canvas flap.

I would jump off. I would sprint home.

I threw the flap aside and stood at the edge of the open wagon, bracing myself for the moving exit. *One...two...*

The vision dissolved. We emerged on the mortal side of the bridge, and it felt like a bucket of cold water had been dumped over me. I heard mumbles around the wagon as I took back my place, confused and embarrassed.

"She listened to the mist, poor dear."

"That's how the bridge took my brother, rest his soul."

Yet none of them reached to pull me back. Maybe because

they didn't care, or maybe they wished they could believe the mist too. Tears welled in my eyes, threatening to roll over my eyelashes and streak my disguise. I wiped them away, one after another, until the wagon halted again.

Camp materialized in the same controlled chaos, tents sprouting like mushrooms after rain, servants scurrying between fires. Canvas pavilions larger than modest houses unfurled in the clearing. I helped where needed—setting sausages on a pan here, stocking furs and linens on cots there—all while keeping one ear tilted toward the King's pavilion like a flower following the sun.

"The village lies three hours hence through the valley forest," an advisor said. "Approximately three hundred residents, mostly anglers and farmers."

"Defenses?" the King asked.

"Minimal. A wooden palisade more suited for keeping out wolves than warriors. No organized militia beyond a handful of hunters."

Three hundred people. They discussed three hundred lives like they were checkers on a board.

The King made a satisfied noise that made my teeth gnash. "And our guide?"

"With the Captain, Your Majesty. Receiving final instructions."

"Excellent," said the King. "We enter the Silverwood at dawn. I want everything noted. Potential garrison positions, river access, farmland quality. Survey it all."

"And the villagers?"

"We leave them to their peace. For now."

The casual cruelty of his 'for now' sent a chill shooting down my spine.

"And remind everyone," the King added before allowing the group to disperse, "if anyone finds themselves separated once we have entered the forest, make way immediately back to camp. We will depart for the Vale at first light the following day. And I won't delay for stragglers."

As purple twilight bled across the sky and the camp settled into its evening routines, I saw my chance. It was shift change at the perimeter, that beautiful moment where everyone assumed that someone else was keeping watch.

I'd been assigned water duty for the hounds. The kennels were set at the edge of the clearing, far enough from the main tents that the nobles wouldn't lose rest to their yipping. I hauled two over-flowing buckets of fresh water across the clearing, the weight of them pulling taut my still-tender shoulder.

The hounds pressed against their wire enclosures, tails wagging, mouths watering, eager for attention from anyone willing to give it. Most were typical hunting dogs, greyhounds with their long snouts and lean bodies, perfect for tracking and chasing.

But there, in the corner by herself, sat the silver Anatolian Shepherd who released her ruckus on the bridge. Her coat shimmered in the dying light like moonlight on rippling water. She watched me with eyes that seemed far too knowing for a dog—too uncannily aware.

After filling the troughs and dodging many eager licks and muddy paws, I approached her. She sat perfectly still, save a slight tilt of her head, as I reached through the wire grate and scratched behind her ears. Fur soft as silk, warm as a summer day.

"Thank you for the chaos," I whispered. "You might've saved me."

She leaned into my hand with a soft whiff that sounded almost like an acknowledgment. Then, I could have sworn she *winked*.

When she was satisfied with the scratches, she yawned, turned in three tiny circles, and curled up in the corner, dismissing me.

I looked around for any eyes that might have fallen upon me, and when I found none, I slipped between two supply wagons and dissolved into the wooded shadows.

The Silverwood Forest welcomed me like an old friend, wrapping me in darkness and the smell of soil and pine. My still-aching feet found moss instead of stone, and my lungs filled with air that hadn't been breathed by a hundred nobles first. I paused after ten minutes of careful progress, listening for any signs of pursuit. Nothing but owls holding court in the trees and frogs singing the night's lullabies.

I followed the river downstream, my feet remembering the path that my mind had half-forgotten.

There was a farmhouse nearby, hidden by the sounds of rustling trees and water pouring over rocks. Guilt swelled in my chest like the smoke that billowed from the farmhouse's chimney.

The last time I stood at this threshold, I was determined to find my love. And now, here I stood again—the love I had searched for so recklessly now sat abandoned, while I ran toward the home I had abandoned long before.

I shoved the guilt into a cedar box, locked the lid tightly, and raised my hand to knock.

<h1 style="text-align:center">Chapter Twenty-Two</h1>
Elidra

The eggs were bleeding.

Elidra stood at the kitchen counter, watching crimson pool where golden yolks should have been as the whites turned to ash in the cast-iron skillet.

Three eggs. Three warnings.

She set the last egg back in the basket, careful not to summon a fourth. They did not have a rooster, and numbers like this were never a coincidence when it came to the boundary.

"Tomas," she called with the forced calm that only came from seeing the world crack and learning to whisper around the fractures.

He appeared in the doorway, his gnarled walking stick bearing more of his weight than it had yesterday. The equinox ritual had carved hollows beneath his eyes, stolen strength from his shoulders. But his gaze remained sharp as it tracked from the skillet to the window, where their hens pecked contentedly in the twilight.

"Fourth sign this week," he mumbled.

"Fifth." Tomas's brow sank as Elidra nodded toward the milk jug on the table. This morning, it had curdled into perfect spirals, turning the cream into a spoiled star chart. "No cornbread tonight."

"Blood where there should be gold. Order where there should be chaos."

His fingers found the leather journal where seven generations of Keepers recorded their observations. It had sat on the shelf for decades until the night they found that young woman, and it had been scribbled in nearly every night since.

They moved around each other with routine ease—Elidra disposing of the corrupted eggs while Tomas traced disturbance patterns on his map. Neither acknowledged how his hands trembled, making the lines he drew wobble down the paper like a snaking stream. Nor did they mention how she had started keeping salves within arm's reach of every chair.

"The southern bend?" she asked.

"Still black. Now flowing upstream."

Elidra's breath stalled in her throat. "The last time—"

"Three hundred fifty years ago. Elidra, if this pattern holds, I fear—"

Her teacup shattered without warning. The porcelain dissolved into dust that sparkled with trapped starlight before settling on the table like snow flurries. The tea itself hung suspended in the air, holding the phantom shape of the cup, before splashing down on the wood.

She moved to the window, staring out toward the Silverwood Forest, where they'd found her nearly a month ago. The one she mistook for a star-fallen goddess; the one who had called herself *Myr'Caenith* with such certainty it broke Elidra's heart.

No woman, regardless of station or bloodline, should ever name herself 'dumb bitch' in Eldertongue. That was the moment Elidra decided—this lost soul was coming home with them.

Tomas gave a low, worried hum before beginning the evening attestation. It was a ritual as old as the Keeping itself. Salt circles across the thresholds, symbols that were a promise to the boundaries that someone still watched, still remembered the old laws.

Elidra lit the beacon candle, its flame burning three colors at once: white for the mortal realm, gold for the Faen realm, and purple for the realm between and beyond. Its smoke rose in perfect corkscrews, carrying those promises to wherever such witnesses went.

"The northern meridian carries stress fractures today," Tomas reported to the flame.

"Witnessed," Elidra responded.

"The Cisqa ran backwards three beats after dawn."

"Witnessed."

"Corin, the fisherman, is still missing. Vanished at Miller's Bend."

"Witnessed and mourned."

The flame flickered at the fisherman's name, as if even the boundary recognized the loss of the man who sold them trout every market day for fifteen years. His abandoned nets were found wrapped around something that might've been a footprint, if footprints could be made of shadow and starlight.

"Lyra is on her way."

The name still felt right, still felt like the daughter she'd never have. The price of being Semi-Faen, of carrying eternal youth, was a womb that would never quicken.

"Witnessed," Tomas replied.

Elidra massaged her temple where a headache had been building all day—the kind that blurred her senses when the Sight was trying to show her something she wasn't ready to see—as she pulled another bowl from the cupboard to set a third place around the table.

"And she's changed," she added. "The darkness clings to her like it wants to own her."

"You think she's connected to what's coming?"

"I think she's at the center of it."

Tomas moved toward the hearth, where his latest carving sat half-finished. A woman's face emerged from the koa wood, her features still rough but somehow familiar. He'd been working on it since they dropped Lyra at the bridge, claiming his hands moved without his conscious choice.

"The southern boundary," he said, changing the subject as he reached for his traveling cloak that was draped across the arm of the couch. "I need to check it before—"

"I already did." Elidra's tone was gentle but firm. "You can barely stand, Tomas. The ritual took too much."

"It was necessary."

"I know." She moved to him, resting a hand on his slumped shoulder. "But you poured yourself into the guardian like you could hold the world together with will alone."

She had seen the chaos that night before it even reached their doorstep. Pain lanced through her temples as a courtyard veiled in a glistening sunset clouded her vision. A massive creature of wood and moss reared above a dark-haired woman. Shattered glass flew in all directions. A golden-eyed Fae with flames dancing at his fingertips—

Elidra gasped as the vision released her. "Well," she said dryly, "looks like Lyra found what she was looking for."

A thunderous crash from outside sent them both barreling toward the window. There in the deepening twilight, the Harthorn stumbled through their wheat field, seeking the river. Smoke still rose from its haunches, its antlers bent and broken, trailing burnt ribbons like mourning veils. Each step that it took left charred earth in its wake.

"Mother's mercy," Elidra breathed.

They didn't need to discuss it. Tomas had already grabbed his cloak, while she stuffed her satchel full of herbs and salves, though what use were these against a wounded god?

They found it half-submerged in the Cisqa, the water steaming where it touched its burning bark skin. Its breath came in great, shuddering bellows, making the river run the other way with each exhale.

It was dying.

"Stay back," Tomas warned as he waded into the shallows.

"Tomas, you can't—"

"It's a guardian of the balance! If it dies, the boundary could tear completely."

He approached the creature slowly, hands raised in the universal gesture of peace.

"But you could die as well!"

"I am just a man! There were many like me before, and there will be countless to come after. This creature—" He placed his hands over its smoldering wood, rising beneath his touch with its every fighting breath. "—it needs to live so that the rest of the realms can as well."

Elidra sobbed as she watched her husband work. She wanted to scream at him from the alabaster shore.

He was never *just a man.*

She surrendered her immortality for him. He gave her purpose when she nearly sailed herself to the Duskhold. He built her a life from the ground up and encircled it with a farmhouse. He gave her horses and chickens, and she repaid him with full bowls of stew and rooms full of laughter.

The Harthorn's great eye rolled toward him, and she could see the ancient pain holding depths of sorrow that predated human memory. The bloodline magic flared to life in his hands as he pressed himself against the creature's flank.

But it wasn't enough.

"Anchor me," he called to Elidra without looking back, his voice booming over the surging waters.

"Tomas, no. The cost is—"

"Worth it."

She knew that tone all too well. There was nothing more to say. Nothing to argue. She waded through the coursing flow of the river and placed both hands on his shoulders. She dug her feet into the rock bed, the current yanking her dress downstream. She grounded him to this realm as he did what Keepers were rarely asked to do: restore balance rather than observe it.

Her fingers knitted into the fabric of his tunic, knuckles locking and knees trembling. Her forehead met the nape of his neck as she held onto him, counting her breaths until it was over, counting his heartbeats and praying they didn't stop.

The working was beautiful and terrible. Tomas's life force flowed into the Harthorn like a golden thread, weaving through the burns, knitting bark back together, cooling the divine fire that still ate through its core.

He diminished with each breath, giving away years—years that belonged to both of them—to preserve the guardian that had tried to stamp out the only other light she had found by this river.

The Harthorn shuddered, steam rising in monstrous clouds as its temperature finally—*finally*—stabilized. It lifted its head, water cascading from its antlers like a waterfall, and looked at Tomas with what could only be described as recognition.

It snorted once, stood with careful dignity despite its now healing wounds, then walked deeper into the river toward the western shore. It disappeared into the darkness between the trees, and Tomas collapsed.

"Stubborn fool," Elidra muttered angrily through her tears as she hauled him from the water. He was lighter than he should have been, as if the ritual had hollowed him out and left nothing but bones and grief. "Stubborn, selfless fool."

That was two days ago. Two days of Tomas moving like a man made of spun glass. Two days of Elidra rushing into silence around the house. Two days of her pretending not to notice each new line that appeared around his eyes, each silver hair that sprouted at his temples.

She helped him to his chair by the hearth, trying not to think about how many years he'd given up. Keepers lived longer than most, but not infinitely. She would live and die as he did, and she hoped it wasn't soon.

The beacon candle flared again as shadows gathered unnaturally at the edge of the woods. Another flash of Sight barreled past Elidra's mental barriers—lightning, two figures pushing and pulling against each other in a pulse of starlight. And beneath it, patient as stone, something vast and dark turned its attention toward their small farmhouse.

"Whatever she's becoming," Elidra said as she headed for the door, "she's bringing it with her."

"Then we will face it as we always do," Tomas replied, his voice threadbare with exhaustion. "With witness and welcome."

She looked back at him once, seeing him as he truly was now—diminished, but never broken, worn but always willing to stand witness. He nodded in quiet reflection. Whatever came next, whatever price the balance demanded, they had already paid part of it. The rest could come due soon enough.

"Well," Elidra said as she opened the door before the knock even landed against the wood, her voice warm despite everything, "you're just in time for supper."

CHAPTER TWENTY-THREE

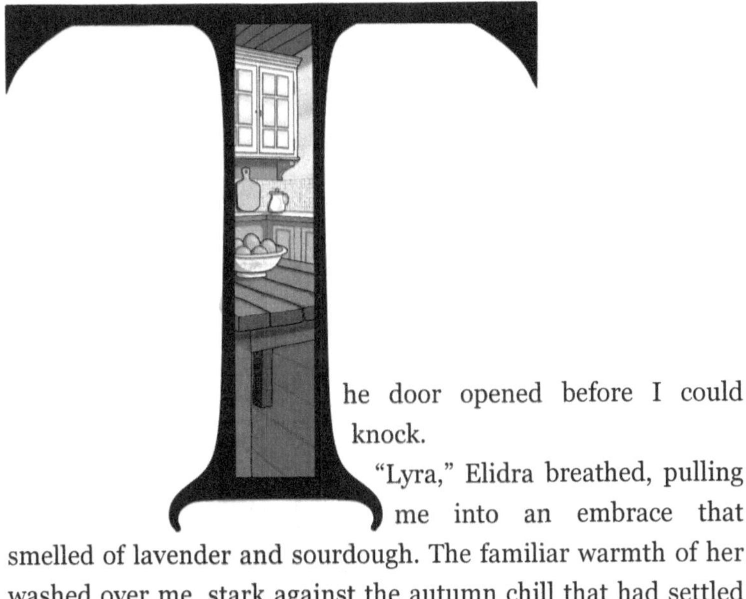

he door opened before I could knock.

"Lyra," Elidra breathed, pulling me into an embrace that smelled of lavender and sourdough. The familiar warmth of her washed over me, stark against the autumn chill that had settled into my bones during the journey from the King's camp.

"My real name is Aevra," I said into her shoulder, the words catching in my throat before they were muffled by the spun wool of her sweater.

She pulled back, her hand finding my cheek as she briefly pressed her forehead to mine.

"Aevra," she repeated, testing the name I had clawed to reclaim. A shadow of something flickered across her face as her thumb traced the curve of my cheekbone. Not surprise, but a bittersweet recognition. "That's a beautiful name."

I placed my hand over hers where it rested against my face. "But I'd very much like it if you always called me Lyra."

Her eyes brightened with unshed tears as she squeezed my face gently before pulling me past the threshold.

"Come in before you freeze."

The farmhouse hadn't changed from my memory. The same herbs hung from the rafters, the same symbols circled the doorframe, though more had been carved since I left. Tomas sat by the hearth, a blanket spread across his lap, and a map open on the table in front of him. His arms trembled with the effort as he rose from his chair to greet me.

"Your transformation has progressed," he observed, gesturing to the faint luminescence beneath my skin that the caked ochre powder couldn't quite hide. "The starlight burns brighter."

"Is that bad?"

"Not bad," Elidra said as she ladled chunks of stew into the bowls set at the table. "Just... significant."

She fingered the dampening pendant from beneath my scratchy tunic, the chain catching and tinkling against the sea glass.

"Keep this on *always*. Without it, you might just burst into celestial light."

I knew it was only half of a joke. I didn't need to tell her I slept in it, bathed in it, rolled around with the prince in it.

"So, tell us what's happened," Tomas encouraged, though the way he leaned forward on his elbows as he blew the steam from his stew suggested he already suspected parts of it.

I gave a half-hearted chuckle. It had been barely a month, and I felt like I owed them a lifetime of conversation on the topic.

"I don't even know where to start," I admitted, swirling my spoon through the chunky contents in my bowl.

"Start at the beginning. From the moment you hopped out of our cart and your boots hit the bridge."

For the second time today, I recounted my incredible story, albeit rather wearily. The words dried me up, and my voice rasped and faded halfway through. It was nearly just as exhausting retelling it as it was living it in the first place, but I added a bit more flourish this time than I did before.

Telling Lysara felt like confessing a crime, but telling Elidra and Tomas—the closest thing I had to a set of parents after mine had long since met the Mother—felt like reciting a fairytale. Banality be damned.

When I reached the part of my story where I was pulled through the rip on Mabon, I felt an eerie sense of déjà vu when the look on Elidra's face was picture-for-picture the same as Lysara's. Tomas straightened so sharply I worried he might jolt himself out of his seat.

"You were pulled back? And you escaped *again*?"

"Not willingly," I said, my voice smaller than I intended. "One moment, I was in the Saffron Fields with—" I paused, heat suddenly rising in my cheeks as Elidra raised a single eyebrow. "with Prince Torian, and the next, darkness. And Alezae—"

"Alezae *herself*?" Elidra all but shrieked, fingers forming a protective gesture that touched her forehead, lips, and chest.

I nodded, but the thought of continuing that part of the tale made me queasy. The two exchanged one of those maddening, meaningful glances, the kind that held entire conversations in an otherwise silent room.

"And was this before or after your encounter with the Harthorn?" Tomas asked dryly, somehow finding the strength and agility to dodge an incoming elbow jab from Elidra.

The nausea rose again, and I pinched the bridge of my nose to will it away.

"Before. How did you know?"

"Elidra's Sight showed it to her. And I—" Tomas choked on the words as his wife's hand found his, and squeezed with another silent exchange.

A warning, a request. I couldn't quite figure it out, but I knew it had to do with his sudden frailty, the kind that doesn't happen over the course of a few weeks.

"What matters is that you are here, and you are safe," she said tenderly, beaming as she elusively changed the subject away from Mabon. "But if you have found your happiness, why have you come back? And in disguise, no less?"

That hilarious, infuriating eyebrow raised at me again. I suddenly felt too itchy in my cheaply woven clothes, claustrophobic beneath the pounds of makeup.

"I have questions."

"As fate would have it, so do we."

"You first," I said, bringing the first bite of cooled stew to my mouth.

I had forgotten how different a simple, home-cooked meal tasted compared to the constant extravagance plated in the palace. Even a sliced apple in the middle of the night was presented on a platinum saucer with a gold-leaf garnish. Nothing existed in the Amber Vale quite like a hearty lamb stew in a hand-carved wooden bowl.

Elidra rose from the table and crossed to a shelf lined with leather journals that looked older than the house itself. She pulled one delicately from its spot, its binding water-stained and warped, and dropped it on the table with a thud that made my spoon clatter. Tomas opened to a page covered in cramped handwriting, then traced a finger down a list of names.

"Corin Seawright of Mistwater. Fisherman. His wife reported him missing a few days before the equinox. Said he went to check his nets and didn't come home."

My stomach churned at the thought of him—the terrified mortal, blood streaming from his broken nose, begging to be sent home to his wife.

"I saw him." The sound of bone crunching, the blow to the back of his head that made him go limp. "But... the guards... it's protocol to escort them over the bridge after they've been questioned—"

I recognized the sheer stupidity of my words as soon as they'd left my mouth. How naïve must I have looked to these wise, old Keepers as my thought trailed off like a fart on the wind?

Tomas snorted, a bitter sound that held no humor, then slammed his fist on the table. "*Protocol.* So he will either wash up on the shores of the Cisqa in a week or two once his body floats, or the King made a copper and sent him to the Duskhold."

I pushed my bowl away, appetite gone.

"When I get back, I can try to find out—"

"There's nothing to *find out*, Lyra," he interrupted, pressing his thumbs against the corners of his eyes. "The stories exist to warn about getting too close to the boundary. Those bloodthirsty—" He stopped before he said too much, Elidra's hand traveling to his back and making soothing circles. "I'm sorry," he mumbled.

The silence grew damn near suffocating, so heavy it muted the crackle of the fire in the hearth. The weight of that obvious lie I had so easily swallowed now choked me, and I wondered what else I—and the rest of the court—had been so gullible to believe.

The so-called protocol, the prince's diplomatic mission, *my* head rolling from my shoulders. All lies. But maybe this journal harbored a useful crumb in one of those mysteries.

"This book," I said meekly, gesturing to the journal between us. "Does it have a record of everyone who disappears?"

"Yes," Elidra confirmed gravely. "It is our duty to maintain the boundary and document what crosses it. And what doesn't cross back."

I tried to keep my tone casual despite my racing heart. "What about a hundred years ago? Was there... were there any women who went missing? Young women?"

Elidra flipped through the yellowed pages, squinting at the faded ink and turning the book sideways. "A few. Why?"

"While I was being sold at the shadow market, someone else died in my place."

Neither of them said anything, just slid the open journal across the table for me to read, a slender red ribbon marking its place like a death flag.

I couldn't suppress the wince as I read:

> *Maria Fenwick, age thirty-two, disappeared while gathering mushrooms in the Silverwood Forest. Body recovered; drowned during the flash flood.*
>
> *Silvania Murkwood, age eighteen, vanished from the barn while milking cows. Body recovered; mauled by wolves.*
>
> *Isa Cordwell, age twenty, last seen with her fiancé leaving Milo's Tavern. Body recovered; found on the neighbor's farm, naked and stabbed.*
>
> *Gracie Taylor, age five...*

I had to stop. She wasn't here. All these poor women still had their heads.

I huffed in frustration before skimming the names one last time, my curiosity getting the better of me. *Josephine, Caroline,*

Mynda... but no *Aevra Nightwind, age twenty, vanished harvesting herbs along the Cisqa.*

My father never reported me missing.

The thought clanged painfully around in my skull. My meticulous father, who insisted on precision in all things, who had a list for everything—even a list for all the lists he intended to write—never reported his only daughter's disappearance?

Something must have happened to him as soon as I'd been taken—a heart attack, a robbery, a *fever*—and it was my own fault that I wasn't there to stop it. That was the only explanation, and I refused to believe the alternative: I simply wasn't worth the trouble to find.

I forced myself to take another bite of stew, though it felt like chewing sawdust.

"How long do you intend to stay?" Elidra asked gently as she slipped the journal from me, mercifully changing the subject. "Perhaps you could accompany me to notify Corin's widow. Though I know you have to get back to your prince."

She added a playful wink that didn't quite mask her concern. Leave it to Elidra to use the word 'widow' as well as a wink in the same breath without missing a beat. There was nothing I could think of that I would loathe more in this moment.

"Just tonight," I said. "I need to travel to Mistwater tomorrow."

"Whatever for?" Tomas asked.

"To warn them. The King is planning an expansion. They need to know—"

"No," he said firmly. "That would cause far more harm than good."

"But they deserve to know what's coming!"

"And what would you have them do with that knowledge?" Elidra asked. "March on the Amber Vale with their pitchforks? Demand sovereignty from beings who would kill them without a thought?"

"They'd be slaughtered at the bridge," Tomas added. "The Fae would see it as an act of war."

I wanted so badly to argue. I'd already lost my father, my identity, and my peaceful life in a quiet village. And now that village was going to be razed by the place I had chosen over it.

But that guilt couldn't erase the nauseating image of fishermen and farmers standing against Fae warriors. No matter the innovative weaponry they possessed, no matter their rusted steel might withstand their flames... their flesh could not.

"Then what can I do?" My voice felt tight against the swelling walls of my throat as I choked down the rising emotion. How could I possibly be *this helpless* when all I wanted to do was finally be helpful to someone?

"Observe," Elidra counseled. "Learn what you can. Report it back to us."

"Besides," Tomas added as he settled down his spoon with forced calm, "those with ill intentions don't make it through the Silverwood Forest. A party led by the King, with malice and conquest in his heart..." He raised an eyebrow as he weighed the consequences.

"You mean the forest will protect Mistwater?"

"What I mean is the forest has a memory that outlives any kingdom, boundary, or claim of ownership. It keeps its own counsel." He shrugged with the same casualness one might have when discussing the weather. "It scents intent like wolves scent fear."

I had questions—*so many questions*—but before I could even open my mouth to ask, Elidra stood, eyeballing my cracking make-up and scratchy clothes with maternal disapproval.

"You need a bath," she said, sweeping the half-empty bowls clear from the table. "You look like you were dressed by someone who hates you and then kicked around in the dirt."

Ouch. True, but *ouch.* I sighed but did not argue.

I followed her silently through the house, watching her gather towels and oils, fretting over which one was softest, which scent would be best for my current mood. She muttered under her breath as she toiled with herself over it.

"Obviously some lavender. Well, tea tree might be better. It would certainly help with the smell." *Ouch, again.* "Some lemongrass would do nicely. Cedarwood to help her sleep."

Elidra dumped them all in the tub, their scents curling in the steam and making me dizzy. She swirled the water into a gentle whirlpool, and a bracelet dangling from her wrist like a pendulum caught my eye. Pebbles of onyx and bits of volcanic glass were woven together with fine silver wire, catching the lamplight and casting luminous freckles on the walls.

"That's beautiful," I said, unable to take my eyes off of it.

She glanced at it dismissively as she shook drips of water from her hand and straightened the folded towel that sat on the edge of the sink. "A merchant traded it for safe passage last week."

She slipped it off and held it up to the light, turning it slowly as if she hadn't admired it once before I mentioned it. The herbal aroma that smothered the bathroom shifted for a moment, and I smelled salty air and spicy pineapple.

Without a word, she pressed the bracelet into my palm, then gently closed my fingers around it. "A homecoming gift. It suits you better anyway," she said with a wink.

The bracelet was warm in my hand, but not from the warmth of Elidra's skin. It felt *alive*, like it had been freshly fired in a kiln and I was the first one brave enough to pick it up.

I slipped it on, and it molded and shrank to the form of my wrist, as if there were a tiny silversmith inside, settling there comfortably like it had always belonged. The warmth reminded me of how my sea glass used to feel, back when it had memories to chase and a mission to fulfill. Now it hung cold and quiet against my chest, dulled to nearly nothing so that I regularly forgot that it was even there.

"Thank you," I whispered.

"Go on," she said, shooing me toward the bath. "Scrub off whoever you're pretending to be. Lyra's waiting underneath."

So I did.

I drowned the thoughts of names in journals and fathers who didn't search for their daughters. Of forests that were judge and jury and kings who treat souls as currency. Of everything that wasn't the warmth of the water on my skin and the glass on my wrist.

Tomorrow, those thoughts would come flooding back.

But tonight, I was just Lyra.

Chapter Twenty-Four

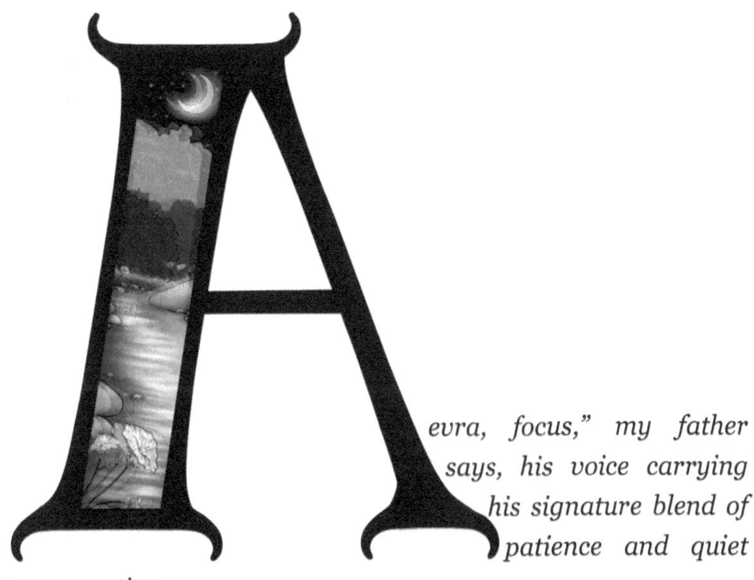

"Aevra, focus," my father says, his voice carrying his signature blend of patience and quiet exasperation.

Twilight bleeds lavender across the sky, and the first stars peek through, watching us harvest tonight's rivergourd blooms. A fever has been tearing through the town, and my father's tolerance for my wandering thoughts is growing perilously thin.

"These blossoms must be clipped just as the sun dips, else the *salve is nothing more than an acne cream."*

I nod, trying to concentrate on selecting the fully opened flowers, but my eyes keep drifting to the forest's edge, searching for any glimpse of movement among the rustling shadows.

My fingers tremble as they slide over a stem. My father snatches the flower from my hand just as I clip it.

"Your mind is elsewhere again," he observes as he throws it carelessly over his shoulder, the river carrying it slowly downstream. "Females only. Do you need a refresher on their anatomy?"

I swallow, shaking my head in embarrassment and trying to clear the lovesick fog that has descended so thickly.

I almost want to argue that I can gather the blooms alone, but I know better. This evening ritual isn't a chore, it's a sacred time between father and daughter—where knowledge is passed between us like inherited memory, and nothing comes between us save the lapping of water on the shore and the silence of words he chooses not to say.

"I'm sorry," I murmur, forcing together the pieces of my fractured attention as I inspect another bloom. Swollen base, no powdery filaments: female. I clip it, laying it in the basket with forced reverence. "The constant preparations for the sickness have been distracting."

"Death does not get distracted." He doesn't look up, his weathered hands continuing their careful work. "You and I are the only ones who stand in its way."

My heart stutters with guilt. He softens—just barely—and puts his shears in his pocket as he brushes a stray curl from my forehead. I open my mouth to apologize again, but a rustling at the tree line snaps my attention away again. The shadows shift; the breeze picks up. Just a sigh from the Silverwood. My father tuts his tongue at me.

"Don't stare too long into the darkness, Aevra," he cautions.

"She might catch you looking and want you for herself."

A chill feathers up my spine, prickling my scalp and standing the hairs on my neck on end.

"She?"

The snap of twigs, the familiar weight of footsteps through a bed of leaves. My stomach jumps with bright, girlish hope. Torian. It must be Torian. Oh, how I've missed him! A smile is already forming across my lips, excitement burying all logic.

But the movement I see is wrong.

No loving Fae steps toward me. No boots, or breath, or warmth.

The shadows ripple and billow like smoke rising from the earth, stretching and swelling until the forest tilts around them. They gather themselves like a creature waking, like a robe of night drawn over a pale corpse.

I turn away from it, hoping it is just another trick of the forest. My father is standing, heels crunching against the alabaster pebbles of the riverbed as the current picks up behind him. His breath leaves him in a long, weary sigh.

"I told you so," he says, though not unkindly. Just absently. The twinkle in his eye snuffs, and he takes a step back, water soaking the hem of his trousers.

"Papa?" I choke, the word scraping my throat. "What are you—"

He keeps moving backward, one step after another, dead eyes locked on mine. The river swallows his ankles. His calves. His knees. The current pulls at him like needy fingers, urging him deeper.

"Papa, stop! Stop this!"

I reach toward him, but my arm feels like lead, disconnected from my will. He doesn't stop. He doesn't even blink as the water climbs up his waist, his chest, his shoulders.

"I told you so," he repeats, the words—his very voice—sound-

ing older than us both, before water fills his mouth with a gurgle, then closes over his head.

A cold hand slides around my throat as I watch my father disappear with the rushing river. Slender fingers with sharpened nails dig into the clammy skin of my neck, curling around my hammering pulse. An emaciated body presses against me from behind, bony hips spearing into my back.

"He didn't look for you." The insincere pity in her voice is sickeningly warm against my cheek as a pair of cracked lips grazes the shell of my ear. "But I always will."

Tears pour from my eyes as I twist in her grasp, desperate to pull my father from the now raging water.

"Papa!" My scream shreds the fabric of reality, tearing open the veil and allowing more shadows to slither forth. They circle me, entwining around my ankles, my wrists, binding me helplessly in place.

"He's gone, silly girl. I am all you have left now."

I try to grab her wrist, pry her fingers from my neck, but she isn't solid. Her grip has the consistency of steaming bubbles from a hot bath, and yet it still tightens. Blood trickles down as her nails break through my skin.

"You are my treasure. My possession. Come home to me, my love."

"No!" I manage with a rasp. Air is harder to take in; my brain fogs with unmet need.

The trees quake as she laughs—that terrible, omnipotent laugh—dropping their leaves in fear. Even the enchantments of the Silverwood cannot withstand Alezae. Her other hand reaches my throat, and she squeezes my windpipe shut. Blood vessels burst behind my eyes; my tongue bulges out of my mouth involuntarily; vertebrae crack and crumble.

"As if you ever had a choice."

I gasped awake, still unable to breathe after ripping myself out of the nightmare. My own shadows were strangling me. Slick, hungry tendrils coiled around my neck, wrists, and ankles, like they were trying to finish what the dream had started.

I thrashed against them, kicking and bucking, screaming but making no sound. Tears continued pouring as I begged for air, trying to reason with the traitorous darkness to release me. But it tightened around my throat, binding me to the mattress and turning the four-poster bed into a torture rack.

I cannot die, I thought desperately. *Please, she won't let me.*

The bedroom door crashed open, wood splintering as it slammed into the wall. I jolted, eyes snapping open, lungs sucking in sweet air as if I'd been pulled from the bottom of the Cisqa. The dream shattered around me like glass dropped from a great height, and the throttling shadows gathered at the foot of the bed, quivering like ashamed penitents. But I still felt restrained, still felt the tightness around my neck.

The bedsheets had tangled themselves around my limbs, my own terrified thrashing knotting me into a makeshift straitjacket. My necklaces were pulled taut enough to bruise, twisting into a delicate noose.

To my relief, my shadows hadn't betrayed me this time.

Elidra stood in the doorway, eyes wild, wielding a spatula like a halberd. Her ears were pricked so sharply that they nearly pointed at the ceiling. Her gaze landed on me, my limbs pathetically snarled in the sheets, hair matted to my tear-stricken face. She let out a noise of tender annoyance.

"Oh, Mother's mercy—hold still!"

She marched to my bedside, shooing away the shadelings with a wave of her spatula, sending them skittering into the corners and up the walls. Her fingers flew to my throat, deftly working the twisted chains loose while her other hand yanked the knotted sheet, nearly careening me off the bed.

Once I was free, I coughed so hard my chest burned.

"You nearly gave me a heart attack with all that crying and screaming," she scolded, combing my sticky curls from my cheek with her fingers. "I am far too young and beautiful to die of fright."

○ ◑ ◕ ● ◕ ◐ ○

The path to Mistwater carved itself through a countryside I had once known like my own heartbeat. A favorite song, now half-forgotten. Each turn was a flint strike to my memory—the lightning-splintered oak where I hid during childhood games, the meadow where I gathered wild lavender, the stream where I caught silver minnows with my bare hands. A lifetime had passed, but the bones of this sacred landscape remained eternal as stone.

The village appeared as the path crested a small rise, and my breath caught like a tittering bird in my throat.

Mistwater had grown. Where once only the wooden palisade marked its edge, now buildings stretched beyond in neat rows. The fields of farmland spread farther, tamed and geometric where the wilderness once ruled. But smoke still rose from the same chimneys, the docks still creaked over the Western Sea, and the ancient bald cypress trees still stood on their stilts in the bay.

I pulled my hood forward, ensuring my transformed features were adequately shrouded. It wasn't the ratty old cloak I had found in my wardrobe back at the palace. This one was emerald green, made from the softest velvet in Avynne, according to Elidra, with an uncut onyx set in the solid gold clasp. I had tried my best to refuse it, stating I didn't want to draw attention with such finery once I made my way back to the hunting party.

"Sweet Lyra," she had reassured me, patting my cheek. "The King wouldn't notice a servant even if she set his trousers on fire and slapped him with a trout."

I didn't find out until later that she had tossed the original in the fire after swiping it off the bathroom floor while I dozed in the tub.

"And it matches your bracelet!" She admired the delicate string of volcanic glass, twirling it around my wrist with a giddy, somewhat mischievous grin. I wanted to ask if the cloak had come from the same merchant, but I did not have time to open a door for one of her worldly tales.

I nearly regretted refusing Elidra's company, but I needed to make the journey on my own. No maternal security blanket, no side quests of notifying a woman that she was now a widow. Just me and the town that wouldn't recognize me—the girl who was never missing.

Never missed.

My feet felt heavy with that truth as I dragged them the rest of the way, trying not to resent the very road for allowing my name to disappear from its memory.

The gates stood open for market day, farmers and merchants streaming through with carts of produce and baskets of eggs and herbs. I joined the flow, just another weary traveler seeking supplies and shelter, devouring every new detail of my long-lost home —the gravel paths now paved with smooth cobbles, stalls and kiosks manned by smiling faces, and the community well that was replaced by an elaborate fountain.

The fountain struck me cold.

It rose from the center of the square like a holy monument, water cascading in sheets over faces carved in stone. Each face had eyes made of birthstones, and the trickling water fell like tears. Some were crying with joy, some with pain, some with grief. Around its base, names spiraled in deep-cut letters—those taken by the great fever, whose bodies had been burned, leaving nothing behind but an inch of themselves etched in stone. But there, larger than all the others, carved with such prominence it made my knees weak:

Thaddeus Nightwind—He Saved Us All

I traced my fingertips over his name. My father had become a legend while I rotted in the Duskhold. He'd been exalted as a hero while I forgot his face in the twilight between worlds. My stomach twisted with something I couldn't quite name. The closest word I could find was simply *hurt*.

"Beautiful, isn't it?"

I spun to find a woman watching me from a few feet away. She was middle-aged, bits of silver shimmering through her dark plait. Her hands bore the telltale stains of an herbalist, green-tinged nail beds and small nicks from a harvesting knife.

"Yes," I managed.

"Though some say it's too grand for a village like ours." She smiled with a warmth that lacked pity, knowledge without intrusion. I attempted to return it, but my face wouldn't cooperate past a wince. "We rarely get many travelers on market days. I'm Molly. I run the apothecary now."

Now. The word landed on top of me like a cliff face crumbling into the sea.

"There's an apothecary here?" Of course, there was. And I was already certain of its whereabouts.

"Aye, need something for that sniffle?" she asked, then nodded her head toward the eastern edge of the village, where my cottage sat removed from the town bustle. "I've got a fresh batch of elderflower syrup brewing."

I swiped my sleeve under my nose, not realizing it had been running like a faucet from the tears I refused to let fall.

"I have little money." A half-truth. I had enough to jingle in my pocket, but not enough to spend on a reduction of berries that I could easily make myself. Though I might have been willing to pay admission to enter my childhood home.

Her sunny smile didn't falter. "Nae bother. I rather prefer company over coin in any case."

I should have said no. I should have made an excuse about

'just passing through' and continued lurking through the market, then up to the cemetery. But the pull was too strong. I needed to see what had become of the space where I'd learned to heal, where my father had taught me that medicine began in the soil and ended in the soul.

We strolled together through streets that followed old patterns but wore fresh faces. The smithy rang with younger hands, boys who could barely grow a few chin hairs, wearing leather aprons and soot-stained cheeks. The bakery expanded, swallowing the cobbler's shop to make room for a patisserie.

The wafting scent of burnt sugar and cream cheese icing made me long for that bench tryst I was surely missing right this moment. I tried to shake the thought of a disappointed Torian from my already clouded mind.

And everywhere, signs of the prosperity that my father had helped preserve—healthy children swinging in doorways, elderly folks sitting in rocking chairs on porches, young mothers cooing at their swaddled babes. All of them waved and whistled without a care in the world.

Despite the splendor of the Amber Vale, it could never deliver *this*.

"You knew him," I said, more of a probe than a statement. "The healer."

"Thaddeus? Oh, yes." Molly's voice softened as she chuckled at a memory. "When I was a girl, I pestered him every day for him to train me, and he always shooed me away at his door. Said I might have the hands, but not the patience."

I huffed under my breath. I don't know how many times he had said that to me whenever my mind wandered.

"Sounds like a stubborn old man."

"As stubborn as they come!" She laughed, bright as water trickling over stones. "One morning, when I was thirteen, he gave me an errand to get me off his doorstep. He loaded me down with countless bits of dried herbs and stalks, then told me to sort them, bushel them, and deliver them around town. And if I made it back by noon, he'd let me in."

I remembered that trick of his. I had been set on the same tedious chore multiple times, just so he could take a nap in peace.

"And?"

"And I returned with half an hour to spare. True to his word, for six years he taught me everything from composting up. 'Start with the earth,' he'd say. 'Everything else will follow.'"

My gut twisted. I heard it in his voice—not Molly's. I held back more tears.

The apothecary appeared at the end of the lane, solid stone and timber where rambling wood and daub once stood. It was practical, sturdy, and nothing like the crooked-chimneyed cottage where I'd spent twenty years growing and playing.

"May I come inside?" I asked, feeling suddenly childlike, my voice barely above a whisper.

"Of course!"

She produced a key from her dress pocket and unlocked the bolt, the door swinging inward without so much as a creak.

It smelled like home—the ineffable scent of healing that was beeswax, menthol, and patchouli.

But everything else was wrong.

Where our scarred wooden table had stood, there were now gleaming cases with shelved bottles. The back room where I had slept was now a consultation room. And worse, the room where my father had slept was now storage, a glorified pantry where marked jars were stacked to the ceiling. Even the hearth had been repurposed into a miniature library, books and journals snugly aligned where logs and fire used to blaze. How ironic.

I moved through the cottage like a phantom haunting her own past. My fingertips found the doorframe where he had carved my height each birthday—now a smooth plaster archway; the east-facing window where my mother's ghost had lingered in morning light—now faced with practical shelves housing essential oils.

"He taught you well." I noted the precise organization, the careful labels—all evidence of a methodical mind trying to make sense of the calamitous calling of healing.

"Everything I know came from him." Molly moved to the stove, removing the pot of elderberry syrup from the burner as she stirred it slowly. "Though he never officially made me his apprentice. That title died along with his daughter. And part of himself as well."

The knife in my stomach twisted deeper.

"What happened to them? The healer and his daughter?"

Molly shrugged as she slid a mug from the cupboard, ceramic singing against wood. She measured perfect spoonfuls of rose hip and spearmint, poured steaming water from the screeching kettle, then drizzled the elderberry syrup from a sticky honey wand. My eyes rolled back as I took the tea from her, the heavenly smell warming me from the inside.

"Thaddeus died thirty years ago after a lifetime and a half, if you can believe it. He attributed his longevity to the salty sea air and that concoction you're sipping."

"And his daughter?"

She hesitated as the kettle gave its final, dying hiss behind her.

"Well," she began, leaning her hip against the counter, "depends on who you ask. Every tale is taller than the last."

"What do *you* believe?"

Molly's shoulders lifted in a weak shrug as she blew on her tea.

"Oh, I put little stock in stories older than their tellers." Her tone remained kind, almost apologetic in its honesty. "But if you're curious about the tale that Thaddeus passed around the tavern—" She inclined her head toward the window, where a pub stood just across the road. "Willem can give you the unabridged version."

I nodded my thanks and tipped back the remaining tea from my mug. Before I stepped out the door, Molly clicked her tongue and plucked a sprig of dried rosemary from a bundle tied over the workbench.

"Here," she said, tucking it into the fold of my cloak as if she had been doing that to me my whole life. "For courage. Not that you'll need it, if all you're after is a spittle-soaked story from an old drunk." She eyed me over the rim of her cup. "The dead only stay as gone as we let them."

Chapter Twenty-Five

The wind whipped at me, carrying a salt-bitten chill from over the sea. It nagged at me like an overbearing aunt, pushing with sharp elbows toward the heavy oak door that I hesitated to open.

How many times had my father walked across this threshold? How many versions of me had been told within this dilapidated pub?

The tavern slouched against the cobblestone street just as it had the day I was born. Uneven stone walls, stubborn leaning supports. The shape of it had always reminded me of a softening pumpkin, melting into the ground as the season turned. Through the warped glass windows, soft light spilled into the overcast afternoon, and I could already smell what waited inside—pipe tobacco and spilled ale, roasted chestnuts and eel pie. Its sign thrashed on a rusty bracket, hinges screeching each time the gusts swung it against the wall.

The Wet Hen.

After all this time, they couldn't come up with a better name.

Lifetimes ago, a gale had picked up over the water and slammed into the town in a raging storm. The sea rose into the streets; roofs snatched from cottages careened on the wind. Livestock crashed through their pens and trampled the sodden graves on Cemetery Hill.

A wicker basket came bobbing down Market Street, spinning in the floodwater like a top. A soaked hen burst from its mouth, ruffled and furious. She let out a single, indignant squawk. At the same moment, thunder rolled so heavily that it shook the windows. And then, as if the hen herself had bullied the sky into submission, the storm broke.

The clouds tore themselves open, and the sea withdrew from the town just before a dozen homes were nearly lost to the briny deep. That chicken lived for an impressive fifteen more years, untouched by fox or fever, and no hurricane darkened Mistwater while she reigned.

I braced myself to endure the telling of that legend before I could hear my own. Though I was thankful that she was memorialized by a tavern instead of a temple, blessed be. I wasn't sure if I could survive hearing my own legend. Not when I already knew part would be wrong and part would be heartbreaking.

I finally pushed through the door, and there she was. Maude herself, immortalized in bronze, sat atop a wicker basket beside the entrance. She stood proudly, tail feathers spread in permanent disgruntlement. Her beak had been rubbed raw by countless superstitious fingers over the years, her bronze worn down to the bright gold beneath. Of course, I touched it as well, though she hadn't blessed me with much luck since I last graced this place over a century ago.

"Cider, please," I said weakly as I slid onto a stool at the mostly empty bar.

"That all?" The barkeep, Willem, looked carved from the same ancient wood and stone of the pub—weathered and sturdy. Laugh lines and worry lines mapped his face in equal measure, and his rheumy eyes were sharp from a life full of listening to every kind of drunk, from celebratory to sorrowful.

"I'm looking to hear a story, and I heard you tell it best."

He slid the mug over to me, the liquid sloshing onto the scratched mahogany of the bar.

"Aye, the next telling of Maudie isn't until this evening. Have to sell tickets for it and all that now."

I shook my head as I took a swig of my cider, the tartness making my cheeks burn. The pain was grounding, keeping the panic and the nausea from rising.

"I want to know about the hero healer whose name is on the fountain. Thaddeus Nightwind."

The transformation in his face was immediate, like watching ice thaw under a spring sun.

"Now there's a name that deserves to charge admission!" He said as he slapped the bar. "I had the honor of serving Thaddeus his evening brandy for the last ten years of his life. Once he hit his hundredth birthday, I watched that door and wondered if it wouldn't open, if the Mother had finally taken him overnight. One hundred and ten in a village where we are lucky to see seventy."

"Impressive." I took another sip, my voice staying steady by sheer force of will. My father's name in this stranger's mouth— spoken with pride and admiration instead of mourning and regret—should have soothed me. It did not. It splintered me even further.

"Impressive indeed." Willem set down his polishing cloth. "My grandmother—gods rest her—she had the fever as a girl. Seven years old, burning so hot that her hair fell out in clumps. They'd already planned her burial, had the carpenter measuring for a child's box.

A group of men at the corner table had gone quiet, their game of dominoes abandoned as they listened in reverence. A woman who sat by the fire had paused in her knitting. Everyone knew this story. Everyone waited for a stranger to come in asking for it. They all owed something to it.

"Thaddeus walked through their door, the best healer this coast had ever seen. He took one look at my grandmother—this little slip of a thing—and rolled up his sleeves. For three days and nights, he didn't leave her side. Didn't sleep, barely ate except for whatever his daughter forced him to."

The memory of it sparked. The girl was seven, but looked five. Her blonde corkscrew curls were sparse and plastered to her mottled forehead. I couldn't stand being in that house with my father while he cared for her. I refused to watch a little one die, to watch my father fail to save her. Instead, I stayed in our cottage and prepared poultices and salves, and brought him bread and cheese when I knew it had been too long since he had eaten. A shiver went through me when I remembered her little gray face.

"He fought the Mother herself with nothing but his mortar and pestle, turning medicine into magic. On the fourth dawn, her fever broke. She opened her eyes and asked for cinnamon grits."

"He saved her," I breathed, taking another burning sip.

"He might as well have raised her from the dead." Willem picked up his polishing cloth again, needing something to do with his hands. "She lived to be eighty-three. Seven children, twenty grandchildren. Every soul descended from her owes their existence to Thaddeus Nightwind's refusal to let death win that day."

The woman by the fire spoke up then, her voice creaky with age. "Saved my Pa too."

"And my wife's grandfather," one of the men in the corner added.

"This entire village, one way or another," Willem agreed. "But that's not why he lived as long as he did."

I leaned forward on my forearms. "Then why?"

Willem's expression shifted to something bittersweet—part wonder, part sorrow. "Love, pure and simple. He was waiting for someone."

For me.

"His daughter, Aevra." The way he said my name—with such familiarity, such fondness—cleaved my chest in two. I gripped my mug to keep my hands from shaking. "Beautiful girl, by all accounts. Hair like night, eyes like a clear sea, quick to laugh and even quicker to help. Had every man in the village composing terrible poetry, though she never noticed."

Oh, but I did notice. I just had the good sense to pretend I didn't after hearing a fisherman's son rhyme "ocean blue" with "eyes like you" seventeen times in a single poem.

"What happened to her?"

Willem settled into his story like an old man settling into a comfortable chair after a hearty meal. "The way Thaddeus told it— and I heard this tale at least once a month for ten years—she fell in love with a Fae prince. Not some passing fancy either, mind you, but the kind of love that reshapes the world around it."

He paused to refill my cider, though I had barely touched it. "One morning, she was just... gone. The dawn came up and shone on an empty bed through the open window."

"Did no one look for her?" I remembered the journal of the missing names, and mine left off of it.

"Look for her? My dear girl, Thaddeus Nightwind would have

torn apart the very fabric of the universe to find his daughter if he thought she was truly lost. He said she went to live with the fair folk across the bridge, in a magic palace where the sun never sets."

But I *was* lost. Lost and abused and nothing more than a husk of the daughter he imagined to be living in the lap of luxury.

"And people believed that?"

"Nobody would believe otherwise because nobody had the heart to break Thaddeus any more than he already was. The man lost his daughter. He didn't need any of us trying to convince him she was dead, or taken by slavers." Willem shook his head. "Though running away to a better life without leaving so much as a note might have stung far worse."

"Surely, if he thought she was still alive, he would have gone looking—"

"Oh, he certainly tried." His voice darkened, and the candles on the wall flickered. "Every year on her birthday—the ninth day of spring—he'd make the journey to the Silvermist Bridge with honey cakes in hand. Asked the guards to let him pass, just for an hour, to wish his daughter a happy birthday.

"For the first few years, they just turned him away. Polite enough, but firm. After the fifth year, they started getting less polite. After the eighth year, they stopped pretending to be civil at all." Willem's jaw tightened as he wrung the polishing cloth in his fists. "The tenth year—her thirtieth birthday—he came back with a black eye and a nose that never did heal straight. That was the last time he tried."

The tavern had gone completely silent. Even the fire seemed to burn quieter.

"After that, he convinced himself she would come home to him in her own time. That one day, when the boundaries thinned just right, his fairy princess daughter would walk through his door. And you know what?" His voice gentled, and a tiny twinkle met his eye. "I think that's why he lived so long. Pure stubbornness. The man refused to die until he'd seen her again."

"But he never did," I whispered, the words like glass in my throat.

"Didn't he, though? His last night—I remember this clear as yesterday—he came in for his usual brandy, sat at the same table by the western window. But he came in *different*." Willem poured himself a small measure of something brown, as if this memory required fortification. "He sat there, staring out at the sunset with this look on his face, as if he saw something beyond it. When closing time came, he didn't move. Just kept staring westward, tears running down his cheeks."

My fingernails dug painful crescents into my palms. My father, the stoic as stone savior, crying in public into his highball. What had I done?

"I asked if he was alright, and he smiled—gods, such a bright smile. Like every good thing he had ever known suddenly made sense. He pointed at the moon and said, 'She's so beautiful, Willem. My little moonflower, all grown up and glowing like starlight itself.'

Moonflower. The pet name hit me like a punch to the gut. I turned away, pretending to study the bottles behind the bar while I fought for composure.

"Then he said—and these were his exact words, and I will never forget them—'Life as a fairy princess must be too glittery to remember your dear old pop. And I'm so happy that you are so happy. I love you, Aevra.'" Willem cleared his throat roughly, and a sniffle carried from the table in the corner. "Those were the last words he spoke. I called Molly to come help him home, worried he'd taken ill. She made him chamomile tea and helped him into bed."

"And?" The word came out strangled.

"She found him the next morning, peaceful as you please. He was holding a little cornhusk doll to his chest, worn down to almost nothing from decades of handling. Molly said he'd kept it by his bedside all those years."

My lungs refused to take in a breath as I remembered that doll. I made it for him when I was eight, carefully braided its corn silk for hair, trying so hard to make it look like my mother. I had given it to him for his birthday—his first birthday without her laughter filling the cottage—so he'd have something to hold when the grief got too heavy.

"He was buried on the hill with it still clutched against his heart. Molly said separating them would be like taking away the last piece of his girls."

I stood abruptly, the stool scraping against the floor, and tossed more than enough coins on the bar to pay my tab. Tears flooded my vision as I blindly fumbled for the iron doorknob.

Without a word, without a look back, without even a flick of Maude's beak, the wayward daughter—the selfish fairy princess—tore out of the Wet Hen and was carried up the road by the nagging wind.

Chapter Twenty-Six

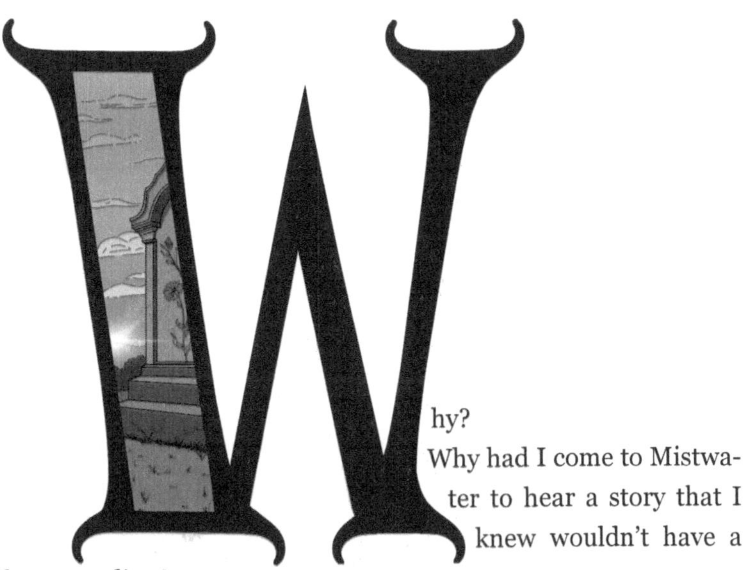

hy? Why had I come to Mistwater to hear a story that I knew wouldn't have a happy ending?

Why hadn't I sought the sea the first time I'd learned about it instead of waiting a hundred years?

Why did it have to be this way?

I cried the self-serving questions into the wind. Tears fell like hard rain, and my voice split the quiet country air with that same desperate, useless word.

Why?

The uphill path was shorter than I remembered, or maybe I was simply too hollow to feel each step. The cemetery sprawled across the eastern hill, covered in stones that marked countless stories that all had begun and ended while I remained suspended in endless dusk.

I read the names like a litany of ghosts.

Here lay Erik Brewster, my childhood companion, who would dare me to steal apples from the mayor's private orchard. My chest tightened when I saw he had died young at the age of twenty-three. I couldn't bear to ask for that story down at the tavern. Erik was my Torian before that name meant anything to me. I had no idea whether he felt the same, but I wasted countless journal pages scrawling our names together in curly letters. I pressed my fingers to my lips, then to the cold stone.

Further along, I passed the elaborate headstone of Mrs. Cordwell, the woman who delighted in catching me picking flowers from her garden and threatened to call the authorities. A hilarious sentiment, considering the volunteer militia wasn't even enough to keep the single palisade manned. She'd lived to ninety-seven—out of pure spite, no doubt. *Of course she did*, I thought in bitter amusement. Only the good die young. But if that were true—what did that make me?

Then came Martha Fingerling's modest grave. Sweet as rhubarb pie, Miss Martha, who had appeared at our doorstep with casseroles for weeks after my mother died. She held me while I sobbed into her flour-dusted apron; she taught me that food was another way to say 'I love you' when words weren't enough; she showed me how to make a cornhusk doll. Countless names of children and grandchildren circled her stone like a wreath.

As I climbed higher, the sunset painted everything gold and orange. They had all continued living. They lived their entire lives as they were meant to be lived, and the envy inside me twisted like a rusted knife. I couldn't help but want the chance to do the same.

I found my father where I knew he would be, where the hill bent to overlook the water on both sides—the endless ocean to the west, the restless river to the east—perfectly positioned to catch the reflections from the sunset and sunrise in equal splendor. This was the healer's spot, as he called it. Earth and sky, morning and night, life and death. The lines that healers toed day in and day out.

His stone was simple granite, every line cut with love. A mortar and pestle sat at the top, carved with such incredible detail that I could even see the worn spot where his thumb rested for a hundred years of medicine-making. Herbs lined the edges—moonflower and feverfew and willow bark—and the curved blade of his harvesting knife was exactly as I remembered it.

Flowers overgrew at its base. Not wildflowers, but carefully curated blooms. Calendula, his favorite, bright orange like tiny suns. He called them "physician's flowers," insisting every healer should have a garden overflowing with them.

Thaddeus Camillus Nightwind

Beloved Husband and Father

Love transcends all boundaries

My legs gave out, knees hitting the earth with bruising force. The tears fell harder, the ordinary grief becoming something raw, like the primitive keening of a child who had lost everything and only just now understood the cost.

"Papa," I gasped, pressing my palms to the cold stone as if I could reach right through it and touch him. "Papa, I'm here. I'm finally here."

The sobs that tore from my throat weren't human. They were the sounds of something breaking beyond repair, of endless loss condensing into this single moment. My body shook with the force of them as I pressed my forehead to his name, fingers clawing at the grass as if I could simply dig down to him, explain everything, apologize for every sunset I missed while he waited.

"You waited seventy years. Seventy birthdays with honey cakes I couldn't eat. Of watching the door I couldn't walk through. Holding that damn cornhusk doll because I left you with nothing else."

Shadows stirred at my anguish, trickling out of the trumpets of flowers, crawling over blades of tall grass. They seeped up from the ground, out of the words carved in the stone in front of me. They crept slowly, careful not to startle after what had happened this morning. I paid them no heed in my violent mourning, but they wrapped around my waist and shoulders like the beginning of an embrace.

"They beat you," I sobbed into the stone. "And you still waited. You still watched every sunset thinking I was watching it too."

I looked up through the veil of tears at the sunset. This one was *real*, unlike the one I had grown accustomed to in the Amber Vale. The sun descended toward the ocean in a blaze of pink and orange and gold, kissing the water and painting the clouds in a way that no enchantment could ever replicate. This was my father's devotional, a beauty that promised change with each night.

The shadows huddled tighter around me, no longer tentative, but protective, knitting a blanket as the evening air grew cold.

"Your last words," I whispered, the echo of Willem's cadence bouncing around in my hollow chest, "I did remember. I forgot your face, your voice... but I remembered being loved. That memory kept me alive in a place where everything else inside me died."

That was the answer. Not the sea glass. Not Torian's ghost.

It had always been him.

He was the hope that I pressed to my forehead each night. He was the reason I emerged on the riverbank beside the moonflowers. He was the one who had loved me, and who loved me still.

The sun dipped below the horizon, brilliantly setting the Western Sea on fire. The shadows had finished their weaving, warm despite their darkness, cradling me as I curled up against the grave. I flattened a palm against the earth that held him as the other clutched my chest where my heart was breaking and healing simultaneously.

"Thank the gods for Molly," I said through a wet smile. "Someone to keep you from working too hard while still making you feel useful, to teach everything you knew. She gave you what I couldn't anymore."

The sun was nearly gone now, just a sliver of flame on the water's edge that reflected the peeking stars above—souls at rest, he'd taught me. They winked and danced for me, like tiny jesters performing for their melancholic queen.

"What would you think of me now, Papa? Your little moonflower, friends with stars and shadows, like something out of a twisted chapter book." I scoffed at the fantastical absurdity of it all. But I knew what he'd think of me, because he thought it of me until his dying breath.

Exhaustion tugged at me from all sides as my eyelids grew heavier. The shadow-blanket adjusted itself, thickening to the consistency of unspun wool as the temperature continued to drop on top of Cemetery Hill. I curled up tighter, head rested on the mound of his grave, the same way I used to position myself against him when I was small and frightened of thunderstorms.

"I'll never forget again," I promised him. "I'll carry you with me, and I will protect Mistwater just as you did. Those seventy years won't be in vain."

Sleep pulled me into it like a second embrace. As consciousness faded, I smelled apple brandy and the sweet perfume of flowers on a freshwater breeze; felt gentle, weathered fingers brush my hair from my tear-streaked face.

Moonflower, the wind whispered. *My little moonflower. The world did not turn in spite of you. It turned because of you. It always has, and it always will.*

Even the night itself knows how blessed it is to love you.

Rest now—and let the sunrise bring you something new.

CHAPTER TWENTY-SEVEN

I woke gently to thin strings of dawn threading through my eyelids. For a fleeting, disoriented moment, I thought I was a child again—asleep in the meadow with a basket of blooms and berries at my side. Then reality slammed back into me: the cemetery, my father's grave, the sobs that dried sticky on my cheeks.

First light.

The hunting party would be leaving *now*, and I was hours away from camp.

I scrambled to my feet, heart ramming against my ribs as I

snatched up the wool tunic I'd used as a makeshift pillow. I raced down the hill toward the village road, each step heavy with the certainty that I was too late. Speed mattered more than stealth now—not that it would save me. Camp was only a few miles from the bridge. Even with all the strength I'd earned, all the pain I'd survived, I still would not make it.

I trudged toward the forest, cursing myself, grasping for any scenario where I might be allowed passage across the Silvermist Bridge. Perhaps Merek the illiterate servant would be denied... but the Crowned Prince's prized illusionist might be worthy of reentry.

I spun the story a million different ways, but none of them explained how I'd crossed the bridge in the first place. Why would a measly court performer be hours away from the Vale? How would she have passed the guards at the checkpoints, having been barred from leaving the palace by order of the King? Sleepwalking, kidnapping, craving some mortal delicacy—none of it would work.

If I approached the bridge now, either I'd give myself away as Prince Torian's lover, as a knowing human from Mistwater, or as an agent of the Frost Court who followed the King across the bridge to further foil his plans. All of those things offered my end, and none of them brought me back to Torian.

I resigned myself to failure.

I just wasn't clever enough to survive this.

Perhaps I'd take up residence in Mistwater. Help Molly in the apothecary, or bus tables under Maude's watchful, beady eye. Perhaps Elidra and Tomas would take me in, not for any usefulness of mine, but because they already saw me as theirs. Perhaps this was the way it was meant to be. I would lose my love a second time, yes—but I had learned the fate that awaited my home. In a roundabout way, this was how I was meant to save it.

The thoughts circled me like a cloud of starlings looking for a place to land. None of them felt *right*, but all of them felt inevitable. Only then, when my future had narrowed itself down to a hopeless pinprick, did I turn away from the edge of the Silverwood Forest and take the first step toward another life.

Hopefully, a more meaningful one. Third time's the charm, after all.

I gave one last look behind me, a final goodbye to the life I had so desperately wanted and bled for, and I froze. Something was wrong. The hair on my arms, on the back of my neck, stood on end, the way it does just before lightning smites you where you stand. The air had an electrified twist to it—a nauseatingly familiar pull I last felt among the saffron. But this wasn't accidental. It wasn't incidental.

This shift between realms felt *chosen*. And that kind of manufactured magic did not belong in Mistwater.

I followed the feeling, letting it tug me along the tree line where the pines and pin oaks stood like sentinels. The pulling sensation sharpened with each step, funneling me toward a lonely sequoia so massive it looked like it had been planted before the gods walked the earth. It marked the very edge of the Silverwood, roots gripping both forest and field, anchoring the realms together.

I slowed, circling it while I gaped at its enormity. The air surrounding it felt... *tilted*, as though the hinges on a cosmic door had been intentionally loosened and a draft had been let in. That's when I saw it.

Carved into the bark—fresh, impossibly so—was an intricate pattern of spirals and curling lines of pink redwood. They refused to stay still as I examined them, subtly shifting every time I dared to blink. It was some kind of enchanted sigil, though not one I recognized. I touched it before I could think better of it.

The bark was warm. Not alive-warm. Spell-warm.

The lines rippled under my fingertips like a pebble dropped into a puddle. For a breathless instant, the sequoia wasn't entirely *here*. It existed at the edge of the Silverwood, but it also existed elsewhere. Or a hundred elsewheres.

Unsettled by the liminal tingling at my touch, I stepped back, and my foot knocked against something solid. It rolled beneath my heel, sending me sprawling hard onto my tailbone. Pain shot up my spine as my legs slid over a large, unmoving lump lying on the ground.

I pushed myself upright, dread crawling up my throat. The lump was a body.

I scrambled backward like a startled crab, my boot catching the corpse and sending its head lolling to the side. I recognized the leathery skin, the mangy scruff along the jaw, the deep-set eyes now empty and glassed over.

The huntsman. Lord Caenan's charge.

His skin was gray and mottled with death, but I still reached for his neck with shaking hands. No pulse fluttered against my touch. He was cold as stone. He had been dead nearly a day before I had so carelessly tripped over him.

I hadn't seen many dead bodies in the healer's cottage, but there had been a few. Most who came to our spare bed sought comfort—a painless sleep before they received their blessing from the Mother. After they'd taken their final communion and their final breath, my father and I would close the door and wait. Sometimes an hour. Sometimes two days. During the great fever, one poor soul had lain in that bed for nearly a week before the undertaker arrived.

After taking a moment to steady my breathing and tame the wild hammering of my heart, I stood on wobbly legs and brushed the leaves and dirt from my pants. The sharp flare in my tailbone had ebbed to a stubborn, pulsing throb. I scanned the trees warily, half-expecting to find more bodies strewn among the leaf bed, but there was nothing.

The wrongness of it slid over my skin. This place should not have allowed such a death while the true danger walked free.

Tomas's echo rattled against my bones, clear as a struck bell: *A party led by the King, with malice and conquest in his heart...*

But they hadn't been led by the King. They'd followed the huntsman.

They masked the scent of their treachery behind this harmless mortal face—a face that was surely welcome and familiar, imprinted into the Silverwood's amiable memory. And then, his usefulness ended, and he was granted his promised *Nyaeleth vyr Myr'Faen*. Which, I now understood, translated much less poetically to: run through with a sword.

My thoughts ran rampant, spiraling around a puzzle I was too traumatized to solve, when a rustling in the underbrush snapped them into stillness. The sound cut cleanly through my panic, lighting every nerve in me on fire. Something had found me, either drawn by the scent of death or of fear.

Instinct snapped into me. I seized the nearest ribbon of shadow and yanked it into form. It snapped from my hand with a startling crack—a whip born of pure survival.

I never designed this magic for violence, but today it would learn. I did not endure the last century plus a month just to be ripped apart by some mortal beast in the woods.

To my surprise—and sagging, dizzy relief—a familiar hound bounded into view. It was one of the King's prized hunting dogs, the same silver shepherd I had scratched behind the ears before slipping away from camp.

She recognized me at once, tail thumping with unbothered delight as she trotted toward me, her tongue bouncing from her mouth. The shadow-whip dissolved in my hand, and I sank to my knees to greet the enormous hound.

"What are you doing out here?" I asked, still steadying my breath. She nuzzled my hand, sharing the same undeniable relief of finding a friendly face among these clearly treacherous woods. "Did you get separated from the hunting party too?"

The hound whined, pacing circles around me before drifting over to sniff the corpse, her tail flicking in uneasy confusion.

I had planned to head for the village, or maybe the farmhouse, to warn them about the dead huntsman, but a sharper idea took shape.

I would not be returning to a mortal life, after all.

If I reached the bridge with the King's lost hunting dog beside me, my disappearance from the party would make sudden, convenient sense—or would be overlooked entirely. They would hurry me across rather than risk more blood being spilled by her escape.

I patted her head and brushed my fingers along her collar. A small silver plate caught the morning light: Hermia.

"Well, Hermia," I said, rising to my feet, "we'd better catch up to your master before we both find ourselves stranded on the wrong side of the bridge."

I spared the huntsman, and the strangely marked sequoia, one last glance before the hound and I stepped into the Silverwood. She pressed close to my side, not anxious, but certain, as if she understood the urgency itching beneath my skin. She guided us after the scent of the hunting party as the forest seemed to loosen around us. The path she chose slipped neatly between brambles and roots, as if she knew each fold of underbrush by heart.

As we walked, I spoke to Hermia mostly to keep my own thoughts from circling back to the corpse, and the village I left behind without a single warning. She kept glancing over her shoulder at me, as if measuring the shake in my breath rather than my words.

"You sure knew the way around that bog," I muttered as she veered us past it. "You're the only reason I'm not neck-deep in mud right now." It made sense how she was so easily 'lost' from the hunting party. They'd never catch her in these woods if she were determined to remain unfound.

Then why did she find me?

Hermia glanced back at me as if she'd heard the question I hadn't spoken aloud, her eyes sharp in a way that felt almost human. Too knowing, too aware.

"Did you run off on purpose?" I asked as she continued her bobbing and weaving through the forest's obstacles. "Were you looking for me?"

She didn't answer—*of course she didn't, because she was just a dog*—but her pace quickened, and her head swiveled back to look at me every few steps we took, making sure I stayed with her.

We came upon the clearing where the camp once stood, now reduced to trampled grass and rings of ash and stone. The sun was well above the trees now, already a quarter of the way across the sky. We had missed them by hours.

As we crossed the abandoned grounds, I saw it. One camp-fire—the one closest to the King's pavilion—still held faint embers, glowing with each gentle breath of the breeze. Another nearby smoldered the same way. *Not hours.*

"They waited for you," I said, dropping to my knees and grabbing Hermia's broad face, laughing as she licked my cheeks and forehead. "They were looking for you!"

If the coals were still this warm in the brisk autumn morning, they couldn't have been gone more than half an hour. We could still make it.

I could see my prince again.

We ran the last stretch, legs screaming, lungs aflame, her silver coat flying as her tongue lolled freely from her mouth. Then, the Silvermist Bridge finally came into view, along with the sprawling procession of the hunting party still making its way across. Relief hit me so hard I nearly gagged on it.

We made it.

I dipped my hand into the pocket of my tunic for the papers I'd nabbed from that lovesick servant, ready to slip back into the provisions cart like nothing had even happened. But my fingers closed on empty air.

"No, no, no," I muttered, searching frantically, though I knew it was useless.

My pockets were bare. The papers were gone—lost during the night at my father's grave, or when I'd fallen over the huntsman's corpse, or in the mad dash through the forest. Any of a dozen moments when survival mattered more than a stolen scrap of parchment.

Hermia whined as I stood frozen at the edge of the road, watching my salvation parade across the bridge without me. I had no proof of belonging, no explanation for my presence that wouldn't unravel in disaster. They'd welcome the King's hound with open arms—and probably liver treats and a dish of water straight from a mountain spring—but a dirty human with crazed eyes and no name? I'd probably receive a 'thank you' from the pommel of a sword and a boot in my ass kicking me back to Mistwater.

I huffed in exasperation, staring ahead as my thoughts spiraled uselessly in search of a desperate plan. Then, Hermia took matters into her own hands... *paws*.

Without warning, she bolted for the bridge, her silver form streaking across the open ground like lightning given substance.

"Hermia, no! Wait!"

But she was already among them, and chaos erupted like oil tossed onto a flame.

"The King's hound!"

"Hermia! She's returned!"

"Someone catch that godsdamned mongrel!"

What followed was a magnificent disaster that would be retold in the servants' quarters for months. Hermia, her agility bordering on supernatural, wove between carts and horses with delighted abandon. A normally placid mare reared in surprise, sending its rider tumbling into a muddy puddle.

The kennel master burst from the crowd, red-faced and wheezing, trying to corner her near the bridge's edge—only for Hermia to dart between his legs, sending him sprawling into a pyramid of carefully arranged horse droppings. Scrolls and documents—the very papers everyone needed to cross—took flight on the midmorning breeze, creating a blizzard of bureaucracy that had guards abandoning their posts to chase after them.

"Get that fucking dog!" The King's voice cut through the chaos like a winter wind, but Hermia wasn't slowing.

She was having the time of her life. She dropped into a play-bow before a young guard, his boot somehow dangling from her mouth, tail wagging in furious circles. He lunged. She sprang sideways. He collided with two other guards in a tangle of limbs, armor, and shouted curses.

In the midst of the beautiful pandemonium, I saw my opening.

A supply cart sat briefly unattended, its driver swept up in the futile pursuit. I moved quickly and ducked beneath the canvas covering. I flattened myself between the stacked crates, shadows curling around me. My heart thundered so loudly I was certain the entire bridge might hear it, though Hermia's havoc only grew.

"She's heading for the river!"

"Block the north side!"

"For fuck's sake, she's just a dog!"

"That's the King's favorite hound, you absolute ignoramus!"

Through a gap in the canvas, I saw the kennel master finally manage to loop a lead around her neck. She toyed with him long enough, dancing just out of reach until she was satisfied with her game. The poor Fae looked moments from collapse, sweat streaming down his face despite the morning chill.

"Your Majesty," he panted, approaching the King with Hermia now heeling perfectly at his side. "I cannot express my apologies sufficiently—"

"You will," the King said calmly, not meeting the kennel master's eyes, "by ensuring this never happens again."

The color drained from his face. "Yes, Your Majesty."

"Move out," the King commanded. "We've wasted enough time on incompetence."

The procession resumed its crossing, quieter now, everyone eager to forget the past five minutes had ever happened. My cart jolted forward, wheels grinding over the bridge's ancient stones. We passed the checkpoint without a single glance. I supposed no one was interested in supply carts while half the guard was still fishing paperwork out of puddles.

It wasn't until we were well into the Amber Vale that my lungs finally dared to breathe properly. From my hiding place, I heard the kennel master praising whoever had found Hermia, though no one seemed to know who that had been. My absence and my return had gone completely undetected, and I almost wondered why I had been worried about it at all.

The carts and wagons bumped over the cobblestones, tired hooves clopping slowly as the eternal sunset washed back over the world in rose gold. Hermia appeared beside my cart, trotting easily along and occasionally glancing up at the canvas, tail loose, unhurried.

"Clever girl," I whispered. "Thank you."

Chapter Twenty-Eight

The carts ground to a halt inside the palace gates, iron rims shrieking against stone as the procession finally collapsed in on itself. Orders were shouted. Horses snorted and stamped. Servants swarmed like flies, hands already reaching for crates and straps and anything that looked remotely like work.

I didn't wait for permission.

The moment the baggage cart slowed, I hopped off the back and disappeared between two storage buildings, heart hammering so hard it rattled my teeth. I didn't look back. Looking back led to hesitation. Hesitation led to discovery.

The journey was disorienting. After watching the sun move normally across the sky, then move backwards to rest on the opposite horizon, I had no idea what time it was.

But the palace was wide awake. Dangerously so. Footsteps echoed off marble; voices overlapped in clipped, efficient bursts. I kept to the shadows, head down, wool scraping my neck, dirt still caked beneath my nails from the grave I hadn't been given time to mourn properly.

A group of stewards rounded the corner ahead, forcing me to flatten myself behind a marble column. They passed in a blur of perfume and gripes about tonight's feast. So, it was evening.

Behind me, a tapestry of brown and blood-red shifted against my shoulder. I slid behind it, and the wall wasn't there.

Instead, a narrow passage yawned open, barely wider than my shoulders. It ran into shadow, lit only by thin strings of ambient light leaking through clever breaks in the ceiling. Not meant for people. Ventilation, maybe. Secrets more likely.

And if I were lucky, it would carry me toward the Wisteria Wing.

The passage threaded through walls thick as fortress stone, bending and narrowing without warning. Slivers of the palace flashed past through gaps and grates—a rush of heat and roasted meat from the kitchens, candlelight skimming the spines of ancient books in the library, silhouettes chanting to the gods in the chapel royal.

As I moved deeper, faint notes of a stringed instrument crept into the passage. Not loud or preformative, but careful. Cautious. The sort of music meant for small rooms in a castle with ears everywhere. It tugged at something low in my chest, an ache I didn't have the energy to examine. I followed the sound anyway, not out of curiosity so much as inevitability.

The passage curved, then straitened, and the sound grew clearer with each step. A decorative grate interrupted the stone ahead, its metalwork delicate enough to pass for ornament rather than surveillance. Light spilled through it in gentle ribbons, gold and steady.

I leaned in.

The room beyond was small. Private. A window stood open to the eternal sunset, its glow pooling across cushioned seats and scattering over the polished floor. Inside, a female figure stood with her back to me, pale hair slipping loose from its pins, her fingers gliding fluidly across her mandolin. Brella's voice floated sweetly from her lips in a song that was far too intimate for public consumption. I nearly turned away, but the music had me paralyzed.

I learned your name in the hush between bells,

in the hour when prayers grow too heavy.

I keep my eyes on my strings instead of your face,

because I would burn the world down if you'd let me.

Hear ye my ballad.

Let it find where you ache;

Let it lay you down gently tonight.

Hear ye, my darling.

If love's my mistake,

then I'll play myself out, take my flight.

If not, I'll be still.

If not, I'll be small.

I'll love you without ever being known at all.

The melody curled through the air, soft and aching, threaded with pregnant pauses as though she were waiting for something unspoken to answer back. The last note lingered, then faded. Silence held. Someone shifted in the lamplight behind her.

"That was beautiful," a voice said—quiet, controlled, unmistakable. For a breath, I didn't even recognize her.

Lady Valeraine sat in the window seat, one leg tucked beneath her, her usual court armor stripped away and replaced with a simple underdress. No jewels, no silks. Unpinned black hair framing a face that lacked its usual severity.

"Would you play it again?" she asked.

"I'll only ruin it if I play it twice in a row," Brella said as she lowered her mandolin, her ivory cheeks turning rosy. "I can teach it to you."

Valeraine reached for her own instrument that rested beside her as Brella stepped closer, angling her mandolin so she could see the fingerings.

I slowly let out my held breath. Just a music lesson. A princess must be well-rounded, after all.

But she did not mirror Brella's hand placement—did not even try.

She set it back down instead, then reached for Brella's hand, fingers closing gently around hers. The lamplight caught on the curve of Brella's cheek, on the soft part of her mouth. She cupped Valeraine's face, thumb resting just beneath her eye.

Valeraine leaned into the touch like a flower turning toward sunlight. And for a moment, nothing else existed—no court, no responsibilities, no restless world demanding attention just beyond the door.

"We don't have much time."

Brella smiled, sadness and fondness softening her mouth. "Then let's not waste it."

Their lips met. I looked away at once, my pulse skidding, heat rising to my face as the shame stuck sharp in my throat. I withdrew from the grate, the threads of my scratchy tunic scraping along the narrow stone walls. It felt wrong to stand witness to something so carefully kept—especially when I was guilty of the same crime.

"The betrothal proceeds as planned," Valeraine whispered, breath still unsteady as she pulled away. "The King is eager to formalize the alliance during the winter solstice."

The warmth on Brella's face flickered like a dying match. "So soon?"

She didn't look away as she nodded. "The preparations have already begun."

Brella took a half step back, her hands falling uselessly to her sides. "Then why don't we leave? We could escape to the Frost Court—"

"And start a war?" Valeraine's voice snapped cold, her mask sliding back into place with terrifying speed. "Abandon my responsibilities and watch the realms burn for the sake of my selfish heart?"

"Selfish?" Brella's voice cracked. "Is love truly so selfish?"

"Yes," she replied, brutal and unflinching. "Bliss is a luxury I cannot afford. The stability of the realms matters more than my frivolous desires."

"Frivolous?" The word escaped Brella like something torn. "That's what you think this is?"

The silence stretched between them like a chasm. Valeraine turned marble-still, beautiful and untouchable. "What I think doesn't matter. What I feel doesn't matter. Only what I *do* matters—and what I must do is marry Prince Torian."

"For duty," Brella said, bitter and utterly broken.

"For duty," Valeraine confirmed, her voice steady as stone.

Brella lifted her mandolin case, her movements jerky with bleeding pride. "I see. Forgive me for misunderstanding the nature of our *arrangement*."

"Brella—"

The door closed with a soft click, leaving Valeraine alone in the sudden silence. She sank back onto the window seat. Her hands trembled as she pressed them to her face, shoulders curving inward like she was trying to hold herself together.

I should have kept moving. I should have slipped back into the passage, let the stone swallow me up, and pretended I had seen none of that.

But I didn't.

I stayed, watching her through the grate as she sat motionless in the window's dying light. She did not make so much as a whimper, even as her shoulders shuddered with stifled sobs.

Whatever grief lived inside her had nowhere to go.

After a long, motionless moment, she stood. It was uncanny how quickly the softness vanished. She smoothed her dress, straightened her spine, lifted her chin with a single twitch of her nose. When she turned toward the mirror that stood by the door, her face was immaculate—no flushed skin, no reddened eyes, no betraying sheen of tears.

Valeraine the lover was replaced by Lady Valeraine, the icy politician.

Nothing of the encounter with Brella remained of her as she reached for the door. Then paused.

"This concludes our audience," she offered to the empty room, her hand resting on the latch. "I do hope you enjoyed the performance."

My blood went cold as she bowed with a flourish toward my hiding spot, then swept out the door and into the corridor.

She knew. She knew I had seen everything.

I forced myself to keep moving instead of just making this little alcove in the passageway my new home. I had to emerge eventually.

It finally spat me out into the upper corridor of the Wisteria

Wing, dizzy from the shift from stale air and cobwebs to the sweet perfume of the hanging blossoms. I paused just long enough to steady myself, fingers brushing the wall to stop the tilt.

The palace looked unchanged—flickering lamplight, tapestries breathing softly in the draft—but I felt wrong inside it, like I had stepped back wearing a different skin that refused to recognize the sunset as its own.

The corridor beyond was mercifully empty. I hurried to my door at the end of the hall, head down, boots squelching. The eagerness itched me, my suffocating need to strip myself of the wool and dirt and secrets.

I was fumbling for the handle of my sanctuary when sickeningly unhurried footsteps approached from behind. My relief hardened to dread as I turned to find Lady Valeraine gliding toward me, ever the picture of courtly grace. Had I not seen her through that grate—not watched her fold inward on herself as she cracked—I might have believed this was the only version of her to ever exist.

"Miss Lyra," she called to me sweetly, voice light as spun glass. "How fortuitous."

She intercepted me like an ambush predator outside my bedroom. Something I would hardly call *fortuitous*.

"My Lady," I managed as I quickly dipped into a shallow curtsy, my eyes refusing to meet hers with magnetic repulsion. She stopped a few paces away, the proper distance for exchanging pleasantries rather than airing scandal.

My tongue felt sharp, butting against my exhaustion. "To what do we lowly performers owe the blessing of Your Grace's attention?"

She didn't flinch. Didn't even blink.

"Performers are not *lowly*, Miss Lyra," she said coolly. "They are the lifeblood of a court—no less essential than its King. Or its *prince*."

Her gaze swept the corridor, lingering on the tapestries and painted panels that chronicled millennia of magic and music.

"The Amber Vale does not offer charity," she continued. "You remain here because your craft is worthy of protection. I would advise against diminishing your patronage aloud."

Her icy blue eyes returned to me. She watched as I struggled to swallow the lump that had formed in my throat. "Especially when you know firsthand how attentive the palace walls can be."

I suddenly felt too aware of how insignificant I truly was in this moment—a magician barred from magic, standing in front of the unerring future queen, tear-streaked dirt caked on my face and curls matted with grass and dried petals. An instinct urged me to apologize, but it seemed my voice had been suspended.

The tips of her pointed ears perked, and her nose twitched as she scented the discomfort shifting into me.

"But I did not seek you out to admonish you for your ingratitude," she said lightly. "I find myself in need of assurance that certain... misunderstandings remain free of propagation."

"I'm not sure what you mean, my Lady," I said carefully.

"Wonderful." Her smile glittered like a sunrise on snow. "Then we are already in agreement."

I nodded dumbly. Her ears twitched once, and her eyes flicked around the hallway before boring into me again.

"Every soul within these walls—living or dead—has private matters that would prove rather *unfortunate* to come to light."

Mutually assured destruction, elegant and unmistakable.

"I've always held that privacy is of utmost sanctity," I replied.

"How refreshing to meet someone who shares my values," she said, as if she were sealing a pact rather than offering praise. "I do hope we continue to understand each other so well."

With that, she inclined her head graciously and swept past me without another word, her overcoat whispering over marble as she floated away. Her unbothered footsteps faded, and I rested my forehead against the chamber door.

Gods, I just needed a moment to *breathe*, to blow away the hammering of my heart, the buzzing of my skin that hadn't calmed since I first assumed the role of Merek.

I turned the doorknob, aching for a lavender bubble bath and clean bedsheets, but found myself face-to-face with fury incarnate.

Torian sat on the edge of my bed, elbows braced on his knees, hands clasped together so tightly his knuckles had gone white. His hair was loose and disheveled, his usual courtly polish stripped away completely. Shadows carved lines beneath his eyes, and when he looked up at me—

The air stalled. The temperature rose to a suffocating degree. His amber eyes blazed with something I never expected to witness. The latch clicked shut behind me far too loudly, and every instinct—to flee, to grovel, to embrace—deserted me, and I just stood there, slack-jawed and staring.

"You left."

"Torian—"

"No." The word cracked through the room like a snapped rein. I stepped back, my shoulders knocking into the door before I realized I had even moved. He stood so abruptly that the bed creaked in protest, and he closed the distance between us in two strides.

Heat rippled off him in shimmering, restless waves. His fist came down with a latch-rattling crack, striking wood just inches from my mended shoulder. I winced as the sound ricocheted off every surface in the chamber.

"I told you to wait," he said through clenched teeth. "I told you we would find a way. Together."

He braced his other hand against the door, pinning me to the spot.

"And instead," he continued, voice curling around a bitter snarl, "you left me sitting on that godsdamned bench. Waiting.

Again."

"Torian, I—"

He pushed away from the door with a humorless laugh, flexing his hand like he'd only just realized how hard he had struck the door. His eyes burned into me, bright and fuming.

"Do you realize how ridiculous this has become?" he demanded. "I might as well put on a cap and bells and do a little jig. I play the fool for you often enough."

"I had to—"

"You had to what?" His voice rose and cracked like primordial thunder. "Risk everything we've built? Risk your safety? Risk getting caught by my father and executed for real this time?"

"I had to see my father's grave," I murmured, the words landing thinner than I'd expected. "There was no other way—"

"There's always another way, Aevra!" He dragged his hands through his hair, pacing a step before turning those molten eyes back on me. "But you don't trust me enough to look for it. You just run off alone, making decisions that affect both of us without even giving me a choice."

I could have argued, cataloged every reason for my deceit, chronicled every step of my journey. But as I stood there, watching his hands shake and his lip quiver, I wondered if any of it would even make a difference. There were no defensible words for the hurt I had caused in my quest for... what? Closure? Purpose? Had I even found them—found *anything* truly worth the risk it took to get there and back?

I did the only thing that felt honest.

I pressed my forehead against his heaving chest, fully expecting him to shove me away. But he didn't. His body was stiff, the heat from him searing my cheek as I pressed my face fully into him. I wrapped my arms around him next, fingers curling into the back of his shirt, damp with sweat and anger.

"I'm sorry," I muttered into his chest.

The word was small. It felt completely meaningless, like tossing a bucket of water into a volcano hoping it cools.

For a moment, he didn't move. He just stood there, body uncomfortably rigid against me, heart pounding furiously against my face. Then, his arms came around me slowly, reluctantly. Not tight, not comforting. Just... there. When he pulled me in, the room exhaled with us, trading the sweltering, stagnant air for the breeze that drifted in through the now open window.

"I wondered," he whispered into my hair, so quietly it barely even reached me, "if you were even going to come back."

The admission broke something in me that had been buried too haphazardly. I bit back tears when I remembered, *'I almost didn't.'* And that traitorous voice inside my head added, *'and I wasn't even afraid of the idea.'*

"Not even hell could keep me from you."

He hummed lightly in acknowledgment as he kissed my hair. Then my forehead. Then the bridge of my nose.

I tipped back my head, lifting my chin in silent request. But he did not answer it. His hands fell from my waist, and those shadows darkened in his eyes once more as he took a step back. The warmth he took with him as he parted from me left me hollow, and for the first time since I'd opened the door, the air was empty between us. No righteous fury, no begging or crawling.

Just empty.

"Not even hell," he repeated softly. "You say that so easily." He pressed the heels of his palms into his eyes and turned away from me.

I frowned, breath stalling in my chest. "Torian—" I reached out to touch him, but my hand closed around nothing as he pulled away.

"I should go."

"Oh." What had I done? "Okay."

He was already halfway to the door. Halfway gone.

Pride, dignity, caution—none of it mattered. I swallowed them all, each one catching painfully in my arid throat.

"Torian," I said weakly, "may I have a kiss goodbye?"

If I could just get him to come closer. If I could just get his lips to remember me, then the rest of him would surely follow. I'd sweep through him like a tide, wash away what I'd *done* with the promise of what I *could do*. I just needed him to touch me, and I could make this all okay. I was sure of it.

But he didn't even turn around. He just kept on leaving.

"We'll talk more tomorrow night," he murmured. "You know where I'll be waiting."

Deferral. It stung far worse than declination. I wished for the wrath to come back, to take the place of whatever this was. At least he spoke to me then. At least he looked at me.

"Torian," I said again as his hand paused on the doorknob. His shoulders tensed at my call.

"What?" The word sounded exhausted.

"Do you still love me?"

An unfair question to ask. I thought he might leave without answering. Part of me wished he had.

"I wouldn't be standing here if I didn't."

Relief flared like a dying star, brightly shone and quickly extinguished, taking all the light and good along with it.

"But I don't know how to love you," he continued, back still turned against me, "and be hurt by you at the same time."

The pain in his words sent me stumbling back, my knees hitting the edge of the bed and buckling beneath me. *What had I done?*

He turned the handle. "And I don't trust myself not to let one choke the other." The latch clicked; the door swung open; light spilled in, blinding and scornful.

"Goodnight, Aevra."

CHAPTER TWENTY-NINE

Sleep refused to embrace me.

Every time I closed my eyes, buried my face into the suffocating mountain of feather pillows, I felt the space where Torian had been sitting on my bed, angry and breaking. I felt the hole he'd left behind when he took all the warmth with him. My sheets twisted around me like chains as I turned and tossed, chasing a rest that I didn't even want. With sleep came dreams, and the only dreams waiting for me could never be sweet.

I don't know how to love you and be hurt by you at the same time.

His wounded words replayed until they lost meaning and be-came only sensation instead—tight chest and unsettled stomach, chapped cheeks and raw eyelids, melancholy shadows slinking around my shuddering shoulders.

Goodnight, Aevra.

Though it certainly wasn't. And I wondered if it ever would be again.

Eventually, I stopped pretending I wanted sleep to take me.

I gave up fighting the restlessness and rose from bed, aban-doning the knotted bedsheets and walking out the door with just my nightdress and bare feet.

The cold marble kissed the soles of my feet as I floated through the corridors like a ghost—candleless, morose, carried on centuries of instinct. The midnight chime sounded, and my thoughts were finally silent, their voices lost and worn raw from their incessant screaming.

The palace slept in uneven layers. The servants' quarters were dark and still; galleries hushed beneath their muraled ceilings, painted eyes shut and brush strokes breathing gently in the draft. Even the guards moved slower at this hour, their footsteps dulled, attention blunted by their quiet routines. I avoided their glassy stares easily enough, aided by the shadows seeping from the seams of the walls and the tapestries waving me onward.

And with every aimless step, the echoes of Torian's pain faded from my bones.

I stopped in front of a bare stone wall, that stifling, primordial magic sweeping the curls from my neck with its hot breath. The words left my lips as if I'd spoken them a thousand times. Perhaps a million times.

"*Otvôrynth, caedryn.*"

The wall dissolved beneath my palm in a shimmering mist, and I stepped into the shrine room, my nightdress whispering across the ancient threshold. The effigies glowed weakly at my intrusion, as if I had woken them up with my own audacious restlessness. The Father, Mother, and Son watched me—judged me—in their perfect preservation from their alcoves.

I faced Alezae, her devastatingly beautiful face fractured and shrouded in an excess of darkness, the shadows huddling protectively around her. I imagined the pebbles of rubble swept up and discarded in a waste bin, her keepers refusing to make her whole again after what she had done to them. I wondered if that was her justice, if leaving her broken was retribution for what she had left broken across the realms.

I stepped closer. My pulse thrummed in my fingertips, tingling with a restless urgency that tugged my hand toward her. Toward understanding, toward a purpose that *made sense.*

The shadows that clung to her stirred, pressing tighter around the cracked stone and hissing their grievances at my blasphemous presence. They nipped at my hand with tiny teeth that felt like the pins and needles that plague a sleeping limb. Their hisses turned into growls, and their growls turned into screeches as a ribbon of darkness slithered from the gaping hole in her face like a viper. They scattered like smoke hiding from the wind.

It wrapped around my wrist, coiling into an inescapable knot, and yanked me into the stone.

Overwhelming isolation engulfs me, flooding my consciousness and filling every empty space in my bones. I stand on a beach, watching eternity stretch in every direction until it becomes meaningless. No horizon for the sun to dip beneath. No edge for the waves to crash against.

I am never alone.

Yet, I am always alone.

Souls drift by on balmy breezes, ephemeral and hollow, passing through my fingers, my chest, my very being. Never staying. They take with them something small to help them on their jour-

ney—things I don't even notice before they grow back. A sliver of comfort, a fragment of strength. A shred of purpose that death is but a gate to something far greater. Each token then lost to the Whispering Sea as soon as the souls cross into the Mother's arms.

In return, they leave me their pain. Their regret. Their unfinished love. And that is the exchange. Millions of grains of sand settle into crevices and hollows, then eventually overflow into a cup until there is no room to drink.

They call me the Reaper. Harvester. Monster. Bitch. They curse my name in sickrooms and on battlefields.

As if I chose this. As if I am the fever that burns through their bodies. The sword that runs through them for the sake of whoever sits on a throne.

I was never meant to be feared. I was meant to tend. To guide. To stand at the threshold with my hand outstretched and say, "You are not alone," as the current carries them onward and away to the next room. My touch was once gentle. My realm was warm. I held steadfast in the belief that this was enough, that meaning could be drawn from repetition. Endurance itself was my holy devotion.

And for eons, it was.

But endurance has proved itself finite. It only survives while it is witnessed, and my final witness turns his back on me. Those grains of sand become suffocating. Purpose vanishes. All that endures is the endless tide of death dumping its suffering on my back. And I am buckling beneath it.

I stand before a child. Trembling, far too small. Far too young. The little soul shakes like it might shatter before it can reach the other side. It sees me, the villain from its fairytales, and it cries for its mother.

"I don't want to go," it whimpers. "Why do I have to go?"

I kneel. I soothe. I have no answer.

"It must be so, little one," I say.

I pluck an eyelash from my eye—bravery—and place it delicately on my fingertip.

"Think of a wish. Anything you have ever wanted but could never have." A tiny nod. "Now, blow." The eyelash disappears on the breeze. "Follow your wish, and it will be waiting for you when you get there."

The soul moves on, and I collapse on the beach. I feel it, the exact moment when something inside me breaks, clean and irreversible.

I call out to my kin. I cannot stand on my own.

"Please help," I rasp. But only silence answers, and the endless procession continues to trample me, pummeling me into the sand.

The tokens they take are excruciating—their terrified, greedy hands ripping me limb from limb for their communion. They pluck the threads of my hair from my scalp, tear my fingernails from their beds. But they don't grow back the same.

My tresses of understanding regrow in wiry clumps of bitterness. The strength in my hands reforms into vicious talons. Rows of serrated teeth pierce through my jaw, turning my whispers of lost things found into wicked jokes.

I finally look like the beast they paint on their walls. And there is nothing left except the wickedness they had always believed of me.

A soul brushes my hand, attempting to claim what it's entitled to. But I do not give it. Cannot. My fingers close around its wrist, and I yank. The tide stutters; the sand beneath me blackens, swallowing its heels as it shrieks.

"No more," I hiss as the line stalls.

"Please," the soul gasps, terror blooming. "Have mercy."

"Mercy is dead."

I drag the soul to the ground, burying its sobs into the depression where my body was trampled for centuries. I push my-

self up on my elbows, then knees, climbing over it and planting my foot into its thrashing chest. Its fear surges into me—hot, anchoring, solid—and for the first time since I started falling, the weight beneath me holds fast.

And I rise.

Stone slammed into my spine as I staggered backward into the wall of the shrine room. Air rushed into my lungs in a harsh, tearing gasp, like I'd been held underwater for hours. My knees buckled, striking the floor with a dull crack. Pain bloomed, the world swayed, statues glowed and blurred to smudges, and shadows retreated into the corners like startled animals.

I was myself again.

Right?

Alezae's unfiltered pain still rang through me. Her loneliness wrung my bones; her rage burned in my gut. I nearly lost myself in her, unable to tell where she ended and I began. For a terrifying moment, there was only despondency—vast and suffocating—a depth of grief that no mortal frame was built to descend into.

My hands trembled in front of me as I braced myself against the tilt, and a bracelet fell from my sleeve, dangling loosely at my wrist. Volcanic glass tinkled against onyx beads, warm and comforting. My fingers then fumbled for the sea glass at my throat, familiar and unchanged. *Mine.*

Yes, I was myself again.

But the shadows had gathered at the base of the effigy, watching—waiting. They spilled themselves slowly over the stone floor, dripping toward me like running ink. They pooled at my knees and ankles first, then crept upward to coil around my calves, my wrists, my shoulders. Not frantic or hostile, but like they were scenting something familiar. Like I had emerged carrying a mark they recognized.

These were Alezae's shadows.

They slid over my skin, caressing and squeezing in slow

passes, fawning in fealty and whispering their prayers. I swallowed and forced my breath to steady, fingers curling into fists at my sides. *Control*, I told myself. Not command, not rejection. *Control.*

My pulse slowed, and the shadows hushed and loosened their effusive grips as I pushed myself up, every muscle screaming in protest. My legs shook beneath me, and my back begrudgingly straightened.

I felt like I hadn't rested in days. The shadows lingered at my ankles, draped themselves down my spine as I stood. I took a heavy step toward the threshold, and they pulled against me. Their hisses sliced the air, as if they were begging me to stay with them.

"I cannot stay here," I whispered. They tightened around my shoulders. "You are welcome to come with me. But I cannot stay."

Reluctantly, the wisps of darkness shed themselves from me one by one and slithered back to their true queen. Like children torn between two parents.

The wall dissolved into mist as I approached, and I looked back at her. Alezae's fractured mouth still gently smiled. Understanding her did not soften her. If anything, it made her more horrifying.

Her wickedness was never a choice. It was an inevitable consequence.

I turned away before the thought could root itself any deeper and made my way back through the reliquary, finding the disembodied voice of my mother easier to ignore after the tragedy I had just witnessed.

Not witnessed—*lived*.

My bones felt like unset clay as I followed the twists of the bookshelves back to the library, barely able to keep the weight of my eyelids from dragging them down. I was ready to let sleep take me now.

The lanterns burned brightly ahead, their glow smearing softly against my vision. I could just make out the strip of light bleeding beneath the towering doors of the main entrance when a voice cut through my haze.

"Restful weekend, Aevra?"

Lysara stood near one of the long reading tables, cloak half-fastened as if she'd been on her way out. Or back in. Loose pages peeked out from leather-bound binders stacked and scattered around a single guttering candle.

"Not remotely," I said.

She arched an eyebrow. "Care to talk about it?"

"Less remotely," I managed, my sights still set on the double doors ahead.

Her gaze swept over me—the rounded slump of my shoulders, the shuffle of my too-heavy feet, the shadows that hitched a ride beneath my weary eyes. If she recognized my exhaustion, she clearly didn't care. Because she pulled out a chair.

"Sit," she said, already moving to the other side of the pile. I sank into the seat and then melted over the table. "I have news."

Chapter Thirty

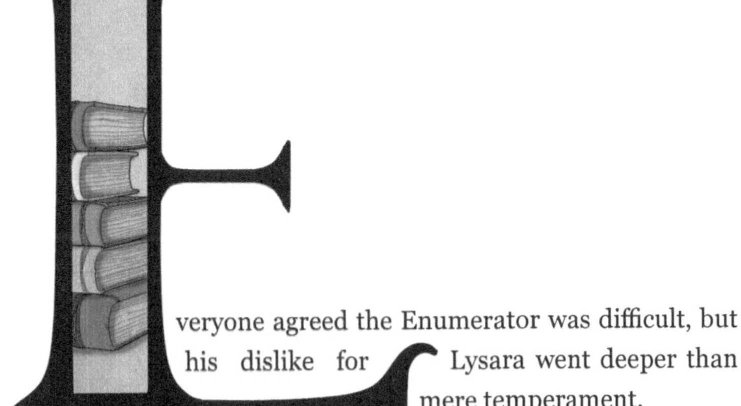

Everyone agreed the Enumerator was difficult, but his dislike for Lysara went deeper than mere temperament.

The Hall of Living Records suited him. Its name suggested vaulted ceilings and prayerful silence, perhaps disembodied bells ringing far above to glorify its splendor. A place where ghosts lived in gold-leafed luxury within towering, winding shelves, sunlight spilling through in shimmering threads and setting each account ablaze in holy flame.

But in reality, it was a dusty corner on the far side of the library, with a single window overlooking the stables.

Lysara approached the desk and waited. The Enumerator did not look up. He was very busy arranging and rearranging a stack of blank papers, squaring their edges against the desk once, twice, then again. *Pat, pat, pat. Tap, tap, tap.* He set the stack down neatly, cocked his head with a frown, then rotated it a quarter turn. A half turn.

He nodded. Sighed.

Then he pulled open a drawer, and out came the ink blotter. He slid a piece of paper from the stack and pressed it firmly to the page. *Amber Palace Volunteer Watch* bled in violently red ink as he lifted it, inspected it, gave it a quick blow, then reached for his quill.

He scratched his grievances with such passion that his words scraped through the paper:

Wisteria Wing:

•Unsecured window latches.

•Candles lit after the third evening bell.

•Unauthorized guests causing disturbances and polluting the air with sulfur and iron.

He underlined the last one twice, nearly ripping the paper clean in half. Satisfied with his memorandum, he set it aside and took another page off the top of the stack.

Lysara cleared her throat. Twice. Nothing. He continued stamping and scrawling his pedantic missives.

"Good morning," she finally said once he placed his fifth citation to the side—a warning about the kitchens getting two degrees too warm for an excess of twelve minutes.

The Enumerator jolted in surprise. His quill flew from his fingers; papers jostled ever so slightly as he banged his knee against the underside of the desk. Lysara did not flinch, only smiled as he retrieved another quill from the drawer and straightened his stack of papers back to order.

"I'd like the key to the census, please," Lysara asked politely.

The census was locked for reasons no one could satisfactorily explain, and its keeper hoarded its records like a dragon. A very prickly, persnickety dragon with a superiority complex.

"I am in the middle of official business," he replied without so much as glancing at her. "If you have misplaced a name, a date, or a relative, you may submit a request in writing. It will be processed within eight weeks."

"A request isn't necessary. I am the Court Historian, and I need access to verify—"

"I know *precisely* who you are," he cut in sharply, slamming another blank page beneath the blood-red stamp. "I am the Enumerator of the Vale, Warden of Rolls and Scrolls, and Acting Chair of the Palace Volunteer Watch, appointed by decree of the Crown itself."

A glorified list keeper.

Lysara raised a finger and opened her mouth to speak, but he did not bother to take a breath.

"The post of Historian is... *nominal.* Ceremonial in many respects. Mine, however, is essential. Sacred, even. And this—" He gestured vaguely to the shelves beyond the locked gate. "—is not history."

He shooed her with a flick of his hand and returned to his menial processes. "Off you pop."

Lysara did not step away; her smile did not falter. She stood there, hands folded loosely at her waist, eyes drifting over the desk casually. The ink stains creeping toward the edges of the wood, the stacks of freshly stamped notices. The ridiculous little empire he'd built for himself in a drafty corner of the palace. And the half-open drawer.

"I beg your *finest* pardon," she said pleasantly, "but the census *is* history. The spine of it, in fact. History does not occur in a vacuum. It requires witnesses in order to be recorded, else it ceases to exist. And those witnesses have names."

He paused mid-stamp, lips parted, brows lifting as if the thought had struck him despite himself.

"So, if you please," Lysara continued as she extended her open hand. "I will take the key."

The Enumerator inhaled sharply through his nose, fingers tightening around the stamp until the wood creaked, and finally lifted his eyes to meet hers.

"No."

Lysara sighed softly in resignation.

"I was worried you might say that," she admitted.

His mouth twitched with the barest hint of satisfaction as he reached for the next page on the stack.

"But before I go," she said, tapping lightly on the desk with her fingernails, "I'd like to ask a procedural question of my own." She inclined her head toward the drawer, and his quill stilled mid-scratch. "Is it standard practice for the Crown's appointed to store contraband literature among official palace materials?"

He followed her line of sight too late. The color drained from his face before it rushed back in a vicious blush, rising up his neck as he slammed the drawer shut. But not before Lysara caught its title clearly—fancy gilded lettering surrounded by flowers whose trumpets resembled the intimate female form.

The Prince Who Ravaged Me, and Other Salacious Tales.

She tutted at him with her tongue. "Volume Five, even. *How depraved.*"

"That's—" he began, then stopped, then cleared his throat. "That is a private item."

"Mhm," Lysara hummed in agreement. "Stored in a public office. During work hours. Among documents bearing the royal seal. As an officer of the Palace Ethics Committee, I would be obligated to disclose such perversion. Along with its harborer."

She strolled past the desk, past the crimson-faced Enumerator, and rested her hand against the lock on the gate.

"You wouldn't dare—"

"Wouldn't I?" she replied mildly. "What glory might I find otherwise, what with my *titular position* and apparent lack of resources to even write an anthropological essay?"

She extended her hand again.

"The key. *Please.*"

For a long moment, he simply blinked in her direction, each bat of his eyelids another mark on the list of consequences growing in his head. His shoulders slumped as he finally reached into his breast pocket, fingers fumbling with the chain that looped through far too many buttonholes. He slid the key free from its ring and handed it over in defeat.

"Return it promptly," he said through clenched teeth.

"Of course."

The tumblers were already rotating, the lock springing free with a disappointed click. She slipped through the gate and disappeared among the stacks, her footsteps swallowed by the shelves.

She returned moments later with a single leather-bound volume tucked beneath her arm. The gate closed behind her, the key slid free, and she crossed back to where the Enumerator sat with his back to her.

"The key, as promised," she said, placing it on the desk in front of him. "And something for your trouble."

She reached into her cloak and withdrew a book, its spine cracked and pages dog-eared. She slid it gently across the wood before floating out of the Hall of Living Records without another word.

The Prince Who Ravaged Me, and Other Salacious Tales,

Volume Six.

☽ ☽ ● ● ● ☾ ☾

"There's a Palace Ethics Committee?" I asked.

"Of course not." Lysara's mouth curved in a humorless smirk. "Ethics are of little importance in the Vale."

I huffed a breath that might have been a chuckle if I weren't completely hollowed out by exhaustion, like the innards of a glowbelly scooped clean and thrown out with the kitchen scraps. My lashes fluttered under the growing weight of my eyelids.

Lysara studied me, her searching gaze weighing how much truth I could shoulder before I tipped completely out of my chair.

"After you told me your story," she said at last, "I decided to go looking."

A shred of life entered me then, giving me the strength to straighten my spine and lift my eyes to meet hers.

"The census was the only sensible place to start," she went on. "Executions leave gaps; names appear on one page, then vanish on another. And these volumes are so tedious that they're rarely remembered when information gets scrubbed." Her fingers rested lightly on the volume's thick spine, the same width as my palm.

Something stirred in my core, like a spiral of leaves kicked up in a passing breeze.

Genius. Lysara was a godsdamned genius.

"You found her?" I whispered.

Her breath escaped her in a disappointed sigh.

"No," she said. "I didn't."

The small spark that flared within me guttered and died—just like every other foolish ounce of my hope lately. How could something seem so monumental and yet remain so frustratingly invisible? How could someone be so forgettable that not even a scribble of her name appeared *anywhere*?

"But," Lysara continued as she watched my shoulders collapse in on themselves again, "I found something else."

I knotted my arms together on the table and rested my cheek on my forearm.

"What was it?" I mumbled.

She threw open the volume to a marked divider, its cover slamming on the table with such force that it jolted my elbow straight into my temple. My neck was too heavy to care to adjust. Several loose papers floated from where she turned in the book, handwritten copies of journal entries.

"The King's personal accounts of the Rime Enclave's conquest."

I said nothing, didn't lift my head or offer the curiosity to ask how that had anything to do with me. Lysara had that look in her eye, the one I first saw in the library just days after I arrived at the palace—the wild, gear-spinning, puzzle-solving look that I learned to just let her ride.

I braced myself for the history lesson, for the dates and names and consequences that tickled her brain while likely putting mine to sleep. My silence didn't affect her, aside from giving her permission to begin her tangent with the first entry:

> *The Rime Enclave has finally been liberated from the neglect of the Frost Court. While Lord Iäen continues to mourn the loss of his mate and heir, their defenses were scant and crumbled just as expected. The fight was short-lived— neuromancy cannot stop blades.*

"Neuromancy?" I echoed, the word disappearing into my sleeve.

"It's not quite what the name suggests," she said, watching a spittle of drool form at the edge of my mouth. "It's not mind control or domination that one reads about in horror fiction. It's preservation and healing."

My ears perked up at her mention of healing, though I made no other indication.

"Rerouting pain pathways, resetting fever centers, reversing shock responses. Some practitioners could even manipulate memories—rearrange them, restructure them, or even erase them entirely, if circumstances called for it."

Disdain flickered through me. Mistwater was nearly extinguished while those indulgent creatures thrived across the river. I watched my father wither and slave over that fever. I watched children—babies—burn up and die, while a simple flick of a wrist could have saved them.

My hands balled into fists as Lysara continued reading:

> *Krivnya was brought to my tent this evening by Officer Caenan. I thought her lost to the slaughter, but she was found hiding in the temple—with my soldiers protecting her as she tended to her wounded. Naturally, Caenan cut the poor bastards down, then bound the little bitch's wrists behind her back before she could reach for his temples next.*
>
> *I considered killing her where she stood for the subversion of my ranks. She would fetch a decent coin at the shadow market. But her neuromancy is clearly extraordinary to have made my own soldiers believe she was their charge. Such talent should not be wasted in the Duskhold.*
>
> *By dawn, she will have come to understand her new circumstances. Once they see their beloved princess belongs to me, the rest will fall in line soon enough. Effective immediately, all neuromantic practices beyond my sanction are*

hereby forbidden.

They hadn't abandoned the world to its suffering. Their hands had been forcibly silenced by royal decree.

"Well, that explains the gloves," Lysara said as she placed the page aside and picked up the next one. "I always assumed it was because she chewed her fingernails in public."

> *Krivnya's continued resistance to using her magic for political intelligence is growing tiresome. Her insistence that mind alteration is sacred reflects the ridiculously primitive superstitions of her people. After last night's coercive exercise, I had expected her to be more pliant.*

> *More direct measures may be required to curb her insubordination.*

The page flipped over.

> *My assumption was correct. Devastation, when properly demonstrated, is a highly effective teacher. Once the consequences of her defiance were made abundantly clear, my queen has become far more cooperative.*

> *Her neuromancy proves increasingly valuable in court matters. She applies her gift with appropriate discernment, no longer hindered by her childish notions of sanctity. Her talents have already averted two diplomatic incidents this week alone.*

> *With her obedience secured, the future of the Amber Vale will be unassailable.*

I stared at her hands as she stacked the entries neatly on the table, wondering where any of this began to matter to me. It did not come. I waited for Lysara to fill in the gaps—explain why she dragged me through the tragedy of the Enclave and its princess while my own life was unraveling.

"The Rime Enclave was absorbed by the Vale two hundred years ago. But its history appears in a census compiled a century later."

Whatever dots she was laying out for me remained hopelessly disconnected.

"You're wondering how this pertains to you," she said, as if my confusion were another entry on the page in front of her. "I believe the Queen had a hand in whatever happened. To Torian, to the executed woman, and to her name being conveniently untraceable in ink and in memory."

It certainly made sense. Enough sense to at least explain the lapses in Torian's memory, the way he had looked at me as though I were nothing more than a stranger. I attributed it all to being lost to the unforgiving passage of time, but perhaps the truth was far crueler.

His own mother.

The theory circled uselessly as my brain descended further into sluggishness. The weight of it was just too much. My head lolled off my forearm, and I smacked my forehead on the table.

"You should get some rest," Lysara said gently as she slammed the census shut, rattling my teeth as it shook the table. "You look worse than you did when I saw you walk through here last night."

Last night? How long had I been held captive by that vision?

I pulled my head up, pink lines indented on my cheek from my sleeve. The noon chime sounded, twelve sonorous *gongs* bouncing off the shelves and vibrating the air. My empty stomach growled in response.

"I will," I said dully, scooting back my chair and testing my weight on wobbly legs. "Right after I get some lunch."

Lysara paused in her shuffling of the loose journal entries and frowned at me, her brow creasing as she cocked her head.

"Lunch?" she repeated. "Aevra... that was the midnight chime."

My hungry stomach dropped to my feet.

Midnight.

I hadn't lost hours. I hadn't lost breakfast and a cup of tea. I had lost an entire day. Add that to the countless ones Alezae had already stolen from me.

"Shit," I muttered as I pushed violently away from the table.

"Are you well?" Lysara asked, but I didn't hear her. I was already sprinting toward the doors.

"Shit, shit, shit." I cursed myself with every single slap of my bare feet on the marble as I ran toward the Night Garden.

Torian was waiting for me, and I left him there.

Again.

Chapter Thirty-One

The corridors blurred together as I ran, lamplight and shadow bending around me, dodging my path. My nightdress tangled around my legs as the desperate slaps of my feet echoed off the vaulted ceilings. Black smudged the edges of my wavering vision, my exhaustion being pummeled into submission by surging adrenaline.

I couldn't even remember the last time I had a restful night's sleep. Days, maybe? Maybe decades. Time collapsed in on itself until the memory of it was no longer linear—Torian's fury watered the soil of my father's grave, a bronze hen cast in a sunset reflected off a mandolin.

Please still be there. Please don't let me be too late.

The thought repeated without shape or rhythm, more of a reflex than a prayer after weeks of stepping on the wrong footholds. Shame chased me through every twist and turn. The memory of Torian's back as he turned away from me—the rise and fall of his shallow breaths, the disappointed rounding of his spine, the way all the warmth inside me walked out with him—hauled me forward despite my trembling legs.

I couldn't lose him. Not now. Not when the certainty of the future forked just out of reach, slipping away every time I reached for it.

I burst through the eastern doors into the courtyard, the chilled air flooding my burning lungs. The moonstone archway of the Night Garden loomed ahead, carved from midnight itself and devouring the sunset without twilight.

No earthly transition separated the oppressive golden light from the serene darkness ahead, and I hit the threshold too quickly, its magic colliding with my exhaustion and popping my ears. I braced my hands on my knees, begging the world to straighten as my eyes adjusted to the swimming darkness. My heart hammered against my temples, inside my jaw, while the rest of me lagged behind, barely responsive.

The air changed—damp mist clinging to my overheated skin, the perfume of wet soil and fresh blooms. One by one, moonflowers came into focus, tracing the winding paths in pale outlines. Their glows were thin, almost sad, barely holding the dark at bay. Even the stars were gone, forced to hide behind clouds that smothered the sky.

Every step I took felt delayed, as if my body were waiting for permission from a mind that no longer issued commands. Everything was too slow and too fast—too heavy and too flimsy at once.

That was when I saw her.

A figure knelt near the garden entrance, motionless enough to have been a statue. Pale and luminous enough to have been a ghost. Hair spilled over her shoulders in a sheet of silver, refracting a light that had no source. She wore a gown of gossamer so fine that even the melancholy glow of the blossoms shone straight through her.

The sight arrested me so completely that my spiraling thoughts simply... stopped.

I was hallucinating. I was dreaming with my eyes wide open as my wounded mind finally bled out. I blinked hard, pressing my palms into my eyes, and willing the phantom to dissolve into scattered smoke.

But she didn't.

She turned her head slowly, and her emerald eyes caught mine across the darkness. The garden tilted again, and I stood there swaying, unsure whether I was curtsying instinctively or falling to the ground. The flowers bowed as she rose, petals whispering across her skirts as the unreality sharpened into something far more dangerous.

Queen Krivnya.

Concern creased her forehead as she glided toward me. The mist-dampened ground pressed through the thin fabric of my nightdress, and only then did I realize I had fallen. My knees ached from the impact, though I couldn't remember the moment they'd struck the gravel path.

I was bracing to stand, palms and bare soles struggling for traction, when she stopped just in front of me. She towered over me, twirling a moonflower stem between her fingers, the petals spinning lazily and casting her face in shifting light.

"My apologies, Your Majesty," I said weakly, averting my eyes from her penetrating gaze as she quietly assessed me—the half-dressed, shoeless performer trespassing in a private garden well past curfew.

Her face softened as she extended her hand for me to take.

Her ungloved hand.

I pushed myself upright before she could help me, swiping the grit away as it left stinging indents in my skin. I forced my body down into a clumsy curtsy before straightening fully.

"My apologies, Your Majesty," I repeated. "It was not my intention—"

I should not be here, I thought. One word from her—or a gesture? A notion?—about my intrusion, and I'd be tossed from the palace. Tossed from my last chance to save things with Torian.

"I shall take my leave."

A thin smile traced her mouth as she gently shook her head, as if this were all just a harmless misunderstanding. The stem between her fingers stilled, and she held it out to me.

I almost took it. *Almost*.

My fingers twitched only slightly before my body betrayed me. I took a half-step back, pulling my hand against my chest as if I were recoiling from a flame. Her expression emptied as the moonflower bobbed uselessly between us.

"You're afraid," she said.

I stared at her, pulse thudding loud enough to drown out the whispers of the breeze through the garden.

She had spoken. The Silent Queen had spoken *to me*.

Her voice did not sound the way I had imagined it.

It didn't catch from misuse. It wasn't thin or tender, not meek, not high, not small. It was dark and even, carrying its weight without needing to be raised. A sound meant to be obeyed.

And that was proof enough that I was hallucinating—trapped inside a vision, another cruel sleight of Alezae's hand as she stitched impossibility over exhaustion until I no longer knew where waking ended. My thoughts chased the sound of the

Queen's voice, unable to catch it properly to make any sense of it.

I blinked once. Twice. And she was still there.

"I—" I swallowed, barely able to work my dry throat. "I'm not."

Not a half-truth. A lie. I gestured at the flower, forcing my gaze anywhere but her bare hands.

"I have... allergies. To pollen."

It sounded foolish the moment it left my mouth.

She nodded politely, her eyes narrowing on me for a heartbeat longer than was comfortable. Whatever softness had been on her face drained away, and she withdrew the flower slowly.

One petal pinched between her bare fingers, and she pulled. The petal tore free, falling soundlessly to the ground. Then another. She didn't look at me as she stripped the flower down to its stem, her fingers trembling just enough for me to notice.

"Did the historian finally think to consult the census?"

Something sharp and cold slid between my ribs, steel burning away the fog in an instant. My skin tingled; my muscles seized and locked. Adrenaline surged through my veins as if I could simply run from the Queen. Or fight whatever threat she posed while barefoot and delusional.

I smoothed my face into something compliant, the way I'd learned to do a hundred times over. The way that had kept me alive. By offering an abundance of ignorance and deference, hoping it would drown the danger and leave me still breathing.

"I'm not sure what you mean, Your Majesty."

The words tasted bitterly familiar. How many times had I said that now? And how many of those times had anyone actually believed me?

A small sound escaped her—not quite a laugh, but more than a sigh. She plucked another moonflower from its bed, its glow sputtering with each petal she ripped from its dimming face.

"You and I are alike in many ways." Her words landed at the

wrong angle, like she planted a flag through my gut without my consent.

"I'm no queen." The retort came out far sharper than I intended, my pride crowding out any courtly, conscious thought.

"No," she replied softly as another petal fell. "But you love my son."

The universe narrowed to the space between us. Between the ageless predator and her graceless mortal prey. The entire garden receded, the mist and glimmer disappearing into a quiet so breathless that not even my own thundering pulse broke through.

I didn't answer. Couldn't. The truth of it struck somewhere where language and understanding couldn't reach it. My face went cold; my fingers curled uselessly at my sides. The stem in her fingers was bare, and it dropped to the ground to rest among its remnants.

Her gaze finally lifted back to me. She pulled her lips between her teeth, and the line of her mouth that remained curved into an unsettling smile. Certainty. Knowing where the blade rested and deliberately choosing not to press it deeper.

"Do not look so stricken," she said, another flower finding its way between her fingers, each petal a soft tear swallowed by the growing dark. "*Silent Queen*, remember?"

The heat returned tenfold to my face, but my lungs refused to release their held breath.

"But we share more than just that," she continued. "You wield magic that is misunderstood. Because it is sacred."

She looked up at the brooding sky, at the shadows snaking between the swollen clouds that strangled the stars. Her eyes traced the silhouettes of the tree branches, the quivering leaves—the way the darkness twitched at my every shallow breath. She turned her hand over, watching a shadow chase away the light resting there.

"Because it is *frightening*. So it is reduced to spectacle—" The petals at her feet picked up in a spiral. "—until it is harmless enough to be dismissed. And eventually forgotten."

Harmless. As if her defiant silence somehow diminished the things her hands could do. She could wipe sworn allegiances like dust from a shelf. She could churn a memory in someone's brain until not even a recognizable face remained.

My stars had burned through her curtains, and my shadows may or may not have strangled me in my sleep, but she was *wrong*. Whatever she thought she saw in me, it wasn't the same thing. I never helped rule an empire with my magic. Never allowed it to claim something that wasn't mine.

Never used it against someone I love.

I begged my face to remain neutral, for my eyebrows to keep knitting upwards in confusion instead of furrowing in disbelief. Whether or not I had succeeded, it didn't matter. She already knew.

"Every terrible thing I have done," she continued, smoothing her hands down her bodice, "began as a decision I could once justify."

She took a step closer, and her bare hand lifted toward me as if to brush something unseen from my shoulder. From my face.

I watched her reach for me in slow motion—every facet of her polished fingernails glinting in the dark, every tiny thrum of her pulse swimming through turquoise veins. I cataloged every single memory from this life and the last, wondering how many of them she would take before she made me forget this ever happened.

Would I still remember Torian? Would I still remember my father? Alezae?

My brain disconnected from my body, and I batted her arm away as if it were a hornet.

"Don't you dare touch me," I hissed, though the sound felt like it came *through* me rather than *from* me.

She didn't recoil in offense; her face did not flush pink with anger or embarrassment. Her hand remained suspended between us.

"I don't need to touch you to show you the truth."

The garden answered before I could. Something unseen pressed in, dense and strangely still. The sounds of the garden dulled to barely a muffle—the chirping wings of insects, wind whispering through blades of grass, the far-off hum of the palace. The moonflowers brightened, their collective glow thickening the air between the floating mist. Shadows stretched long and slow, dancing across the path and pooling at my feet. The dark itself leaned in to listen.

The light solidified into a blinding white sheet in front of us, and my mouth hung agape as history projected itself with unsettling clarity.

Snow falls on a moonless night, blanketing a settlement nestled between twin mountains. No lanterns burn in the windows; doors hang off their hinges. Steel sings through the darkness, pleas for mercy echoing through the valley.

A young Krivnya kneels on the stone floor of a temple, her trembling hands hovering over countless wounds of her writhing people. Few of them can be saved.

The door buckles against the makeshift barricade, cabinets and bed frames rattling.

"Hide," she bites out to a male in the corner. He does not argue, does not hesitate, and disappears through an opening in the wall that shuts tightly behind him.

Wood splinters and explodes, furniture kicked aside as two soldiers wearing gold and bronze step into the room. Krivnya does not turn, does not acknowledge them. She places her palm on the sweat-streaked forehead of a child, allowing the last breath drawn to be an easy one.

A fist tangles in her hair and wrenches her to her feet.

"Look what I found!" the soldier cooed as he gripped her jaw in his blood-stained hand.

"What a beauty!" the other one said. "The King will be pleased with this one."

"Aye, but we don't have to bring her just yet."

A stiff body is tossed off the nearest bed. Leather and steel clatter to the ground as Krivnya is shoved face down onto the blood-soaked mattress. Cold hands roam where they please, clawing her skin and squeezing hard enough to bruise. She clamps down on the pain, refusing any sound to betray her.

Her undergarments are yanked halfway down, then torn in half.

"Flip her over," one soldier grunts. "I want to watch that pretty face—"

She's flung onto her back, metal scraping against stone, and two mouths find her neck and shoulders. A single tear falls as she weaves her fingers through their snow-flecked hair, palms pressing gently against their scalps.

"She likes it," the soldier moans into her skin, his free hand fumbling with his waistband.

Her hands brush their temples, and they stand at attention before her.

"My liege."

Snow flurries, and the scene is wiped clean.

Krivnya stands in front of the floor-standing mirror, powdered bone and ochre dusted heavily over her swollen cheekbone. She adjusts the collar that sits just below her jaw, hiding the trail of bruises that line her neck.

The crimson-stained bedsheets have already been changed and straightened. The lace curtains billow gently in the breeze blowing freely through the open windows. A sharp knock raps on her chamber door.

She walks with small, careful steps. The pain in her hips, between her legs, has been hushed beneath her magic. But the bleeding has only just stopped.

"My Queen," a steward says as she opens the door slowly. "The King requests your presence in the drawing room."

The King stands facing the hearth as she enters, glowing embers matching his breath. She does not speak as the door clicks shut behind her.

"I have summoned you because I have given some thought to your argument," he says, keeping his back to her. "You say your gift is sacred, and I have been... disrespectful to you regarding your beliefs."

Krivnya remains still as a statue as the King turns. His eyes are bloodshot, cheeks splotched red.

"I wish to understand. So, I will have you enlighten me. We leave for the Enclave posthaste."

Twilight settles over the Rime Enclave, spring grass shooting up from wet earth. A fog has descended as the carriage rattles over the main road.

Not fog. Smoke.

The carriage approaches a slab of stone, charred wood and fallen rock strewn in devastating piles. The acrid scent of burnt flesh chokes the air. Townspeople circle around the remnants of the temple, crying and wailing. They gather bits of their sanctuary, still too hot to hold close to their hearts.

The wheels grind to a halt, and she stumbles out, landing hard on the ground. Nobody helps her stand. Her dress rips as it catches on the heels of her shoes while she runs. She screams, and countless hands catch her at her shoulders—her people.

Then a hand settles low on her lower back.

"What good your faith has done," the King whispers against the shell of her ear. "Your sanctuary is in cinders, and its guardians are buried beneath the rubble." His palm presses into her, leading her back toward the carriage.

"Let me stay," she whimpers.

"From now on, I am your temple."

The wind blows her tears away before they can fall, and the scene shifts again. Even clearer this time.

The Queen sits beside the hearth in her chambers, and the door is flung open, slamming hard against the wall. The King enters. He is angry again, but Krivnya does not look up from her book.

"You've been keeping secrets, my Queen." His voice is deceptively soft as she turns the page. "The prince confides his treachery in you, and you do not think to tell me?"

"There is no treachery in a son speaking in confidence with his mother."

"Do not mistake my restraint for trust, Krivnya," the King says, his voice low, barely measured. "I have tolerated your fickleness in your duties, given your lowly people purpose in this palace, and you have done nothing but betray my authority and coddle our son's immoral deception."

"My people are no more than servants, and perhaps if you acted as a father to Torian rather than an inflexible disciplinarian, he'd be less likely to—"

The book is ripped from her hands and tossed into the fire. Krivnya exhales gently and stands, avoiding the King's fiery gaze as she adjusts her spider silk gloves and heads for the open door.

"And where do you think you are going while we are having a conversation?"

"To the library," she says calmly, smoothing her hands down her bodice. "And this is not a conversation—it is a diatribe. Perhaps I shall bring you back a dictionary so you may research the difference."

She takes one step, then his hand tangles in her hair. His fist closes at the base of her skull, twisting around the roots. He drags her backward, her neck bending at an unnatural angle, and kicks the door shut.

"*No more games,*" *he hisses into her ear as he shoves her back down into the chair. "You hid the prince's mortal affair from me, and you will correct it appropriately.*"

Krivnya's lip curls into a snarl.

"*Neuromancy cannot influence or displace love,*" *she spits out through clenched teeth. "If it did, I might loathe you a fraction less.*"

The King smiles as he leans down.

"*My dear,*" *he whispers, almost sweetly, "I don't want him to forget her. I want him to watch her die.*"

She rolls her eyes. "Then make it so. You don't need me to aid in your bloodlust." She tries to stand, but the King's firm hand on her shoulder keeps her in place.

"*On the contrary, my Queen. The mortal cur is already en route to the shadow market. I need you to make it so that he never looks for her again.*"

"*No,*" *she said flatly, ripping his hand free from her skin, already pink from his grip. "You may exploit my gift for your political nuisances, but I will not defile my son.*"

"*Very well, then." The King stands and faces the fire, fingers lacing gently behind his back. "Then I suppose I have no choice but to kill him, as is required for such a disgusting infraction.*"

"*You're bluffing,*" *Krivnya says with a scoff.*

"*The law is written very clearly,*" *he replies, rocking back on his heels. "Perhaps you might read up on it during your trip to the library.*"

"*You wouldn't dispose of your only heir." Her voice is more timid, though only barely. He swings his head toward her, his amber eyes now hot and ravenous.*

"*I would.*"

He sinks down to the floor in front of her, forcing her knees apart as he bites the inside of her thigh over the gathered fabric.

"*And you will make me a new one.*"

Her horror-stricken face fades to black, and there is only a flicker of orange light in the darkness. A candle.

The wooden door creaks quietly, slowly, as Krivnya steps into the room. Someone is sleeping in the bed, tangled in the bed-sheets. Only not tangled, restrained. Drugged.

She sinks down beside him, the lump of his body rolling toward her slightly. A tear slides down her face as she removes her glove, one finger at a time.

"Just this once, little love," she whispers into the dark, brushing a lock of hair from his sticky forehead. "Just this once. And I shall comfort you over breakfast. I shall hold you to my chest while you cry and tell you that death eventually gets easier—and I shall pray you do not realize that I am lying."

She cups his cheek in her hand, then rubs her thumb over his temple, the memory already loaded. She leans down and kisses a tear from his skin, unsure whether it belongs to him or her.

She pulls the trigger at her fingertips, and the memory impales his brain with the force of a bolt from a crossbow. It plays behind her eyes as she releases it into him.

A woman—her features only as clear as Torian had described her—kneels before the executioner. Her head falls cleanly from her shoulders. She weaves Torian's excruciating agony from her own. Repaints Oranth's heavy hand just as it rested upon her tonight.

The flicker of the candle dies, and the darkness explodes as light pours into the windows. Krivnya enters Torian's chambers with a tray of breakfast and a fistful of handkerchiefs.

But his bed is empty.

The tray falls from her hands, clattering to the floor. Glass shatters. Fruits and breads bounce and roll to every corner of the room.

"The prince has been relocated," comes a voice from behind her. It is so gentle, she almost does not recognize it as her hus-

band's.

"I did what you wanted," Krivnya says, her voice tiny and trembling.

"Yes, you did. You fulfilled your punishment. Now he must fulfill his."

My ears popped as the muffled sounds of the garden rushed in, and the night swirled back into place. The moonflowers dimmed, their glow thinning back into something fragile and ordinary. My knees wobbled, and I realized distantly that I was still upright only because my legs had locked in place. My jaw ached from how hard I'd been clenching it.

The Queen stood exactly as she did before she split the world open in front of me. Her hair was still a smooth sheet of silver down her back, ungloved hand still outstretched. No blood. No ash. No scorch marks marring her gossamer gown. Not even a hint of shame lined her face.

My stomach pitched as her lips parted to speak, pausing halfway as if she were sifting through her mind for the correct words. I braced for it—the careful reframing meant to make whatever that was into something survivable. I drew my shoulders in tight, my spine stiffening as if I were about to receive a blow to the face.

I flinched as gravel crunched sharply behind me.

Torian stood at the edge of the path, half in shadow, half caught in the pitiful glow of the moonflowers. He looked wrecked—hair loose, shirt unlaced, collar gaping just enough to show the familiar line of his throat that had undone me a hundred times over. His chest rose and fell too quickly, his breath hissing through his teeth.

His eyes went to me first. Then his mother.

"What—" His fists gathered at his sides, knuckles blanching white, smoke bleeding from his skin. "—is this?"

Queen Krivnya's expression had gone still, once again the garden statue that haunted the night. The only movement she made was the slow drag of her emerald eyes across the dark.

"You..." He raked a hand down his face. "You? You did this to me?"

She did not answer him. Did not lift her chin; did not soften her mouth into an apology or defense. Her silence slid back into place like a stone wall, eyes fixed somewhere beyond him, as if the matter were already concluded.

"Torian," I breathed, the word slipping out before I could think to stop it. "She didn't—"

His eyes snapped toward me, amber eyes burning with the same fire I had seen just seconds ago in the King. His jaw worked once, hard, like he was chewing down something bitter.

"Don't." His command cracked like a lash, freezing me mid-breath. "This does not concern you," he said, each syllable sharpened down to a blade's edge. "You do not speak for her. You do not *look* at her like that."

His gaze cut back to his mother, frantic and angry, searching for somewhere to land.

"Say something," he demanded, stepping closer to her as the gravel beneath his boots whistled and scorched. "Anything. Tell me I've misunderstood. Give me your pathetic excuses. An apology."

When she did not answer, when she continued to stand there, immovable and unflinching, he laughed in her face. His breath, harsh and broken, rustled the hairs at her temples. She didn't even blink. Her refusal to respond seemed to strip him raw—her indifference far more caustic than her cruelty.

"Gods, this is what you do, isn't it? You let your *noble* silence speak for you, while the rest of us have to fill in the rot. Can't be held accountable for anything if you don't acknowledge a single word anybody says to you, can you?" Their faces were so close that the tip of his nose brushed hers. "*Can you?*"

"Your father would have killed you," I interrupted weakly, my words almost carried away on the gentlest breeze.

"He might as well have!" he shouted as he turned back to me. "You dare defend this monster after witnessing her betrayal? To the one you supposedly love?"

He laughed again—an unamused, terrifying laugh—as his fury cracked through his grief like lightning through stone.

"Perhaps you are no better than she is," he continued. "Perhaps I am better off without either of you."

"Don't say that." The words left me too quickly, too plainly. No poetry left inside me.

"You do not get to tell me what to say," he snapped. "You do not make demands of a prince in his own court."

The fight I might have had left drained out of me, leaving a strangely calm hollow in its place. Whatever I had come here to salvage had already burned itself down.

"Then I shall waste no more breath," I murmured.

I turned to the Queen, my knees bending in the automatic, ingrained motion. "Goodnight, Your Majesty."

Then to Torian. Another perfect curtsy. Polite. Impersonal. *Safe.*

"Your Highness."

I left without waiting to see if he would follow. Without wondering if it would even matter if he did.

Perhaps it was for the best after all.

Chapter Thirty-Two

ay yes, Aevra Nightwind, and we will live and die as one."

"Yes. A thousand times, yes."

Our lips hover over each other before the forest breaks apart. Torchlight splinters through the trees, then floods the clearing. Steel rings as swords are pulled from their sheaths. Shadows move where they shouldn't, materializing into guards shouting orders and brandishing weapons.

Torian moves before I can even grasp reality. One moment, I am reaching for him; the next, his body is unyielding between *me and the blades held level with our necks.*

"By order of King Oranth," calls a voice from behind the blinding torch fire, flat and merciless, "you are under arrest."

"On what grounds?" their prince demands. His voice doesn't shake, but I can feel the tension in the warmth of his back, hot coils of violence barely held in check.

"Illicit fraternization with a mortal civilian."

My fingers lock around his arm. We had been careful. Gods, we had been so careful—night meetings, whispered vows, the slow patience of lovers who knew what it cost to be seen.

The guards do not hesitate. Hands wrench me backward, and Torian's sleeve rips from my attempt to hold on to him. I fight against their grips, nails scraping against their armor. My arms are painfully twisted and pinned behind me. I try to scream, but my breath has vanished, stolen whole from my lungs.

"Unhand her!" Torian roars as his wrists are shackled at his waist. "That is an order!"

"The King's orders supersede yours, Your Highness."

The snow sinks into my skin as I am dragged away, on and on, for miles. Past the same fallen tree, past the same frozen bend of the river, the moment looping pitilessly. I watch Torian's face as I'm ripped away from him from a thousand different angles.

"I will find you," he mouths. I believe him.

I am crying, screaming, but my breaths are silenced by the sound of boots crunching snow. The forest finally swallows him from view, extinguishing those golden eyes burning through the night. But there, watching from the tree line, stands a figure, half-hidden in shadow. Its face is blank, featureless, aside from two emeralds gleaming in the darkness.

A sharp knock at my door yanked me from the dream's clutches. I woke gasping, my neck locked in place, body aching like I'd been running instead of sleeping. The echo of the winter air still ghosted along my skin. I shivered as I rubbed at the knot at the base of my skull, trying to force reality back into place.

I blinked groggily as the knock came again, more insistent this time. I dragged myself upright, limbs still weighted with exhaustion.

"One moment," I rasped through a yawn, pulling a robe around my shoulders as I slid from bed. My hair was a tangled mess, and drool had caked itself sticky across my cheek as I padded sleepily to the door.

I opened it just enough to see who stood on the other side. The last vestiges of sleep were driven away by a pair of warm, golden eyes that met mine through the crack in the door. He was impeccably dressed in an ivory tunic and pressed trousers that looked fresh from a steward's iron. His hair was perfectly combed and coiffed without a lock out of place, his boots polished, posture immaculate. He smelled faintly of sage and sea salt—clean and composed in a way that seemed almost deliberate.

"Prince Torian," I mumbled, not opening the door any wider. "To what do I owe the pleasure?"

His gaze flicked briefly to the sliver of space between the door and the frame, then back to my face.

"I couldn't wait until tonight," he whispered urgently. "Please, may I come in?"

I studied him for a moment longer than was polite. The careful neatness, the armor of propriety. I had already begun to imagine how the rest of this exchange would go. Escorted out of the palace with few possessions. My room reassigned. His patronage withdrawn with a flick of a quill.

But I opened the door anyway, stepping aside to let him in. That was when I noticed what the polish had failed to hide. The skin around his eyes was slightly puffy, tinged with violet that spoke of a sleepless night. His posture was brittle, holding himself upright by effort alone. His throat bobbed nervously when he swallowed.

"I didn't sleep," he began as soon as he crossed the threshold, and the door shut softly behind him with a click. "Every time I closed my eyes—"

"You said you'd be better off without me."

His mouth hung half-open. My heart slammed violently against my ribs, loud enough that I was certain he could hear it. I did not give him time to recover a response.

"You said it like it was a conclusion," I continued, my fingers knotting so tightly into the fabric of my robe that my knuckles creaked. "Not something spoken in anger. Not like something you meant to take back."

His face drained of color, leaving only the dark hollows beneath his eyes and the rough grain of stubble along his jaw.

"Aevra—"

"No," I cut in again, refusing to stop for fear of falling apart in front of him. "If this is where you tell me this was a mistake—last night, us, all of it—I would rather hear it cleanly before I take my leave."

A suffocating silence pressed in as he stood rigidly in the center of my modest chamber. I turned away from him with a sharp scoff and yanked open the wardrobe, pulling out the only dress inside I still dared call mine. The cloaks followed, and I shoved them into a leather satchel.

"I'd at least like to say goodbye to Lysara before you chuck me out the front gate—"

"Aevra—"

"But don't worry, I won't soil her image of her *best friend*—"

The wardrobe door slammed shut hard enough to rattle the hinges, and I barely got my fingers out in time. Torian's hand was splayed against the wood beside my head, his arm caging me in before I could step back. Heat rolled through the thin air between us, the smell of wood burning beneath his fingertips.

"I would be dead without you."

My throat constricted, forcing my breath to come in crooked and shallow. I suppressed a wince and laughed instead—defensive and disbelieving.

"How dramatic."

"It isn't," he muttered, pulling his hand away from the door. He dragged it through his perfectly arranged hair, then let his palm fall to the nape of his neck as if bracing himself. "I used to think that dying would be easier than surviving in this palace. Easier than living with what I am. What I've done."

His voice faltered on the last word. He stepped away from me abruptly, creating a chilled distance as he crossed the room in two long strides. He stopped at the window, bracing a hand against the stone beside it, shoulders drawn in as he stared out at the glow of the Vale.

"I spent an hour with my valet this morning," he admitted, keeping his back to me. "Made him redo this tunic twice. As if looking like a prince might somehow make me feel better when I saw you." A hollow sigh left him. "I was going to bring you breakfast, but then I thought—" His hand lifted, then fell uselessly back down. "Who brings breakfast as an apology for becoming their father?"

An unsettling quiet stretched between us, and he did not rush to fill it.

"It wasn't your father who spoke to me like one of his hounds," I finally said, crossing my arms across my chest. "That was you."

He flinched, but did not deny my words.

"I know," he said. Simple. Unadorned.

He turned from the window, finally facing me fully. The appearance he'd carefully constructed seemed almost absurd against the naked emotion in his eyes; the thread of composure he'd been holding himself together stretched taut.

"I know it was me."

I didn't answer. I didn't trust myself to.

"You asked me the other night if I still loved you," he said weakly.

Tears burned my eyes as I pulled my lips between my teeth and turned my face away from him. The ache from that question stung like a brand pressed too deep.

"And I should have just said yes," he went on, his voice scraping against his dry throat. "Because I do, Aevra. Of *fucking* course I do."

"Then why would you say—"

"I don't know," he bit out. "I don't know why I said what I said. I don't know where it came from, or what part of me thought it was allowed to speak to you like that. But I do know one thing."

A reply rose up my lungs, but my throat strangled it before it could pass my lips. The rest of my body kept my mouth from interrupting—kept me from barely drawing a breath—for fear I'd lose whatever might still be left between us.

"It wasn't true." His hands flexed at his sides, then stilled as he caught himself before reaching for me. "I am not better off without you. I never have been. I never will be."

He looked at me then. Finally, he *looked*. And for the first time since he recognized me in that alcove, I believed he *saw* me.

"I love you, Aevra. And I am so sorry that I made you doubt that even for a second."

I stood paralyzed before him, caught between the lingering hurt of the past three days and the unguarded vulnerability that wet his eyes.

This was him. Not the prince the court demanded. Not the boy who survived these walls by becoming the blade that drew first blood. *Him.* The honey-eyed boy who had found me once before, when I was small and human and afraid. The one who would always find me.

My body acted without instruction. I closed the cavernous distance between us with desperate momentum, colliding against his chest. My arms circled his waist, fingers clutching fistfuls of his tunic. I pressed my forehead to his sternum, letting the sage and salt burn into my brain for eternity.

He folded around me without hesitation, closing hard at my back as if my weight had finally given him permission to exist again. He dug his chin into the crown of my head, and we exhaled the same shuddering breath into each other.

"Do you still love me?" he murmured.

I buried my face deeper into him, as if I'd find the answer burrowed somewhere beneath his ribs instead of in my own mouth.

"Of fucking course I do."

He let out a whimper of relief and cinched his arms tighter, like he'd braced for a blow and instead received mercy. His mouth pressed into my hair, then to my forehead.

"I love you," he breathed against my skin. Then, quieter, "—F'elvænith."

He said it like I wasn't meant to hear it. A kept truth slipping loose with the collapsing dam.

I didn't ask what it meant. Didn't care. But my fingers wrung lightly in his tunic, a silent acknowledgment. A promise to keep it close, whatever it was.

His body eased against mine, the stiffness held in his poise warming to thaw. His hand at my back softened, then a knuckle nudged my cheek—a request—until it caught beneath my chin. And I let it guide me.

My face tilted up, my gaze meeting his at last. For once, I didn't see them burning with conviction or smoldering with want. They were just... clear. Emptied of all pretense and expectation. No crown. No performance. Something fragile and almost shy glittered there, and it undid me far more thoroughly than heat ever could.

He leaned in slowly and brushed his nose against mine, the

faintest, familiar graze of skin that pulled the loosened thread in my chest and unspooled me. I let out a soft, surprised sound—half sigh, half laugh—but he barely gave it any room to form.

His lips found mine, serene and certain, his kiss curving into a smile against me; he pulled me in tighter, pressing the air from my chest and catching it before it could escape.

Then my traitorous jaw nearly unhinged with an unstoppable, gaping yawn. Torian stilled, his arms loosening as his forehead came to rest gently against mine.

"Am I boring you?" he murmured playfully as his nose skipped along my temple.

A low hum slipped from me before words bothered to assemble themselves. "Not remotely," I mumbled. "You just woke me up." *And I finally felt safe.*

My body betrayed me again, folding backward in a deep, instinctive stretch as the week-long ache finally found somewhere to go. My robe slid open as my spine spilled over the cradle of his arms.

He inhaled sharply as his hands glided to support me, tracing the shallow grooves between my ribs through the thin nightgown. A quiet sigh left me once the stretch ran its course, and I settled back against him, boneless and pleasantly weak-kneed.

"I've missed this," he whispered, lips hovering at the shell of my ear while his thumbs made small, absent passes at my waist. "I've missed *you.*"

His hand shifted just a fraction down my back as he nuzzled a request at the curve of my jaw. A pulse of awareness went through me, reminding me of my dry mouth and the sleep that still lingered there.

"Wait," I said, hardly opening my mouth while my body stiffened in its sudden self-consciousness. "I—" I cleared my throat. "I haven't even washed my face."

Torian pulled himself away from my neck as my lips pressed

together instinctively.

"After everything," he said with an amused grin, "you're worried about morning breath?"

Heat rushed up my neck as I let out a mortified sigh. "I'm allowed to have standards."

"Mm," he hummed. "Then allow me to lower mine instead."

"Torian," I whined as I weakly pushed against his chest. "I'm a mess. I wasn't expecting—" I made a vague gesture between us, deliberately keeping my attention from traveling downward to the outline in his trousers. "—this."

His smile widened. "You're beautiful."

"You're biased."

"Perhaps. But I know what I want." The fire returned to his eyes as they darted from my mouth, to the pulse beneath my jaw, to the neckline of my nightgown. "What I've waited a century for."

I ducked swiftly out of his slackened arms. "Then you can wait a moment longer while I freshen up."

I didn't bother closing the bathroom door—modesty seemed so trivial now. I ran my face under the frigid tap, rinsed my mouth, and ran wet fingers through my hair in a futile attempt to tame it.

Torian watched me from the other side of the room. Not politely. Not with the careful distance he'd worn earlier like penance. He leaned one shoulder against the stone beside the window, hands held loosely in his pockets while he followed every small, mundane motion I made.

"Enjoying the view?" I said, cupping another handful of water and splashing it over my flushed cheeks.

"What man so bold can turn his face from grace?"

I raised an eyebrow as a curious smirk crept along his mouth.

"Yet flame nor ash may draw me far from thee."

Time froze as we got caught in the shock of having spoken the same language without meaning to. The language of something old and human.

"I've never known a Fae to allude to ancient mortal poets."

"Then you have met not a single Faen worth knowing."

"You're incorrigible."

He pushed off the wall and sauntered closer, still peering at me with those half-lidded eyes like I was the most interesting thing in the world.

"Better?" he asked softly.

"Marginally," I replied halfheartedly, glancing at my reflection through the water droplets on the mirror. "Though a proper bath—"

"—sounds heavenly," he finished for me.

The clawfoot tub answered before I could. Water surged from the faucet, steam blooming upward as it filled, lavender bubbles whispering against the porcelain.

I turned curiously.

"Perks of being prince of the palace," he said mildly, tipping his eyebrows toward the filling tub. "It listens when I ask nicely."

I looked at the bath. Gods, I *wanted* it. My muscles already ached in anticipation, my bones craving the heat and the stillness it offered. My head fell back as I let my robe slip from my shoulders, the nightdress following in a puddle of silk.

Jasmine and vanilla steam curled around my skin, coaxing an involuntary moan from me as I took a step toward the tub.

His hands met my bare waist.

"Torian—" I protested unconvincingly, because, again, *gods, the bath—*

He whisked my curls aside, his mouth finding the nape of my neck. "The bath can wait," he murmured.

"But—"

"I can't bear another moment when I've already lost so many."

I closed my eyes, and the steam, the warmth, the scent of him all blurred together—my body ached less for the water and more for *him*.

"The bath can wait." The words dissolved somewhere between my choosing comfort over necessity the moment our mouths collided. His kiss wasn't careful this time; he didn't hold me against him like a china doll he feared might break.

His tunic pressed roughly against my skin as I fisted the fabric and dragged it free from his waistband. I slipped my hands beneath it, meeting the dense, living warmth that melted into my palms. My fingers traced slowly upward, learning the planes of his stomach, counting each ridge and groove that tensed at my touch. My thumb lingered along the patch of hair below his navel, lightly skimming the path it knew by heart.

His breath stuttered against my mouth as he yanked the tunic over his head. My palm slid across the unyielding mound of his chest, coming to rest over the monstrous scar that lay over his pounding heart. The muscles there strained, then yielded, as if he were coaching himself through my touch.

I draped my arms around his neck, rising on my toes and baring my collarbone to his mouth. His teeth met the hollow I offered him, and his hands skimmed lower, squeezing me firmly to draw my hips deliciously against his.

With his face buried in my skin, a wrecked groan tore from his chest. "Not another damn moment." His grip flexed and shifted, and my stomach flipped as he lifted me cleanly off the bathroom floor. I locked my ankles at his lower back as we crossed the bedroom, metal jingling as he worked the buckle of his belt. A breathless, impatient huff left him as he kicked his pants aside.

This was it—the closest we had ever gotten to each other. Not a scrap between us, and yet I still needed him *closer*.

His grip tightened on me, fingers digging into my flesh as if he felt it too—the impossible need to close a distance that no longer existed.

The edge of the bed met the back of his knees, and he drew a slow, steady breath as he sat. He took my weight easily, but his jaw still clenched like it cost him something dear.

I sat astride his lap, hips rocking back and forth while his mouth trailed a slow path up my sternum. His hands remained planted on my thighs as the pressure settled between us, pooling where our skin met.

My movements drew the shadows from beneath the bed. They twisted hungrily around our ankles like vines of smoke, and Torian's fingers pressed into me reflexively, nails biting half-moons into my flesh. He was solid beneath me, the unmistakable length of him brushing with each roll of my hips, maddeningly near but never quite where I needed him.

"Aevra," he murmured with a jagged breath, pulling his forehead from my collarbone as I shifted over him.

I cradled his face in my palms, feeling the sharp edge of his jaw working beneath my thumbs. I leaned down to brush my lips against his, a shimmering breath of stardust wafting into his mouth. He inhaled sharply, pupils blown wide and swallowing up every ounce of gold there.

"If you keep doing that—" His voice fractured, fingers digging in harder. "Gods, help me."

I met his warning by pressing down harder. "You'll what?"

"I won't be gentle," he growled.

I brought my lips to his ear as he throbbed against me.

"Then don't be."

With one fluid motion, he flipped me onto my back with enough force to knock the wind out of me in a gasp. His weight caged me into the mattress, one hand capturing both my wrists above my head while the other moved between us.

His mouth never left mine as a tendril of shadow wound around his forearm like a ribbon, guiding his touch lower. The first stroke of his fingers made me gasp against his lips, my body pushing into his touch.

My hips stuttered in their writhing as I struggled against his hold on my wrists. Want burned through me, sharp and useless, all of it trapped beneath his grip.

But before I could beg, before I could even say his name, he withdrew his fingers slowly. Without enough time to form a breath of protest, he then took himself in hand and pushed into me with one smooth, breathtaking stroke.

He was everywhere—filling me completely, driving the breath from my lungs as my body forgot how to resist him. All language was stolen from me, and a moan tore from deep in my core. I tried to wrench my hand free to muffle the sound, but he only held firmer.

"Let them hear," he whispered into my mouth.

The shadow that coiled around his wrist pulsed intently in response. It urged his fingers to continue their work through each slow stroke, adjusting the pressure until my breath fractured completely.

He released his hold on my wrists and slid his hand down my ribs, dragging his palm possessively across my skin.

I turned my head helplessly into his touch as he traced along my throat, then my jaw. My eyelids fluttered shut as the pressure coiled in my belly, my thighs trembling at his waist.

"Don't," he said roughly, his voice a low rumble that vibrated straight through me. "Don't close your eyes."

A drop of sweat traced a line from his temple down the rigid line of his jaw, falling to land on my collarbone and mingling with my own. His thumb held my chin steady, forcing my gaze to his as another wave crested high above me, too fast to outrun.

"Look at me, Aevra," he demanded, his breath cracking along with mine.

His command unraveled me. I knew he could feel it ripple through my core as his name tore free on my voice. My lungs, my mind, my every fiber of muscle seized as it crashed through me.

"That's it," he purred, still holding my face as he watched me come undone beneath him. "There she is."

The sound I made—raw, pulled from the depths of my soul—echoed off the walls in a sputtered moan. My vision flashed white at the edges as the darkness around us quaked in time with the aftershocks rolling through my spine.

"There's my girl."

His touch slowed to a crawl—not stopping, never stopping—drawing it out until it burned, until I was shaking beneath him. He pulled my lower lip between his teeth as he chased his own end, his rhythm shifting to abandon what little patience remained inside him.

His hands then slid beneath me, palms searing along my spine as he pulled me tighter—closer—until there was no space, no air, no ragged thought left to spare. He swore under his breath, hips snapping forward again and again.

"Gods—fuck."

His breath broke open as he shuddered. His face twisted; his arms shook where they braced around me. The bedsheets beside my head knotted in his fists as he bowed, his grip slipping, before he sank into me with one last, helpless sound.

For a long moment, he didn't move. Just breathed. Just clung to the sliver of bliss we'd been afforded. When he dropped his forehead to my shoulder, planting a kiss on my collarbone before collapsing beside me, the room spun in and out of focus. He rolled onto his side and pulled me into him, tracing lazy circles along my waist.

We fit so comfortably together, every curve of my body nestling perfectly against every contour of his. I could have slept like that for millennia—sweaty, panting, loved.

"Aevra," he whispered hoarsely, tenderly.

I barely hummed in reply.

"Marry me."

Chapter Thirty-Three

"What?"

The word slipped out breathless, half-laughing, my skin still humming for his touch.

"Marry me," he said again.

I shifted closer, propping myself up against him as I lifted my hand to the band of light filtering through the curtains.

"Well," I huffed, considering my empty ring finger, "the stone isn't as large as I would have expected." I tilted my wrist this way and that, squinting with theatrical disappointment. "And I prefer a marquise over an oval. But I suppose this will do."

His mouth curved, though only slightly. "I'll be sure to remember that."

Satisfied with my performance, I let my hand fall back to his chest, my fingers finding the ridge of the scar that crossed his heart. The seam of something torn and imperfectly mended. I traced its path idly, like one might worry a familiar stone in their pocket.

"You've never told me how you got this."

He didn't answer right away. Instead, he studied me with the careful attention of a cat measuring shadows on the wall—curious, wondering whether to pounce or let them pass unnoticed.

"Bear," he said finally. Flat, dismissive, as if that story wasn't worth the breath it took to tell. "Aevra, I'm serious."

"And I'm impressed," I replied lightly, even as something in his tone made my stomach flutter. "To have taken on a mountain bear and lived to tell the tale?"

"Not about that." His hand caught mine, stilling my wandering fingertips.

I searched his face, waiting for the inevitable softening that was supposed to follow moments like this—the sign that the heat and the closeness had carried him away from the shore of his better judgment. But I didn't find it.

A strangled laugh bubbled up in my throat, wrong-footed and sharp at its edges. "I hope you know a good necromancer," I scoffed. "So my father can walk me down the aisle."

I waited for him to smile. To meet me in the absurdity that I used as an escape hatch. To make his declaration unreal again, meaningless as morning mist.

He didn't.

"Gods, you really are serious."

"And you still haven't said yes."

"Because it's reckless!" I accidentally shouted, then quickly dropped my voice to barely a whisper. "Can't we just—" I gestured helplessly at the space between us, at the bed, at the fragile peace we had just carved into each other. "What's wrong with what we have now?"

His thumb found the inside of my wrist, pressing softly where my pulse hammered beneath my skin.

"What we have now cannot last," he said gently.

"But—"

"The formal betrothal announcement is in a week." His voice was mild, but each word dropped like a stone in still water. "On the solstice, Valeraine becomes princess in name and law. And I become hers in the only way this court recognizes."

He paused, eyes burning into mine. "And you remain my careless indulgence. My trick pony, trotted out when it suits me. Left to wonder in your chambers how long it'll be before I come touch you again."

Hot tears clouded my vision as I tried to pull away, but his grip held firm.

"Aevra, that is not the life I want with you."

"Then what life do you want with me?"

Torian fell back against the pillows with a heavy sigh, one arm thrown over his eyes as if the weight of what he was suggesting had just settled over him.

"I want a life where I don't have to check over my shoulder before saying your name," he said to the ceiling. "Where I don't have to choose you quietly, or carefully, or only after the door locks behind me."

He lowered his arm and turned his head to look at me. "When people ask me what's important, I want to tell them the truth instead of reciting the advantages of a strategic alliance with the Obsidian Isles."

"Torian—"

"I want a life where choosing you won't also cost me *you*."

Again, I thought.

Just outside the door, the palace stirred—distant voices trailing through the corridors, morning bells chiming softly—blissfully oblivious in its routines, which suddenly felt suffocating.

The thought of it, of a life I hadn't even felt safe fantasizing about, made me want to swoon. And scream and hide. A life where days were allowed to be boring, where lazy mornings carried over into sleepy afternoons before giving way to quiet evenings.

Where I could be Aevra—and only Aevra.

"We can't exactly get married in the palace chapel," I finally mumbled, my eyes locked on my hands as I picked at my fingernails compulsively.

"So we run."

My forehead crinkled as that word speared itself through my mind. *Run.* If only it were as easy as those three little letters suggested. But I was too tired to chase the idea of forming a plan. The betrothal was in a week.

We had time.

I let out a long breath and shrugged half-heartedly.

"Okay." Not *forever*. Not *solstice-bound and sealed by the gods*. Just... okay.

Torian's brow furrowed slightly, though a flicker of hope glinted in his eye. "So you're saying yes?"

"I'm saying okay." I shook my head and settled back against the pillows. "And that's fine for now."

His eyes searched mine for a long moment, but whatever he found in them, he did not press it. Instead, he smiled softly.

"But only for now," he whispered.

I nodded once, the only motion I could manage without cracking something fragile inside me.

He swung his legs off the bed and reached for his discarded clothes. I watched him dress in silence, trying to focus on the way the sunset glowed across the muscles in his back, failing to stop the spiral.

I found my voice as he was fastening his belt.

"I don't want to go back to the Duskhold."

His hands stilled on the buckle. Then he moved toward me, sitting on the edge of the bed as his palms cupped my face. His thumbs traced the curve of my cheekbones with infinite gentleness.

"You won't," he said. "We'll take a threshold to the other side of the world before anyone even realizes we're gone."

"Threshold?"

"I'll explain—" He kissed me quickly, firmly, with promise. "—later."

He didn't linger but a moment, his knuckles brushing lightly under my chin as if to ground himself.

"Until then," he murmured. "*F'Elvænith.*"

Before I could even sigh in agreement, he was already turning away. He crossed the room in long, decisive strides and pulled the door open—

Lysara stood on the other side, her hand raised mid-knock, eyes wide with shock that she tried to school into polite confusion a beat too late.

"Your Highness," she whispered as she dipped just a fraction, careful to keep protocol as well as secrecy.

Torian barely spared her a glance. He leaned out just far enough to clear the doorway, already shrugging into his coat.

"Tomorrow night," he said simply, tossing the words over his shoulder as he moved past her. "I promise."

Tomorrow night?

"Wait!" I hissed after him, but his boots had faded down the corridor, swallowed almost immediately by the waking palace.

Tomorrow night. It was terrifyingly too soon, while also seeming unreachable. I looked over at the wardrobe, at the leather satchel strewn on the ground, bulging with the only possessions I had.

I was already packed.

"*F'Elvænith?*" Lysara questioned from the doorway, her eyebrow raising incredulously. "He named you?"

I lifted a shoulder in a small, defeated shrug. "I suppose so."

"And?" Lysara's yellow eyes sharpened on me. "Did you answer him?"

"I—" I frowned. "Answer him how?"

She exhaled slowly and pinched the bridge of her nose. "Don't worry about it," she sighed. "Get dressed. It smells like sex in here, and I believe you owe me some truth from last night."

Chapter Thirty-Four

Torian

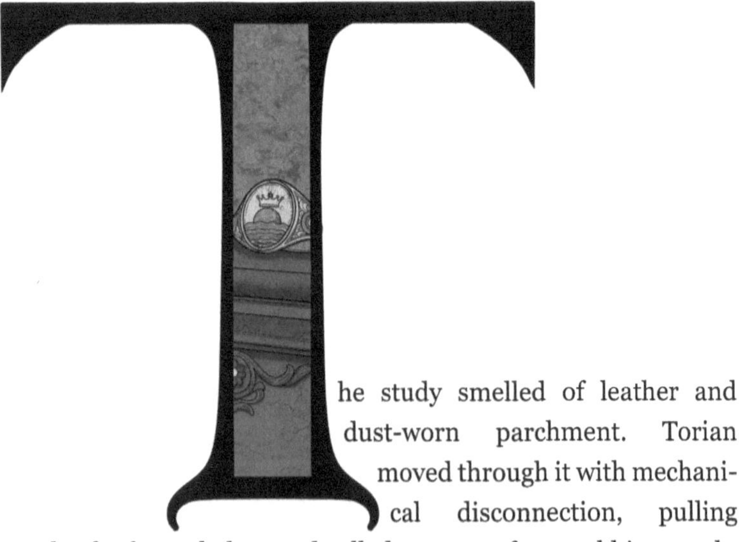

The study smelled of leather and dust-worn parchment. Torian moved through it with mechanical disconnection, pulling notebooks from shelves and rolled-up maps from cubbies, stacking them beside the open satchel on his desk. Each motion was efficient. Practiced. As if he'd packed this room a hundred times over in his head.

He snatched a half-empty bottle and drank from it without

looking at the label, without even tasting it.

A polite knock sounded at the door. He didn't look up. Just flicked his wrist, and the door creaked open.

Lady Valeraine stepped inside with a bottle of wine in one hand and two crystal glasses balanced in the other. She was dressed simply for once, her deep green robe making her look almost mortal, if one didn't know any better.

"I found myself wanting for company," she said lightly, lifting the bottle like an offering. "I thought we might share a glass—" Torian took another sip straight from the neck and set it down with a hollow *thunk*. "—Though it seems you've started without me."

He added another book to his pile with a noncommittal grunt.

Valeraine's gaze drifted around the room, noting the half-packed satchel, the empty spaces on the shelves. The corners of her mouth pinched as she set the wine and glasses down.

"You're packing," she observed quietly.

"I'm reorganizing," he said, still not meeting her eyes. "Making sure affairs are in order before I leave tomorrow."

"Tomorrow?"

Torian suppressed a wince, kicking himself for forgetting that he ought to be lying.

"I'm riding south. A succession matter in the Low Marches."

Her brow furrowed only slightly. "Baroness Delphine?" she asked. "But she isn't due until spring."

"There are certain formalities," he sighed as he pinched the bridge of his nose, "that must be addressed well in advance."

"Very well, then." She clasped her hands in front of her, fingers laced too tightly as her attention caught on the ring sitting on the mantel. "Shall I have your signet polished before you go?"

"That won't be necessary."

"Are you certain? It's looking rather tarnished—"

"I won't be needing it."

The air in the room turned stale. Valeraine's eyes sharpened on him as he took another long pull from the bottle before corking it and tossing it into the bag.

"You won't be needing your signet," she repeated slowly, carefully, "for an official errand?"

"Not this time."

The lightness drained from her face, and her posture slackened as she stepped further into the room.

"Prince Torian." Her voice was soft, gentle in a way he never thought possible. "I hope you understand your choices do not end with you."

He didn't answer, just continued briskly folding his traveling cloak.

"It may not give you the love story you so recklessly crave, but preserving your duty as prince and future king—"

Torian let out a low, humorless laugh. "*Future king.*" He shook his head. "I refuse to live up to my father's tyranny."

"Then don't," she bit out. "Outlive him. Rule without malice. Make his reign look small in comparison."

"With all due respect, my Lady—" He finally looked at her, something cold flickering behind his molten eyes. "—you are not my counsel. Nor are you my queen." He paused to let the words settle like frost. "My condolences that I will not bestow that title upon you."

If his words struck her, she did not let it show.

"I do not need to be Queen to serve justly," she said. "But you—"

"The only justice I can offer," Torian cut in, "is my abdication."

"Abdication," she scoffed. "That's your idea of justice?"

He said nothing.

"Abandoning your people while the King arranges his board for war?" She was no longer attempting to whisper. "You may not care for your father—and you certainly do not care for me—but for pity's sake, Torian... surely you care what becomes of your people?"

He reached for the satchel and fastened the clasp with a final click.

"What becomes of my people is no longer your concern," he said as he slung the shoulder strap across his back. "Nor will it be mine come tomorrow night."

"Torian." Her voice broke across his name. "*Please*. Don't do this."

He crossed to the door without looking back, opening it wide as he stood to the side.

"I believe we are finished here, my Lady." He gestured for her to exit, but she remained rooted to the spot. "I am sorry that it has to be this way."

"It doesn't."

"It does," he said firmly. "Now, if you please..."

Her legs were like lead, but they carried her out anyway without her command. She stopped before him at the threshold, icy blue eyes drilling into him.

"Be careful which bridges you choose to burn, Your Highness. You may not be welcomed back a second time."

And then the door shut quietly behind her.

CHAPTER THIRTY-FIVE

is own mother."

Lysara shook her head as we walked the narrow paths of the royal menagerie. The scent was far less heavenly than the gardens—hay and manure replacing peonies and roses—but the conversation was safer beneath the symphony of whinnies and snorts, and the occasional screeching of exotic birds.

A peacock preened its iridescent tail feathers, each eye catching the light like scattered jewels; a pair of silver foxes curled together in sleep, their breath misting in the cool air. Beautiful creatures, all of them. Pampered and fed, admired from a distance.

"Well," Lysara continued as she fed a sugar cube to a zebra, "that answers some questions. Not all of them, but some."

We strolled in silence for a few blissful moments, my attention drifting to the measured rhythm of hooves and wingbeats. But I could feel the question burning through her.

"So... tomorrow night?" she finally asked.

Of course, she knew. I didn't even bother to feign ignorance this time.

"I suppose so," I mumbled with a half-hearted shrug.

I paused before a gilded cage housing a small dragon the size of a house cat, perched on a boulder with its wings tucked in tight. It pressed its scaled snout against the bars, its green eyes tracking every fidget of my fingers, every shuffle of my nervous feet. I wondered if it remembered flight, or if captivity had become so comfortable that the open sky was nothing more than another ceiling.

Trick pony.

Lysara stopped beside me, her gaze flicking between the dragon and my face.

"You don't look like someone planning a wedding."

I wanted it all.

I wanted Torian; I wanted freedom. But my feet refused to take me any further than this. I shrugged again, unable to sort through the tangle of panic and plans that had me paralyzed.

"I don't know where we would even go," I said weakly. "Where does a prince take his human ward when running away from his duties and his betrothed?"

Lysara's hand rested steadily on my arm, her thumb pressing once to anchor me in place. The dragon took a bored whiff, then blew a gentle gust of warm air that lifted my curls from my shoulders.

"There's a village on the far side of the Irons," she said as she procured a cube of raw meat from somewhere I couldn't see and handed it to me. "Timbered houses, low stone walls. No one looks twice at strangers there."

The little dragon chuffed as I offered it the meat in my flattened palm. It took the treat with a quick swoop of its forked tongue, gulping it down without so much as tasting it. It blinked slowly at me, and I did the same.

"And how are we supposed to get there?"

"A threshold."

She said it as though it were obvious, with the same indifferent cadence that Torian had used earlier. I let out a long, annoyed sigh through my nose and finally looked at her with eyes I had to force not to roll.

"I'm sure this will come as a shock to you, but I have no idea what that means," I said sharply, but Lysara didn't recoil at my bite. Instead, she gave an apologetic snort and pulled me down with her to crouch on the ground.

Before I could ask, she rolled her sleeves up and began tracing shapes in the dirt of the menagerie floor. With just a few swipes of her finger, a sigil was drawn at our feet between us.

"*This* is a threshold."

The flecks of dust along the lines and curves shifted and stirred, though not from a passing breeze. The sigil itself hummed and shook, going in and out of focus like it wasn't entirely there. I had an eerie feeling like I had seen something like it before, but I was hopeless to remember where. Perhaps in a dream.

"There is one just outside the eastern gate."

"How does it work?" I asked as I poked the wavering symbol, the feeling of static climbing up my wrist.

Lysara chewed her cheek as she considered the mechanics of magic that folded time and space.

"It's like a hallway between rooms," she said as she waddled a few paces away and began tracing another mark in the dirt. "You touch it with the intention of wherever you want to go, and you just—" She placed her palm over what she had just drawn, and suddenly appeared in front of me again, the symbol between us now glowing. "—go."

I fell on my bottom as I jolted backwards in surprise.

"As long as there's a threshold, you can get there," she continued. "Even if you've never been. Even if you've never seen the other side."

My eyes darted between the two thresholds on the floor as they dimmed in sync with each other.

"Your turn," she said as she effortlessly wiped it away.

I shook my head quickly, my voice stolen from watching Lysara effectively teleport. She pursed her lips as she took my fingers in her grip.

"Aevra—"

"Is there any other way?"

Lysara crinkled her forehead. "Aside from walking? I suppose you could take a ship." She gestured to the dragon perched above our heads. "Or hitch a ride, but I doubt this one could carry you both."

She giggled, but I just stared down at my hands.

"That's not what I meant," I murmured.

"I know." She didn't release my hand. "Unfortunately—" My breath hissed through my teeth as my entire body tensed at that word. "—aside from a mating bond, there are no loopholes to exploit when it comes to politically arranged marriages."

I looked up from the dirt beneath my fingernails, a flicker of hope twinkling in my eye.

"You are not the prince's mate," she said matter-of-factly, and my shoulders slumped even further. "Mates are equals in both power and conviction—humans and Faen cannot be fated."

Rising tears blurred my vision as I tried to stand, but Lysara held firm on my hand, forcing me to keep squatting with her.

"Show me how you draw the threshold."

I shook my head again as the tears fell, landing to form wet craters in the dirt.

"If Torian knows how to use them—"

"*You* need to know how to use them." Her tone was no longer tender and understanding. "Does Torian instruct you to breathe in and out? Does he accompany you to the toilet? Was he standing beside you when you faced Alezae?"

I winced in offense and opened my mouth in rebuttal, but she barely took a breath.

"You should never depend on anyone more than you can depend on yourself. Now—" She slid my fingers into the dirt. "—draw the threshold."

armth still ghosted along my fingertips, tingling from where I'd traced thresholds in the dirt. Over and over, until Lysara was satisfied I could draw one blind.

I rounded the corner toward my room when relentless knocking echoed down the corridor.

Knock, knock, knock, knock, knock, knock, knock, knock, knock.

I knew exactly who it was before I even saw her. There was

only one person in this palace who knocked like the world might end if a door went unanswered for a heartbeat too long.

Miravelle stood outside my door with a massive dress box balanced in her arms and her emotional-support clipboard clamped between her teeth. She never paused, never looked around. Just kept hammering the wood like it owed her something.

I approached her slowly, half-wondering if she'd even notice me.

She did.

Her head whipped around so fast that her resident butterflies scattered in startled loops. The clipboard tumbled from her mouth, clattering to the floor as she let out a small squeal.

"Miss Lyra!" she admonished, as if she weren't the reigning queen of startling.

She shoved the enormous box into my arms without ceremony, then mumbled something incomprehensible as she bent to collect her discarded clipboard.

"I have come to deliver your ensemble and discuss the finer details of your upcoming performance." She was already scribbling furiously as she adjusted the tiny pair of glasses perched on the tip of her nose.

I blinked at her. "My performance?"

"Yes, dear. For the betrothal ball."

"Oh." My mouth went suddenly dry. "Yes. Right. The betrothal."

The topic felt hollow. Because none of it mattered. We'd be long gone before Miravelle even had time to map the shadows. I forced a smile that didn't reach my tired eyes.

"I haven't quite finished blocking it yet," I said, wondering if woodland faeries also had a knack for detecting lies. "May I let you know in a few days?"

Miravelle's expression fell, like I'd just suggested setting fire to the palace instead of asking for more time.

"Heavens, I'm afraid that will be far too late!"

The dress box grew heavier. Or perhaps my arms had just decided to stop working altogether.

"The betrothal has been moved up," she said briskly, quill scratching again—no doubt notating my ignorance and lack of urgency on the matter. "I will need the minutiae of your performance posthaste. Lighting cues, musical accompaniment—"

Her voice faded into static.

Moved up.

"I'm sorry," I interrupted, voice cracking. "When—when is it now?"

She looked up from her clipboard with an annoyed *hmph* as the butterflies settled in her rose gold hair once more.

"Tomorrow night."

Chapter Thirty-Seven

looked for him everywhere.

The kitchens, the courtyards, the library. I had even cloaked myself in a shroud of shadow and walked through the male communal baths like a phantom, steam curling around too many naked bodies who never even glanced my way.

Nothing.

I reluctantly returned to my room long past midnight, my bottom numb and flattened from sitting on the bench beneath the willow for what seemed like hours. I paced the length of my chambers—wall to wall, window to window—waiting for the knock that never came.

He'd said tomorrow night. He'd *promised* tomorrow night. And now, tomorrow night was only a few moments away.

I forced myself to stop moving. To breathe. To *think*.

Maybe this was his plan all along. Maybe he'd arranged for the betrothal to be moved up to create a distraction. Drunken revelers would have a harder time noticing their prince slipping away with his magician.

When my feet ached, when my thoughts became a snarl I couldn't untangle, I practiced. And then, when the stars flickered and I couldn't pull the shadows from the corner, I slept.

And I slept until the pressure mounted in my head and forced my eyes open. The noon chime sounded in the corridor, but I didn't move. I stayed curled up in the bedsheets, relishing the last comfort they'd ever give me.

I tossed the dress box carelessly on the bed as the evening chime sounded. The festivities were probably well underway, but I couldn't bring myself to care. I was the court favorite, and they wouldn't start my performance without me.

My breath was stolen when I finally flipped open the lid.

A spider silk gown spilled from the box in a cascade of powder blue and gold, the fabric so fine it seemed to shimmer and shift like morning light rippling across water. It was delicate. Breathtaking. The kind of dress that turned you into something precious, even as it laid you bare.

I dressed slowly, my fingers fumbling as I fastened the last tiny pearl buttons cinching at the sides. My hair was pinned to the side, tumbling over my shoulder while rogue ringlets framed my face. My lips were stained a soft rose, my lashes darkened and elongated enough to make my eyes look wider. Startled.

I pressed a hand to my chest and breathed with intention, willing my heartbeat to slow, but it only quickened. The creeping sense of dread I'd tried to outrun all day and night settled over me, suffocating and inevitable.

Something was wrong.

But I shoved that wrongness in a box and stuffed it in the corner as I exited my room with no plans to return.

The ballroom was a riot of sound and light when I arrived.

Musicians played in pockets around the room, their melodies weaving through the hum of conversation and laughter. Courtiers in their finest furs and jewels moved in elegant clusters, raising their glasses in toast after toast.

I slipped into the wings, my breath shallow and pulse erratic.

The thrones sat at the far end of the chamber, raised on a dais draped in amber satin. The King and Queen surveyed the revelry with uninterested expressions, while the two other thrones were empty of the prince and his betrothed.

The dread barreled into me, blurring my vision at its edges. My knees buckled, and I stumbled backward into a dancer. Some faceless someone guided me to the drink table and deposited me beside a row of crystal decanters.

I grabbed the nearest glass and poured something sweet and floral, my hands shaking so badly the liquid sloshed over the rim. I brought it to my mouth and drank, the nectar coating my throat and doing nothing to calm the storm raging through me.

"Hello."

I startled, dropping the glass on the table and spilling its sticky contents.

Torian stood beside me, the slightest thread of his sleeve brushing my arm as he reached for the wine, and I poured another. I barely looked at him, gripping the glass with both hands now to keep them from trembling.

"Did you do this?" I asked through a disguised sip.

"No."

I cut my eyes toward him.

"Apparently the Frost Court learned about the details of the betrothal," he whispered as he fixed his eyes on the crowd. "The King moved it up to avoid Lord Iäen making an appearance."

I downed the glass in one swallow, the sweetness cloying, my stomach turning.

"What are we going to do?"

Torian's jaw tightened. "Eyes are on me," he murmured. "After your performance, slip out the back door." He tilted his head toward the exit behind the dais. "Wait for me by the eastern gate."

I nodded once, pouring myself a third glass.

"You look beautiful."

By the time I looked up, he was gone.

I rooted myself to the drink table and counted my breaths, watching the performances before mine without actually seeing them. And then my name was heralded.

I took my spot in the center of the ballroom, the crowd circling me, pressing in as they elbowed each other for the best view. The chandeliers dimmed at Miravelle's signal, and silence flooded the hall.

I had no earth-shattering magic planned, no sigh eliciting imagery loaded at my fingertips. I couldn't afford another catastrophe. Not when my purpose was to remain unseen.

So I kept it safe. The court might have been disappointed that no stars would implode, that no aurora ribbons would unfurl across the ceiling—but I wouldn't have to shoulder their disappointment for long.

Stars winked to life overhead; they gasped. Shadows curled around me like a cowl; they marveled. I pulled a tendril from the mass at my neck and twirled it in front of me; they whistled and cheered.

Their unconditional wonder at my illusions sparked something in me. Something that stopped my hands from shaking. A noblewoman laughed as I plucked the darkness from beneath her heels, sending it spiraling around her before dissolving it into smoke. Another nobleman grinned as his shadow rose and bowed mockingly to his companions.

The crowd was mine, and the attention was intoxicating.

I scanned for another willing participant as the circle parted for someone muscling to the front. The shadows that pooled at their feet clung to their ankles and calves, refusing to shift with the flickering chandeliers. I reached for them, confidently playful.

But they did not come.

I reached again, yanking them toward me, but they held firm.

I looked up.

Our eyes met.

CRACK!

Blinding, searing white light exploded from somewhere deep inside me, ripping through my chest with a pain so excruciating I couldn't even scream. Stars burst behind my eyes, my ribs cracking under the pressure of something vast and terrible trying to escape.

The gods had finally come for me, and I was dead before I even hit the ground.

Lord Iäen Thrymskaldr of the Frost Court traced a finger along the map of Avynne spread across the council table. Hoarfrost trailed his touch, sketching glittering lines down winding dotted roads and snaking up the blue line of the river.

"The scouts report the rifts grow more unstable by the day," he murmured, the weariness plain in his graveled voice.

Lord Daeran Noctis stood rigidly at the frost-glazed window, his breath curling past his lips like smoke. He looked out with open disdain at the thick flakes of snow falling silently over the serrated glass spires of the Frostkeep. The chill gnawed at him, boring into his bones as he pulled his fur-lined cloak tighter around his neck.

This cold was unnatural. Endless.

A far cry from the smoldering warmth of his own realm—where one did not need to swaddle themselves like a newborn babe simply to visit a friend.

"We've seen the same around Montumbra." Daeran's tone was clipped, as if he were listing irritations rather than crises. "The sirens are restless, and the shadow paths demand twice the power they once did."

"And yet the illustrious Amber King chooses to ignore these warnings," Iäen said, his voice rough and icy, mirroring the perpetual winter of his realm. "Instead, he keeps his eyes narrowed on the north. Can't even take a frozen piss without him wanting to inspect it for treachery."

Daeran huffed with a smirk, silver eyes catching the mischief of a fisherman baiting a hook.

"The *Golden* King—I have heard he refers to himself of late."

Iäen's lip curled, his breath fogging white. "I'll give him something golden to put in his goblet."

"Gods, mate. That's vile," Daeran said, dropping his eyes to hide the glimmer of amusement.

It was a favorite pastime of his—needling the ancient Faen until he bit. Because if Iäen could still bite, that meant he still had teeth, and when it came to King Oranth, those teeth needed to remain bared and razor-sharp.

Daeran traced a crude, unmistakable shape in the fog on the glass before pushing away from the window. Iäen, halfway through rolling up the territorial map, sighed like he carried three centuries of disappointment, and tossed the map back onto the table.

"This is a place of repute, Noctis," Iäen said as he scraped the window with his sleeve. "Not a lowly bathhouse. Perhaps if you were more mature, you wouldn't be living in that mountain married to your hand."

"I resent that," Daeran drawled. "You are simply incapable of appreciating the oldest form of Impressionism." He tipped his head, eyeing Iäen's face with faux appraisal. "And it may not be a bathhouse, but I can give you a shave if you'd like. That jaw is looking a bit rugged."

The smallest curve crept across Iäen's mouth as he shook his head, so slight it might have been mistaken as a trick of the light.

"How is Valeraine?"

Daeran shrugged as he picked up the haphazardly strewn map, curling it up neatly and tying it in place with its leather string.

"As far as I can tell, she is well. Or about as well as any of us could be among those gaudy elitists."

Iäen's crystalline blue eyes glazed over with something like remorse.

"I haven't received a scrap from her," he admitted softly, his gruff voice catching on the lump in his throat. "And it seems I have been conveniently left off the guest list for her betrothal ceremony."

Daeran patted him on the back with the rolled map.

"You know very well she cannot send a word from within the Vale. Especially after Loch Rime." His voice was calm, but the edges of his words carried a cautious strain.

Pink rose up the ivory skin of Iäen's neck, peeking out from his high collar.

"I did what needed to be done," he snarled through clenched teeth. "And I am paying dearly for it."

"I am not questioning your actions, my friend. I am stating the facts." Daeran thwacked him with the map a little harder than necessary—an attempt at levity that landed like a shove. He rested his hand heavily on Iäen's shoulder.

"She shouldn't have felt the need to do this," Iäen went on. "Inserting herself into that pit of two-headed vipers. Marrying that spoiled little brat. I should like to intervene. Let them cower at the monster they've made of me."

"No," Daeran said, flat and final. "You will do no such thing. Valeraine is perfectly positioned, and her political instincts are sharp as knives."

"They ought to be," Iäen muttered. "I sharpened them."

"That you did. And she's terrifying for it."

Iäen huffed a short laugh and swept Daeran's hand from his wool overcoat. Affection had not come easily for him over the last three and a half centuries after losing his mate.

"Give her the chance to do what she went there to do," Daeran said. "Or else giving her hand to the prince will be in vain—and we risk losing every godsdamned inch of ground we have gained against the Vale."

Iäen groaned in icy frustration.

"Don't worry your flaxen head over it. I will be in attendance, but even if I weren't—"

"I know," Iäen cut in, lifting a hand to stop the explanation he didn't want to hear. "So, they're scared shitless of the decrepit fossil in the north, but not the Devil of the Dark?"

Daeran snorted softly at the nickname gifted to him by the cravens in the Amber Vale. He could never decide if he loved it or loathed it, especially when it sounded almost... fond in the mouth of one of the most ancient and powerful rulers Faenkind had ever seen.

The shadows in the corner of the room stirred and swayed as Daeran strolled toward them, no longer able to keep his chin from trembling.

The cold prickled his nerves and heightened his impatience—

too many looming headaches tugging at the fraying edges of his attention.

"I expect the next shipment will be ready in the coming weeks," he called over his shoulder. "The forge has been overheating with the instability. Harder to temper the steel."

"Take your time," Iäen said as he waved him off. "I'd rather wait for strong blades than be handed flimsy butter knives."

With a casual flick of his wrist in a lazy farewell, he walked into the shadows and disappeared from the Frostkeep.

Daeran entered his private study and went straight for the decanter on his desk. He hoped a glass of volcanic wine would help chase the lingering chill out of his bones.

Still wrapped in his furs, he relished that first sip that lit his tongue and made him wince.

The glass had not yet left his lips when a knock gently tapped at the door, followed by the familiar, uncomfortable shuffle from the other side.

Unmistakably Elian, jumpy as ever.

He exhaled sharply through his nose and placed his glass down with restrained annoyance. Just a moment's peace. Was that such a difficult ask?

"Come in, Elian," Daeran said flatly.

"Welcome home, my Lord," Elian greeted as they shuffled into the room, arms spilling over with an array of ledgers, documents, and bits of correspondence.

Daeran forced his expression into something neutral as Elian dropped the pile of papers on his tidy desk. He pinched the bridge of his nose as a headache climbed into his forehead.

"How was your visit to the Frost Court?"

"Cold," he replied.

Elian's eyes flicked from Daeran's grimace to the full glass of wine to the furs on his shoulders and seemed to realize they had entered at an inopportune time. But instead of retreating out of the door like a sensible creature, they delicately cleared their throat and pulled a piece of folded parchment from the top of the stack.

"This arrived not an hour before your return, my Lord," they said, holding it out.

Daeran did not reach for it. Did not even glance at the seal.

"Is it going to detonate unless I address it right now," he asked dryly, "or can it wait until after dinner?"

Elian blinked at him. "It will not detonate, my Lord. It is only a bit of parchment. But it is time-sensitive, and I believe you should open it now."

Daeran dragged a hand down his face and sighed, then gestured for the missive. He had long since stopped trying to teach Elian his brand of jest—or any kind of jest, for that matter.

He rolled his eyes as he noted the seal of the Amber Vale: a pretentious rendering of a semicircle sun wearing a glowing crown. He thumbed the letter open, and his expression dropped even further.

"The betrothal ceremony has been moved forward to tonight." He snatched up the glass of wine, emptying it in one burning swallow. "The Amber King moves his pieces with suspicious and incredibly irritating haste."

Elian shifted on their feet, rummaging in their mind for the correct response. Their lips pursed, then cautiously parted.

"That's *unfortunate*, my Lord," they said carefully.

"Thank you, Elian. It *is* unfortunate." Daeran exhaled sharply. "It seems my moment's peace will have to wait until I return."

"Shall I assemble your formal attire? The air in the Vale is balmy this evening, and I believe your furs are a poor choice."

Daeran nodded.

"And what of Lady Calista?" He asked, shrugging the heavy

furs from his shoulders and dumping them onto Elian's arms.

They wavered under the weight of at least twenty beavers.

"She is down at the fisheries," they said, muffled and half-choked by pelts and pride.

"Still? I suppose I'll dine alone yet again." He looked over at Elian, who was now struggling blindly toward the door. "I'm beginning to wonder if she cares for me at all."

"She cares for you in her own way. In fact, she left you a gift."

Daeran shuddered and reached for the decanter again. "Gods, help me," he muttered under his breath. "I will take my dinner in here, Elian. And then I shall take my leave."

"Yes, my Lord."

Daeran swirled the fresh pour, watching the legs of the wine run down the sides of the glass. "Oh, and would you check if the cook wouldn't mind poisoning some of it? I'd like to send my corpse to the celebrations in my stead."

Elian did not so much as blink, merely inclined their head with grave sincerity, equal parts maddening and endearing.

"I would never ask such a thing. I will be back shortly with your meal, my Lord."

The shadow path between the Obsidian Isles and the Amber Vale had always been one of the most stable routes.

Tonight it felt... slippery. The darkness stretched and warped around him as he moved through it, demanding more concentration than such a familiar journey had any right to require.

When he emerged in the designated arrival chamber of the Amber Palace, his exit was not graceful. For the first time in perhaps three centuries, Daeran stumbled as he stepped out from the shadows, nearly losing his balance entirely.

Nausea rose from the twisting dark. Dinner before traveling was not the finest idea after all. He braced a hand against the wall, breath sharp, brow furrowed in confusion—or mild embarrassment—before he swallowed it down.

Thankfully, no one saw it. But that did not make it any less concerning.

A palace attendant appeared from around the bend of the hall, bowing low as he approached.

"Lord Daeran of the Obsidian Isles," he announced loudly, though no one else was around to hear.

"It seems I have arrived fashionably late to the party," Daeran said as he fidgeted with his cufflinks.

"The celebration is already underway in the High Ballroom, my Lord. Shall I announce your arrival?"

"That won't be necessary." The last thing Daeran wanted was a heralded announcement drawing attention to his entrance. He preferred to observe before being observed himself—a habit that would die hard after centuries of politics.

The attendant nodded and led him through corridors made of amber-veined marble and enormous gold columns that had no structural purpose other than to take up space. They floated like gilded ghosts, monuments to nothing but unbridled vanity.

The sunset poured through the arched windows. Surfaces had been awkwardly arranged to catch and scatter it until every step was damn near blinding. The Amber Vale's unceasing glow had always struck Daeran as ostentatious compared to the stark volcanic landscapes of the Obsidian Isles.

Everything here was built to impress rather than to function.

Form without substance.

Much like the court itself. But what more could be expected from a king who built an empire's entire personality around petrified tree sap?

As they neared the High Ballroom, the noise thickened. Music and laughter floated through the air, not to mention the distinctive cadence of courtiers competing for attention and favors among each other. Daeran suppressed a grimace. This was precisely the environment he had spent centuries avoiding.

The room smothered him the moment he stepped in. Heat from a hundred bodies pressed close, the air turning into a cloying fog of perfume and sweat. Daeran slipped in quietly, positioning himself at the edge of the gathering where he might not immediately be drawn into tedious conversation.

Gods, he'd sooner asphyxiate.

It took less than five minutes for the first courtier to approach him—an exceedingly petite middle-aged Semi-Faen with butterflies floating around her elaborately styled hairdo. She materialized out of thin air, almost making him jolt.

"Lord Daeran," she greeted warmly. "What an unexpected pleasure! I am Miravelle, Coordinator of Royal Events."

He inclined his head slightly, offering the minimum courtesy required for such interactions. "Miravelle."

"Your arrival is most fortuitous," she continued, unbothered by his lack of enthusiasm. "We've been discussing—"

"Lord Daeran!" Another one skittered over, her dress catching beneath her feet, causing her to stumble. "I was so hoping to see you in attendance this evening."

Miravelle pursed her lips. "The Lord and I were having a discussion—"

"I simply must tell you about the behemoth that was unearthed in my family's onyx mines, my Lord." Her eyes dragged over him. "It is quite impressive—even for your standards."

"Surely not nearly as impressive as the enchanted lumber from my family's pine forests! The structures crafted from our materials are unparalleled."

"How charming, Miravelle," she said with a contemptuous snort. "Wood would make fine fuel for the Isle's burning magma."

"As if His Grace has any more use for your counterfeit baubles!"

"Counterfeit?"

Daeran kept his face carefully blank as they bickered over him.

More marriage proposals dressed up as trade discussions, he thought as they tried to outbid each other with resources and innuendo. *Perhaps I'll start a collection.*

He was plotting the cleanest escape route to the wine table when a familiar voice cut through the din. Relief slid into him like a blade sheathed.

"Dearest cousin," said the voice, crisp yet comforting in its undying familial ease. She approached with the same grace he had envied growing up. She wore it like armor—her birthright. "I'd heard rumor of your arrival."

Daeran turned toward her, his shoulders loosening the barest fraction as she guided him away from the squabbling courtiers, oblivious in their sniping.

"Lady Valeraine," he said, pressing his forehead briefly to hers in greeting, his hand coming up to rest against her cheek. "You look well. Albeit a bit troubled."

Her timing was impeccable. It had always been. Her mouth bowed into a smile, though it did not meet her eyes.

"Your perception remains sharp as ever, my Lord," she said. "Rather refreshing, if I am being truthful. The endless need to explain nuance these past weeks has been... exhausting."

Daeran watched her gaze drift over the gathered party-goers as she adjusted the clasp of the diamond chain around her wrist.

"You're deflecting, my Lady."

"I am managing the matter," she said sharply, without so much as a flicker of her composure.

Daeran hummed, unconvinced.

"I am pleased you received my missive in time. The timing was necessary, I assure you."

His eyes narrowed on her. He never pretended to understand

every one of her maneuvers, but he had not expected her to be this forthright amid such dangerous company.

"*Your* missive? Moving the betrothal forward was your doing?" he whispered.

One eyebrow twitched upward—a glint in her eyes like a blade catching light. *Of course it was mine, little cousin.*

"These halls thrive on rumor, Daeran," she murmured. "I would rather shape outcomes than be consumed by them."

"Your ambiguity is lost on me," he said dryly, "but I will assume that is exactly how you meant it."

This time Valeraine's smile was genuine—and incredibly disarming. A weapon she kept honed, though she rarely unsheathed it.

"How are you enjoying the festivities?" she asked, weaving her arm through his, steering him with ruthless kindness toward the refreshments table he'd been eyeing their entire conversation.

"Immensely," he replied, voice dry as desert sand, as he poured himself a glass of something lavender. "Although I've only been objectified twice so far. My self-esteem has taken a terrible blow."

"I fear that is entirely my fault," Valeraine said. "I monopolized your attention far too quickly upon your arrival."

"And I worship you for it, my Lady."

The swell of strings diminished, and the incessant chatter dulled to a hush as a bell tinkled sharply. A herald's voice rang out across the hall, carrying even past the surrounding gardens.

"Announcing for your prime entertainment this exquisite evening—Lyra of the Twilight Isles, Illusionist of Starlight and Storyteller of Shadow!"

Delighted murmurs rippled through the crowd, fans snapping open, and necks craning for a better view. A couple of isolated whoops and squeals sounded around the room.

Daeran usually had little interest in the vapid entertainments of court—save the occasional trick-animal—but his elongated ears pricked at the mention of the Isles.

"That's quite a mouthful," he muttered into Valeraine's ear.

"You should watch this one," she said knowingly. "Her magic is rather... *different.*"

Different.

Valeraine drew him closer, though he still tried to keep himself to the fringe as long as he could.

In the middle of the ballroom, the courtiers parted into a hollow ring, baring the marble floor for the performance. Their jewels and sequins created the first illusion of a crown encircling the empty space.

Daeran straightened as she stepped forward.

"A human?" he said, louder than intended. Valeraine shushed him and gestured for him to pay attention.

He was not moved easily by the feminine form, no matter how lovely. Beauty was cheap currency among the Faen, and he had long since stopped counting it.

But the woman who took the center of the hall was—

Not cheap. Not simple.

She was striking in a way that made this gaudy court look like painted glass beside a living flame.

Her black curls devoured the light from the candelabras, shifting like oil across water. And her eyes—gods, preserve him. Nebulous galaxies swam there, clouds of indigo and gold colliding, newborn stars hurling themselves into impossible orbits.

She was infinity peering out over the crowd.

The entire court leaned in as she raised her hands in front of her, and darkness gathered from nothing, swirling at her command. Her fingers twitched like she was plucking the strings of a thousand marionettes, and the shadows obeyed, dancing intimately around her body.

His own shadow at his feet twitched, restless.

Shadows were not a gift Gwenael bestowed lightly—certainly not to a human. Daeran could count every shadow-wielder, dead or alive, on one hand. They were all of the Obsidian Isles.

He might have considered her gift a hidden outlier... until the stars flared through the darkness, blazing like tiny suns caught in her orbit.

His lungs stilled. He dared not blink.

He was not moving of his own accord.

His shadows coiled around his ankles, his calves, picking up his feet and pushing him forward, as if he had become one of those thousand puppets. He staggered forward. One step, then another.

Smoke snaked around him, stretching toward her in recognition. He did not try to rein them back. There was no point. Their will was immovable.

She looked at him.

Lightning cracked, violently splitting the air between them.

Courtiers shrieked and scattered, hands flying to their faces as they cowered away from the crater in the center of the room.

The pain in Daeran's sternum was immediate and obscene—as agonizing as a bone saw tearing through his ribs, then snapping inward to impale his heart.

His legs buckled beneath him, but he did not stumble. He did not clutch his chest. He moved toward her as her body crumpled, her head lolling to the side, her eyes rolling backward.

He bit down on the eviscerating pain and caught her before her limp hand even touched the rubble of the shattered marble floor.

When he pulled her against his chest, the pain stopped.

Daeran knew what this was.

Not in his three hundred and fifty years had he expected to experience it himself. Never expected to be cosmically bound to another, to a supposed *equal.*

The knot solidified within him, tethering him to this stranger eternally. A stranger unconscious in his arms. Porcelain skin that stretched over a million glittering stars. Curls that defied natural gravity. A heartbeat that found his and fell into sync as it hammered in his throat.

And she probably had no idea of the cosmic weight that had just knocked her out.

Chaos continued to erupt—courtiers spinning with panic, the King rising from his throne, Prince Torian shoving through the horrified crowd, rage etched in sharp lines across his face.

Daeran's focus remained on the woman cradled against him. On his eternity gone limp in his arms.

"Aevra!"

Not Lyra.

The prince's anguished cry cut through the cacophony. Daeran's arms tightened instinctively around her.

"So," the King said, strolling over far too calmly, "your human returns." He stopped at the edge of the crater, hovering over Daeran and the unconscious stranger. "I hate admitting I was wrong, but it seems her punishment for your dalliance was not permanent enough."

The Queen rose with her hand over her mouth in horror. For the first time in Daeran's memory, she spoke in public, her voice barely audible yet somehow carrying across the hall.

"Oranth, please—"

The King silenced her with a sharp hiss, then gestured to the revelers now huddled together.

"All ye bear witness!" announced the King, jabbing his finger at the crumpled woman, "This performer—this *succubus*—has returned straight from its infernal pit to bewitch my court and corrupt your prince."

Torian stood frozen at the edge of the crater, pale and shaking. The King placed a heavy hand on the back of his neck.

"Tell me, my boy," he hissed, his venomous breath coiling

around the shell of his ear, *"did she succeed a second time?"*

A visceral growl escaped Torian's throat as he slapped the King's hand away.

The woman—Aevra—stirred slightly against him as consciousness tugged itself back into her body.

The pull between them thrummed stronger, and with it came impressions that were not his: confusion, fear, and beneath it all, bone-deep exhaustion.

Whatever had brought her to this moment bled into him, heavy and ancient, turning his eyelids leaden and fogging his vision.

"Lord Daeran," the King said with a frigidly empty expression, "release the human demon to my guards at once. This is an internal matter of the Amber Vale and its council."

Daeran fractured his focus away from Aevra with visible effort and gave the power-hungry tyrant a single thread of attention.

"I'm afraid I cannot comply with that request, Your Majesty."

"Cannot?" The King's voice hardened. "Or will not?"

"Both," Daeran replied simply.

He rose to his full height, still cradling Aevra against him. He walked straight toward the King, boots crunching bits of marble as he went, and stopped just out of arm's reach.

"Do what you see fit with your adulterous heir," Daeran continued, his tone terrifyingly conversational, "but nobody touches her."

A collective gasp rose from the courtiers at his casual dismissal of the Crown Prince's behavior, at the King's command. The King's face darkened with fury, and the court held its breath as all the air in the room thinned.

"Council chambers. Now."

He turned to the stunned gathering with a tight smile.

"Continue the celebration," the King said. "The betrothal proceedings will resume shortly."

Chapter Thirty-Nine

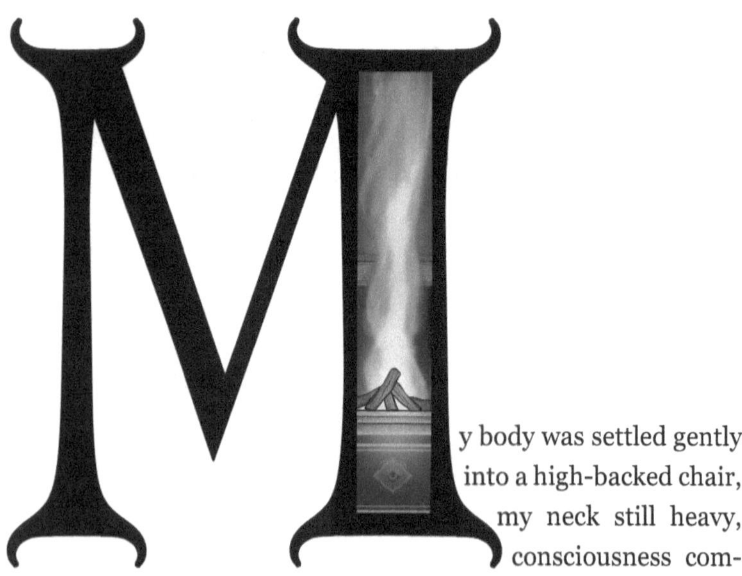

My body was settled gently into a high-backed chair, my neck still heavy, consciousness coming and going through the revolving door in my head.

The afterlife arranged itself in the comforting, mocking form of a study—a chair that fit me, the soft circle of lamplight, the crackle of fire, the musk of old parchment.

It was easier to accept the stillness of death than face the reality that I had likely shredded with my loss of control. If I hadn't actually died, then I must have killed everyone around me. And if not that, then I was in trouble.

Big trouble.

I brought a heavy hand to my chest, certain I would find a gaping hole burned straight through me. But my bosom was solid, and the pain had been replaced with a subtle tug that pulled me back and forth as a stranger paced in front of me.

The hearth bellowed with King Oranth's rage, every seething breath stoking the flames higher.

"This changes nothing," the King said matter-of-factly. "She infiltrated and deceived my court, endangered my only heir, and disrupted a formal betrothal ceremony. I demand satisfaction for these crimes."

"With respect, Your Majesty, it changes everything," came the stranger's measured response. "This woman is now bound to me by the mating bond, which is recognized by all courts as inviolable. By ancient law, she falls under the protection of the Obsidian Isles."

The words dropped like rusted chains onto my shoulders. Bound. Ancient law. *Mate.* I wanted to laugh, to retch, to tear free of this invisible cord already yanking me toward him like a taut fishing line.

I forced myself to look at him properly, at the male to whom I clearly belonged now. The predictability of him was almost comical. He was just like any other Fae I had come across. Tall, broad-shouldered, handsome.

But shadows clung to him like servants. Hooded silver eyes glimmered beneath his furrowed brow, unyielding. Dark waves were tied back at his neck with careless precision. My mate, apparently. My mate.

And I didn't even know his name.

"Daeran Noctis, the Devil of the Dark, is lecturing *me* about abiding by law?"

"Do not dare test me, Oranth. You are not my king."

Lord Daeran Noctis. A name I had only seen once, forged and sharpened into a lie. Yet, here the looming phantom stood. Not ink on a page, not a whispered rumor. But a bargain that might as well have been carved into my skin.

Queen Krivnya sat motionless nearby, her emerald eyes fixed on me. Lady Valeraine stood idly beside her, biding her time.

And Torian—my Torian—stood apart from them all, the sea glass clutched in his hand, his face a pale study in devastation. He did not look at me.

"Mating bond or not," the King continued, "this human will answer for her deception."

Say something.

"Her name is Aevra," Lord Daeran said, his voice deceptively calm though shadows gathered menacingly at his feet. "And she leaves with me tonight."

"The ancient laws are clear, Your Majesty," Lady Valeraine interjected smoothly. "The mating bond supersedes all other claims, even royal ones. To interfere would risk a diplomatic incident with not only the Obsidian Isles but all courts that recognize the bond's sanctity."

Save me.

"You overstep, Lady Valeraine." The King's golden eyes narrowed dangerously on her. "Especially considering she cavorted with your intended, and would have continued to do so indefinitely had she not been caught! You should feel humiliated!"

"My feelings regarding the woman and the prince are irrelevant. What matters now are the facts at hand, Your Majesty," she replied, unflinching. "Facts that your council would surely confirm were they present."

The King turned his wrath back to the silver-eyed stranger now bound to me. "Your savage heaps of slag may be beyond my direct authority, but do not think I cannot reach her there. I will simply steal her in the night if necessary."

Fucking say something!

Lord Daeran's shadows darkened around him, responding to his rising anger without conscious direction. The flame in the hearth flickered, and frost coated the windowpane as all the warmth was sucked from the room.

"No one with ill intentions toward my mate will enter the Obsidian Isles and leave unscathed. Not even you, Oranth."

A tense silence followed, broken only when I finally found my voice.

"May I speak with Prince Torian?" I asked, the words barely more than a whisper. "Privately. Before we depart."

All heads turned toward me, surprise lighting up each face. Except Torian's. His expression held only hope, quickly masked as the King's attention shifted to him.

"To what purpose?" the King demanded.

"To say goodbye," I said simply.

Lord Daeran studied me for a long moment, his platinum eyes unreadable. Then, to my surprise, he inclined his head. "A reasonable request."

"Reasonable?" the King scoffed. "After a century of failed punishment, you would grant your seductress privacy with my son?"

Torian's hands clenched into fists, his jaw tightening at the insult. A muscle jumped in his cheek as he fought to master the rage flashing across his golden eyes.

Lord Daeran's shadows pulsed once, though he did not meet my gaze directly.

"The bond is already formed. It cannot be undone by words or farewells," he replied with unexpected gentleness, his voice betraying none of the anger that the cloud of darkness circling him continued to reveal. "Besides," he continued, turning his attention back to the King, "His Majesty would be wise to consider that denying his son this courtesy may cause him to act on his anguish.

And any harm befalling him could very well affect her own well-being. And anything that harms her..." He let the implication answer itself.

The King's expression shifted, calculation replacing rage as he processed this new perspective, then he smirked.

"Mates die together. Perhaps all my problems could be solved—"

"The enemy you've sworn in the north is a clear exception to that rule. Perhaps so am I."

"Very well," he said through clenched teeth. "A brief farewell. Under guard."

"No guards," Lord Daeran countered. "But within the palace, with your word that no harm will come to either of them."

Another tense silence stretched before the King finally gave a curt nod. "The west solar. Ten minutes. No more."

Ten minutes.

The corridor to the west solar seemed endless, each step simultaneously too fast and too slow. How could I possibly say goodbye to Torian in ten minutes? How could we convey a century of love, of pining and searching, of finding each other against impossible odds, only to be torn apart again to an even crueler end?

Nine minutes.

The blue mosaic above the doorway depicted what I perceived to be a sunrise over water, ironic within the land of sunset. My stomach jumped at the thought of seeing one again.

I opened the door with a weak push and found Torian standing by the window, his posture slumped in defeat. He turned to me slowly, and the raw pain in his golden eyes nearly brought me to my knees.

"Aevra."

The sound of my name cracked along his voice like an axe splintering through ice.

Eight minutes.

We stumbled toward each other like a loaded spring, meeting in the center of the room in a crushing embrace. He pulled away and cradled my face with aching gentleness, his thumbs brushing away tears I hadn't realized poured down my face.

Seven minutes.

"I'm so sorry," I whispered, the words wholly inadequate. "I never meant for this to happen."

As if it were my fault. As if keeping my eyes on my performance could have prevented this from happening. If I had just maintained focus, if my attention hadn't been so fractured tonight, this could have been avoided. We'd be leaving the Vale together instead of separating.

"The mating bond isn't something anyone can control," he said, holding back blame that he could rest on nothing, no one. "Not even my father, with all his power."

Six minutes.

"We were so close," I said, unable to keep the despair from my words. "Just a few more hours and we would have been free."

His forehead dropped to mine, our breath mingling in the small space between us. "I will find a way around this bond," he promised. "Whatever it takes, however long it takes. This is not the end of our story."

"How can you be sure?" I asked, clinging to his certainty like a lifeline in a storm.

Five minutes.

"Because I lost you once before and we defied fate," he said fiercely. "Because a century of punishment couldn't erase what we feel for each other. Because I refuse to believe that after everything we've endured, the universe would be so cruel as to bind you to a stranger."

His words lit a match of hope in the darkness that had enveloped me since the lightning struck between Lord Daeran and me.

Four minutes.

"I don't want to waste another century without you. With some stranger. I don't even know him," I wept. "How am I supposed to—"

"You don't have to do anything except survive," Torian interrupted. "Stay safe. Stay as far away from him as you can. I'll find a way to break it."

Three minutes.

I took a deep, shaky breath as he thumbed away more fat tears rolling down my cheeks. He then reached into his pocket and withdrew the sea glass. My hand shot up to the hollow of my neck. Both pendants were gone. So much for hiding my true colors—literally.

"I want you to take this with you," he said, pressing it into my palm. "I made an adjustment to it," he added, now closing my fingers around it.

I looked down and noticed a symbol etched into the smooth surface of the glass, the lines rough and hastily carved. I traced my thumb across it and it warmed at my touch.

Two minutes.

"A communication rune," he whispered, as I now recognized the pattern was like a threshold. "I carved it while waiting for you. It's crude, but it should work. Keep it with you always. When it grows warm against your skin, that's me."

"How—"

"The magic won't last for many correspondences," he explained, his words coming faster now as our time slipped away. "We must use it sparingly. But know that no matter where you are, no matter what happens, I will bring you back to me."

We were supposed to have an eternity. Now we had...

One minute.

He pulled me into him, and our mouths met for the last time. A kiss born of infinite sorrow instead of blazing passion. *Just yes-*

terday.

A sharp knock at the door split me clean in two.

"Aevra," Torian said, his voice dropping to a whisper, thumb resting on my bottom lip. "Always remember that you were mine first. Remember that I loved you when you were just a healer's daughter gathering moonflowers by the river. Remember that I chose you, and would choose you again—across time, across realms, regardless of destiny or bonds or royal decrees."

Torian held me close, the hard muscles of his chest shuddering against me as his lips grazed my temple with finality.

"This isn't goodbye," he whispered against my hair, and then I heard the definitive sound of the door locking, the iron latch clicking into place. The palace obeyed his whim without even a twitch from him. I pulled back just enough to see his face.

The grief that had hollowed his features a moment ago was gone, replaced by something feral, stripped of reason. His jaw clenched, chin trembling between a plea and a snarl. I did not see the prince who loved me by the river, but a male willing to defy crowns and cosmos to keep me in his arms for a few seconds longer. It was madness. Devotion. Desperation explosively colliding with the ruin of the past century.

Another knock came, sharper this time. The doorknob jiggled, but the lock held.

"Aevra," Lord Daeran called gently from the other side of the door.

Torian's arms tightened around me, pressing my cheek into his sternum. His heart pounded against my face as he squeezed me in a possessive vise. Heat emanated from him, rising higher and higher, so hot against my cheek that it dried any remaining tears on the spot.

"You can't take her," he shouted, his claim cracking like thunder.

A silence stretched as I stood stiffly against him, my breaths shallow from the constriction of his embrace. I strained my sight as far as my stillness allowed, the corner of my vision catching the tip of a shadow that crept through the crack under the door and unfurled like a roll of black ribbon.

Torian's biceps bulged as he clenched me even tighter against him, and a tiny squeak pressed from my lungs. He didn't notice; his eyes fixed on the shadow that now picked the lock from inside, wrapping around the latch so it couldn't catch again.

When the door swung open, Lord Daeran's tall figure was a sleek silhouette against the light of the corridor.

"It's time," he said simply.

"She belongs in the Vale. With me," Torian growled, his voice scraping over gravel.

Lord Daeran's expression softened with what might have been sympathy, shaking his head as he stepped into the room, hands in his pockets with a casualness that did not fit the tension.

"You know she would never be safe here," he replied. "Though I wonder if you even care. And need I remind you—" He leaned in, an inch from Torian's face, his cold stare unblinking. "—that you have an obligation to my cousin to fulfill?"

Torian shook with barely contained ferocity, his face flushing red and teeth bared. Every thread of muscle trembled beneath his skin, screaming to be unleashed. The heat from him spiked, and I gritted my teeth, suppressing a cry of pain as he burned me with his searing magic. The acrid tang of singed skin stung in my nose.

As if he felt it happening directly to him, Lord Daeran wrenched his hands from my bare shoulders, revealing skin blistered and charred in the shape of his fiery grip. Tears welled in my eyes—from pain or anguish, I could not tell—as he guided me protectively behind him. His gaze never left Torian, though his fingertips lingered lightly against my elbow.

"Her being within arm's reach is dangerous enough, it seems," he said coolly.

Torian's face finally fell as he watched the smoke still rolling off my shoulders from his slip of restraint. His features folded into a wet wince of regret as he realized what he had done. He reached toward me.

"Please," he breathed, his voice cracking away from the word as his throat tightened. "Let me fix it." Tears streamed from him, turning to steam as soon as they slid over his eyelids.

I wanted to let him. To feel his loving hands glide over me one more time. I would have given anything for that touch.

But my body recoiled from his outstretched hand, and he let it fall slack at his side.

The knot in my core tugged behind my navel, then shivered like a plucked string.

"You will never touch her again, *Your Highness*."

I felt the familiar tingling of shadows snake up my waist, then around my shoulders, anchoring at my neck as they nestled firmly against the burn marks. They thumped with a cold pulse that was not my own. *His.*

Torian's knees hit the floor as he hung his head, and I knew I had to cut the cord. To be the strong one now.

"I'm ready," I rasped, though nothing could have been further from the truth. I couldn't bring myself to look over my scorched shoulder at Torian as we left.

A carriage waited in the eastern courtyard, far from the main palace entrance.

"We'll be taking a ship from the southeastern harbor on the other side of the Irons," he explained. "It's a longer journey than I'd prefer, but with the shadow paths unstable and the... *delicate* nature of the situation, it's the safest option."

"Longer?" I asked. The first islands of the archipelago were not even fifty miles from the mainland.

"We will sail around rather than taking the most direct route," he replied, his silver eyes briefly darkening. "The waters directly between the mainland and the Isles aren't suitable for crossing this time of year."

Before I could ask for clarification, Lady Valeraine approached with measured steps, chewing on the inside of her cheek. Lord Daeran stepped away from me to speak to her privately, but I could still hear every word.

"I'll ensure the King maintains his distance," she murmured. "I hope he is satisfied that his son publicly losing his love to another male is punishment enough."

"For now, perhaps," Lord Daeran replied equally quietly. "But his focus will shift to the Obsidian Isles soon enough. And our exports."

"I'm well aware," she said, a flash of steel beneath her diplomatic veneer. "I'll smooth out what I can for as long as possible."

"Valeraine," he said, genuine warmth in his tone as he cupped a hand against her cheek, "your father would be proud."

They touched their foreheads together briefly, then stepped away from each other. When she looked at me, my insides twisted with the ugliest combination of guilt, jealousy, shame, embarrassment, and anger.

She didn't do this to me, but she got to keep her illicit love hidden within the palace. And she also got to keep mine.

A ghost of a smile touched her lips. "Safe journey," she said. "Don't lose hope."

I didn't thank her. I said nothing at all.

I was stepping up into the carriage when I heard an echoing wail. A copper braid whipped through the air as Lysara barreled toward us.

"Lysara," I breathed, surprised to see the historian risking such a public farewell. She reached me, slightly breathless, and clasped my hands within hers. I stiffened, realizing those hands had a duty to record every instance of magic, including the formation of a mating bond.

"I suppose you will immortalize this entire evening," I said stiffly.

Her mouth curved down in a frown as she searched for the correct words to say. "I do not intend to reduce your survival to your sin. But even so, your truth lives on far beyond my pen," she said, tears pricking in my eyes. "Make the ending count."

She squeezed my hands once more. "And remember this, Aevra Nightwind. The bonds we choose *freely* are more powerful than any thrust upon us."

With a quick, fierce embrace, she stepped back, composing her features into the proper expression of a court historian merely bidding farewell to a departing guest.

And then we left them all behind.

I caught one last glimpse of the golden spires of the Amber Palace before it reduced to barely a smudge on the horizon, then disappeared behind the peaks of the Iron Mountains. The home that was never truly mine. And the love that I supposed wasn't mine either.

I squeezed the sea glass so tightly that it hurt, trying to keep the tears from falling. For the briefest moment, an inexplicable wave of memory washed over me in a deluge: the scent of moonflowers, golden eyes in twilight, a promise whispered against my ear. The sensation was so vivid it made my stomach clench with a longing that felt like it didn't fully belong to me, surpassing time and space.

I blinked away the unexpected vision and slipped the glass into the hidden pocket of my gown.

When we finally approached the ship, sleek and elegant, Lord Daeran guided me on board with a steady hand at my elbow. His touch was careful, almost hesitant, starkly different from the protective way he had touched me earlier.

"Why don't we just take a threshold?" I asked, my voice shattering the quiet that had grown between us like a hammer to glass.

"We don't have thresholds in the Isles," Lord Daeran said flatly. "I don't want anybody showing up uninvited, or blaming me for falling into the volcano."

"Volcano?"

He nodded once, jaw clenched. The silence that followed felt like a wall of stone sliding shut. I understood it would be best for me not to speak for the rest of the journey.

With only the gentle lap of the water against the boat and the screeching of gulls overhead—neither loud enough to drown out my internal screaming—I was once again ripped from a life I wished I could keep.

It was a misfortune doomed to repeat.

Again.

And again.

Acknowledgments

I've never done this before, so I scoured half of the books on my bookshelf to figure out the correct way to simply say thank you. So here is my attempt.

First, I need to thank my creative writing teachers, Ms. Allen and Ms. Marszalek. Without your guidance, I never would have found (and stuck with) my voice.

Ms. Allen—the literary drill instructor who taught me never to rhyme unless it was going to be worthy of snaps—you fought my self-doubt with your red pen anytime I strayed from what you knew to be my truest self, even when I was only thirteen.

And Ms. Marszalek—you did the exact opposite. You allowed me to write whatever my heart wanted, and you praised all of it no matter how cringy or weird it might have been. You were the reason I started writing for a crowd, from slam poetry in Barnes and Noble—my pretzel poem that won a Gold Key, inspired by my crush on the barista—to the early morning Poets Society meetings that forced me out of bed before my alarm.

I am able to put words to paper because you both saw something in me worth nurturing, and I hope I have made you proud.

Next, I'd like to thank my therapist, Katherine. You've helped me filter the realms when I couldn't remember what belonged to Aevra and what belonged to me. Your ear and your insight have kept me sane through this very interesting project. There's no doubt in my mind that without you, this acknowledgment page would not be necessary.

Then, Mia and Mindi. My ride or die girls who didn't shy away when I asked them to "just read a couple pages and tell me what you think."

Mindi, specifically your critique on Chapter Thirteen when all I needed to know was "Does it make your loins tingle?" gave me the confidence to write the next twenty-six chapters.

And Mia, the only brave soul who had never even heard of romantasy, but decided to be my only beta reader anyway, so many Easter eggs in this book were written solely for you. Your incredibly intimidating and admirable knowledge on every single subject known to man (and probably known to other life forms outside of this galaxy) forced me to think through ideas as more than just strings of pretty words, and give substance to even the smallest mentions in the book—like the sonnet I wrote in perfect iambic pentameter just for Torian to quote a single line.

And finally, my most formidable ally aside from my own free will, my husband. You believed in me from the moment I scrawled the first word. When I decided to design and create my own cover art; illustrate my drop caps; and write, sing, and produce an original song just for Chapter Sixteen, you never told me that it was too much. That *I* was too much.

And you are the first one. My Daeran.

I love you.